Kira Shay

FSF Publications

Cover art and design by TJ Geisen

e-Book ISBN 978-0-9961485-2-8
Print ISBN 978-0-9961485-3-5

Manufactured in the United States of America.

www.fivesmilingfish.com

Dedicated to Will.
Your belief in my madness is astounding.
I love you.

Endless Thanks and Appreciation to:

Sidney Reetz and Megan Vaughn for pretty much everything. I am lucky beyond measure to have you both in my life.

TJ Geison for the amazing cover art.

Meaghan McGovern for the edits.

Brad Williams for being a beta reader without knowing exactly what you were getting into.

Tom Dushku for the technical assistance.

And thanks to YOU for reading!

An Angel twice born within the realm of man
The Father's creation stands guard over Divine Hand
A Human blessed with the Mother's gift
The catalyst for the healing of the rift
Together will bring forth the next stage
Summoning the start of the New Age
Return what was lost when the stars were formed
The family united that once was torn
Sacrifices made cannot be undone
End the war and three realms become one

Chapter One

Something was coming—something that would change everything.

I had been watching the hills since nightfall. As the stars turned above me in the darkness, a stirring excitement grew in my stomach. I wondered what the approaching dawn would bring. Anticipation pulled at me, an incessant tug drawing me towards whatever was calling out.

My back rested against the old Serra Cross of Ventura, California. The dampness of the morning mist crept over me from the concrete platform I sat upon. I ignored the sharp chill from the ocean that penetrated my layers of clothing and kept my gaze dutifully trained on the horizon. I listened to the heart of the city stir and hoped whatever change those distant hills held would hurry up and arrive.

It was dark under the cross, mostly because the city had removed the lights that once illuminated the religious symbol. I liked the darkness, though. Because of it, the cross had one of the best views in the city and glaring spotlights would have lessened its appeal.

A cement pathway surrounded by manicured lawns of lush grass connected the platform to the parking lot. At the bottom of the landscaped hill, downtown Ventura awoke to the rhythm of the waves against the not-so-distant shore. Lights, which had kept their vigil through the long winter night, winked at the coming sun.

"What are you doing here?" a familiar voice asked as it came towards me. "You should be out doing whatever it is kids your age do." It was Uncle Azra, my father's best friend. I'd been entrusted to his care when my father died centuries ago.

I glanced over as he settled himself next to me. "I don't think there are any kids my age."

The smile he gave me showed his pearly white teeth. He didn't look much older than twenty-five, all bronzed and blonde from surfing. Only a couple of things gave away the fact that he wasn't human: the gold flecks in his impossibly blue eyes and the slight shimmer that accented the air around him, which most mortals couldn't discern. Well, that and his outfit; he wore only a pair of board shorts and flip-flops in the middle of January.

"Uncle Az," I sighed, "put some clothes on. It's only twenty degrees out here. The humans will notice."

He laughed. It was a booming sound that always seemed to cheer me up. "There's no one around to see us, Orion. It's just you and me." He spoke his words with a conglomeration of accents. The syllables brought to mind all the world's languages and, at the same time, a language unheard of on Earth. He didn't bother to mask his speech either. He preferred to let people wonder about it.

"Don't call me Orion," I grumbled. "I told you, I'm going by Ryan now."

"Fine, Rye-anne." He said the name with a jeering emphasis to illustrate how ridiculous it sounded. "Why don't you tell me what's got you all bothered? You're too mopey lately. Don't glare at me like that. I can tell when you're upset."

When I didn't say anything he settled back on his elbows and tilted his head back to gaze up at the stars, confident that I would break eventually. We sat in companionable silence for a while. I with my eyes set firmly on the horizon and his on the heavens.

Unexpectedly, a horrible noise erupted from my uncle. After a second or two an equally noxious smell wafted around us.

"Ugh!" I covered my nose and mouth against the fumes. "Dude! What the hell did you eat?"

Azra burst into a fit of giggles. "Sorry, kiddo. Had

some angel food cake earlier."

Though I fought it, I couldn't help but laugh. Uncle Azra had that effect on people.

With the mood lightened, we resumed our observations of the sky and Azra asked me, "You know what they used to say about the stars? They said stars were the campfires of the angel army."

"When did they say that?" I'd heard this story countless times before and knew my cues well. Sometimes I wasn't in the mood to listen. This morning was one of those times. With the nagging sensation in my stomach and the persistent tugging of my awareness towards the horizon, I only listened halfway.

"Back in the good old days—when the Sumerians came to power—there wasn't any of this non-belief idiocy. Mankind had more realistic views about the Creator. There wasn't any of this 'my god can beat up your god' crap. Well, there was, but it wasn't as intense. It was more of a, 'you sacrifice to that god and I'll sacrifice to this god and we can have wars over the real estate.' They knew what it meant when—"

I stopped listening and allowed my mind to wander.

We'd been living in Ventura, California for almost two months now and, until this morning, there hadn't been anything to indicate that we were in the right place. We had come from Toronto, and before that a village in Cambodia, and before that . . . well, I lose track. Azra loved living in California, but I think that was more for the surfing rather than being where we were supposed to be. While there hadn't been any sign of others of our kind skulking nearby or our cover being blown, I'd been more than ready to move on out of sheer boredom. Unless. . . The nagging feeling in my stomach twitched.

Unless something happened.

It wasn't the first time that night I wondered if the strange calling I felt was real or if I was just hoping for some sort of change. I could do with some action, even if it meant having to uproot for the umpteenth time.

Almost as if in response to my thoughts, the faintest sound of footsteps and hissing came from the left. I sprang to my feet, disrupting Azra's tale. He was right behind me, crouched and ready to launch himself at whatever was approaching us, the story already forgotten. This kind of reaction was typical when you have been hunted for most of your life.

By the shadows that danced around the approaching figure, I recognized the outline of a man and knew it to be a Fallen One; an angel turned demon when the Angelic War had first started in Heaven. I could hear his sinister chuckling as he stepped into view.

The Fallen One mused loud enough for us to hear him, "Two Watchers. Who would have thought I would find those of the exiled choir. Your kind are rare these days. Tell me, do you still believe the Creator loves you?"

My uncle, ever quick with his wit asked in return, "Tell me, does the devil know you are out here? I can't believe the all-powerful Hell Bat would allow something as stupid as you out of the Great Easy Bake Oven willingly. After all, he's got a reputation to uphold."

A condescending grin spread across his narrow, pale features as he addressed my uncle. "Still fighting the good fight, I see. You're still trying to rid the world of our influence so you can gain the favor of Heaven. What a fool you are." In the darkness, the red gleam in the Fallen One's black eyes was the only color he had. Behind that gleam, though, were millennia of torments. He hid it well as he sauntered closer and as his gaze flicked between Azra and me. His eyes met mine long enough for me to feel the sorrow and hate of the damned echo across my mind. Sleepiness washed over me, making my limbs feel heavy.

I blinked and tensed, ready to fight. My anger bubbled, dispelling the drowsiness of the Fallen One's attempt of taking me over. I would show Uncle Azra that I could beat him on my own.

"I got this," I assured my uncle.

"You think so?" Azra asked, the ghost of amusement

lacing his words.

The Fallen One considered us, ignoring our whispers and calculating the opportunity for attack. "I wonder. . . Will you die like a human or like our holier-than-thou brethren? I've never killed a Grigori before."

Faster than thought, he darted forward. There wasn't time to dodge out of the way, so I braced for the assault. At the very last second, Azra's hand clamped onto my shoulder and he shoved me towards the edge of the hill and away from the coming attack. The propulsion my dear uncle gave me was a little more forceful than I could handle, and I bounced over the edge of the plateau.

The coarse plumes of grass and scrubby underbrush made my fall both perilous and itchy. I grabbed desperately at whatever plant life I could, trying to stop my bumpy descent. It was to no avail; I landed with a painful thud on the access road that wound up the hill, roughly half a mile away from where I started.

Furious, I got to my feet and brushed the dirt from my clothes. The fight was in full swing above me; the clash of energies reverberated off the surrounding hills. I heard Uncle Azra taunting his opponent as well as the low pitched growl of the Fallen One. It was a good thing most of the humans in the area, even if they could hear the fight, would refuse to understand what was happening. The majority of humans only saw and heard what they could easily explain, all else was ignored to the point of obstinacy. It was both a blessing and an annoyance.

I ran back to the cross, angry that the battle was taking place without me. He hadn't needed to push me out of the way. I could have handled it.

The jeering taunts my uncle issued were getting louder with every step I took. "Sing like a Choir Boy! Oh, wait, you can't can you? That's why you were kicked out of Heaven, wasn't it? They couldn't stand your screeching!"

The Fallen One hissed, so enraged that he couldn't even formulate a response.

"Oh!" Azra went on louder than before. "You're one of *those* Fallen Ones. It's okay. I hear Jesus loves everyone so you aren't completely screwed. By the way, your mother was a stinky pirate! No, wait—that would make you kinda cool . . ."

I groaned, but kept running. Just as I crested the hill, the sun emerged, cutting through the clouds. The Fallen One stopped his enraged charge at Azra as the brightness of the dawn threatened to dispel the shadows in which he surrounded himself.

Taking advantage of the momentary distraction, Uncle Azra lunged and stabbed the Fallen One with a knife that he had taken out of a hidden pocket in his shorts. I recognized the celestial blade (this one was a small dagger that was a miniature of his real sword) by its otherworldly glow. With a growl and a furious curse in the old tongue, the Fallen One dissolved into what appeared to be a sticky puddle of tar that absorbed into the ground. Every Fallen One's physical form that I'd seen dispatched vanished the same way— in a sticky gooey mess. Why that was I couldn't say. Whatever the reason, it saved on cleanup and awkward questions with the mortals.

Azra wiped the slime from the Fallen One off of his blade and onto the grass. He beamed at me as I came closer. "Man! That was fun! You should have stuck around, kiddo! You missed one hell of a fight!"

I glared at him as I went to retrieve my backpack from the base of the cross. "Why did you push me away? I could have taken him on my own."

"Why are you so anxious to get yourself killed?" Azra asked as he watched me pull out my headphones from one of the front pockets of the dark blue bag. "I made a promise to protect you, you know?"

I rolled my eyes at him and flipped on my iPod. Irritation crossed Azra's face and he shouted to be heard over my music. "Your father would have done the same thing! He wouldn't have wanted you taken down by some sleazy—"

The mention of my father was the last straw. Cutting him off, I yelled, "My father would've taught me how to defend myself by now! He would have given me the chance to stand up for myself, to see what I could do! He wouldn't have pushed me down a hill to keep me from fighting a stupid Fallen One."

This startled him into a stunned silence, something that rarely happened. While we had argued this point many times before, my aggravation was magnified by the insult of being literally shoved out of the way of the fight. Usually, I tried to respect Uncle Azra as my elder. After all, there was a reason why my father had left me in his care, even if he was erratic at the whole parenting shtick.

I looked at Uncle Azra's stricken face and sighed. He looked so pathetic standing there all crestfallen.

"You're right," I conceded, softening my tone. "My father wouldn't want me taken out by some worthless, every day Fallen One, but he wouldn't want me cowering in fear every time one crossed my path, either."

As he opened his mouth to argue, I turned my back and headed for the road.

"Do you at least have your beads?" he hollered.

In response, I lifted my left wrist, showing off the wooden prayer beads. The sigils burned into the spheres were a charm meant to disguise my psychic presence and make me appear nothing more than a Watcher or, to those not paying close attention, a human. They were also a constant reminder to keep my anger in check.

The volume of my iPod increased, drowning out whatever else Azra yelled at me as I walked away.

Punk music formed the soundtrack of my trek back to the studio apartment I called home. The building wasn't in the best repair; however, it was close to the ocean and had an amazing view. The location, of course, made rent insanely high. That didn't matter too much to me, though. When you have been around for most of human civilization, you just sort of accumulate stuff that appreciates in value over a few hundred years.

As I trudged up the stairs, the sounds of my neighbors waking up came through the thin walls. I envied them. Humans had the option to believe in the illusion they were safe. To not know what I knew, to not be as trapped as I felt by the sheer weight of what I was; well, it seemed like a great life.

I thought about the fight at the cross. The majority of the Fallen Ones we found, or who managed to find us, were stupid and easily tricked. There were a lot of them on Earth and it seemed no matter how many were destroyed, more would crop up. Running into one like that was almost an everyday occurrence. Given that fact, it still confused me why Uncle Azra refused to train me to defend myself against them and the Heavenly Host. Both were a threat and only being able to hide and evade them wouldn't win me any fights if they cornered me.

I sang the chorus of the song blasting through my headphones under my breath when I reached my door and pulled out my keys.

The early morning light shone weakly through the windows in my apartment. I tossed my keys onto the table tucked into the corner and slung my bag onto the ground. Despite Azra's attempts to keep the small, cramped space clean, it was cluttered and disorganized. Empty plates and cups lounged among the bits of crumpled paper littering the floor. Patches of beige carpet showed through the piles of stuff. The walls, or at least the parts not covered by artwork (both my own and others) were in need of new paint.

My furniture was an odd mix of the very antique and the very secondhand. This was also my choice. Azra had wanted to decorate and buy new things, but I preferred the pieces I already had. Still, he bought several items in an attempt to class up the place, ranging from a Tiffany lamp to a bearskin rug. I had disposed of them after he left. Overall, the apartment was rundown and cramped, but it was home.

With the day already underway, I didn't have much

time to get changed for school. I set my iPod next to my keys and turned to the armoire on the other side of the room. I had to move one of Uncle Az's abandoned surfboards to get it open and, once it was, I cursed the emptiness of it.

I forgot to do laundry. Again.

I kicked at the clothes littering the floor to find the least dirty pair of jeans and the least wrinkled hoodie, all the while grumbling to myself. When I told Uncle Azra this apartment was what I wanted, he pitched a fit. He said it was too low-class—this from someone who preferred camping on the beach instead of his own high-end apartment a block over. I stuck to my decision, though, and eventually he let me lease it.

It turned out to be an unfair deal because half the time he stayed at the apartment anyway. He stayed and criticized. I think it's his second favorite pastime, next to surfing. Uncle Azra's main contention was that he didn't agree with the state of disarray my apartment was in.

I could hear his voice ringing admonishments in my head: 'Cleanliness is next to Godliness, Orion' and 'Lysol kills 99.9% of germs'. I swear, he memorized the cleaning commercials just to torture me. Not only that, but I also kept finding various cleaning products in random places. Like a bottle of bleach placed benignly on the TV, hinting at the promise of gleaming white shower tiles without mold or mildew.

Unearthing a decent pair of jeans and a minimally wrinkled hoodie, I headed into the bathroom.

There was a note written in lipstick and taped to the mirror above the sink. "Beware of Norman."

"Thanks, Uncle Az." Scowling, I ripped it off the mirror, allowing my image to frown back at me for the briefest moment before I looked away. I knew what I looked like and I hated it. My brown hair was streaked with natural highlights, proof of my time in the sun. Laziness on my part meant that it was long enough to be considered shaggy. If it were cut any shorter, the angular structure of my face would look more awkward than it already did.

What I loathed the most about my appearance, though, were my eyes; my father's eyes. I hated their color, the strange mix of grey and deep blue that oftentimes took on a purplish hue. The silver flecks that accented the irises didn't help. My eyes marked me as different in a world of brown, blue, and hazel.

As the hot water from the shower sluiced over me, I thought about the pull I had felt up at the cross, the nagging feeling that something was coming. I allowed myself the briefest flickering of hope. Maybe it was the one I was supposed to find.

There is a certain prophecy among the angelic community which promises that an angel born on Earth would, with the help of a human, end the Angelic War. Some believe this to mean that all of the Creator's creatures, more specifically the Grigori, would return to Heaven. According to Azra, I was the foretold angel in the prophecy. This human we were looking for would know what to do to fulfill our destiny to end the war.

I had my doubts about this. The prophecy wasn't very specific, but then, I didn't think it was their nature to be clear and concise. My father and Uncle Azra used to tell me about it when I was younger. I believed them back then. With both sides of the angelic divide gunning for me it made a certain amount of sense to think I was a threat to them somehow. Uncle Azra explained that most beings feared the unknown and I was nothing if not an unknown entity. That's why they wanted me dead: to stop me from ending the war and, possibly, their lives.

As I grew up, I realized it wasn't necessarily the prophecy that had everyone up in arms; it was my parentage. You see, my parents, like Uncle Azra, were part of a choir of angels called Grigori or Watchers. I'm the child of two angels and the only of my kind.

When my existence became known, the news exploded across both sides of the angelic community. The only thing the councils of both Heaven and Hell could agree on was that I should not exist. I was a dangerous anomaly.

I turned the shower off, stepped out of the tub and dried myself with a towel. I ran my hands through the wet strands of my hair, smoothing it out of my face.

After pulling on my clothes, I hunted for a pair of socks. There was one last pair rolled up and stashed in the back of my sock drawer. Though old and mismatched, they were better than nothing.

"Orion!" Uncle Azra burst through the front door, his anger radiated off him in waves. "We need to talk."

I tied my shoes, unimpressed with his blustering authority figure act. "I'm going to be late," I told him in a bored voice.

"I don't care. We can't have this fight every time a Fallen One shows up. They're like roaches. You're too important to risk your life on them!"

I didn't want to go through the lecture. So instead, I jumped up and grabbed my backpack and skateboard on my way to the door as Uncle Azra shouted, "Orion, stop and listen to me!"

"Late for school." I waved him off and shut the door behind me. With my headphones in place, I set off down the stairs.

Chapter Two

Ventura High School was a sprawling campus full of loud, rowdy kids even at seven o'clock in the morning. Through my music, the chatter of teenaged morons surrounded me. It took most of my self-control not to turn around and leave.

I was here for a purpose. As much as I wanted to be doing something else, I had to live up to my end of the bargain. School was something new that Uncle Azra decided I should try in the last few decades. His reasoning was based on some article about networking with large groups. He thought I needed more exposure to the human population and what better way than to make me go to school. I'd been around humans all over the world for a couple thousand years, and though a few had caught my attention, they hadn't been the right ones. Azra thought that if I went to some high school, that would change. Because of some embarrassing mistakes in the past, I didn't have any room to argue.

Luckily, I'd been able to negotiate my own living space for repeating my entire high school career for what would have been my fourteenth matriculation. Azra saw it as a test to see how I'd do on my own if it ever came down to that. I figured if I had to put up with hordes of kids, it wasn't fair for me to put up with living with Uncle Azra too. As I already said, that backfired.

I watched the other kids mill about in large groups, laughing with each other. Another reason why I hated going to school was the way the joking teenage cliques made me feel every bit the outcast that I was not only in my social life, but in my very existence.

My music was the only thing that helped push back

the loneliness. I could escape into the beat of the drums and the resonating thrum of the bass. Lyrics ripped my soul apart and glued it back in a space of a chorus. Every note was felt. Music gave me the ability to face day after repetitious day of spiraling boredom and was just as, if not more important, than skateboarding.

I suppose it could be summed up that while music was what released my mind from the tedium, skating is what released it physically. The feel of the pavement below my wheels and the wind in my face was intoxicating. When I skated, I understood why Uncle Azra liked to surf so much; it was a powerful high that made you forget for a moment that you were meant to do anything more. I suppose it's akin to flying and the feeling of being closer to Heaven than ever before. Closer to the home I've never seen.

I couldn't wait to get out of school to go skate. Usually, I wouldn't think twice about ditching a couple of classes, but the strange pulling sensation I felt up at the cross was back and a lot stronger than before. Whatever was causing it was here and I didn't dare leave until I knew what it was.

The bell rang, signaling the commencement of first period. I pushed my way through the crowd, bumping into the people who never seemed to watch where they were going. Snippets of conversations, whole worlds and lives that I would never know about, flowed around me. For the most part, I blocked it out of my mind. Reaching my locker, I stored my deck, wishing that I didn't have to leave it. I pulled out my English book and allowed the flow of students to pull me to my first class.

That's when I saw her.

She was tall, not quite as tall as my six foot five, but almost. The majority of her sandy blonde hair was twisted up with the rest hanging to frame her narrow face. It was her eyes that really grabbed my attention, though. They were big and chocolate brown, edged with impossibly full lashes. They sparkled and I found I couldn't look away.

She stood against one of the columns in the breezeway, surrounded by a group of girls. By her stance, I could tell she was participating in the conversation politely, but reservedly. It was as though she didn't know any of them very well. For one terrifying and exhilarating moment, she glanced up and caught me staring at her. A delicate eyebrow rose in question and a surprised smile sprang to her lips as her eyes met mine.

Everything faded away; all of the people and the noise until all that remained was the two of us in a field of blackness. Just as I felt the sorrow and pain of the damned when I locked gazes with the Fallen One, I felt the joy and peace that must be Heaven when I looked into hers. A tingling sensation crawled over my skin, its intensity making me shiver. She was the one. She had to be. The nagging pull I had felt all morning propelled me towards her and I took a step forward.

"Who are you?" I asked in a whisper, my voice trembling with amazement.

She smiled and the joy inside grew until it was on the verge of exploding out. My heart pounded in my chest and the draw towards her intensified. I took a couple more steps forward before the bell rang—a sharp jarring sound that startled me enough that I broke eye contact.

As quickly as the school faded, it came back with sharp clarity. The connection with the serenity was severed and I gasped at the sudden loss of it. The thud on the cement made me realize I had dropped my books. I bent to pick them up. The rush of students scurrying to class helped to further break the stupor that had overcome me. Kids bumped into me and acted genuinely surprised that I was there. I ignored the jostling though, my mind instead whirling with the implications of what had just happened. When I had hold of my books and my senses, I stood up and looked to where she had been. She was gone.

Damn it! Should I go after her? What would I say to her? Mentally, I slapped myself. What was wrong with me? My stomach did a flip as I recalled her eyes and the irresistible draw I felt. Something wasn't normal about that. But what if I was wrong, like before? The second bell rang and, still kicking myself for acting like an idiot, I made my way to English class.

I took my seat in Mrs. Foster's classroom, still sorting out what I had just experienced. Nothing like that had ever happened to me before. Did that mean it was the human I was looking for or was it something else entirely? I turned off my iPod just as the teacher came into the room. She went to the head of the class and began writing something on the board. Once the last bell rang and most people were in their seats, Mrs. Foster turned her attention to her students.

"Alright everyone, settle down," she called out. The room lapsed into silence. "Today we're going to start our unit on American poetry. Open your books to page two hundred and fifty-three."

Poetry, I thought with a certain measure of disgust. I hated poetry. Begrudgingly, I opened my book to the page listed on the board.

The door to the classroom opened just as Mrs. Foster was starting the lesson. I glanced up to see the girl from the breezeway walk into the room. My muscles tightened. I was ready to spring into action, but for what I wasn't sure. The tingling sensation returned and the overwhelming urge to go to her scared me enough that I stayed in my seat.

She walked to Mrs. Foster with a slip of paper held in her outstretched hand. The teacher inspected the note carefully before announcing to the class, "Everyone, this is Stella Evangeline, she will be joining us for the rest of the semester. Please make her feel welcome." A muted chorus of hellos echoed from around the classroom. A low whistle sounded from the across the room. I scowled in that direction, catching one boy's eye in the process. He cocked his eyebrow at me challengingly as a confident smirk stretched over his face. I narrowed my eyes at his arrogance. Let's see him try. My gaze returned to the front of the class in time to see Stella wave shyly. Mrs. Foster told Stella, "There's a seat next to Jody in the third row. You can share a text book until you get one."

"Thank you," the girl replied and walked to the empty desk. She sat gracefully, a mere two rows up and one over from my own seat.

Mrs. Foster called the class to silence once again, "Two hundred and fifty-three."

The rest of the class passed in a blur. I stared at her the whole time, my mind working hard at memorizing every detail. Her name repeated itself in my head. Stella Evangeline.

The little details of her appearance had my undivided attention, even as my mind rebelled against the swirling emotions she evoked. How her hair was twisted up captivated me. Her pink and green shirt came just to the top of her jeans and was tight enough to show off her figure. The way that she would shift in her seat enthralled me. I couldn't understand why. The tugging, tingling sensation lessened when she wasn't looking at me, but it was still enough to put me on edge.

There was movement out of the corner of my eye. The boy in the back of the class who had whistled at Stella (I think his name was Ben? Brad? Something starting with a B) poked the girl in front of him and slipped her a small folded piece of paper and jerked his head towards Stella. The girl passed along the note.

I watched all of this transpire with an inexplicable fury building inside of me. I held my breath as she received the note and discreetly unfolded it. I counted the seconds that passed as she read whatever the jerk had written. Her face was partially hidden from the angle I was sitting, but I could still see the wrinkle in her nose and the disgust that washed over her.

Stella glanced back at Ben/Brad/Bozo, who watched her with the same lazy arrogance that he had challenged me with. I heard the subtle rip of paper. The stricken expression on Ben/Brad/Bozo's face relieved me so that I let out the breath I'd been holding and relaxed my grip on the book I'd been subconsciously bending in half. A soft laugh escaped me and Ben/Brad/Bozo, whoever he was, shot me a dirty look for it. I returned it with my own victorious smirk before I could stop myself.

He broke eye contact first and when he did, confusion swept in. What was I doing? All of this emotion over a girl? She couldn't be human. Humans never affected me like this. She had to be something more.

But she wasn't. Was she?

What was wrong with me? I grew up with the horror stories of what happened when angels were attracted to humans. The very idea should have been revolting. Still, she called to me, superseding everything I was ever taught, and I had to wonder. Was she the one I was looking for or just some strange infatuation?

With difficulty, I tore my gaze away from Stella as she got up from her desk when the bell rang. She left the room before I did with twenty other kids between us. By the time I was out of the door, she had disappeared.

My instinct was to track her down and demand to know what the hell she was doing to me. But I knew better than to do that. Instead, I forced myself to go to my next class and away from her distracting presence. The last time I thought a human was the one I was supposed to find, it had turned out to be a disaster. They had only been a fascination; they had known nothing about the Angelic War. But, if I remembered correctly, I hadn't been this affected by just being around the human either. I took my math class as a welcome chance to get my head on straight and to decide on how best to approach her.

By the time I arrived at the classroom, I'd almost convinced myself that I'd imagined the entire episode. I sat down and pulled out my notebook. My thoughts wandered as my pencil flew over the page. Someone tapped my shoulder. The contact sent electricity down my arm and my back and I jumped as though I had been stung by a bee.

"Sorry," Stella said, her voice rich and warm. It was like music. I gazed at her, completely dumbfounded as she went on. "I didn't mean to scare you. Can I sit here?"

Without thinking, I blurted, "What the hell are you doing here?"

Giving me a quizzical look, she hooked a strand of hair behind her left ear. She was nothing short of gorgeous, even with how confused she looked. "Um, I'm in this class. I was just looking for a seat."

"Sorry," I amended. "Of course you can sit here."

She smiled, making the heat return to my cheeks. It took all of my self-control to sit still.

As she took the desk beside me, she extended her hand. "I'm Stella. Stella E—"

"Evangeline," I finished. The puzzled look returned to her face, so I explained haltingly, "You're in my English class." Not knowing what else to do, I took her hand in mine intending to shake it. The electric shock grew more powerful, but I found I didn't mind.

"Ah," she nodded and let go of my hand. The tingling stopped as soon as the physical contact ceased. She frowned at her fingers and I wondered if she felt the strange tingling sensation as well.

To fill the growing silence, I said, "I'm Ryan."

She stopped contemplating her hand and looked at me. "Hi. Oh!" She gasped and I panicked at the sound. "Your eyes..."

Hastily, I bowed my head, forcing my gaze to the ground. Damn. Why hadn't I remembered my sunglasses before I left the house this morning?

"No," she said sounding apologetic. "I didn't mean it like that. They're amazing."

I glanced up, surprised. She flushed at the admission and opened her binder. There was a strained silence between us for a moment. I was about to ask if she had noticed the strange electric sensation when we touched, but Mr. Pooler, the math teacher, called for our attention.

The disruption was probably for the best. I would have probably made an ass out of myself and, for some reason, I really wanted to impress her.

Pooler began class with his usual charm and grace. "Alright, listen up! Today we are going over Integers. Open your books to page three hundred twenty-seven," he boomed. Pooler liked to treat class like boot camp. He believed that discipline was in order to keep the young minds on the straight and narrow.

I wasn't able to talk to Stella because of Mr. Pooler's diligence and swift consequences for talkers. The last thing that I wanted was to get her in trouble. I sketched absently, trying not to stare at the beauty sitting next to me. It gave me time to gather my thoughts.

Was she the one I was supposed to find? How could I know for sure? If she was, what happened next? Azra had never told me what I was supposed to do once I found the human. The more I thought about it, the more I realized that I needed to talk to my uncle.

But I was reluctant to leave the school. More specifically, I didn't want to leave Stella. There was something magnetizing about her. It was an odd feeling, this attraction. I wasn't used to wanting to be near someone, let alone a human. The revulsion that had been bred into me was still there, but in the background. It was surprisingly easy to bury it and focus instead on the mystery that was Stella Evangeline.

As my mind whirred, my hand was busy sketching, too caught up in my thoughts to pay attention to what I was drawing.

When Stella leaned over and whispered in my ear, "Wow, you are good," I nearly fell out of my chair.

There was an almost perfect rendition of Stella sitting at her desk on the paper. Her head was cocked to the side and her fingers drummed on the top of a book.

"I—I didn't," I stammered, covering up the picture with my own book.

"Mr. Gregory!" Pooler shouted from the front of the

class. He crossed the room before I could even begin to respond, and stood over me. He snatched the sketchbook from my desk and sneered. "This is not Art class."

The whole classroom fell silent, waiting to see what would happen. I met the teacher's gaze arrogantly and that made his already red face brighter. The tension was palpable. My own anger rose to match his. Who the hell did he think he was talking to me like that? We stared at each other, neither willing to break. My control began to slip. Power seeped into my limbs, coiling and ready to strike. Taking in a deep breath, I fought it back. It wasn't worth it. If I blew my cover now, I wouldn't get to find out if Stella was the one in the prophecy. I had to stay focused. I closed my sketchbook and slumped in my chair. Mr. Pooler glared at me for a moment longer before going back to his lesson.

When I glanced over at her, Stella shot me a grin and handed over a piece of paper. Still feeling my rage swirling inside, I returned the smile a little bitterly and unfolded the note.

She had beautiful handwriting, halfway between the elegant old time penmanship that was more common in the last century and the modern scrawl that passed today. It was a fascinating combination, distracting me from the message.

I'm sorry I got you in trouble. I read and her voice echoed the words in my head. *You are an amazing artist.*

A combination of excitement and fear coursed through me, banishing the anger to the back part of my mind where it sat and waited for the next opportunity for violence. I glanced over to her and found her watching me expectantly. That bolstered my elation, and I wrote back, regretting my own messy chicken scratch lettering. *Thanks. Don't worry about Pooler. He's an idiot. I didn't mean to draw you. It just sort of happened.*

Her response was quick and subtle. She slipped the note back to me with a lot more grace than I had in handing it to her in the first place. *I don't mind. In fact, I like it. Would you want to hang out sometime? Show me around town?*

I wrote without thinking. *How about tomorrow around six? Meet me at the Ventura Pier?* Never had I been so bold. The prospect of a date was new but at the same time exciting. With a sort of thrilled apprehension, I slipped the piece of paper back to her.

I tried to act nonchalant as I watched her read my response out of the corner of my eye. She grinned and penned a hasty reply.

By this time, Mr. Pooler instructed us to work problems out of our books. He walked around the room, making sure that everyone was on task. Stella had to wait until his back was turned to slip me the piece of paper. It was just in time too because he swiveled around and glared at us as if he knew what we were doing. We appeared to be hard at work, however, so he resumed his pacing.

His almost supernatural ability to detect sneaky behavior made him keep a close eye on me through the end of class. I didn't want to risk being kicked out, so I wasn't able to find out her answer until after the bell rang. As soon as it did, most of the students jumped up and headed quickly to the door.

I finally turned my attention to the note. I had succeeded in unfolding it halfway when Stella interrupted me. "So what do you have next?" she asked as she hugged her notebook tightly to her chest.

"Um. History. You?"

Pausing to consult the front of her binder, she said, "It looks like French."

"Oh," was all I could say. The disappointment was more than it should have been.

She bit her lip and watched me as if waiting for me to say something. When I stood there mute, her face flushed and she ventured, "I guess I'll see you tomorrow then. I have to go find my next class." She swept a loose strand of hair behind her ear and ducked out of the room before I could say anything more.

At once I felt like an absolute idiot. I should have said something. Anything. I could have at least walked her to her next class. Sighing, I opened the note.

I read her reply with a growing sense of disbelief. *Tomorrow sounds good. Text me. 805-555-2734.*

"Shit," I muttered. I couldn't believe it. Not only had she accepted, but she had also given me her number. "Shit!" I repeated, my excitement ebbing away.

I didn't have a cell phone.

I grabbed my bag and headed out into the melee of teenagers. Forget the rest of school; it was definitely time to talk to Uncle Az.

Chapter Three

Earthbound angels have the ability to teleport themselves from one place to another with only a thought. Usually they could do so undetected, but because my energy pattern was so unique, I was the exception to that rule. Every time I tried to teleport myself, even if it was just into the next room, an attack from either a Fallen One or a Heavenly Host soon followed. The enchantment on the prayer beads wrapped around my wrist couldn't stand up to the strain of teleportation and the carefully crafted Watcher disguise would fall away. The Heavenly Host would pinpoint my location in a second. As a result, if Azra wasn't with me, I was left with the public transportation system or cabs as my only options. I was barely permitted that because Azra wasn't a big fan of motor vehicles.

"Horrible idea," he told me when Ford's Model T came out. "They're nothing more than deathtraps. It'll never take off." Well, it wasn't the first time my uncle had been wrong.

While strange and infuriatingly dense, his logic was simple enough for me to follow. Angels, while on Earth, can only be killed by a celestial blade; a weapon forged in Heaven from the particles left from dying stars. Nothing else could harm them.

Because I was the only angel ever to be born, we weren't sure if I was impervious to a mortal death or not. On several occasions, mostly out of the careful watch of my uncle, I tried to see how far I could go. From the various injuries of an active childhood I discovered that I could pretty much heal myself. While it was accelerated by human standards, it still took some time. A few hours would mend a broken bone while a matter of minutes would render gashes into barely noticeable scars. I still didn't know how much damage I could take or if it was even possible for me to die. Since there was no known afterlife for angels, let alone for a creature such as myself, it wasn't something I was too keen to test out.

From a local payphone, I called a cab to get to Azra's favorite surfing spot in Malibu. Why a cab? Well, it was so I could bring my surfboard with me. It was times like this that made me want my own ride. About thirty minutes later, the cabbie deposited me on the side of the Pacific Coast Highway and I hauled my surfboard through the sand towards Leo Carrillo State Beach.

It was January, so only the die-hard surfers were there to pay homage to the waves. My uncle was one of them and a good distance out, perched happily on his board as he watched the horizon for the next wave. I launched into the water, hoping I would catch him in a good mood.

"Hey, kiddo," Az called when he saw me paddling out towards him.

I angled my board at him and let myself bob up and down with the small waves.

Az asked with immediate suspicion, "Hey, why aren't you in school? You're going to fail! You'll be kicked out because of your attendance record! I knew that letting you fake the flu in the fifties would come back to haunt me."

It always amazed me how fast he could switch from best friend mode to over-reacting parental mode and back again. It also amazed me how short his memory could be. It was like our fight that morning never happened. It was just as well. This was more important than the earlier squabble.

"I'm not going to fail or get kicked out of school. Nothing is wrong," I said. Then I amended, "Well, not quite nothing." I found I could barely look at him for the sudden embarrassment I felt. How could I even hope to explain?

The thought of Stella made my head spin and I couldn't get the right words. "There's this girl," I began.

To my dismay, Azra laughed. "A girl, huh?" His amusement served only to irritate me.

Taming my annoyance, I got to the point. "I need a cell phone."

His smirk was replaced with confusion. "A cell phone? How did you go from girl to cell phone?"

"Because I have a date. She gave me her number."

"Whoa!" Azra burst out. "Little Orion scored a date? How in the hell did that happen? I didn't even know that you were interested in—"

"No," I interjected, frustrated. "No, you don't understand. This girl, she's not like anyone else I have ever met. I get this feeling when I am around her. There's this tingling sensation whenever I well, anyway, when I touch her, it gets so much worse, like my arm falls asleep or something."

Azra's face was one of abject horror. "Do we need to have the talk? Damn it, I'm not ready. I thought I would have more time to prepare. We need to go back to my place. I have puppets." He started to turn his board back to the shore.

I rolled my eyes. "It's not like that."

Azra stopped moving and regarded me. The sound of lapping water hitting our boards filled the air. "Right," he said, his conclusion reached. "Come on. Let's get some grub and we can talk about this." Without even looking back to make sure I was following him, he started paddling towards the beach.

"Oh, man," I muttered to myself, dreading the lecture I was in for.

There was a restaurant just up the beach from where we washed up. An open shack really, it had a long bar as wide as the building and less than a dozen picnic tables under the tent-like umbrellas. It was one of Az's regular places to eat. The fish tacos were his favorite.

We left our boards leaning against the outside wall

before seating ourselves on the rickety barstools. Azra called out a greeting to the bartender named Frank and requested an order of six fish tacos and a Corona.

"You got it," Frank said. He turned to me, his thick Italian features at odds with the Hawaiian shirt and beach shorts. "What about you?"

"A coke is fine," I answered.

Once the man ambled off to put in our order, Uncle Az turned to me. "Alright, kiddo. What's going on?"

I took in a breath and said as quickly as I could, "A girl at school . . . she's new. I got her number. She said to text her before our date tomorrow, so I really need a cell phone, like now."

Frank returned with our drinks and, in the way of most bartenders before him, he felt the need to comment on his client's predicaments. "Getting a phone to impress a girl," he tsked looking at Azra. "Good luck, my friend. He's discovered the fairer sex."

Azra saluted the bartender with his bottle. "Thank you, Frank. It's about damn time." He took a deep swig.

What did he mean, 'about damn time?' "Uncle Az," I said, "I think she's the one I am destined to find."

"Oh, Lord," Frank moaned as Azra sputtered out his mouthful of beer. "Not even been on the first date yet and already he is talking destiny. He's what, sixteen? Azra, you better set him straight, man." The bartender wandered to the other side of the bar to tend to some of the other patrons.

It took a moment and the rest of his beer for Az to organize his thoughts enough to face me. In the silence, he wiped his mouth with the back of his hand. His voice was pitched low and his tone was serious when he finally asked, "What makes you think this girl is the one, exactly? What has she done to convince you?"

I watched him gesture to Frank for another beer and answered, "When I first saw her, everything else faded away and just looking at her sent shivers up my spine. There's this draw I feel to her, like I must be right there with her or I don't feel whole somehow. The feeling when she touched me was strange and tingly. I don't know how else to describe it."

Azra developed a sudden fit of coughing which I soon realized was meant to cover up his laughter. My glare only made him hack louder before it dissolved into a mess of giggling.

Aggravation must have been written all over my face because he struggled to get his laughter under control. "Oh, c'mon kiddo. You have to appreciate the humor of the situation."

"I guess I don't," I said icily. It was ridiculous that it was this difficult to talk to Uncle Az. He could have made it easier on me. After all, this was the whole reason why he put me through the hell that was public high school year after year, wasn't it?

Azra took in a steadying breath, his shoulders still shaking with amusement. "Kiddo, what you just described is lust at first sight. It doesn't mean she's the one. It's just that you're attracted to her. It happens all the time, believe me."

"Don't you mean love at first sight?"

"Ha!" Uncle Azra slammed his palm against the bar.

By then, Frank returned with Uncle Azra's tacos and his other beer. "Set him straight yet, Az?" He asked, chuckling a bit.

"I'm just about to."

Frank ambled away again, leaving me with my still chortling uncle.

"Orion, just because a girl makes you feel that way, doesn't necessarily mean she is the one in the prophecy. Remember what you are—a Grigori. You're going to be attracted to human girls because it is part of who we are. As long as you don't succumb to the temptation, it won't matter if you have a crush."

"My parents were Grigori's. There isn't a term for me other than abomination."

"Oh, stop it, Orion." Azra made a face at me as he

doused his tacos with hot sauce. "What I mean is that these attractions happen all the time. You can't believe that all of the ones that make you feel tingly or whatever are because of the prophecy." He took a bite of a taco. "Do you remember last time you thought you found the one? What was his name? That painter, the one who cut off his ear?"

"Van Gogh," I answered sullenly.

"Right! Van Gogh! He wasn't the one in the prophecy; you were just really getting into art about then. It's the same thing this time around because now you are getting into girls. This girl is someone you are attracted to so, of course, you want her to be the one."

I began to have serious doubts about the situation. If Uncle Az wasn't concerned about it, then why should I be? Then I remembered Stella's voice, her smile, and her penetrating gaze. The obvious power she held over me was more than disconcerting. Confusion built up inside of me as I sipped my coke. I decided on a different line of questioning. I had my doubts, but I still wasn't convinced Stella was just an infatuation.

"Then how will I recognize the human in the prophecy? You always said that I would just know. I feel like Stella is the one."

He took a healthy swig of his beer. "Does she have any special superpowers that most humans don't? When she touched you, did you feel your life draining away? Can she fly? Does she have a streak of white hair?"

I scowled. "She isn't a mutant superhero."

He gave me a smirk. "Well, how about you start out slow then? Find what she knows about us angels. See what she knows about the war. Keep an eye out for any supernatural abilities."

I toyed with the ice in my cup as I thought about what he was saying. "Find out more information before jumping to conclusions? That is really unlike you."

He shrugged. "What can I say? When it comes to the prophecy, I'd rather be safe than sorry. Do you know what kind of a ruckus we would cause if you told every girl you fell for that they were going to help end the War of the Angels? The last few times you thought you found the one were disastrous enough. "

I made a face, but he had a point.

"Now, you want a cell phone because you have a date with this chica, hmm?" Az asked between bites of his fish taco.

"Yeah, something like that."

Azra considered the idea. "I suppose that it's a good thing. I mean, a cell phone is a lot more convenient than me getting in touch with you the regular way."

I snorted. The regular way was for Azra to muscle his way into my head and give me whatever message he wanted. Angelic telepathy was anything but subtle. More often than not it left me with a splitting headache. Anything was better than being reduced to a crumpled form on the ground for an hour. Cell phones would require a lot less explanation and I could to turn it off.

"Yeah. We'll get cell phones." He nodded, confirming the decision to himself, then wrinkled his nose. "How do we get them?"

I wondered if he was messing with me. "The mall. You know the building with all of the shops inside it?"

"Don't be a smart-ass, kid," Azra told me curtly. "We'll get them before the afternoon set. Here," Azra said gruffly and handed me a taco. "Eat up."

***

Several hours later, I wearily tossed the bags from the shopping excursion to the floor of my apartment. I didn't have the courage to look in them for fear of what Uncle Azra had bought. Instead, I flopped myself face first onto my unmade bed and kicked off my shoes. "Never again," I mumbled into my pillow.

As soon as we had entered through the big glass doors of the Ventura mall, Uncle Azra's whole demeanor changed. I had forgotten the danger that was Azra inside one store, let alone in a building with dozens of them. When it came to shopping, Az reverted immediately back to the bartering and haggling methods used in the bazaars centuries ago.

Nowadays, he was the reason why working retail made people go mad.

He was determined to go into every store regardless of what they sold, so I had to drag him out of all sorts of places just to get to the cell phone retailer.

At one terrifying point I lost him. I ran through the mall, hoping I would get to him in time to save some poor clerk's sanity. An hour later, I managed to find him in a children's clothing store with an armful of bags already dangling at his side. He was arguing with one of the sales clerks over a pair of two-year old sized overalls.

"Fifteen dollars? For a pair of cheaply made pants with straps? They don't even glow in the dark! Has the world gone mad? I'll give you seven for them."

"Sir," the woman said, "the price is fifteen." By the edge to her voice it was apparent they had been going in circles for a while now. "If you don't want to pay the price, don't get them."

"This is ridiculous," he seethed, tossing the overalls onto a nearby table. "This is robbery. How can you sleep at night, woman?"

I grabbed him by the arm and tried to drag him away, apologizing profusely to the woman for his rude behavior. "I'm so sorry. He forgot his medication."

She glared at both of us and threatened to call security. I was able to get my uncle away from the irate clerk and into the general area of the mall.

"You can't do that," I told him as we set off again.

"A ridiculous price is a ridiculous price, Orion."

With my arm locked onto Uncle Azra's and with much pulling, we made it to the phone store. By then, I convinced him to let me do most of the talking. Even with Uncle Azra's interruptions we spent only thirty minutes in the store. I'm sure that was some kind of record. We got phones and a plan that would cover everything from talking to browsing the web. The representative was even nice enough to give me a quick lesson on how to work the thing.

By the time we were ready to leave, Azra had called me twice from inside the store, exclaiming that it worked.

The representative looked at him oddly.

"He doesn't get out much," I explained and then quickly changed the subject.

When we left the phone store I thought it was over. I thought we were done, but Azra had a different idea.

He linked his arm in mine and said with a wicked gleam in his eye, "We are going to go shopping!" There was no way to get out of it. Whenever I tried to guide him to an exit, he veered off into another store. My limits were definitely tested.

After the purchase of seven shirts, five pairs of jeans, two pairs of shoes, sunglasses, and a new lamp for the apartment, I was able to get him out of the mall. The second he breathed in the fresh air, the madness induced by commerce left him.

As he gazed up at the sky, he told me, "Alright, kiddo. It's time for some sets. The waves are calling my name. I'll catch you later." He slipped on his new pair of sunglasses and wandered off, leaving me with all of the bags to take back to my apartment and a seething temper.

"Never again," I repeated into my pillow. I'd heard other kids mention how much they dreaded shopping with their parents. Were their parents anywhere near as bad as my uncle was with stores? I wondered how long one of them would have lasted on one of Uncle Azra's shopping binges.

I sat up and reached for the bags at the foot of the bed and dug around until I found the one from the phone store. With all of the craziness in trying to corral Azra, there hadn't been time to really look at it.

I plugged it in and pressed the buttons to make sure

that the settings were changed to my preferences. I pulled out the note with Stella's number on it, adding her to my short list of contacts along with Azra and the phone store.

I fiddled with the phone for another minute before I discovered how to create a text message. I muttered to myself, "It's now or never," as I typed a message to Stella. *Hey, it's Ryan. From math class.*

Before I could change my mind I pushed send.

Immediately I regretted it.

What if I put in the number wrong? I double checked the number in my phone against the note. It was the same. More worries sprang into its place. What if she didn't remember me? What if I bothered her? What if she just deleted it? What if she had meant for me to text her on Friday only? What if it wasn't really her number? What if it was a way to get rid of me without having to tell me so?

I sat there on the bed, staring at the phone, absolutely terrified that it would ring yet eagerly waiting for it to do something. After ten minutes of sitting in tense silence, I got up and started rounding up the clothes that littered the floor. New clothes notwithstanding, I needed to do laundry. I loaded the washer, not bothering to sort them.

As it started going, I pawed through the bags from my inadvertent shopping trip, separating my things from Azra's. In one bag I stumbled upon a leopard print bra and a pair of black pumps.

"What the hell, Azra?" I exclaimed and stuffed them quickly back into the bag. What had he been thinking when he got those?

"There was probably a sale or something," I muttered, shying away from the thought. I placed the bags near the door so I could give them back to him.

Just as I started unpacking my new lamp (a gaudy yellow glass base with mauve tassels hanging off of the lampshade), I heard it; the high pitched, dancing melody of my phone receiving a text message.

I dove onto the mattress with more momentum than

necessary. I slid off the bed and onto the floor on the other side. Luckily, I grabbed the phone as I slid. Lying there on the floor, tangled in the comforter, I looked intently at the phone. Sure enough, on the small screen was Stella's name and a message that read: *Hey. Have you ever had history with Mrs. Thompson?*

She texted me back! And she was asking me a question! My mind worked furiously for a full minute before I typed back my witty, yet informative reply: *I don't think so. Why?*

In no time, there was a response. *That harpy of a woman assigned a ridiculous amount of homework on my first day.*

Oh, I typed, unsure of how to respond. Who was she talking about? I mentally ran through what faculty members I'd encountered at Ventura High in my time there. *Is she the really tall one with the wig?*

Yes. She told me that I needed to catch up or I'd never pass the final. Who says that to a student on their first day at a new school?

Someone who has never moved somewhere new in their life, I said. While I hadn't had the pleasure of Mrs. Thompson, I'd had plenty of other teachers with similar attitudes in the past. *What do you have to catch up on?*

It's U.S. history, so everything from when Columbus discovered it through the Civil War.

Columbus didn't discover America, I typed automatically. *He landed in the Caribbean. It's said that Vikings were the first Europeans on this continent.*

There was a long pause between texts and I grew anxious. Maybe I shouldn't have corrected her. I set the phone down, and tried not to check it every second for a new message.

The washer buzzed suddenly. It was time to switch the clothes over to the dryer. Leaving the phone where it lay on purpose, I made my way over to the machines. The conversation replayed in my head. Ugh. Why did I have to be such a show off?

I'd just barely started up the dryer when the phone went off again. There was no easy way to get to the bed from where I was so I jogged around the obstacles and flopped on the mattress taking the phone in hand.

Hey, you're right! She had sent. *Looks like the history book is wrong according to the internet.*

Before I could answer that, another text came through. *You're pretty good at this history stuff. Maybe you could help me out with my homework sometime?*

Sure. Inside I was giddy. She wanted my help with her homework? That was a good sign, right?

So what are you doing right now? she asked.

Laundry, I tapped, smiling. This whole texting thing wasn't as difficult as I thought it would be.

Well that doesn't sound very fun.

No, it's not. But I'm gonna go skating soon.

You skate? So do I! What kind of board do you have?

Her response instantly intrigued me. What were the chances that she skated too? *Actually, I make my own boards.* I looked over at my favorite, but battered deck. It was almost time to switch to a new one. It always seemed that as soon as they got comfortable, they broke. *How about you? What kind of board do you have?*

A Sector 9. Where did you learn to make your own boards?

My uncle was into making surfboards. It kinda just happened, I guess. I need to make another one soon. My thoughts wandered to the storage sheds that Uncle Azra rented out downtown. One of them was where we stored my wood press and his surfboard shaping tools. The other was filled with evidence of Azra's shopping addiction throughout the centuries. The buzz of my phone brought me out of my thoughts and back to the conversation at hand.

Have you ever been to Venice? I used to cruise down there a lot.

It took me a moment to realize that she was talking about Venice Beach, California and not Venice, Italy as I originally read. *Oh yeah, I've been there, but I didn't go to skate. My uncle took me surfing down there. It's really crowded though.*

Yeah, it can be. But it is the best place to people watch. It's amazing the different kinds of people you find down there.

People watch? Was that really something people do or was she trying to hint that she knew I was looking for someone? I didn't have a chance to even formulate a response before another text came in. She was quick!

I have to go. It's dinner time. Text you later?

My mouth twitched with a mixture of disappointment and relief. There were so many things I wanted to say to her. In the end, I typed back, *sure*, and got up looking for something to occupy my mind. But I couldn't get Stella out of my head.

As I waited for my clothes to be clean, I wound up analyzing what it was that drew me towards this strange girl. Despite what Azra had told me, the attraction wasn't just physical; it was all encompassing and in direct contrast to the disgust I usually felt at the very thought of being with any other human. All I could think about was being near her, breathing in her scent, and wrapping my arms around her—which was completely disturbing. The consequences of a Grigori being with a human were too big to ignore.

The Grigori were made to blend in amongst the humans. The problem was that they were made a little too well. Several Grigori started falling in love with the mortals and the children that came from those unions of angel and human were huge monsters that were dubbed the Nephilim.

Legend had it that they were grotesque beings who had an insatiable hunger. It was said that one of the monsters devoured three whole villages, people and all, before being stopped.

Once, when I was much younger, my father told me a story about a Nephilim. It had been found in one of the remote areas of China, decimating the mountain villages. The Nephilim was huge, easily twice the size of the Heavenly Host that came to subdue it. The monster had immense power, because it swept its arms and took out three of the Heavenly Host in one blow. But it didn't go after the other ones. Instead, it continued to eat the remaining humans who were cowering below.

The rest of the Host managed to kill the thing, but it had cost them dearly.

"That's what happens when our kind mate with humans," he had explained to me. "Our choices have dire consequences. You must be careful."

Ever since that lesson I made sure to steer clear of human girls and not let my feelings get the best of me.

But Stella Evangeline had somehow caught my attention and wouldn't let me go.

My phone rang, interrupting my thoughts. Without looking at the caller ID, I pressed a button and answered. "Hello?"

"HEY! GUESS WHO BLEW INTO TOWN?" It was Azra, shouting into the phone with a great amount of background noise in competition with his words. He rushed on before I had a chance to reply. "IT'S ASCHER! COME DOWN TO DARGAN'S!" There was a loud noise in the background that made me think he dropped the phone onto the ground. A moment later, after some scuffling, Az was back, screaming, "I'LL SEE YOU WHEN YOU GET HERE!" He hung up.

I groaned. Ascher was another of the Grigori choir and had been my mother's best friend. He was a very sedate, forbidding angel. But then, anyone would seem that way next to Azra. Ascher came and went. He checked in every so often, but never stayed with us for long. Whenever he was around I felt the power coming off of him like poison-tipped spikes. Unlike my uncle, whose energy flow was similar to the natural rhythm of the ocean, Ascher's left a bitter taste in my mouth and put me on edge.

Uncle Az said we were lucky Ascher was on our side because he would hate to have him as an enemy. I could understand why. Ascher gave me the creeps, even though Uncle Az reminded me countless times that he was the only other angel that hadn't tried to kill me. He had even saved my life once.

After the Grigori choir had been exiled and their deaths called for, the name of the game was survival. As a result, most of them avoided any contact with me so they wouldn't get a bigger target painted on their backs. Some had even tried to kill me to get back into the good graces of Heaven. So, because of me, my parents had been ostracized from the last scrap of family they had. When they died, Azra took on the lonely burden of keeping me alive.

Uncle Azra never let on if he regretted being shunned by what remained of his choir, but it didn't stop me from feeling guilty. He assured me many times that it was good that we were on our own. He said that trusting a lot of people with my whereabouts would be too dangerous, so he opted not to tell anyone. The only exception to that was Ascher.

I sighed as I picked up my board. As much as I disliked it, tolerating Ascher was a small price to pay for my uncle to have a friend. Besides, he would distract my uncle enough to let me figure out this Stella thing.

Chapter Four

Dargan's was an Irish pub in downtown Ventura and one of Azra's frequent haunts. It was a weeknight, so the small building wasn't packed. I waved hello to Marie, the matron who ran the pub. She nodded briskly in response to my greeting and pointed me in the direction of my uncle's table. His laughter boomed through the building as I approached the corner booth. Noticing that the table was covered with plates and beer glasses, I braced myself.

"ORION!" Uncle Azra exclaimed happily, waving at me. His hand was wrapped firmly around a pint of Guinness which sloshed dangerously close to the edges. Based on how loud and glassy-eyed he appeared it was a safe bet he was drinking more than just beer.

I plopped myself down next to Uncle Azra in the booth and gave a nod to Ascher.

Tall, like most others in the Grigori choir, Ascher had dark brown hair which was slicked back and curled slightly at the nape of his neck. His hooked nose reminded me of a vulture's beak and his eyes were just as beady. The dark bags under his dark eyes made him appear exhausted, like he had been working months without any reprieve. Even his suit, normally more common in some big corporate office, sagged as though it had seen too many hours in use.

"You look bigger than the last time I saw you. It still astounds me that you age, even if it is abysmally slow. How have you been, Orion?" Ascher asked. His voice, which was normally sharp and clear, was hoarse.

Before I could respond, Azra said in a whisper that most of the pub could hear, "He's got a DATE!"

I closed my eyes, willing the embarrassment to

subside. When I reopened them I found Ascher smiling thinly at me. It didn't quite reach his black eyes.

"Congratulations," he said.

I didn't want or need his approval, but I shrugged in acknowledgement. I wondered why he looked so worn, but couldn't think of a polite way to ask. Marie appeared at that moment with a glass of water for me.

"I'm glad you're here, Ryan," she said as she plunked the glass in front of me.

I looked at her, puzzled. "Uncle Azra hasn't been causing trouble again, has he?"

"Oh no. I'm just glad that you are going to be able to take him home." She pointed to my uncle who grinned and waggled his eyebrows suggestively at her. She gave Uncle Azra a withering look and said as she turned away, "He's in no shape to drive."

"Ha! No shape to drive! That is a good one," Azra guffawed, slapping the table. He took a huge swallow of the pint in his hand. "What shape can drive? A circle? A square? Not parallelograms. They're just bastards."

I raised an eyebrow to Ascher. "How much did you give him?"

This is inevitably what happened when Ascher met up with us: he would bring Uncle Az a bottle or two of Heavenly Nectar. Similar to wine (but much more potent), it's the angel's drink of choice. Uncle Az didn't have the ability to get it on his own due to the self-imposed exile because of me, so Ascher made sure he had a supply. The result was the same; Ascher and Uncle Azra would proceed to get completely smashed.

Ascher shrugged in response to my question. "A little over half of a bottle. I think mixing it with beer makes it more ... effective, let's say." A bemused expression spread across his features.

I sighed, "How about you? How much have you had to drink?"

The smile grew wider as he watched Azra slurp down the liquid in his cup. "Oh, I've been matching him drink for drink. His tolerance is just very low."

"Pshaw!" Azra said loudly. "My tolerance is just dandy. And even if it is a little low, that is your fault for not visiting sooner. What kept you away for so long? Where have you been?"

Ascher took a thoughtful sip of his drink before answering. "Mainly in the Middle East; the war is really heating up around there. Neither the Host nor the Fallen have committed to a specific set of humans. Instead, they're making them attack each other without any rhyme or reason. There's no way to determine who's influencing which humans. Both sides are playing the religious fanaticism card a little too liberally." He snorted and took another drink. "As if the humans needed any prodding in that department."

Azra chuckled. "But that's how they were made, my friend. It's part of their charm. I didn't know you were getting more involved in the war. It seems kinda stupid to go where all the enemies are if you are trying to hide from them."

Ascher laughed. "I assure you, my friend, I'm not involved with any of the fighting. I was looking for the mirror. There were some rumors that it surfaced somewhere over in Jerusalem, but those were false."

"Mirror?" I asked. "What mirror?"

Ascher looked surprised at my question and addressed Azra. "You haven't told him about the legend of the mirror? I thought you would have, given that you believe he is the one in the prophecy."

Azra shrugged looking bored. "The prophecy has nothing to do with the mirror. We have other things to worry about."

"Oh, yes. That human that you are searching for," Ascher sniggered in return. He poured the contents from a black bottle into his beer and tipped some into Azra's as well. "How's that going for you?"

Azra stiffened slightly next to me. "It's going," he answered defensively, slurring his words. "We are a lot closer than you are to your mirror."

Ascher had never agreed with Uncle Azra on his interpretations about the human mentioned in the prophecy. He didn't believe a mere human would have the mettle to help me end the war. He saw them as weak creatures, easily swayed from one side to another. With all of the fighting he saw, I could understand that assumption. Uncle Azra, however, didn't think there was a way for me to end the war without one of them.

"What mirror?" I asked again, trying to head off the argument that was brewing. I could see the hard setting of both their jaws and the fire of disagreement kindle in their eyes.

At my question, the two Grigori looked at each other in a silent communication that I couldn't miss.

Uncle Az waved his hand and said, "Go ahead and tell him, Ash."

Ascher leaned forward over the table, a light of excitement dispelling the anger in his eyes. "Long ago, after the creation of the Earth, there was some kind of a breach in Heaven. Because of that breach, living mortals managed to get through the gates."

"How is that even possible?" I interrupted. "Living humans can't get into Heaven."

Ascher answered simply, "No one has figured out how the humans did it. It's a mystery how they were able to escape the Cherubim guardians that stood watch; none of them even detected a human presence. It was only when one of the tools the Creator used in the construction of the Earth was discovered missing that any alarms were sounded. It's said that the object they managed to steal has the power to completely unmake not only this realm, but all of existence."

"The Creator's giant eraser," Uncle Az interjected from the rim of his glass, earning him a withering glare from Ascher.

"You can imagine, I'm sure," the dark haired Grigori turned back to me, "the havoc it would cause if it fell into the wrong hands."

I could imagine. The thought of that much destructive power at the disposal of a Fallen One sent shivers up my spine. "But, if it was a tool from the Creator that was stolen then why are you looking for a mirror?"

He nodded as though proud that I had pointed that out. "Sharp observation. You see, it changes every so often. Mankind found a way to disguise this relic as ordinary objects to hide it from the angels who have been searching for it ever since. I'm sure you've heard of the Holy Grail? The Philosopher's Stone? Both are incarnations of the object that was stolen from Heaven. The last proof we have is that it had been turned into a mirror in Italy around World War Two. From the information I've gathered, I don't think it's changed yet."

"But how can a mirror erase all of creation? How does it work?" I asked. "And how could a mortal alter a tool of the Creator? I didn't think they had that much power. I mean, what being can influence that which helped create it in the first place?"

Ascher opened his mouth to answer, but Uncle Azra interrupted in a frightened whisper, "The witches can."

"Witches?" I couldn't keep the skepticism from reaching my voice. I glanced around at the other patrons in the bar. None seemed to be paying attention to our particular conversation. Even if they did, they would pass it off as the drink talking. "You can't be serious."

"Call them what you will," Ascher said, irritated at being interrupted again. "There are humans who are not like their brothers and sisters. They have enough power and talent to force their will onto things, to alter and create objects into what they desire. It's believed that a group of these humans, or witches, have the mirror and are trying to discover how to use it against the angels in order to claim the Earth as only theirs."

I frowned at this. "Why would humans want to erase the only existence they have ever known? That doesn't make any sense."

Ascher sighed. "Think about it. Humans are easily influenced by the simplest of suggestions. What if one of the factions of the war has already gotten to them? I know quite a few on either side who would love to eradicate this world simply to end the war." His tone held a certain quality to it that made me pause. Was it longing I heard?

He took a drink and I followed suit, deep in thought.

"Why do you want the mirror?" I asked again.

"Isn't it obvious? It's in the best interest of us all to neutralize the threat of the mirror. If it falls into the wrong hands, no one would be safe from the unraveling of existence."

Uncle Azra burst out laughing causing both Ascher and I to jump. "You are on a fool's errand, Ash. What makes you think that you're going to find it after all of this time? If something like that did exist, it's been lost to antiquity."

I thought Azra's outburst would infuriate Ascher, but instead he laughed along with my uncle and shrugged his slender shoulders amicably. "I could be, Az. But I'll never know unless I try. Besides, I'm working a lead I got in Rome. It's from a reliable source and worth checking into."

"Chasing rumors," Azra snorted into his nectar spiked beer. "Meanwhile, we are fending off Fallen Ones over here every other night. Just this morning, I had to stop one from attacking Orion."

I bristled. "You pushed me off the hill and wouldn't even let me try to fight him."

"You would have just gotten hurt, kid."

Ascher raised an eyebrow at this. "You mean to tell me you haven't taught him how to fight yet?"

Azra set his glass down on the table firmly. "He doesn't need to know how to fight, Ash. He knows how to hide and evade just fine. I made a promise that I would take care of him."

"Hiding and evading is fine," Ascher said, "but sooner or later, the boy is going to have to learn how to defend himself."

"How am I supposed to teach him when he doesn't even listen to me? He could get hurt... and then what?"

"Uncle Az," I interjected, "I won't get hurt. Ascher is right—I need to learn how to take care of myself."

Ascher spoke up, "What if something happened to you? What would he do then? It's your responsibility to make sure he is protected, even if he is the one that has to protect himself."

It must have been the Heavenly Nectar that made Azra sniff loudly. "They grow up so fast, Ash. I remember when he was this big," he held his hands a foot or so apart. "I had to change his diapers."

"I know," Ascher soothed. "But now he has to learn how to be an adult. I'll tell you what. I'll stick around and help get things started. How's that?"

"Okay." He peered into his empty pint and sniffled again. "If you can stick around and help, then we will teach him to fight."

It was hard to contain my excitement. Finally, they would treat me like an adult!

"We will start on Saturday, bright and early. That will give us all of tomorrow to work out who will teach him what and to go meet those business men." Azra raised his glass as a salute and Ascher and I did the same.

After swallowing a large gulp of water, I inquired, "Business men? Why are you meeting business men?"

Az clanked his glass on the table. "Never you mind. It's something Ascher is helping me with." He ruffled my hair affectionately, all of his previous weepiness gone.

Ascher, who was finally showing just how much he had to drink, commented offhand, "He looks so much like his mother."

My uncle cocked his head at me; looking for similarities to someone I couldn't even remember. "Yeah, now that you mention it, he does have her bone structure. Thank the Creator he didn't take too much after his father."

The two Grigori's laughed over this and Ascher snorted, "Thank the stars. Rasheym, as good as he was, was not a looker."

"Do you remember when he pretended to be possessed that time in Macedonia? He had a bunch of mortals around him and he was twitching and convulsing on the floor. He kept screaming out, 'I'm Legion. No, I'm Legion! Shut up, I'm Legion!'" Azra chortled at the memory.

Ascher joined in. "We had to drag him away from the crowd to get him home. Indra was so angry that night! She always did have a soft spot for the mentally deficient demons. She said they couldn't help it because they weren't all there."

"That's right! She yelled at us for an hour for making fun of him. Man, she had a tongue on her! For weeks afterwards I couldn't even look in her direction for fear that she would go off again." Uncle Azra shook his head.

This was the part I loved the most when Ascher came to visit; I got to hear them reminisce about my parents and their unguarded ramblings about the past. Don't get me wrong, Uncle Azra would happily tell me anything I wanted to hear. The problem was that I rarely knew what to ask. Besides, mostly what I got from Azra were stories about my father. Ascher, however, had been closer to my mother. When the two Grigori were together, I heard about both of my parents without struggling to ask the right questions.

"Remember that one human artist who kept hitting on her and tried to get her to pose for him. You know that Greek guy. . . what was his name?" Azra snapped his fingers trying to remember. "Orthodontist?"

"No, no," Ascher slurred. "It was Hermodenatis."

Azra scrunched up his nose. "No. Are you sure it isn't Oracles?"

"Oracles was that fellow who performed Oedipus Rex by himself in Athens."

"Oh yeah. . ." Azra lapsed into a thoughtful silence,

lost on a tangent in his mind. "Anyway," he roared once he had gotten himself back on track, "you know who I mean. Indra fixed that lecherous bastard good."

"What happened?" I asked, eager for the story.

Ascher swallowed the fry that he had stuck in his mouth before answering. "The stupid human wouldn't stop bothering her. Day and night he called on her, regardless of her hints and outright demands that he stop. He hounded her so badly that it finally got to the point where Rasheym was ready to take him out."

Azra picked up the story as Ascher stuffed some fries into his mouth. "Rasheym wanted to get rid of him and be done with it. He wasn't appreciative of his wife having a stalker. But, with your mother being who she was, Indra told Rasheym there were better ways to handle it than brute force."

Ascher continued, "She told the human she would pose for him, but their meeting would have to be in secret because of her husband. The stupid man agreed to meet her in Dionysus' temple the following night."

"She convinced him to disguise himself as her handmaiden so as not arouse any suspicion. He does all of this and the next night he showed up . . . he showed up . . ." Uncle Azra was overcome by a fit of giggles and Ascher resumed the tale.

"He showed up, in one of his wife's chitons, and she led him into the temple where she asked him to show her the pose that he wanted her to hold. Just as he's in the most embarrassing position possible, the door bursts open and in come a bunch of drunken worshippers of Dionysus ready for a mini Bacchanalia. Indra slipped out just as they began the carnival of excess pleasures and noticed what's-his-name all dolled up." Ascher couldn't hold it in anymore and dissolved into a fit of hysterics. I imagined my mother walking out of the temple with a smug look and grinned.

When Ascher recovered enough, he said, "Your parents were very much in love. Indra adored you both."

"Pity we never got the bastard that killed her," Azra whispered and we all fell silent.

This was typically how these conversations ended—with my parents' deaths. I glanced around the pub. Last call had sounded a while ago and it was time to leave. I waved Marie over to get our check.

"Are we going?" Az blinked at me from over the rim of his pint.

"Yeah," I told him as I eased myself out of the booth. "We're going."

"Ash, you got somewhere to go?" Uncle Azra asked as he slid out of the booth and onto his feet. He wobbled before regaining his balance.

"Yeah. My secretary booked a hotel for me." He patted Uncle Azra on the shoulder in a brotherly manner. "I'll see you on the beach, my friend."

Uncle Azra nodded as he leaned on me for support. "Tomorrow it is." Ascher headed out before us because Azra had to stop in the restroom to relieve himself.

"Damn physical body. Always needing something," he muttered, his rant echoing off of the tiled walls. At last, we left. Az blew a loud kiss to Marie as we headed out into the cool night air. She returned it with a slight wrinkling of her nose.

The beautiful thing about Dargan's is that it's fairly close to my apartment. I only had to drag Azra a few blocks and we would be home.

As I tried not to stumble with the awkwardness of supporting him, Azra told me drunkenly, "You know, Orion, I'm proud of you."

I rolled my eyes. "Why's that?" I asked.

"Because you have a DATE!" he exclaimed. "I was beginning to worry about you. I guess you're just a late bloomer. Your Dad would have been proud of you."

This was not what I expected him to say. When he was alive, my father treated me more as a burden than anything else. It was hard for me to believe Azra when he said my father would be proud.

I shifted away from the topic and replaced it with something that I was genuinely curious about. "Uncle Az, why don't you think the mirror has to do with ending the war? It sounds like it could be a very powerful weapon."

"Orion, you have to understand something." His speech was slurred and punctuated with hiccups. "Ascher's on a treasure hunt and the dangerous thing about that is when you are on a treasure hunt, you start seeing treasure everywhere, especially where it isn't. That's why you shouldn't jump to conclusions. You aren't a cricket, after all. "

I kept my thoughts to myself. It was obvious that he wasn't going to answer my questions right then. At least they wouldn't be answered coherently. "C'mon," I sighed, "let's get you home."

We turned down an alleyway that was a shortcut to my apartment building.

Something hissed from the shadows behind us.

I turned to see a tall figure cloaked in darkness. The aura around the figure was murky and radiating outwards in a wispy line. The little bit of light thrown by the surrounding buildings gave the shadowy form the appearance of a young man. Dark hair fell over one eye, obscuring it from view. The other eye that stared back at me was rimmed in black eyeliner and glowed pale yellow. I groaned. Fabulous. A Fallen One ready to attack and my uncle was completely drunk. Why couldn't we have started my lessons tonight instead of Saturday?

Inebriated or not, when my uncle spotted the threat, he pushed me aside to sway on his own two feet. He declared in a loud, arrogant voice while shaking his finger angrily, "You stupid emo-demon! Can't you see we're walking here?"

I caught Azra before he toppled over. The Fallen One was lithe and the only similarity to the one earlier that day was the glow to his eyes and the way the shadows clung to him. This Fallen one gave no preamble speech, no rhetorical questions and speculation, just a violent hiss as he leapt to attack.

I didn't know what to do. Even a stupid looking Fallen One was dangerous if you didn't know how to handle them. There was no time for me to react, but Azra twisted us out of the way, allowing the Fallen One to bring himself up short.

"Ok, kiddo. You wanted to learn how to defend yourself. This is your first lesson." I could smell the Heavenly Nectar on my uncle's breath and fought to keep my heart from racing too much. He was going to let me fight this guy on my own?

"Here's what you got to do. Hit him, but don't let him hit you." He smacked me on the ass and gave me a little shove forward. "Go get 'em, kiddo!"

There wasn't even time to blink before the Fallen One charged me, an unearthly cry issuing from his mouth. I danced out of the way, but wasn't quick enough. The Fallen One slammed into my side, sending me into the brick wall of the alley. Seconds after I hit the wall, the Fallen One was on me, his arm pressing into the back of my neck. His other fist punched me repeatedly in the back and sides.

It hurt like hell, but I didn't allow myself to focus on the pain. Bracing my palms against the wall, I pushed backwards as hard as I could. The Fallen One tripped and fell, taking me with him. We landed hard and I squirmed out of his arms and got to my feet as quickly as I could. I kicked him as he tried to get up. He latched onto my foot, but I was able to shake him off.

In a flash, he was up and coming after me. I backed up with my hands outstretched. Azra grabbed my hand and yanked me sideways and out of the way of the charging Fallen One. In a single, fluid movement that belied his drunkenness, he released my grasp and met the coming assault full force. He performed an impressive series of punches and kicks all while making an odd monkey-like sound that reminded me of old Kung Fu movies. He wasn't stopping long enough to allow the

Fallen One to strike back, so there were a few well-placed blows. The majority of the moves, however, only connected with air.

I stood there, stupidly, watching him and wondering what he was doing. Then it dawned on me. I held my breath, watching the exchange of blows and listening to the ever increasingly shrill noises. He couldn't be. . . Could he?

A groan escaped my lips. He was. Right before my eyes, Uncle Azra re-created Bruce Lee's moves from the ending fight of *Enter the Dragon*.

I shifted nervously as the Fallen One dodged the seemingly random moves Azra was performing. He wasn't even bothering to aim. I had to do something.

As soon as the Fallen One had his back to me I took my chance and launched into a sprint to close the distance between us. When I was close enough, I flung myself at his back in order to tackle him to the ground.

At least that was what I meant to do. As soon as I was close enough to touch him, the Fallen One swiveled around and his left arm connected with my shoulders, sending me sprawling to the ground. Before I hit the pavement, the Fallen One wrenched my arms behind me and twisted them together with only one hand.

I sucked in a sharp breath at the pain, but didn't give the Fallen One the satisfaction of a scream. The more I struggled, the more pain lanced through my arms. More pressure was added as the Fallen One shifted to sit on my arms, keeping them pinned in place. Fingers grasped my hair and yanked hard. My vision swam and my eyes watered.

The Fallen One drew a wickedly curved black blade out and waved it in front of my face. It was a celestial blade, blackened and as damned as its owner. Uncle Azra hadn't seen it, so intent was he on his memory of the action sequence.

I struggled against my assailant, trying to maneuver myself out from under him. It was no use. He had me pinned effectively.

"Uncle Az!" I yelled, hoping to draw his attention away from his reenactment. The electric crackle of the knife at my throat made me panic. The sudden burn of the blade's energy seared me.

I froze, holding perfectly still to keep the cut from getting deeper.

My shout was enough to break Azra out of the furious punch he aimed at a wall. "What, kid? I'm busy over here." Annoyed, he glanced over to see me trapped by the Fallen One.

The drunken stupor on his face morphed into a snarl of rage. He charged the Fallen One at full speed, an ancient battle cry screaming from his lips. His aura flared: a bright vibrant aquamarine edged in white, like the Mediterranean Ocean against its white beaches. In a flash, his human guise melted away and his astral form—the true form of all angels—took its place. Huge gunmetal grey wings materialized on his back. Each feather was sharp enough to slice through concrete. His swim trunks and flip-flops evaporated and in their place was shiny, elaborate battle gear complete with breastplate and mail.

He was an inspiring and horrifying sight.

From the scabbard attached to the side of his armor, he pulled out his own celestial blade. It glowed with heavenly fire, ready to be plunged into the corporeal mess of the Fallen One. It had been centuries since I had last seen him in his astral form. Gone was the stupid surfer persona and in its place was an amazing and terrible image of what the Creator had intended to be the face of balance.

The sight of Uncle Azra charging at us in all of his angelic glory was enough to shake the Fallen One's confidence. The blade slid from my neck and the grip on my hair let go. My face fell into the pavement as my arms were released and the weight of the Fallen One disappeared.

When I turned to see what happened, the Fallen One

was running away fast, but Uncle Azra was faster. He caught up with the demon before the fight could be carried out into the street. The silent, yet deafening mental scream of the Fallen One as Azra dispatched it was eerie and disquieting. A shiver ran through me as the energy that was the Fallen One dispersed.

A moment or two later, a hand reached down and grabbed my shirt, lifting me off of the ground. Uncle Azra, looking once again like a surfer, smiled at me. "That was fun." He put his arm around my shoulder and let me support his weight once again as he lost his balance. My arms hurt like hell and my shoulders weren't much better. I shook him off of me, letting him stumble back. As soon as his weight was off of me, I rotated my arms, just to make sure there wasn't any permanent damage. I'd be sore and bruised, but overall I would be fine.

"Uh-oh. You're bleeding a bit there." He pointed to my neck.

I dabbed at the wound and glared at my uncle. When I pulled my fingers away, I saw the deep red of my own blood.

"If you're lucky you'll get a scar out of it. Just think of all the stories you could tell the ladies about how you got it. You could make up literally anything."

I wiped the blood on my jeans. "All of that was a little overkill don't you think?"

"Bah," Azra waved off my sarcasm. He wobbled slightly. "Bruce Lee is never overkill. Come on, kiddo."

I scowled at the childhood nickname he pulled out just to annoy me. "Don't you think it's a little bit odd to run into two Fallen Ones in one day? It's like they were waiting for us. Or maybe they were working together?"

Uncle Azra didn't answer me. Instead he started humming to himself some tune from an old TV show and I had no choice but to drop the subject. I was more eager to get back to the apartment and clean up than pressing the issue right then. Besides, if there was something to worry about, then Azra would already be making plans to leave this place.

When we walked through the door of my apartment, Uncle Azra tumbled face first onto the couch. In a matter of seconds, he was snoring loudly.

I shuffled to the shower, sore and still mulling over what happened. It wasn't often I saw Uncle Azra transform out of his human guise. We were lucky that none of the Heavenly Host had picked up on his transformation. It had been a completely reckless move. That being said, I had to admit it was still really cool.

After inspecting the healing cut on my neck in the bathroom mirror, I turned on the water to the shower and stepped in.

I was going to have to find Uncle Azra's stash of Kung Fu movies and hide them.

"Crouching Turkey, Hidden Featherbrain," I muttered.

Chapter Five

The next day I rolled through streets of Ventura earlier than normal, weaving my way between the groups of people on their way to offices and breakfast meetings. It wasn't long before I escaped the bustling downtown area and reached the more sedate and outlying residences.

It was a typical Southern California winter morning: overcast and dreary. The sun wouldn't actually make an appearance until mid-morning or so. Being so close to the ocean, there was a permanent damp chill in the air that seemed to soak through even the thickest clothes. Gradually, the sounds of the ocean faded as I made my way closer to the school. My music choice that morning was West Coast punk because it always put me in the mood to skate. I pictured Stella's impressed face as I practiced kick flips and ollies.

Looking at the school from a distance, I could see the likeness to many prisons I had seen in both real life and film. That fact served as an appropriate analogy. The parking lot was mostly empty because not many of the other students had arrived by the time I got there. Usually I would have skated past the gates as the last bell sounded. But this time I hoped to catch a glimpse of the enigmatic new girl.

I scanned the parking lot as I cruised up to the school. Cars slowly pulled in and students wandered in the general direction of the buildings. Just as I had reached the main gate and was ready to go around again, an old rusting '79 Ford Fairmont rumbled into the parking lot.

It was mostly black and looked like small children were unleashed upon it with finger paint. Brightly colored hand prints and designs were dotted all over the car's original black paint with dozens of stickers holding up the rear bumper. The sounds that emanated from the beast were interfering with my own headphones; it was actually drowning out my music.

Frowning, I yanked out my ear buds just in time to catch part of a song—one of my favorites, incidentally—before the car sputtered and turned off. The driver side door eased open and Stella slid out.

Her hair was down and framed her face. The jeans she wore made her look taller than she was and the cropped black jacket displayed the bottom of a lacy shirt.

Plucking up my courage, I skated over to her car. She saw me and leaned against the side of the vehicle, watching. Seeing her gave me a giddy feeling and I couldn't resist doing a couple of kick flips as I approached.

"Impressive," she laughed.

I motioned to the car, "So is that. Is it yours?"

"Yeah," she made a face. "I inherited it when my brother went into the Army. Not the Mustang I wanted, but it serves its purpose." She patted the top of it affectionately.

I stared at the paint job and the bumper stickers with a raised eyebrow. "Your brother did all of that?"

"Oh, no. My cousins and I did," she said with a certain amount of pride. I glanced over to the back of the car. The little stickers covered every topic from religion to politics to band logos. She must have seen my look of incredulity because she said cheerfully, "We call it the Gospel of Spike."

I blinked. "The what?"

Her laughter was better than any music I'd ever heard. It made it difficult for me to concentrate.

"It's his name," she explained.

"You name your cars?"

"Well, yeah." She looked at me with a bemused expression. "Don't you?"

"No. I don't have one."

"Oh. Well, what about your board? Do you have a name for it?"

"No." I glanced down at the beat-up board in my hands with a slight twinge of something I couldn't readily define. Was it guilt? The idea was ridiculous.

The unexpected awkwardness descended upon us swiftly. We stood silently for a moment, looking at anything but each other.

I broke it by asking the first question that came to my mind. "Did you finish that homework last night?"

She looked at me oddly, like she wanted to say something else entirely, but changed her mind at the last moment. "Yeah, I did the reading part of it."

Out of embarrassment, I studied the pavement. Of everything I could have asked her, I chose to ask about her homework? Ugh.

Just then, the bell rang, rescuing us from the awkwardness.

"Come on," Stella said and took my hand. "You can walk me to class."

The prickling sensation caught me off guard, but I stopped myself in time from yanking my arm away from her in surprise. But despite my best efforts not to let go of her, she released my hand. I wasn't so proud to admit that it disappointed me. But I had to stop thinking like that. It would only lead to trouble.

I pretended not to notice her anxious expression as she subtly wiggled her fingers, as if they had gone numb. Had she felt it too?

As we wove our way through the crowds, I snuck peeks at the beautiful girl beside me. The other students melted away and all I could see was her. I still felt the echo of her hand in mine. I should have said something, but I was at a loss as to what.

Stella's courage was greater than my own because she asked, "Do you have a girlfriend?" Her arms hugged the books and her bag hung off her shoulder haphazardly.

"Uh, no," I answered uncomfortably.

"Why not?" Her questions were direct and to the point. I got the feeling that she would expect the same in the answers that I gave her.

"I just never met anyone I was interested in," I tried to say nonchalantly. Instead it came out rough and short. Mentally, I kicked myself. I sounded like a jerk.

"That's too bad," she said and I thought I caught the hint of hope in her tone.

The walk to Mrs. Foster's english class took both a lifetime and only a few moments. She went into the class, biting her lip as though deep in thought. I followed her, reeling with unexpected giddiness mingled with apprehension. The conflicting emotions inside me declared war and it was all I could do to maintain a careful composure as a million questions zinged through my mind all at once.

Each of us took our seats quietly. Just as Ms. Foster came to the front of the room, Stella turned and smiled at me widely as she got a pen and a piece of paper out. Despite my divided mind, my heart leapt. She smiled at me! That was a good sign, right?

"Good morning everyone," Mrs. Foster called out bringing the class to attention. "We're finishing our unit on poetry today before we begin our unit on Hamlet tomorrow. I want you to pair up with a partner to read and compare these poems by Frost and Longfellow and complete the worksheet attached. It's due by the end of class." She placed the packets on the table next to her, ready for students to come up to get them.

I groaned while the kids around me started talking excitedly. I loathed group projects. It was like being picked last for sports teams: it illustrated even more that I didn't fit in. Why was everything in high school—even the in-class assignments—a popularity contest?

My fellow students paired off and I glanced over to Stella, hoping to work with her. My hopes fell when I noticed several people surrounding her desk. Of course, working with Stella for the entire hour would have been too much to ask for. Heaving a sigh, I looked around, wondering who I would have to put up with. Usually I ended up stuck with the slacker of the class that no one else wanted to be partnered with. That was like doing all of the work on my own anyway, so there really was no point to it.

"Hey, you with anyone yet?" Stella's voice made me whip my head around. She stood just to the right of me, holding a packet in her hand. A pen graced her ear.

"Uh, sure," I said. "I mean no, I'm not with anyone."

She gave me a hopeful smile. "Would it be okay if I worked with you? I don't know anyone else here."

"Sure." I tried to sound nonchalant.

"Thanks." She scooted the nearest desk over until it was flush with mine. "The first poem we have to interpret is by Robert Frost and it is called . . ." She looked on the packet. "'Into My Own'. Oh good. This is one of my favorites."

"Why is that?" I asked, still overwhelmed at being paired with her.

She grinned as she handed me the packet. "Read it. You will see."

Blinking, I read through the poem, trying to understand what she meant.

"No." She put her hand over the words. "You have to read it out loud."

I eyed her with skepticism. "Read it out loud?"

With a gentle roll of her eyes, she explained, "There are some things that need to be read out loud. It's the kind of poem that needs a voice to be complete. Besides, it's beautiful the way you talk. It makes me think of far-off places."

I refused to allow her compliment to affect me. "I'm bad at reading out loud," I told her, keeping my face straight. I focused on my accent. Usually, it blended seamlessly with whatever dialect I was speaking without my thinking about it. Could she hear something other than a Southern Californian accent?

"Nonsense, you will do just fine. Trust me," she encouraged.

Trust me.

A chill ran down me and the words echoed with consequence, like a sort of divination. Could it be a coincidence? I looked at her, trying to see the traces of an oracle. She just gazed back at me, seemingly unaware of the otherworldly authority she spoke with. I must have been imagining it.

Taking a deep breath, I decided to trust her and hoped none of the other students were listening. The poem wasn't long, but I read it slowly and carefully so as not to stumble over the words. Reading for Stella alone was more nerve-wracking than making a speech in front of millions.

When I finished reciting and raised my eyes to her, she wore a dreamy expression. "Do you see?" she sighed.

"It's a poem about forsaking the world," I said, sort of confused at her reaction. "But it's naive to believe the world won't change who you are. Everything changes. It's because of the adaptability to change that humans have advanced as far as they have. If not for change, there'd be nothing but grunting Neanderthals living in caves. There wouldn't be any progress."

The dreamy expression was gone from her face; now, there was astonishment and a certain fire in her eyes that told me she disagreed.

"You talk funny," she said with the utmost serious expression on her face.

I blinked at her. "I what?" Frantically I thought over what I said. Was it the accent she somehow heard in my speech? How was that even possible? That couldn't be what she was talking about, could it?

"You don't sound like a teenager," she clarified. It didn't help at all. I must have looked stricken because she went on to say, "It's not a bad thing. I understand what you are saying, but you sound older. It's . . . nice."

"Oh," I breathed a sigh of relief. Not sure what else to

say, I simply left it with, "Well, okay."

The smile was back on her lips, letting me know she found my reaction to her observation amusing. She went back to the subject of the poem. "This isn't about not changing. It's about having the courage to leave what's familiar to confront the unknown. It's the guts to maintain your beliefs and stay true to yourself despite what the world throws at you."

Just as she was pleasantly surprised by my words, I was impressed by the opinion she put forth. Her argument was a welcome change to the typical insipid teenager I usually worked with and it was definitely a more interesting conversation than I usually got from my uncle. I found I wanted to discuss things with her. Things that I had learned over the centuries, things that I hadn't talked about with anyone, just to see what she thought.

The classroom had grown louder as the other students discussed their assignments. I leaned forward in my seat to ask, "Why is this one of your favorites?"

"I told you," she said sharply, but there was a smirk on her face.

"No," I countered. "You told me to read it out loud. You didn't explain why this is your favorite."

I sensed her hesitation and wondered at it. After such a decisive argument just moments before, this reticence was perplexing.

"I. . ." she started, but somehow lost her nerve. After mentally forming her response she answered, "This poem is a reminder for me to not to get too attached to the way things are."

I wondered what had happened for her to need such a reminder and what she was expecting to change.

I was about to ask just that, but what came out of my mouth was a shaky and whispered, "Who exactly are you, Stella Evangeline?" The power in those words crackled around us. I hadn't meant to infuse the words and I wasn't even sure I was the one who had. It was like when Stella told me to trust her. There was a hint of foretelling, an elusive command from on high.

At my question, her face instantly became unreadable. Could she feel the charge in the air as I did? I reached out to touch her hand, meaning to reassure her. The tickling sensation came back full force. She pulled it away at the second I made contact.

When she spoke, it was more subdued and held a certain amount of distance to it. "I am who I am."

I could feel the confusion on my face, but I smoothed it out carefully before saying, "Stella, I know this is strange, but please just hear me out. I haven't experienced anything like this before and I was wondering if you feel it too."

"Feel what?" She looked at me, both expectant and guarded at once.

I grappled for words to describe the sensation. Everything that came to mind sounded so stupid in my head. Why was asking her about the prophecy so difficult? I chickened out in the end, thinking I might have a better chance later that night. That is, if she still wanted to go out with me. "Never mind. We better finish the assignment," I abruptly switched topics as I withdrew my hand from the desk. I kept my gaze trained on the paper, avoiding her eyes.

What the hell was wrong with me?

We went through the questions quickly and formally, not sure how to handle the sudden embarrassment that sprang up between us. The reserved way she spoke made me keep quiet and hope she just thought I was harmlessly weird.

The class ended and Stella grabbed her stuff and strode to Mrs. Foster's desk to deposit our completed worksheet. I waited for her to return and when she did, I cast a brief smile as we made our way to Math class.

We spoke of inconsequential things as we walked. I was still kicking myself for the awkwardness earlier, but the tension had eased. It wasn't anything we would talk about, but the fact that it passed rather quickly gave me hope. Mr. Pooler yelled at the class in his normal way of greeting. The students pulled out their homework and passed it forward.

My attention was not on the lesson. I was more focused on the subtle sounds coming from Stella's general direction. If I wanted to, I could phase out every other sound in the room except for her. It would be a simple thing for me to get lost in the beating of her heart and the rhythm of her breathing.

I was so busy listening that I wasn't aware of the passing time. When the bell rang, I wasn't ready for it. Students filed out the door and Stella leaned towards me. "Still on for tonight?"

"Absolutely," I confirmed, thanking my lucky stars that the tension hadn't put her off completely.

She rewarded me with a slight blush of her cheeks. "Ventura Pier at six, right?"

I nodded. "I'll be there."

She waved as she left the classroom and I watched her go, feeling a mixture of emotions I wouldn't have thought possible.

"Tonight," I muttered to myself, the dread and anticipation overwhelming me. If I couldn't talk to her about the prophecy and the Angelic War right then, what made me think that being alone with her later on would help matters?

***

My music was at war with Uncle Azra's TV show. Every time I turned up my stereo, he would increase the volume on the TV. Soon it was a horrible mish mash of Saved by the Bell re-runs and The Foo Fighters. I'm sorry, but Dave Grohl and Screech just do not mesh.

Enough was enough.

"Would you turn that off and help me?" I snapped as I gathered the empty wrappers and cans that littered the area around my uncle's prone form.

In response, he held up his hand. "Shhh! Zach is totally about to kiss Kelly!"

I heaved the pile of junk I gathered in my arms on top of him. "I have only an hour and a half until I have meet her at the pier. I need you to get off your ass and help me get this place decent!"

Azra twisted to look at me. "Dude! I didn't know you were bringing her here! I thought you two were going out, as in out on the town or something."

"Yes. No. I don't know. We could come back here. She said she wanted to see some more of my artwork."

My uncle snorted. "You think you are going to score by bringing her to this dump?"

I fought the urge to punch him. "I'm not trying to score. I'm just trying to make it decent. I need your help."

"You really like this girl, don't you?"

I spread my arms out as if to say, 'duh!' "Will you help me already?"

He shifted the garbage I had thrown at him onto the floor. "If you kept it clean in the first place, you wouldn't be scurrying around like this. I can only impart so many cleaning tips. But, I will give you some of the finer points of dating." He clicked off the TV and, to my dismay, he also turned off my stereo. "You need to pay attention," he explained, rubbing his hands together, "This could be the difference between coffee after dinner or a drink in the face, if you get my meaning."

"I don't need that kind of help," I told him sourly and resumed my tidying up. Once he got on a roll will his well-intentioned, but ultimately stupid advice, he wouldn't stop. I glanced around the apartment and grimaced. There was too much to do before I had to leave. I didn't have time for his yammering.

"You really want to wow her, right?"

"Yes! Which is why I have been asking you to help me with the chores." I threw a rag at him to emphasize my point.

He scoffed. "Believe me, kid, I'm gonna help you.

What are you planning to do on your date?"

"What?" I asked as I scrubbed at a particularly stubborn spot on the rug. I'd abandoned my brimming garbage bag by the door. I began hunting down rogue stains with the carpet spot remover that had been left innocently in the refrigerator two weeks ago.

"Are you going to take her to a movie? To dinner, maybe? Or perhaps a long moon-lit walk on the beach?"

An uncomfortable feeling bloomed in my stomach and I stopped scrubbing. "Dinner?" I echoed faintly. "I— no. She said she wanted to hang out and look at my artwork. I thought that we would . . ." I let the sentence trail off. What were we going to do? Just come to the apartment? What was she expecting?

"You don't have any idea what to do, do you?" Uncle Azra grinned. He got up and went to the kitchen for another drink.

"No," I admitted.

A soft chuckle came out of his mouth. "Art, huh?" It was as though he had never considered art to be an opportunity to impress the 'fairer sex.' He stood in the kitchen, watching me scrub. "You have to do something before coming to your apartment. Girls don't like to feel like they're being used."

I pulled my eyes away from the surrounding mess and regarded Azra indignantly. "What do you mean? I'm not trying to take advantage of her at all!"

"Look." Azra leaned on the counter. "Take her out on the town or bring her some flowers. Make her feel like she's special. Don't take it too far on the first date. That's what the second date is for." He smirked wickedly.

"And you call yourself an angel," I muttered, disgusted. Getting off the floor, I grabbed a different rag and started dusting some of the flat surfaces that I had cleared. "After all of the horror stories about Nephilim you and my dad have fed me over the years, what makes you think I even want to get that close to a human?"

"You missed a spot." Uncle Azra pointed to a section

of the floor that was underneath an errant magazine. He ignored the glare I gave him, "Oh, you will still want to get close to her. That is perfectly natural and acceptable. What isn't acceptable is getting her knocked up; that's when you will be in way too deep. But, for the meantime, have a little fun. Take her out to dinner; it's a good sign if they feel comfortable enough to eat in front of you. Also, if you can 'accidentally' spill a drink on her, it'll give you a good measure of how far you can go and if she is the forgiving sort. Bonus points if she's wearing a white shirt. Get her a corsage, but be careful with the pins. You don't want to hurt her. I recommend duct tape instead. That stuff will fasten anything."

This was getting ridiculous. "That's enough. You're starting to freak me out." I shoved Uncle Azra out of the kitchen and ushered him to the door. "You need to go. I can't listen to this anymore."

"Wait, one more thing," he protested as I was trying to close the door on him. He pushed back to have his last word. "Be upfront and honest, Orion. That's absolutely crucial. Tell her you have a condom and show it to her, preferably before dinner."

"Do you want me to get slapped? Just get out of here!" I slammed the door and leaned against it in case he tried to come back inside.

My peace only lasted a little while though. Fifteen minutes later, Azra was back and with a moderately sized box in hand. I was working on getting the kitchen to a non-biohazard state when he came in.

"What do you want?" I asked as he dropped the box onto the table with a thud.

"This," Azra motioned to the box, "is for your protection. I wasn't sure what would work for you, but I figured one of these is bound to get the job done."

I was scared of what was in the box, but I was too curious not to ask. "One of what?"

Azra upturned the box, letting the contents spill over the table and onto the floor.

My eyes nearly popped out of their sockets when I saw what it was. "What the . . ."

It was a box full of contraceptives, and not just condoms, though there were plenty of those. There were birth control pills, patches, as well as several bottles full of strange liquids and bunches of dried herbs. It looked like he brought me every contraceptive known in the history of mankind.

Azra began sifting through it. "Like I said, something has to work."

I could barely formulate any sort of response. "I—I—" I stammered.

"No need to thank me, kiddo," Azra smiled. "I'm just looking out for you."

"What exactly do you think I'm going to do tonight?" I asked, horrified.

Az brushed off my concern, "You never know when you'll need protection. Since we don't know what will work and what won't, I recommend using them all at once. It's better to be safe than sorry."

I closed my eyes for a moment, trying to abate the sudden throbbing in my temples. "I don't need condoms. I'm just trying to find out if she is the one in the prophecy."

"Whatever you say, kiddo." Azra headed towards the fridge, leaving me to clean up the pile of contraceptives. He grabbed a beer and watched me. "By the way, you aren't going to wear that, are you?"

That was the last straw. I dropped my rag and lunged, intent of knocking some sense into him. His reflexes were quick and I landed gracelessly on the floor.

"What's gotten into you?" My uncle asked, offended. "I'm only trying to help."

I sputtered as I got to my feet. "Trying to help? I asked you to help me get this place clean and what do you do? You get me contraceptives!" I was yelling and I knew I should stop, but I couldn't help it. The stress of my uncle right then, not to mention everything else going on in my mind, was too much for me to handle. I fought to keep my composure. With my right hand, I started rubbing the prayer beads on my left wrist.

A faint glimmer of understanding sparkled in his blue eyes. "Alright, Orion. What else has to be done around here?"

I exhaled loudly as I brought my temper back under control. "I need to finish the kitchen, then the bathroom, and then I need to get my art hung up."

"Ok," Azra looked at the clock on the microwave. "Don't worry about all this. I'll take care of it. Why don't you go chill and figure out what it is you want to do with the girl tonight? The last thing you need is to be so tightly wound on your date."

"What? You mean leave you here alone?"

"Of course I mean leave me here alone. I can work quicker without you underfoot."

"You'll be gone by the time I get back?"

There was a moment's worth of hesitation. "I'd really like to know who you are hanging out with, Orion. I mean, as a responsible guardian angel, it is my duty to know what sort of characters you are influencing." At my hard look, he chuckled. "Fine. I promise I won't be here. Go on. Let me get to work."

I asked, eyeing him, "Why the sudden change? What's the catch?"

"There's no catch. I see that you are freaking out and I'm supplying a resolution. The place will be ready for you when you bring the girly home, I promise." Uncle Azra held his fingers up as though he were taking a Boy Scout oath.

I thought about his offer. "Promise it'll be perfect?"

"Absolutely," Azra shooed me out of the kitchen. "Go on. Good luck tonight. And remember, don't stay out too late. You have training in the morning."

With a more than a little reservation, I snagged my board and my iPod and left my uncle to do his thing. I prayed that Azra wouldn't sabotage my date.

Chapter Six

I leaned against the railing of the pier and stared out into the crowd milling around me. The sun had begun to set, making the clouds streak the sky with pinks and grays in its dying light. People wandered past me on the hollow-sounding planks of the wooden pier. I watched the couples that strolled by hand-in-hand, studying their actions as I tried to quell my nerves.

My plan for the evening wasn't the best first date in the world, but it was all I could come up with. I just hoped that I could bring up the prophecy at some point without sounding like a complete idiot.

"You better treat her right tonight. You'll be one sorry angel if you don't," a thick Brooklyn accented voice murmured in my ear.

I whirled to see where it had come from. "What the hell?" There wasn't anyone near me. I scanned the people walking around the pier. I could have sworn someone had spoken to me. It had sounded so close. I must have overheard a conversation as someone passed by. Yeah. That had to be what that was.

My phone rang then, driving the voice out of my thoughts. Fumbling, I pulled it out to answer it. "Hello?"

"Hey," Stella responded. I could tell she was smiling by just the tone of her voice. "I'm in the parking lot. Where are you?"

"Um, I'm on the pier. Do you want me to meet you out there?"

"Nah," she said. I heard the slamming of her car door. "I'll come to you."

I made sure my phone was set on silent before returning it to my pocket. The last thing I needed was

Uncle Azra checking up on me.

The time it took Stella to get from the parking lot to the end of the pier seemed endless. All of the doubt and insecurity rushed back into my head as I waited. How was I going to get through the whole date without scaring her away completely?

When she walked onto the pier and started towards me all of the questions disappeared. "Hey," she greeted. She was dressed casually in jeans and a zip-up hoodie with a cartoon character emblazoned on it. A small messenger bag was slung over her shoulder.

"Hey," I responded. She walked over to the edge of the pier and leaned over the railing, her eyes down at the foaming water beneath the wooden planks. I joined her with my hands clasping the rail. The sun ended its descent into the watery horizon.

"I love this time of day," Stella said. "It's like the world is caught between light and darkness."

This was the perfect time to bring up the Angelic War! As I tried to phrase the question in my mind, the voice that I thought I had imagined scoffed, "There she goes being all weird. She isn't going to get anything accomplished if she keeps that up."

The glare Stella gave my left shoulder was murderous. What the hell was going on? Could she hear the voice too? I hazarded a glance over my shoulder. There was nothing there.

Stella looked at me fully, her anger disappearing in a blink, "Sorry. I was writing before I came here, so I'm all dreamy. What is the plan?"

It felt like I was in the middle of an argument between two people and one was desperately trying to ignore the other. Not sure how I should react, I decided to keep it simple for now and to give myself some more time to ease into the topic of the prophecy. I responded to Stella with a grin, drumming up some excitement in my voice. "Did you bring your board?"

"Yeah, it's in Spike."

"Good," I picked up my own skateboard and grabbed her hand. It was a bold move, but worth it. I was ready for the tingling sensation, so it didn't bother me as much. She didn't pull away this time either. "Come on. Let's go get it."

To my delight she gave me a confidence-boosting squeeze. "Alright."

We walked hand-in-hand to her car. "What were you writing about?" I asked.

She shrugged, but was happy enough to explain. "I write down feelings I get."

"I see. Any particular feelings jump out at you today?" It was a loaded question and by the expression on her face, Stella knew it too.

"A few," she conceded with a coy smile. "Mostly they had to do with you."

"Me?" I didn't even have to feign surprise.

"Of course. You're a real boost to a girl's self-esteem," she laughed and took out her keys from her bag.

We reached her car and she opened the back hatch. She pulled out a beautiful, green and blue board about three feet long.

I eyed the craftsmanship of the board appraisingly. "Nice," I commented.

"Thanks." She set the board down and closed the hatch of the car. "Where to?"

I pointed to the hills that shadowed the downtown area. "Up there."

Without any more conversation, I dropped my board and started rolling. I looked back to make sure she followed. She kept up easily, so I increased my speed, to see how she handled it.

"Hey! Are you trying to ditch me?" she yelled, amusement peppering her words.

"What's wrong?" I taunted, glancing back at her. "Can't keep up?"

"Oh, you think not?"

The game was on and I was more than impressed. Most girls who say they skate usually only have the board as an accessory. Stella was definitely not one of those girls. She not only kept up, but she even passed me a couple of times. When she did fly by I really had to push myself to get back in the lead. Our laughter only increased each time we passed each other. The people walking around downtown got out of our way for the most part as we approached. Only a few of the older crowd yelled for us to get off of the sidewalk. We laughed even harder at their angry shouts.

"We're going to City Hall?" Stella asked, squinting at the ornate architecture of the building we momentarily stopped at.

"Not exactly. We're going up there." I pointed up to the hill where the Serra Cross of Ventura resided.

I was fairly certain it would be safe tonight. The Fallen Ones wouldn't be roaming around quite so early. Besides, she had to see the view.

Stella wrinkled her nose. "What's up there? It looks like it is just a hill."

"Trust me. The view is amazing. It's too steep to skate up, but the walk will be worth it," I assured her.

We started up the hill, leaving the noise of downtown nightlife behind.

"What's your favorite movie?" Stella asked to fill the quietness of the night.

I'd seen so many movies; it was difficult to pinpoint just one. I went with the one I identified with the most. "I think it would have to be Tod Browning's *Freaks*."

Stella frowned with unfamiliarity. "I haven't seen that one. What is it about?"

"It's an old movie from the nineteen thirties about a bunch of circus freaks who have been rejected by 'normal' society so they created one of their own. They have their own rules, their own code. Well, one of the performers falls in love with one of the normal circus people and it is about how the freaks accept her, or not."

Stella looked impressed. "That sounds interesting."

"It is. We'll have to watch it sometime." She smiled at

my suggestion and I asked her own question back. "What's yours?"

There was no thinking, she just blurted out, "*Edward Scissorhands.*"

"Ah," I said. "Tim Burton or Johnny Depp fan?"

"Can there be one without the other?" she quipped. "Where are you from?"

I looked at all of the brightly lit houses as we passed while I formulated my answer. "A little bit of everywhere. Uncle Azra and I go so many places, sometimes it feels like I'm from everywhere and nowhere at the same time." It was a half-truth, but it worked.

"That explains the accent then."

"Is it really that noticeable?" I asked, feeling self-conscious. No one had ever mentioned it before.

"It is to me. But then, I have an ear for them. So, you live with your uncle, huh? What happened to your parents?" After the words came out of her mouth, she blushed and I saw the hesitation in her eyes, like she was afraid I would be offended.

To ease her mind, I answered affably, "They died a long time ago. I was a baby when my mother passed, so I don't even remember her. I think I was about eight when my father died. It's hard for me to remember. Sometimes it feels like Uncle Azra's been looking out for me forever."

"Oh jeeze. Ryan, I'm so sorry," she said, her eyes fixed on the ground in front of her. She looked horrified that she had asked.

"It's okay," I replied, trying to reassure her. "Really. What about you? Where did you move from?"

"My family is Italian. My grandmother and I go back every summer to her home village. When we aren't in Italy, we live in L.A. Well, we did until recently. Nona said we were needed here, so this is where we moved." Stella said this rather stoically, like she was trying to be more accepting about the situation than she really felt. When I peered at her questioningly, she continued, "Nona gets these . . . instincts and she is very insistent on following them. When she said that it was time to leave, we did."

I knew all too well what that felt like. "That's kind of random, but I understand the feeling. Uncle Azra does the same thing."

Stella shrugged. "There's always a reason for what Nona does. She believes the consequences of ignoring them would be greater than acting on them."

"I suppose that makes sense." It sounded like her grandmother had enough precognitive ability to see the path that she needed to be on, but not enough for specifics. Interesting.

We came to the end of the housing area. The darkness of the night became thicker without streetlamps to break it apart. Headlights flashed and we moved to the side of the road.

As the car passed us, I cleared my throat to break the silence "You said you moved here with your grandmother. What about your parents?"

Stella took in a breath as we hiked further up the hill. "My mom died giving birth to me. My dad wasn't the same after that. We moved in with my grandmother after her death. He left about seven years ago." She said this matter-of-factly, like she distanced herself from the emotions of the situation.

"I'm sorry. Do you ever hear from him?" I asked. Her lack of feeling seemed cold to me. Or was she filtering the emotions out like I was? Losing your parents wasn't anything you really get over, no matter how much time you have.

"He calls every once in a while. Mostly it's to ask for money or something." She reached up to twist a strand of her hair between her fingers. "To tell the truth, I don't really understand him. I mean, he's family, but he doesn't act like it. Nona says that it could be that he doesn't want to be around my mother's ghost."

"Your mother's what?"

Stella flushed. "I meant her memories. She isn't really a ghost."

"Oh." I allowed the silence to stretch into the night until I could latch onto the next logical topic of conversation. "So . . . do you believe in ghosts?"

Stella gave a sharp chuckle as she kicked a rock to the side of the road. "Of course I do."

"Really? Why is that?"

"Well," she took in a breath and focused her gaze on the road in front of her. "We don't really die; our energy just changes. Ghosts are the transition into something else. Some transitions take longer and are more annoying than others is all."

I had a feeling that her last statement wasn't meant for me, but, at the same time, I wasn't entirely sure who it was meant for. To stay on the safe side, I ignored it. "That's an interesting theory."

"Do you believe in ghosts?"

We had crested the hill and come to a sort of plateau fork in the road. We could turn right and head through the gate to the cross or continue left to follow a steep incline to get to the top of another hill.

"I'm not sure what I believe in," I answered as I paused just before the fork in the road. I strained to listen as far up the road as possible. There wasn't any indication that a Fallen One was there.

Stella looked at me. "Which way?"

Sure that I didn't hear anything out of the ordinary, I pointed up the incline. "Left."

"You're killing me!" she groaned jokingly. "I've never worked this hard on a date before."

I assured her with an encouraging nod, "It'll be worth it, I promise."

"Will you at least tell me what we are doing?" she asked. "I mean, it would be nice to know what I am climbing for."

"Let me ask you a question," I replied, savoring the expectant look that she gave me. "Have you ever gone luging before?"

"What?" Her brows furrowed, making her rounded

face even more adorable.

"I'll take that as a no. More or less, we're going down this hill sitting on our boards."

"Are you kidding me?" Her mouth dropped open.

I grinned. "Don't tell me that you are scared."

"No! Of course I'm not scared," she shot back defiantly. The anxious look on her face told me otherwise.

"Good. The last one there has to go first!" I started to sprint up the hill, leaving her to struggle after me.

"Hey!" I heard her shout from behind me. "That's not fair!"

The sound of our feet hitting the pavement brought a staccato echo in the quietness of the night. I knew I was a lot faster than she, so I purposefully slowed down, letting her overtake me.

"I beat you!" she panted as I rolled up next to her.

"Yeah," I breathed heavily, giving the appearance that I had been laboring as much as she. "You win." We stood there, catching our breaths. "But before we go down, I want to show you something." I walked with her to the edge of the precipice. Before we reached the perfect spot, I told her, "Close your eyes."

"You aren't going to throw me off the cliff, are you?" She joked.

"Nope. Pushing you down the mountain comes in a few minutes. But you have to see this first." I maneuvered behind her and placed my hands over her eyes. "Walk forward slowly. I'll let you know when to stop." We moved awkwardly as I tried to keep a respectful distance from her. "Stop," I said. "Ready?"

"As ready as I ever will be," she answered. There was a lightness in her tone that sounded like she was enjoying herself.

I removed my hands from her eyes and heard her gasp. She was positioned perfectly so that she would see the lights gently twinkling from downtown contrast with the darkness of the ocean. The view was phenomenal.

"It's beautiful!" she breathed.

"Not nearly as beautiful as you are," I countered and immediately cringed inward. Ugh. Why did I say that?

A tense silence threatened to overcome us before she burst into laughter, shattering it into a million pieces. She turned to face me, a giant grin on her face. "That was really cheesy."

I laughed along with her. "Yeah, it was. Sorry. Forgive me for the cheese?"

She pretended to think. "I don't know. Being cheesy isn't what I usually go for, but I kind of like it coming from you."

I grinned. She didn't mind me being cheesy and romantic? That was definitely a step in the right direction. Wasn't it?

"All the streets look so far away," she said, peering down into Ventura's downtown scene. From this distance, the cars looked little more than toys. "No wonder you like this place. It's so high up. It must be kind of what heaven is like."

"Yeah," I replied, wondering what she meant. "It's one of my favorite places in this town."

She stared at the inky blackness of the ocean beyond the lights for a while. I stayed quiet, allowing her to take in the view

We went back to the road and I showed her how to sit on her board for the trip downhill. It was easier for her because she had a long board at least half her height.

"Make sure that you hold on like this." I positioned her hands under her bent knees.

"Steer by leaning your weight to one side or another. Use your feet to brake."

"Are you sure this is safe? I mean, I haven't been that bad of a date that you want to permanently injure me, have I?" she asked. Her voice, though light and playful, held a tremor of something else. Not fear exactly, but excitement mingled with trepidation. Like she didn't think that this was the smartest thing to do but, at the same time, she didn't really care.

"Don't worry. I'll be right behind you. I won't let anything bad happen."

Stella nodded and took a deep breath. "Alright. I'm ready. Let's do this."

I was amazed at her fearlessness. Placing my hands on her back, ready to push, I called out loudly, "One. Two. Three!" I heaved on the last syllable and she went flying down the hill. Her squeal of delight filled the night air and I lost no time in sitting on my own board to follow her down. She negotiated the turns like a pro; her gasping shrieks were filled with pleasure.

Headlights flashed against the darkness of the night and I yelled, "Stella, stop!" I didn't know if she heard me over the wind and the grating noise of the wheels over the asphalt.

Suddenly, her board tipped like it hit a rock. She veered sharply to the left, over compensated for the adjustment, and wound up colliding with a mound of dirt. To my horror she fell, crumpling like a rag doll to the ground and then was still as stone. The car cruised past us without even slowing.

Shit! I stopped breathing for a second as I skidded to a stop a few feet away from her. "Stella!" What the hell had I been thinking? Was I demented putting her in danger like that? What if she was seriously hurt? It would be my fault. Did I have to push her so hard? What if she snapped her neck?

In the seconds it took me to reach her, I was already picturing how I would have to break the news to her grandmother that I killed her on our first date. "Stella," I stretched out my hand to her.

As soon as I touched her shoulder, she leaned back uncovering her grinning face. She was laughing. My heart stuttered a few beats as it kick-started up again. I watched her giggle uncontrollably.

"Are you alright?" I asked her, refraining from searching for injuries.

"That," she gasped between crows of laughter, "was

so much fun!"

I coughed to cover up my overwhelming relief. "I'm glad you enjoyed it." In my head, I berated myself for being so irresponsible.

She looked at me piercingly, the smirk still on her face. "I scared you," she stated. The leaves and brush around her gave her an unearthly look.

I explained thickly, "I didn't want to break my promise. I thought you were hurt."

"Don't worry," she said as she held up her scraped arm. "It's no worse than I can manage on my own without your bad influence."

We stayed like that for a moment; me holding her in my arms and she gazing up at me. Something indefinable passed between us. My instinct was to lean in and kiss her, but I held back. I couldn't do that. She saw both my intent and denial. Awkwardly, I helped her up.

"Want to check out downtown?" I'd had enough daredevil antics for the night.

Stella must have picked up on my thoughts because she nodded. "Sure." She brushed her hair back from her eyes. "You know, I was nervous that this date would be all formal and stuffy. I'm really glad that it isn't. I'm having fun."

Her compliment eased more of the tension inside of me. She was having fun in spite of all that had gone disastrously wrong. She placed her board on the ground and made to sit on it when I grabbed her shoulder. "You know, let's walk."

"You're silly," she snickered. Still, she entwined her arm in mine and we walked carefully back down the steep winding pavement. I was very aware of how close we were and I savored the feel of her leaning into me.

Chapter Seven

I led Stella down Main Street, each of us holding our boards as we wandered among the crowds and peered into shop windows.

So far the night had been a moderate success. I managed not to kill her, though I certainly tried. Why hadn't Azra warned me that extreme sports shouldn't be on the agenda of a first date?

Being with Stella was so easy though. Even with my missteps, I was having a great time. She was funny, relaxed, and confident. I found it difficult to remember the main purpose of this date: to see if she was the one that I was destined to find. I was going to have to find a discreet way of fitting it into the conversation.

As it turned out, the subject was brought up by a shop window. The display was a mishmash of knick-knacks. There must have been a special sale or something because all of the items were angels in some way or another.

Stella laughed and pointed to a plastic figurine. At first, it appeared to be a frog with wings contemplating a water lily, atop of a pad, with a dragonfly at his feet. Upon closer inspection, it was an angel dressed up as a frog. Perforated golden metal wings were attached to its back and golden ringlets poked out of the hood of the costume.

I eyed the frog angel in disgust. "That's ridiculous."

"I take it you're against cutesy frog angels," she commented wryly as she shifted her board from one hand to the other.

"You mean the kind dressed up like frogs? Absolutely. What do you think about angels?" I ventured the question cautiously.

Her answer was relaxed, "You mean cutesy angels or the real kind?"

I choked out, "Real kind?"

"Yeah," she said it like I should have known. "The real kind. The halos and whatnot aren't real. At least not in this realm. When real angels are here on Earth, they appear to be like you and me."

We continued down the sidewalk. She peered curiously into windows and I stumbled next to her. "Is that so?"

"Yeah. It's said that there's a war going on between Heaven and Hell," she continued, still looking at the merchandise in the windows. My attention was riveted on her. "Part of that war is being fought here on Earth over the souls of mankind. The angels and the demons fight through the humans. It's sad, really."

"I've heard that too," I admitted, thinking this was my chance. I fought to keep my excitement to myself. She had to be the one. She knew more about us than ninety percent of the world's population. "Most people don't know that much about it."

"Oh, well Nona explained it to me. She. . ." Stella trailed off.

Just before the last syllable left Stella's lips, there appeared a sickening sense that something was watching us. Something sinister. I turned my head to see where it was coming from. A Fallen One was behind us, mingling with the crowd. Panic threatened to overtake me. No. Not tonight. Why did it have to show up here?

"Stella," I said, quietly without taking my eyes off the Fallen One. "What do you say we get out of here? You wanted to see my artwork, right? Let's go to my place." I could have slapped myself for the way I handled that. The Fallen One hadn't shown any signs that it recognized what I was, but, at the same time, I definitely didn't want to stick around long enough to give it a chance. Anxiously, I rubbed the prayer beads into my palm and focused on them, hoping that my disguise would hold up.

Stella was looking in the same direction I was. Her answer was quiet and quick as though she knew of the danger too. "That sounds good. If you don't mind, can we get my car before we go to your place?" Was there a tremor of fear in her voice?

"Sure." I forced my gaze away from the Fallen One and tried to look casual.

"Come on," she said putting her board down on the concrete with a clank. "I'll race you." She took off without a second glance and I followed suit.

We skated our way through the streets. I glanced back several times, but the Fallen One didn't come after us. That had been too close. Had Stella recognized the Fallen One? Is that why she agreed to leave so quickly? I used the moment with the wind in my face to breathe deeply and refocus. I didn't have much time left to get information from her. I had been so close! When would I ever get a chance like that again? My gut said she was the one, but Azra was right. I needed to be one hundred percent sure before I told her about me. I didn't want to risk her leaving.

"Where do you live?" Stella asked, placing her board in the back of the vehicle.

"Over on Main Street, just past the mission." I pointed in the general direction of my place. "Oceanside Apartments."

She unlocked the door next to me and made her way over to the driver side. The rusting metal squeaked as I eased it open. The interior of the vehicle was just as run down as the outside. The seats were worn and ripped in places. The floorboard was riddled with holes. I wondered what would happen if we went over a puddle. The entire thing looked unsafe. Azra's warnings about cars came unbidden to my mind. He would never let me live it down if I got hurt in this thing.

I guess I hesitated too long because Stella asked from the driver's seat, "Hey, what's wrong? Too good for my car? Get in already."

"Okay," I responded with some trepidation and eased my way into the passenger seat. I slammed the door behind me and bits of rust rained down from the roof. I looked at Stella in alarm. She wasn't paying attention, though, as she revved the engine to life. I clutched onto my skateboard, worried that it would be lost if the rusted floorboards managed to disintegrate beneath my feet. A punk rock song blasted from the surprisingly decent stereo.

She gripped the steering wheel lightly, obviously at ease with her junker of a car. "Which way am I going?"

"Turn left at the next light," I advised, pointing towards the next intersection. "Then take the third right into the complex. Then a left and park wherever."

"Okay," Stella confirmed. There was a moment or two of silence when the music seemed to get louder as she maneuvered her large, rumbling vehicle around the turns and finally settled into a parking spot.

My apartment building was a single structure that could have passed for an office area. Its pale yellow stucco walls were common enough along Main Street to render it very nondescript.

"I can park wherever?" Her voice rose higher than normal at the end of her question and I realized she sounded as nervous as I was.

"Yeah." I glanced up at my apartment windows. The sight of them dark sent a glimmer of hope running through me. Was Uncle Azra truly gone?

Spike parked in an open space in front of the entrance. We looked at each other as she killed the engine. Without the music, the silence was deafening.

"Well? Here we are," I said. There was no way to keep the anxiousness from my tone.

"Yep," Stella nodded. "We are indeed."

We sat there for a moment, not sure what else to do. The air had changed between us. We were both more on edge. I could have killed that Fallen One for ruining it. But surely murder was also frowned upon on a first date as much as extreme sports were. Finally, I motioned to the apartment building. "Well, shall we?"

"Sure." Stella undid her seat belt and creaked open the door. I followed her lead, shutting the passenger door as gingerly as I could. It took nothing less than a firm slam to get it completely closed and I winced when I saw bits of rust rain down onto her seats.

She must have seen my grimace because she told me, "Don't worry. He does that all the time."

Giving the barest of nods, I asked, "You don't mind stairs do you?"

"Nope. What floor are you on?" She eyed the tallness of the building.

"Only the fourth," I assured her. "It's not that bad."

"Penthouse, huh?" She started towards me, brushing her arm against mine as she passed. "Why thank you, sir." I guided her to the stairs, happy that she relaxed a bit more and wishing with all of my might that Uncle Azra was gone. This was my second chance and I didn't want him wrecking it.

"How long have you been into art?" Stella inquired as we ascended the steps.

"I've been drawing since I was a kid. Are you alright? You're slowing down a lot."

"Yeah," she breathed. She stepped up another stair in an obviously exaggerated motion. "Just not used to so many stairs."

"We're almost there. This is the last flight," I assured her. We emerged from the stairwell and entered the tiled hall a few moments later. "Here we are," I said, pulling out my keys.

There was a note taped to the outside of my door. Snatching it up before Stella could notice, I unfolded the piece of paper and read Azra's message.

Orion,

I wish I could have been here to meet your new girlfriend, but I had a meeting to go to. I fixed the place up as best as I could. Remember you have training tomorrow morning so this soiree needs to conclude by midnight. Don't forget to use protection! Good luck!

> *See you on the beach,*
> *Azra*

Crumbling the note and stuffing the ball of paper in my hoodie pocket, I said a quick prayer before unlocking my apartment.

The sight that greeted us brought me up short. This was not my apartment. It couldn't be. Candles that were placed in hideous ceramic holders burned around the room. Azra had hung my artwork as promised, though he had draped red fabric over the frames. Presumably, this had been done for atmosphere. Flowers were scattered over every available surface, both in vases and alone, intermingled with random condom packages. Some sort of crooning music played on the stereo. It felt like a scene from a bad romance movie. I stepped forward in panic. Rose petals and leaves littered the entryway. A decadent chocolate cake with red sugar hearts and strawberries studding the chocolate icing was placed with care on the table as a center piece.

A murder scene couldn't have made me more ill.

"Oh, wow," Stella breathed behind me.

I wanted to smack myself for letting her inside. I hadn't intended for her to see this train wreck. "This was not my idea," I said, trying to push her back into the hallway. "You have to understand this isn't how I left it. I don't have any idea what this is. Well, I do have an idea, but mostly it is because my uncle likes to embarrass me. I am so sorry." I forced myself to stop babbling and held my breath, waiting for her to react.

Stella didn't say anything. She simply brushed past me to step fully into the room. There was no way to prevent her from seeing Uncle Azra's decorations/innuendos. Helpless, I watched her, a sense of doom welling up in my chest. This was the end. In about another minute I was going to get slapped and I wouldn't be able to look her in the face ever again. My gut still told me that she was the one and all of the hope that the prophecy gave the remaining Grigori choir was going to be crushed just because my uncle didn't understand the phrase overkill.

"For the love of God, did you think you were gonna get laid on the first date?" The mysterious voice from the pier said what Stella must have been thinking. There was no time to wonder what the voice was; I was too focused on Stella's reaction.

At last she spoke. "Ryan, what's this about?" Stella didn't sound angry, just wary. Her expression was one of puzzled curiosity bordering on panic.

"I'm so sorry. Uncle Azra. . . " Words failed me right then so I pulled the crumpled note from my pocket and smoothed it out as best as I could. I waved the note in my hand at her and finished lamely, "He's got these weird ideas and he thinks that he's doing the right thing, but then it turns out like this." I motioned to the room. This was it. I was done for. My shoulders slumped and I tilted my head towards the ground. I couldn't even look at her face, I was so embarrassed. "If you want to leave, I completely understand. To tell you the truth, all of this is really freaking me out right now. I'm not even comfortable here. I'm so sorry about this."

She looked as though she were deciding something that would shape any chance of a relationship, or even friendship for that matter, going forward. The intensity with which she gazed at me made me squirm and the silence was unbearable. "I think I should go," Stella murmured, her decision reached. She made her way past me to the door. I watched her go feeling completely shattered.

"Wait! Please Stella. Let me at least walk you out," I called and ran after her.

I could see the debate being waged behind her eyes. "Alright," she consented.

I breathed a sigh. At least this whole thing hadn't completely freaked her out if she was willing to let me walk her to her car. "Let me close up the house of horror over there." This elicited a soft laugh from her so I knew that all was not lost.

I closed the apartment, locked it and was thrilled to find she hadn't bolted when I turned my back. Even with that encouraging gesture, we descended the stairs in uneasy silence.

"Stella," I began when we walked through the main doors, "I hope this doesn't ruin the night. I mean, I hope you won't judge me on what my uncle did."

"I know how obnoxious family can be," Stella offered.

Hope flared inside of me. Maybe she wouldn't leave.

As if she heard my thoughts, she said, "I still better go. It's getting late."

I tried not to sound disappointed. "That's cool. I had fun tonight. Well, before we came here," I amended.

Stella squeaked open her car door. "I was going to say the same thing."

"Yeah? Good. Maybe we can do it again sometime. Without this last part."

"Definitely," Stella agreed, her tone giving me further hope. She stayed standing just outside of her car and I couldn't tell if she was waiting for me to say something or if she was thinking of what to say.

"So, about earlier. . ." she began. She must of thought better of what she was going to say because instead she said, "Never mind. I have to go. I'll text you tomorrow?" The question in her voice made it sound like she was asking permission.

"Yes," I agreed quickly. "I mean, I would like that."

"Alright, then, I will." She came closer and hugged me, taking me completely by surprise. The press of her body against mine sent the tingling sensation into overdrive. We held onto each other for a long moment and I savored the feel of her against me. All of my thoughts vanished in that embrace and it felt natural to kiss her to amplify the electricity between us. She must have felt the same way because she leaned up as if to kiss me. Our lips were inches away from touching, but something stopped her. She backed away, unable to look me in the eyes.

"I really have to go, Ryan."

Silently, I cursed and fought to keep the disappointment from my face.

After a moment of awkward silence and longing looks, she got into the car and started the engine. I smiled and waved at her, feeling horrible as she drove off. What an absolutely disastrous night! Not only did I not ask her about the prophecy, but I managed to run her off too.

Disgust filled me as I headed back inside my building. No, I hadn't been the one to run her off. I had help in that department.

I was going to kill Azra.

***

I sat at the kitchen table contemplating the chocolate cake in front of me. I had long since disposed of Uncle Azra's frightening attempts at mood enhancing décor and the cake was the only evidence left of the horrible night.

On top of being completely humiliated, I was no closer to figuring out if Stella was the one I was supposed to find or not. There were indications, but those could be explained away. What I needed was something definitive.

Sure, I had messed up pretty badly in the past when it came to finding the one. But none of those humans felt the way Stella did. None of them had known so much about the Angelic War, let alone actual angels as Stella did. But Uncle Azra wasn't just going to take my say-so. I would have to find a way to research the prophecy on my own. But how? There's no *Apocalypse Prevention and Angelic Prophecy for Dummies.*

Sure, it said that a human and I would end the war, but how? I was a wanted man on both sides, after all. The Heavenly Host and the Fallen Ones weren't likely to get together at Starbucks to share the Venti Caramel Frappuccino of peace with me.

I pawed at the cake with a fork, mulling over my options. Haphazard words were stabbed into the chocolate frosting. 'Kill Azra' was the message. Well, he certainly deserved it after his little stunt. I'd be amazed if he even remembered what he did to ruin my life by the time he came back. It was the sort of thing he would have to write down to remember.

I slapped my forehead with the obviousness of it. Uncle Azra had to have something tangible relating to at least the verbiage of the prophecy! He must have discovered some hints and clues throughout the years and knowing my uncle, he probably had them stored somewhere. There was no way he could remember it on his own. It would have been just like him to withhold information until I had found the right human.

I began to pace. If I were Uncle Azra, and I were keeping information regarding the prophecy that would potentially end the Angelic War, where would I put it?

My answer to the question was the mental equivalent of a stutter. That way of thinking wasn't going to work. New tactic.

Uncle Azra stored things. He was the ultimate hoarder and had the storage units to prove it. I could start with the one he had in Thousand Oaks; it was as good of a place as any. That was also where my board press and his surfboard tools were kept, so I could use needing a new board as an excuse to get at his keys.

I glanced at the digital clock on my microwave. Three o'clock. I had training at dawn. Even if I did manage to get the key this morning, I doubted I would be able to go until after my lessons with Ascher and Azra.

I needed a backup plan. If Azra didn't have any information on the prophecy or the Angelic War in that storage shed, who would?

Ascher! He had to have at least some information from all of his travels. He wasn't the social leper that Azra was and he would have heard things from other angels. I remembered the derision with which he spoke of the human helping to end the war and my excitement dampened.

Maybe he would tell me if he paused long enough before laughing.

At least it was better than nothing, I rallied myself. It's definitely worth a shot.

I glanced down at my phone and a wave of regret washed over me. Would Stella call? After the date I wouldn't be surprised if she cursed whenever my name came up.

I picked up the fork, ready to attack the cake once more when the phone rang. Nearly falling out of my seat, I reached over and answered it. "Hello?"

"Dude!" Uncle Azra's voice greeted me. "How's the date going?"

My lips pressed together forcefully, creating a thin line. "It's been over for hours thanks to you." I threw the fork at the cake, embedding it halfway into the thick frosting.

"Oh." There was a slight pause. "Too much, huh?"

"Too much? My apartment is not a bordello!"

"Hey, I can't help it if your definition of classy is lacking. Anyway," Azra went on, oblivious to my stony silence. "Come down to the beach. I've got something to show you."

"What is it?" I asked, more out of habit than genuine interest.

"You'll see. I'm at the Ventura Pier."

The line went dead before I had a chance to refuse. Resigned, I got to my feet and grabbed my skateboard. I needed to get the storage keys from him anyway.

Chapter Eight

Even though it was dark, I found Azra on the beach sitting in a portable chair with both of our surfboards standing in the sand next to him. Beside the boards a stake had been driven into the ground. That was odd, but what really caught my attention was the pungent smell that wafted around him. As I got closer, a brown and white spotted goat peeked out from behind the surfboards. It regarded me with doleful brown eyes, bleating at me from around a mouthful of foliage. A pail of what looked like various lawn clippings from a very prosperous landscaper was nestled into the sand next to her. My uncle flipped through a thin children's paperback book with a picture of a goat on the front as he lounged on his beach chair. He had a headlamp strapped to his forehead which emitted a bright enough light to illuminate the pages.

"Uncle Az," I said as I watched the animal warily, "what are you doing with a goat?"

Azra glanced up from the book, his lamp momentarily blinding me, and gave a wide smile. "Oh good, you're finally here. Orion, meet Bethesda." He beamed at the goat proudly.

"Bethesda?" I repeated.

"Beth for short. She's the first."

Beth chewed a palm frond in response.

The question to my uncle came out hesitantly. "The first of what?" Before he could answer, a dismayed and horrified question left my mouth. "You're not going to try to breed it are you?"

"No! Well, maybe? She's the first of my new petting zoo," he said as if I should have known from the mere sight of the animal that he would do just that.

"You're going to have a petting zoo? Here?"

He kicked off his sandals and amended, "Well, no. Not here specifically. I don't have an exact location yet."

"What are you going to do?" I asked, the incredulity seeping into my tone. "Walk around town with a herd of goats and sheep on leashes?"

I could almost see the gears turning in his head.

"Stop," I said holding up my hands. "You can't walk around the city with a menagerie on leashes. I'm sure there are city ordinances that prohibit that."

"It'll be fine, kid," Azra assured me. "Ash is working on all of that legal stuff. He will have it sorted out in no time. Once I get the okay from him, as well as my permits, I will be in business."

I blinked at my uncle. "Wait, Ascher's in on this?"

"Well, yeah," he scoffed. "We met with the financial backers last night. That's why I wasn't there to meet your girlie. One of them sold me Beth to get started."

I stood there on the beach, completely dumbfounded. "One of your financial backers sold you the goat to start a petting zoo? Doesn't that seem a bit strange to you?" I had to remind myself that it didn't matter what Azra wasted his time on; my immediate priority was to get more information on the prophecy. "Alright, whatever. Look, I want to make a new board today after I am done with my lessons. Can I have the keys to the storage place in Thousand Oaks?"

I ignored the goat as she stared at me, still chewing on the palm frond in her mouth. Her gaze alluded that not only did she know what I was up to, but also that she didn't approve of it one bit. I did my best not to look at her; do you know how hard it is to avoid a staring contest with a goat, let alone win one?

Azra frowned as he handed me his giant key ring. I sorted through them until I recognized the two for the units in Thousand Oaks. The numbers printed with black sharpie were the only thing that differentiated them from the others on the ring. I slipped them into my pocket and handed the rest of the keys back to my uncle.

"Thanks," I said.

"Well, since you are here, we might as well start early. Come on, we are going out." Azra motioned to the ocean with an expansive wave of his arm.

"What about Beth?" I asked, gesturing to the goat.

"She'll be fine where she is. I've got her hooked up to a stake. Besides, she can't swim for at least two hours after she is done eating."

"I thought it was only thirty minutes."

Azra shook his head. "Not when you have four stomachs."

"Whatever." I shrugged and stripped off my shirt. The water would be freezing to a human however, to my desensitized skin it felt no more than chilly.

Azra was already in the water by the time I had stripped down to my trunks. I knew better than to come to the beach with my uncle and not at least have a pair of swimming trunks. Taking a quick glance around to make sure no one was watching, I removed the board Azra had brought for me from the sand and plunged into the water, paddling past the breakers after him.

After living with Uncle Azra for so long, it would have been very difficult for me not to pick up a few things about surfing. While I typically preferred my board to have wheels, I still knew my way around a wave. But that morning I was not at all ready to have my board almost yanked out from underneath me.

"What the—?" I gripped the edges of the board to keep it underneath my stomach. Whatever it was had a hold of the tail end. Even with my exceptional balance and death grip on the sides, it wasn't enough to keep me on it. After much struggling, I was tipped into the rocking ocean and my board was ripped out of my hands.

Uncle Azra popped up out of the water with both my board and his. He grinned at me and wiped the water from his face.

"First lesson: be prepared for anything to happen."

I glared at him as I bobbed in the ocean. "Can I have my board back now?"

"Have you learned the first lesson?"

I let out a disgusted sound and was rewarded with a whap on the head with my own board.

"Hey! What was that for?" I cried out when I surfaced again.

Uncle Azra's expression was smug. "Lesson not learned apparently." He hoisted himself up onto his own surfboard and shook out his blonde hair. My board floated along next to him. "We'll work on that one sporadically. It requires the element of surprise. Now, lesson two: stamina."

"Stamina? What do you mean?"

"I want to see how long you can tread water. You know, in case you fall from a boat or something."

I made a face. "You mean how long I can bob here before I get too exhausted to swim back to shore?" It sounded more like torture than training.

"Let's face it, kiddo, we need to know how far you can go. Once we know that, then we can work on extending it through training."

I hated to admit it, but that made a certain amount of sense. "Why this particular activity?"

"When you tread water you're using all of the muscles in your body to stay afloat; especially against the natural flow of the ocean. It's the perfect place to test your endurance without damaging something I'll have to pay for later."

"What if I damage myself?" I asked, flippantly

"Don't worry about it." Azra flashed me a brilliant smile. "I'll be here with you. Just think of me as your guardian angel. I won't let you drown."

I groaned. "You've got to be kidding me."

My uncle ignored my comment and said in a definitive tone, "While we are waiting for your exhaustion to happen, I'll quiz you on what you should know and what you think you know."

"What I *think* I know?" I asked acerbically.

"Precisely," he said, completely un-phased by my tone. "You think you know a lot, but really, you don't know much at all. From what I've read in those parenting books, it's a teenage thing. Since I'm not sure how many more centuries I'll have to deal with this phase of yours, we better just set you straight now." He adjusted himself on the board so he was lying on his back with his hands clasped behind his head. He bobbed up and down with the current. "You see, Orion, sometimes you have to look at things differently in order to make them make sense."

"You make no sense," I muttered, my arms and legs working to keep me afloat. The seagulls flew overhead, calling out to each other. They were probably commenting on how ridiculous I looked floating here.

I regretted my previous excitement about Ascher and Uncle Azra training me.

"Now then. Down to business. What is your best bowling score?"

The question caught me off guard so there was a hesitation in my response. "I don't know. I don't bowl."

"That will have to change. It's a good way to gain accuracy. Tell me somewhere in that vast education I've paid for that they've taught you how to Tango."

I shook my head, concentrating on keeping my limbs moving and not so much on his line of interrogation.

"Nope."

"Did they teach you how to blow glass?"

"No."

"Knife throwing?"

"No."

"What kind of an education have I been paying for all this time?" He shouted at the world in general.

"I've been going to public school— you haven't paid for anything. What sort of schools did you think you were sending me to? Listen, I made a spice rack in woodshop last year. Doesn't that count for something?"

Azra looked over at me with a scowl. "Don't be cute,

kiddo." He turned his face back towards the sky as the sun came up. "It's a pity about the glass blowing. Mindful breath and how it can affect your control . . ." His voice trailed off distractedly. I thought that was the end of his questions, but I was wrong. "How about tracking? Did they teach you how to track something?"

"Look, what is the point of all these questions?" I asked, my frustration mounting. I started to feel a twinge in my muscles from fighting the current to stay in place.

"The point is to figure out where we need to start with your training. I want to know if you've learned anything even remotely useful in all those years of schooling."

I sighed heavily. It sucked when he had a valid point. "Fine. Ask away then."

He eyed me skeptically and briskly nodded. "Alright then. Next question. When did the Angelic War start?"

"Wasn't it around the beginning of time itself?" I asked. Uncle Azra pressed his lips together in disappointment. "What, you want an exact year?"

"A history lesson is in order," I heard him mutter to himself. I could almost see the checklist forming in his head. "Ascher should be able to take care of that today."

Hours passed. The sun steadily rose as I continued to tread water while Uncle Azra floated on the board next to me and bombarded me with question after question on the most random topics. All of my answers seemed to confirm to him that I knew next to nothing.

"I'm getting hungry," Azra mentioned as he sat up straight on the board and looked up at the sky. The sun had climbed well over head and its weakened winter rays beat down on the water. "Are you getting hungry?"

"Yes," I answered, hoping he would let me take a food break. This wasn't as hard as it first seemed to be, but even if I could, I definitely wasn't too keen on floating out here for hours on end.

"Are you tired yet?"

"Yes," I answered promptly. The slight ache in my

arms counted, right?

Azra narrowed his eyes. "Well, keep going until you're exhausted. I'm going to get some tacos. Stay here. I'll be back in a while." He flipped onto his stomach as easily as a monkey switching tree branches and paddled off towards the shore with my board in tow after him.

"Hey!" I shouted. "Hey, you can't leave me here!" When he didn't turn back, I began to flail desperately sending big, loud spatters of water into the air. "Help! I can't do it anymore! So much water!" I allowed myself to sink under the surface of the ocean for a few moments. When I came back up, Uncle Azra was nowhere in sight. Damn. "So much for guardian angel," I sighed.

I settled back down, moving my legs and arms in the familiar pattern that kept me afloat. Out of boredom, dunked my head under the surface and came back up, shaking off the excess water. It was quiet this far out. The only things that I heard were the far off cries of the seagulls and the lapping movement of the water as it struck my body. I watched the clouds drift overhead, identifying shapes and patterns that they made.

Something brushed against my leg. Peering into the water, there was a shadowy from of a big fish, possibly a shark, passing beneath me.

"Okay," I said to no one in particular and fighting against my anxiety. I was pretty sure getting eaten by a shark wasn't supposed to be part of the training. "Time to go in."

"It took you this long to figure out you had been ditched?" A voice called out scathingly. It was the Brooklyn accent from the pier the previous night.

Startled, I turned around in a complete circle to see where the voice was coming from. There was no one around. "Who said that?"

It is disconcerting to hear someone talking to you when you are alone in the ocean.

My question was met with silence. "Too much sun," I muttered to myself, though I had my doubts. Was I losing my mind?

Another brush against my legs had me swimming in earnest towards the distant shore. Getting munched on by a confused shark wasn't going to get me any closer to my destiny.

Every so often, when my head broke the surface, I would hear distant laughter. Once I even thought I heard Stella's name, but when I popped up to see who had spoken, no one was in sight. It must have been my imagination playing tricks on me.

Despite my best efforts to stay in the spot I started out in, I had drifted away from where Azra and I had gone into the water so many hours ago. I ended up having to hike a few miles of beach, alternating between rocky to smooth sand until I reached the point where Azra and Beth were lounging comfortably.

Uncle Azra reclined in the beach chair, flipping through a large book. Beth was laying dutifully by the left side of the chair. Wrappers littered the sand surrounding him.

"Thanks for bringing me some," I said and sat on the sand across from him with my back to the water.

Uncle Azra looked up from his book and shrugged. "I figured you'd come in if you were hungry enough. Did you get tired?"

I nodded. "Well that and a shark was eyeing me as a snack." I grabbed for the hemp bag which was sprawled in front of me. Some of the contents had spilled out into the sand. A couple of weights, a few books and a medicine ball lay innocently at Azra's feet. The sight of a bright red book cover caught my attention and I stretched to get it. It was a copy of the *Malleus Maleficarum*, the leading witch hunting for dummies book of the Middle Ages.

Holding it up for Uncle Azra to see, I asked, "A bit of light reading?"

He snorted in derision. "Hardly. There's some information in there about the Fallen Ones. It's best to read up on the enemy. I want you to read it and report back to me about the first two parts. You should be able to distinguish the differences in the descriptions of Witches and Fallen Ones. It seems Kramer and Sprenger didn't understand they were describing two different beings." He thought about it for a long moment and added, "I don't know how they could get them so mixed up. Even though Witches are dangerous, they're much better to look at than Fallen Ones any day of the week. They're also generally softer and nicer smelling."

I put the book off to the side, resigning myself to reading it later.

My uncle went on, tossing me the yellow notebook that I had discarded earlier. "Here's your syllabus. It outlines the training schedule I set up for you."

I scanned through the formal typed pages. "How does making sushi count towards dexterity?"

"Do you know how difficult it is to make a California roll? It takes sushi chefs in Japan years to even be able to make rice!"

I rolled my eyes and continued scanning the page. "Why are we going to the zoo?"

"It's to work on your mind control. We'll start with the smaller creatures and work up to the monkeys. Eventually, you'll get to where you can recognize when a human is being influenced by an angel."

"Why don't I just try it on Beth?" I commented under my breath.

Azra ignored my remark, even though we both knew he heard it perfectly well.

A little louder, I said, "I don't think I have ever seen a human influenced by an angel. What does it look like?"

He let out a light chuckle. "You know about zombies, right? Well, they are kinda like that, except they talk and have better motor skills. Though, really, it depends on the skill of the angel controlling them. I've seen some humans being influenced that you wouldn't have known they were being swayed. The trick is to look in their eyes. If they are vacant, like no one is there, then most likely they are most likely being controlled. Or they are high on something. Sometimes it's hard to tell which."

I nodded as I processed the information he gave me and continued to rifle through the bag's contents.

"Hey, Uncle Az, I gotta ask you something."

"Shoot, kiddo." He kept flipping through his book.

"Have, um, have you ever heard voices before?"

Uncle Azra looked at me, concerned. "Voices? What do you mean, voices?"

"I thought I heard something out there," I said quietly. It sounded crazy saying it out loud. I wished I hadn't said anything.

"What did you hear?" Azra had put aside his book and was paying close attention to me.

"Oh, nothing much. Just thought I heard Stella's name out there or something."

He peered at me seriously for a few heartbeats and then burst out laughing. "Oh, kiddo. You've got it bad! If you are hearing voices say her name, she must be one hell of a girl."

I rolled my eyes and turned back to the handwritten notes. "Ugh. Whatever. Forget I said anything."

"Well speaking of your girlfriend, she called while you were out playing in the water." He waggled his eyebrows suggestively and, with a crooked grin, waved my phone at me.

I leapt into action. Springing from my sitting position, I lunged towards my uncle to snatch the small plastic device out of his hands.

Sand flew in all directions as the beach chair he had been sitting in tipped over backwards with the force of my dive. Azra held the phone high up over his head, keeping it from my immediate reach. He fought me off with his other hand and both of his legs. Because he was a little bit taller than I was, he was able to keep me well away from my phone.

"Give that to me!" I yelled, struggling against his flailing limbs.

Uncle Azra laughed. "Is this all you've got? I've got a lot of work ahead of me if this is how hard you can hit."

I punched him in the stomach. He groaned, but kept the phone in the air. "Come on," he urged. "If you want it so badly, just take it."

I threw my body towards his outstretched arm, but he was too quick. The shiny black plastic went sailing through the air and landed a few meters away. There was a flurry of sand as we scrambled to where it fell. Instead of my phone, we found a pair of finely made leather sandals attached to pale feet.

Both Azra and I tilted our heads up to find Ascher smirking down at us. He held my phone aloft. "Fighting over this?" he asked. He was dressed in a pristine white button-down shirt that looked as though it doubled for nights out at the opera. His khaki shorts were pressed and starched with creases still visible from the folds.

I made a grab for the phone and Ascher gave it to me. Quickly checking the call history, I breathed a sigh of relief that my uncle had lied. Stella hadn't called. She probably wouldn't after last night either.

Beth still stood among Azra's things, watching us reproachfully. Ascher saw her and strode towards the animal, his hand outstretched.

Beth didn't appreciate Ascher's proximity, let alone his attempt to pet her. She made a horrible noise somewhere between a bleat and a choking sound. It brought Ascher up short and he stepped back just as she spit and scampered as far away from him as her leash would allow.

"Beth! That's no way for a lady to behave!" Azra admonished. My uncle righted the beach chair and began gathering the items that had been scattered in our tussle. "What's wrong with you? It's just Ascher. You were fine with him last night. Crazy goat."

"So, what's the plan now?" I asked.

My uncle was the first to speak. "Well, kiddo, you and Ascher are going to continue your training. He's going to

- 100 -

give you some pointers on basic fighting moves and start you on the magic side of things." He looked at Ascher. "I tested him to see where his limits are."

"I see. How did you test him?" Ascher eyed me. It was a look he would give a potential purchase; impressed, but still waiting to see the features before he committed.

I didn't appreciate feeling like merchandise. That appraising look put me on edge.

"He's been treading water and fighting the current since sunrise. He's got a lot more stamina than I would have expected— and a lot more strength in general than I do in my physical body."

The admission from my uncle was startling to me. Was I really that much stronger than him? How was that even possible?

"Well, we thought that might be the case," Ascher reminded my uncle. "After all, he was born in this body and ours were given to us fully made."

"Yeah well, he is going to need a history lesson. I'm afraid I've been pretty lax with him on his angelic knowledge."

"Alright, we can start that today." Ascher gestured for me to follow him. "Come on, Orion. We are going to the gym." He started back towards the road. I followed with the hemp bag Azra had brought for me and my sand-covered skateboard. I reeled with the realization they considered me strong and wondering what he had in mind as far as training went.

"Orion, wait!" Azra called after me. "I want you to take Beth with you!"

I turned to look at him incredulously. "No, I'm not taking the goat. They don't allow goats in public buildings."

"C'mon," Azra pleaded. "I can't just leave her here while I'm out surfing."

"What did you do with her earlier?"

"There wasn't anyone out here earlier. She's been alone for too long today. She needs to be with someone."

I waved him off. "So teach her how to surf."

Azra eyed the goat and I just knew he was figuring out how to stand her up to balance on a board.

Chapter Nine

Ascher had reserved one of the aerobics rooms at a nearby gym so we could work uninterrupted. It was large, with a wall of mirrors adjacent to a small dais where the instructor would usually be. The aroma of stale sweat and a dying air freshener assaulted my nose. Ascher set his gym bag on one of the benches lining one side of the room and I stashed my skateboard and bag underneath.

"We are going to start off with some basic drills. What do you know about hand to hand combat?" Ascher asked once the door was closed and we were settled in the middle of the room.

I shrugged. "Don't get hit?"

Ascher's mouth twitched into a smile. "More or less. Let's see how much you know and we will go from there. I'm going to start off slowly. I want you to block me."

His fist connected with my stomach in a sudden and silently painful jab. My breath was gone and I doubled over, clutching my belly. I didn't see his foot coming at my knee until it was too late.

The next thing I knew, I was gazing at the ceiling fans. Ascher leaned over me and I detected the barest traces of amusement in his eyes. "I told you to block me."

Sitting up, I fought to keep my anger in check. "Let's try again."

He helped me to my feet and we squared off. "Ready?" he asked.

I nodded, putting my hands up in front of me. He didn't attack straight off; instead, he sidestepped to the left, circling me. I mimicked his movements, never letting my eyes off of him. He rushed forward, his fist pulling back to strike. My hands flew up to protect my face and I shut my eyes.

The punch never came.

"You can open your eyes now. I'm not actually going to hit you."

Reluctantly, I dropped my hands and opened my eyes. Ascher stood in front of me and this time, I could hear the mocking laughter come from his lips. I felt like an idiot.

"Never take your eyes off of your opponent. You have to know where he is and what he is doing at all times. Focus your attention on their chest. It will help you to anticipate their next move. Now, I want you to attack me. Give it your best shot." He kept his hands at his sides and his stance relaxed.

I studied him for a moment before launching myself forward, swinging wildly. He sidestepped me easily and I wound up unbalanced with my face on the ground.

"We have a lot of work ahead of us," Ascher commented with a sigh as he helped me to my feet. "Should I even ask about how you are with the magic part before we get into it?"

I glared at him and straightened my shirt, not bothering to answer.

"I didn't think so. Azra was never good at the wards." He frowned at my wrist. "But if you can't do the wards either, then what's the deal with those beads? Azra doesn't have the patience or the talent to make something as subtle as that."

I glanced at my prayer bead bracelet and held up my hand. "This? It's something Azra got for me to help me blend in. It hides my psychic presence. I'm not sure where he got it."

"Why would you need that? You should be able to hide yourself without it."

I shrugged, trying to appear nonchalant. "My ability to blend in like other Grigori doesn't work. If I don't have this on, I would be a beacon to the Host and the Fallen Ones." I contemplated the little wooden beads. "If I don't keep myself calm and focused, things could go really badly. Like it did with my father."

Ascher blinked at me somewhat startled. "You remember what happened that day?"

"A little," I admitted with shame. "The memory is a bit hazy, but I know more or less what happened. I know that because I was out of control, I got my father killed and I don't want that to happen to Azra."

I could almost see the thoughts spinning in his head. Whatever it was he was thinking, he kept it to himself. Instead, he proclaimed, "We will start you out with Jujutsu. The first thing I'm going to show you are the stances. We can build on those."

We went through several moves and poses slowly and Ascher corrected me every so often on my footing and posture. When he was sure I had it, we began practicing the moves in tandem with gradual speed.

"So, tell me what you know about the creation of this world?" he asked.

"Not much," I said, focusing on my movements. Was he really going to quiz me while I was trying to learn this? "I know some of the creation myths that the humans believe in, if that's what you mean."

Ascher responded with a grunt of derision, "None of them have it right, but if they put all those theories together, they would be pretty close."

"Really?" It was difficult to focus on the moves and the conversation all at once, but I think Ascher did it on purpose. I did my best to keep up, but I stumbled on a few moves a couple of times.

"Yes, really. Take, for example, the two biggest extremes of thought in the theory of origin: Creationism and Evolution. On one hand, you have the Creationists who believe that the Creator just snapped Its fingers and from that sprang life as they know it. Then, you have the Evolutionists who believe that everything evolved from a single-celled organism in primordial muck." He paused to watch me as I continued the movements without him.

"Keep your feet forward and your back straight."

He stepped in front of me and halted my movements. "Let's switch it up a bit. This is called a front snap punch." He demonstrated the move. "Do one of those after every position. Flow into it, alright?"

I did as I was told, striving to make my movements smooth and seamless. It was harder than Ascher made it look. As I practiced, Ascher continued with the lesson.

"If you take those two extremes, the Evolutionist and the Creationist, and overlap them then somewhere in the middle is what actually happened. There was quite a bit of evolution involved and a fair amount of finger snapping as well. The problem with humans is that they have an extremely limited perception when it comes to the Creator.

"What really happened was that the Creator made Earth and appointed the angels to be the caretakers of it. Angels were created to obey and because of that, they felt nothing but adoration for their lot in life."

As he spoke, his tone became more and more sardonic. His entire attitude and demeanor became mocking and harsh, though his movements were still smooth and fluid. It made me wonder how long he had felt this way. Was it even possible to stop being enamored with the Creator if we were made to just obey? I'd heard bits and pieces about the start of the Angelic War from my father and Azra. It was a sore topic for them, so I never really got the whole thing. It was surprising that Ascher was willingly talking about it.

"If the angels wanted nothing more to care for Earth, then how did the war start?" I asked, pausing from the drills.

Ascher gave a slight chuckle and motioned for me to continue the movements. "Keep going. This is your warm up for the magic lesson. But, to answer your question, the war started because of the humans."

"Humans? What do you mean?" Settling back into the stances, I started the drills again.

"When humans came into being, the other choirs watched as they crawled through the darkness of prehistoric time and ascended into power. They saw how humans grew and learned and, most importantly, they saw how humans reacted to the Creator, or rather, their lack of reaction. You see, humans never did figure out that the Divine was among them.

"Some of the angels were appalled by that lack of recognition and they believed that it was their duty to force the humans to give that respect. Others believed the Creator made the humans that way for a purpose and didn't think they should question it."

He paused again as I kept up my routine. He went to the duffel bag near the door and returned with a handheld paddle-shaped target. "Your form is good. Let's see how your aim is."

"How is this going to help me do magic?" I asked, unable to keep the frustration from my voice. I'd been looking forward to learning the magic portion with Ascher. Plus, my muscles still ached from my buoy impression.

For his part, Ascher didn't react to my snappish tone. He positioned himself a few feet away from me and answered, "How you handle these drills gives me an idea of how you will learn wards. The types of wards I am going to teach you will mostly revolve around fighting and defense. If you have a good grasp on some sort of fighting style, it will make the wards much more effective. Now. Hit the target."

With my lips pursed I did what I was told. Or at least I tried to hit the target in his hands. I missed the first few times, but once I focused on aiming and not on my form, I landed a punch.

My teacher didn't let me rest though. "Don't get sloppy, Orion. Put some force behind it. Don't forget to watch your stance. Keep going."

I did; my fist smacked against the vinyl target loudly. The sound was the catalyst for Ascher to start talking again. "Where were we?"

"The debate about humans," I answered with my eyes firmly on the target.

"Ah, yes. Attempts were made to educate the humans, which lead to the creation of the Archetypes. All of the deities in human history are based off of the four Archetypes of the Divine. One was assigned to each of the Ages of Man."

I couldn't help but laugh. "I've never heard that before."

Ascher smiled at my disbelief even as he insisted that it was true. "First came the Age of the Mother. This was during the hunter-gatherer period of human existence. There were a lot of fertility cults and goddess worship going on around then. After a while, humans grew out of that particular archetype. Next came the Age of the Father. This is when the patriarchal pantheons came into focus, like the Sumerian, Greek, Egyptian, et cetera. After the Father came the Age of the Son—whose reign we are still in, by the way. Someday there will be an Age of the Daughter."

I paused in my punches to wrap my head around the idea. He was really serious about it. "You mean to tell me that all religions on Earth originated from these Archetypes and not the Creator?"

"Sort of. Think of them this way—the Creator made the Archetypes as a way for humans to comprehend divinity. The gods of human belief are simply their interpretations of the Archetypes. For example, the Father Archetype is the same as Odin or Zeus or Yahweh. The Son Archetype is the same as Jesus and the same as Mohammed. Do you understand?"

I nodded slowly, running through it once more in my head. "So, the Archetypes are the reason why there are so many religions; because humans interpret things differently, depending on their culture and society."

"Right. Now, the Archetypes were created similarly to us angels, but they aren't nearly as restricted. The four carry all of the power and wisdom of the Creator. Their reigns have helped shape humanity and guided it along the path the Creator set for them."

"Why did the war start?" I asked, slightly out of breath. My muscles strained with the constant effort. I was going to feel all of this later on.

"While the Creator was away one time, a human managed to get into Heaven. One of the tools used to construct Earth was stolen."

"The mirror," I confirmed.

Ascher nodded, "That's right. Ok, now go through your stances again, but this time, I want you to punch and kick between each move. Get used to the movements and the flow."

Nodding, I blew out a breath and started the stances all over again. The constant movements made me build up a sweat, but there was something satisfying about the motions. I was enjoying them.

He watched my moves with approval. "Snap your leg more when you kick. Give it power. Yes, that's right."

"Okay, so the mirror was stolen," I panted. "Then what?" This was a lot more information that I had ever gotten out of Azra and I was determined to take advantage of Ascher's talkativeness.

"The theft of the tool was what tipped everything over the edge. What had our fellow angels up in arms wasn't just the invasion of territory; it was the sheer gall of stealing a holy relic directly from the Creator. The outrage pressed the human debate into an all-out war, which is what caused the Fall."

I delivered another combo at the target, landing each blow with a vicious thump. "After that, the Grigori were created to balance the scales, right?" I said, reiterating what little I had heard from my uncle.

"You are correct. We were made to make sure the humans maintained their free will and stayed out of the clutches of the Fallen Ones. We were designed to blend in with the humans. The problem was that we blended in a little too well." Ascher made a face and I knew what he was referring to.

"You're talking about the Nephilim, right?"

"Time for a break," Ascher responded. He let the target drop onto the floor.

Together we wandered over to the benches. Passing me a water bottle, he continued the story. "The choirs were furious about the procreative ability of the Grigori. After all, angels weren't supposed to be able to procreate and the fact that the Grigori could partake of the more sensual side of humanity must have irked some of our brethren.

"Others saw the destruction the Nephilim were capable of and feared for Heaven. With angelic blood running through their veins, there was nothing stopping the Nephilim from storming the gates of Heaven and wreaking total havoc, especially if the human part of them were being controlled by a Fallen One.

"The fear escalated into a call for a full extermination of us and our offspring. They killed most of us off with the flood. The few of us who survived had no choice but to scatter. Since we blended in so well with the humans, they couldn't be sure we were all gone. The rest of us were banned from Heaven. We weren't damned, but we were still cut off from home."

I watched Ascher blink back tears and I felt for him. To lose everything, to be exiled and hunted for just being how the Creator made you was an almost unimaginable pain. He wiped at his eyes, a startling show of emotion from the most reserved angel I had ever known.

I didn't know what to say to make it any better, so I asked the question that had been on my mind all day. "What about the prophecy? When did that come about?"

He blinked a couple of times and covered his emotional vulnerability with a sharp derision. "Az does have you chasing dreams, doesn't he? The prophecy was a legend. Some said it was a secret that the Creator imparted to the leaders of the Grigori when they were sent to Earth. It was a promise that eventually the war would end. It was a myth that was kept alive within the Grigori ranks as a hope that someday their unjustified exile would end. But it was a lie."

"What do you mean it was a lie?" If Ascher didn't believe in the prophecy, what was he doing training me like this?

"Even if it is real, the end of the war won't be all sunshine and rainbows," he said. "It will be sheer destruction. The three realms, Heaven, Hell, and Earth will collide and will rip the fabric of existence to shreds. That is what the prophecy is really about— the complete annihilation of everything we know. If that happens, there wouldn't be any redemption for us. We would never be accepted back into Heaven because there wouldn't be a Heaven left. If that is really what happens when the war ends, then we are all better off dead."

My mind was alive with unanswered questions and warnings not to ask them. Ascher's outlook on the situation was fairly skewed, even to the point of sounding suicidal. Except . . . the last sentence of the prophecy flashed through my thoughts. *End the war and three realms become one.* What if Ascher was right? What if it meant the end of the world? I was more confused than ever.

"What about the mirror? At the pub the other night you mentioned it had something to do with the prophecy."

"Yes. If the prophecy is in fact real, then I think the mirror is what is going to bring it about. It is the only object on Earth that has the power to create and destroy entire realms. That's why I'm searching for it. If I manage to find it, then I might be able to get it back to Heaven and end this senseless exile."

It was then that I realized that Ascher wanted nothing more than to return to Heaven. The longing almost dripped off of him. How had I not noticed it before now?

With the exception of the mirror, I hadn't heard of

anything else that had enough power to stop the war. Ascher said the mirror was in the hands of a human, and that I was searching for one particular human to fulfill the prophecy—it made sense that the mirror was linked.

"Alright," Ascher got to his feet. "Let's teach you some basic wards. Maybe you won't be as abysmal at it as Azra."

I got to my feet, still thinking about the prophecy.

Ascher positioned us in the middle of the room. "Wards are angelic spells. They vary in purpose and design, but they all start out the same; they require your own reserve of energy to function. Do you know how to tap into your energy?"

My blank look must have said it all because he gave a smirk. "Yeah, I didn't think so. Okay. Close your eyes and take in a deep breath. Relax your body and focus on your center."

"My center?" I repeated, skeptically.

"Yes. Your center. When you find it, then you are going to mentally siphon the energy from your center and into your hands. Imagine it like a ball of light."

Ascher had his own eyes closed and was taking in deep breaths so I did as I was told, wondering if this was even going to work.

It took a while for me to find my center. Turns out it was in the pit of my stomach. Once identified, the warmth threatened to break my concentration.

I must have made a noise or something because Ascher said calmly, "Move that energy into your hands. Feel the warmth move from your center to your palms. Envision it."

Slowly, inch by inch, the warmth traveled up from my stomach to my chest and eventually my shoulders. The concentration it took to keep it moving was astounding. There was nothing easy about this at all. It was hard to imagine that I would be able to do this in the middle of a fight without getting killed.

When the energy finally found its way into my palms, the heat was almost unbearable. Gritting my teeth, I forced into my mind an image of a ball of light bobbing an inch or two in the air above my hand. I focused on that image as hard as I could and eventually opened my eyes.

Instead of the perfectly symmetrical ball of white light I had envisioned, there was a glob of purple light coating my fingers. Out of reflex, I shook my hand, trying to dislodge what looked like glowing purple slime. It didn't budge.

Ascher opened his eyes, a perfectly formed ball of red light at his fingertips. He regarded my attempt at it with a mocking grin. "It's a good first start," he said after I glowered at him.

"Now what do I do with it?" I asked. When I spoke, the purple energy faded and disappeared completely.

Ascher flexed his fingers and whispered something under his breath. In response, the ball of energy flattened and splintered into strange glyphs arranged in a tight circular formation. With a gesture, Ascher placed the energy sign into the air between us. The light flared and shimmered outwards, spreading a wall of light in the space. Just as quickly as it came, the light disappeared.

"Go on. Try to pass your hand through it," Ascher encouraged me.

I raised my hand and tried to tap Ascher on the shoulder. I was stopped halfway between us as though there was a wall there. "What the?!" I tried again to get my hand past the ward, but without any luck.

"That," Ascher explained, "is a ward. It can be used defensively, like this, or," he spun around and thrust his hand out in front of him. A sudden flare of red energy leapt out like a burst of flame. "It can be used to attack."

My jaw was on the floor. "How did you do that?"

"Wards. They can be used for anything you can imagine. But to get to that point, you have to learn how to access your power source quickly and how to control the energy once you have it harnessed. Now, for the rest of the hour I want you to practice summoning the energy until you can form the ball in your hand, like this." He placed his hand palm up and immediately a perfectly formed ball of light appeared as before.

Eager to get this down, I got to work. It was tough— a lot tougher than the physical training I'd had throughout the day. This required patience and finesse, which were two things that I apparently didn't have.

After about two hours, I dripped with sweat from the sheer effort of summoning my energy over and over again. The practice was worth it though. By the time Ascher said we were done, I could manifest my energy after only a minute of concentration. It even came out as a passable, if not wobbly, purple sphere.

"You've done very well," Ascher complimented as we went to rest a minute on the bench against the wall. "Much better than I thought you would. You must take after your mother in more than looks." A peculiar expression graced Ascher's face. It was a mingling of sadness, regret and something else I couldn't quite define. "She wanted so much more for you than all of this nonsense."

I knew I might regret it, but the question was out of my mouth before I could stop it. "Did my mother believe I was the one in the prophecy?"

The sigh that Ascher let out was a heavy one. A look I couldn't quite identify passed across his features briefly; like a flash of pain, or anger. He was silent for a long moment. I was about to tell him to forget that I had asked when he spoke.

"You have to understand, the prophecy is more of a legend than a fact. Those tales were centuries old by the time you came into being. When Indra found out she was pregnant, she had more immediate things to worry about than some story.

"When the word got around she and Rasheym were going to have a child, there was a complete upheaval in the choirs," Ascher explained. "Indra just wanted to bring you into the world safely and then to stay alive long enough to be a good mother." He gave a bitter laugh. "I told Indra that you could be a Nephilim, but she didn't believe it for one second."

"Really?" The admission stirred something inside me. My mother had believed in me from the very beginning. To cover my sudden emotion, I reached down and grabbed a water bottle from Ascher's bag.

"Absolutely," Ascher confirmed. "Indra wanted nothing more than to be your mother. After Rasheym realized you weren't the monster you could have been, he put two and two together with the prophecy. When your mother died, he clung to the idea that you would save the world as a way to deal with his grief."

"How was he so sure?" I asked. "You said it was all just a rumor. My father wasn't the type to buy into something so vague."

Ascher shrugged. "I don't know. That's something you might want to ask Azra. All I know is that your mother wanted only the best for you."

Now that the ball was rolling, I couldn't stop it. "Will you tell me about her?"

He leaned back against the wall and closed his eyes as though the memories were just behind his eyelids. "Your mother was amazing. She was sharp, funny, and beautiful. When the Grigori were first sent to Earth, we were paired up for our missions; just as Azra and Rasheym were partners. One day, the four of us met in the Indus Valley." He chuckled at the memory. "Your mother didn't like Rasheym at first."

"No?" This surprised me. I never would have guessed. I suppose I always thought it had been love at first sight.

"Absolutely not," Ascher chortled. "She described him as a pretentious idiot with an ego that could rival the Satan himself. Rasheym was persistent though. I never saw anything like it." Ascher shook his head.

I hesitated, screwing up enough courage to spit out my next question. "How did my mother die? No one ever told me the whole story."

Ascher tensed as though my words physically

injured him. He opened his eyes to stare at me in wonder. "No one told you?"

"No." The silence that followed was strained.

Ascher sighed and kicked at the gym bag. "I guess I'm not surprised Rasheym and Azra haven't told you. They were the ones responsible for it."

"What? My dad and Uncle Azra killed my mother?" My hands clenched around the water bottle forcing the liquid out and over my hands. Rage threatened to overtake me. It took a few deep breaths and the better part of my mind to build up denial at what he said. When I came back to my senses, I realized that not only had I gotten to my feet, but the giant wall to floor mirrors had been shattered. The contents of Ascher's bag had been bent, broken and scattered all around the room.

"You were just a baby when it happened," Ascher said, calmly watching me. Was that fascination in his eyes? "You and your parents were living in Rome at the beginning of the Republic. Your father and Azra went out one night, leaving Indra home to tend to you. Azra and Rasheym liked to drink excessively. It made them careless.

"As usual, they got into some trouble. That was routine for them. Some angels from one of the other choirs found them. Who knows why they were slumming down on Earth? Anyway, they recognized Azra and Rasheym for what they were: two exiled Grigori's who were to be killed on sight. Rasheym and Azra managed to kill one of them, but the other got away."

Ascher closed his eyes as if he were witnessing the scene in his head. "I was there when your father came home after that. Indra was furious at his recklessness. She admonished him for his stupid behavior once she got the whole story out of him. Well, your father wasn't about to be reprimanded like that, so he stormed out.

"I visited her the next day. She was still angry, but worry started to take its place. She begged me to go look for him since she had to watch after you. I left the villa with promises on my lips that I'd convince Rasheym to come home. It was the last time I saw her alive."

I kept silent and focused my gaze on the floor. I was having a hard time controlling the fury and sadness inside of me. Why hadn't anyone told me this? Biting back my anger, I glanced at Ascher as he spoke. He looked haunted by the memories I was asking him to drag into the light.

"I traipsed all over Rome, trying to locate either him or Azra. I never found them. By the time I returned to the villa, it was ablaze. Azra was there, covered in ash and he held you in his arms. You were screaming at the top of your lungs. Azra didn't speak, just pointed to the burning building. I told him to take you away from the fire and run, but he didn't move. I think he was in shock. Rasheym's cries came from inside. He must have come back while I'd been searching for him.

"He came out soon after, carrying your mother in his arms. She was covered in blood and ash. He got far enough away from the building not to have it fall on him and sank to his knees. Out of that wall of fire came an Archangel. I couldn't recognize which one it was because of all of the flames and the smoke. The Archangel took off abruptly leaving a trail of blood in its wake. I remember wondering why it hadn't attacked us. We would have been easy enough prey. To this day, I don't know why we were spared."

A weight had settled in my chest. The seven Archangels were the top of the angelic hierarchy. Of the Seraphim Choir, they were like the Creator's generals. They executed the law of the Creator with fanatical zeal.

I couldn't quite believe what I was hearing. It wasn't real; it couldn't be real. It was just another story. Still, the pressure in my chest moved to my throat. I swallowed but it wouldn't go away.

Ascher's voice hitched a bit and I thought that I saw a tear in his eye. "Rasheym picked Indra up and told Azra to take you away. He would catch up once he put her to rest and just like that, he walked away. I was furious. How could he just leave us there? I tried to go after him. Every time I made a move to follow, Azra prevented me. We did what Rasheym asked. We waited for him for a week and all the while I looked for ways to get away, to find him and demand to know what he did with Indra. There were always reasons, always the logic that I didn't want to listen to. I resented Azra for keeping me with him for so long, but I knew he couldn't take care of you by himself; you were too young and he was too inexperienced. I resented your father for being so selfish. He wasn't the only one who had lost Indra.

"When Rasheym did catch up with us, he refused to say what he did with your mother's body." Ascher's face was twisted and bitter at the hard memory.

Abruptly, the emotion was gone. Ascher picked up the gym bag and got to his feet. "Is there anything else that you would like to know?"

It was clear that the conversation was over. I shook my head, my thoughts swimming with dozens of revelations and a flurry of anger and confusion. What Ascher told me shook loose everything I thought I knew about my father and Uncle Azra.

A small, tense smile graced his lips. "We will continue your lessons on Monday. Azra has you tomorrow. You need to practice though. I expect at least two hours every day."

I couldn't bring myself to speak, so I just nodded.

"I'm going to go pay for these damages. Azra was right; I should have kept our lessons outside." He gave me a brittle nod and left the room. I sat there alone long after he was gone, just thinking things through.

If my father and Azra hadn't been so reckless. . . Well, my life would have been very different.

The stories Ascher told me colored in my black and gray memories. I remembered my father as a very imposing figure. He kept his dark hair short in the Roman style and a celestial blade on his person at all times. He had seemed so infallible to me. But then, I had been looking at him from the eyes of a child.

Why hadn't Azra told me any of this? Why had that Archangel let me live? There was something missing from the story— something that Ascher hadn't told me.

In the wake of unburied memories, my decision to search the storage shed for more information on the prophecy and the Angelic War seemed like the best thing to do. Ascher had brushed it off as a rumor, but if it was just a rumor, then what made Uncle Azra and my father so certain about it? There had to be something physical they found that would prove my involvement; something I could reference.

I grabbed my skateboard, more confused, but also more determined. With my music blaring and my board under my feet, I went out into the world ready to find out the truth.

Chapter Ten

I thought about my mother and all the things Ascher told me on my way to the Stash-Ur-Stuff storage facility. Was that really how she had died or had Ascher made it up? There really wasn't any reason that I could see as to why he would do that though. His pain was real enough for me to believe. The more I thought about it, the angrier I became. Not just at my father, but at my uncle too. How would my life have been different if my mother had lived? The questions of what could have been plagued me as I travelled.

My timing was perfect. The moon rose just as I rolled up to the storage place on my skateboard. It was an easy thing to maneuver past the distracted closing employee and straight into the facility itself. I walked through the long, grey concrete halls with rows upon rows of red metal garage-like doors listening with my entire body for anyone else in the building ahead of me. All I heard was the thudding of my own pulse and the squeak of my shoes on the hard polished concrete floor. Suffice to say breaking and entering was not my forte.

I ascended the stairs to the second level where our units were. The stairwell echoed with my every move. I thought I heard the elevator ding, but I must have been wrong. Beyond that momentary imagined noise, the silence of the building resounded.

Each row held twelve red doors with numbers stenciled in spray paint on them. Our two storage spaces were at the end of the third row next to the window that overlooked the front entrance to the building.

I peered out of the wire-laced glass of the window as I pulled out the keys. Below, the teenage boy who had been covering the closing shift locked the front door and hopped into a waiting car which drove off leaving me alone on the premises.

I went to Azra's storage, mentally bracing myself. It took more than a couple of deep breaths before I was ready to open the door. I hefted the padlock in my left hand, inserted the key and twisted it until the lock clicked open. Yanking off the lock and lifting on the handle at the bottom of the metal door resulted in a hideous clanking as the metal slid upwards revealing the dark, hulking shapes inside of the room. I stood back and regarded the cramped rental space.

Even after the deep breaths, no amount of mental preparation could have equipped me for the maze of stuff inside that room. Even knowing Azra as I did, I was still awed by the sheer magnitude and the randomness contained inside. I couldn't go in one step without taking some of the stuff out. How was I going to have time to deal with all of this? I wrinkled my nose at the musty smell that came from unused things and dug in, moving them to the hallway.

It was good that I chose to do this after hours seeing as it would have been impossible to go through it while the establishment was open for business. There simply wouldn't have been enough time and, considering what might have been in there, too many questions.

Nothing was packed in boxes. No, Azra could never be that neat. Instead, the myriad of items were crammed in Tetris-style, making it a puzzle to take apart. I wasn't sure that I could put it all back when I was done. Hell, I wasn't sure if I could get through it all in one night, but I was here now and I figured that I'd cross that bridge when I came to it.

Since I wasn't sure what might pertain to the prophecy, I had to inspect every item carefully. That meant opening all of the 80's cartoon lunch boxes and peering into all of the ancient pieces of pottery to look for anything out of the ordinary. That, in and of itself, was a tall order since there was no rhyme or reason to what I pulled out.

The first layer of Azra's possessions seemed ordinary enough; there was an old grill, a broken lamp, some shoeboxes full of action figures. But the deeper in I went, the more unusual the items became. Soon, I was pulling out jars labeled 'mummy dust' and several beer steins, flasks and drinking horns that looked like they belonged at a Renaissance Festival. Knowing Uncle Azra, they were probably authentic.

Really, who else but my uncle would have a four-foot Mayan calendar carved in granite? Or an old chariot from the races in Rome that had been stacked full with finely woven Persian rugs?

There was a whole pile of pirate paraphernalia, including a ship's helm swathed with an old, tattered flag. It was evidence of Azra's pirate phase and the relapse he had after watching *The Goonies*. I could see some recognizable bits of merchandise from the movie amongst the treasure chests, swords and boots. It was surprising that there wasn't a complete skeleton somewhere in the pile just to complete the ensemble.

By the time I finished inspecting the pirate stuff, it was going on midnight. I had been working for almost five hours and still no sign of any information that would help me understand the prophecy better.

A quarter of the way in, I hit a barrier of furniture. There was a wall that consisted of a chest of drawers, a china hutch, a couple of armoires, an old writing desk, as well as four tall filing cabinets. All of it was filled to the brim with small knick-knacks and papers.

I wiped the dust from my hands onto my jeans. "You have got to be kidding me," I groaned. I checked my phone. Azra hadn't called yet. Maybe Ascher told him about what we talked about. Maybe he was avoiding me. It was just as well. I wasn't sure what to say to Azra anyway. There were just too many raw emotions that I needed to work through; too many what-ifs I needed to get out of my system.

Regarding the wall of stuff, I decided to start with the filing cabinets. I approached the first one, which was a simple beige color with five single file drawers stacked on top of each other. The metal handles were small and the placards meant to advertise what was inside were blank, leaving no indication what the contents were. Preparing myself for anything to jump out, I slid open the bottom drawer.

There were papers crammed inside, sloppy and disheveled and in no particular order. I was taken aback by the appearance of my own handwriting. Upon further inspection, I realized that I was holding a report I did on *Dante's Divine Comedy* back in the eighties.

Uncle Azra had kept this? Flipping through a few more files it became apparent that wasn't all he held onto. I opened more drawers and was met with my school work again and again. Uncle Azra had saved what looked like my entire school career in these cabinets.

Once that thought was realized, a pang of guilt shot through me. He was proud of me. If he wasn't, he wouldn't have kept all of this. Here I was rummaging through his stuff when I should have just told him outright what I was up to. He probably would have helped me. But then, I remembered my mother and how he was partially responsible for her loss. He couldn't even tell me what happened himself. Why should I believe that he would be upfront about anything else, including the prophecy?

I shoved the guilt out of my mind. I wasn't doing all of this for the hell of it; I was looking for information on what I had always been told was my destiny. I was doing this so I could make the right decisions to fulfill my end of the deal.

Looking through all the paper took me back to my childhood. Bittersweet nostalgia washed over me with every new discovery. As I shoved the filing cabinet aside, I came face to face with the marble bust of my mother; it looked as pristine as it had centuries ago when I had last seen it. She had a quixotic expression that made her lips turn up in a sort of half smile. The eyes were blank, having never received the paint they required to make them seem alive. Gently, I touched her cheek, wishing I could talk to her. Things might make a little more sense then. What would she say to me if she could? Would she be proud of me, of the prophecy I was supposedly involved in? There was no way to know.

Behind the bust was a suit of armor. The faint ghost of my father's face in the opening of the helmet made me gasp. The image faded and my heart beat wildly. I placed the armor off to the side, facing it away from me. Touching the leather and the metal that my father once wore brought back even more memories. This was what he had been wearing when he died.

Even as I tried to push the memory away, it was pulled into the light. I found myself speaking to the suit of armor. "We went hunting. It was my first time tracking a Fallen One. We were in England. The Fallen One we tracked led us into the forest. Something happened. I lost control; like someone hit the switch to turn me into the monster I should have been."

Snatches of the memory broke free of their protective confinement. The storage shed faded away, replaced with the shadows of the trees racing passed me, the labored breathing of something large and angry running behind me. No. The panting was coming from me; I could feel the burn of my lungs as they contracted with air. I saw the Fallen One; a dark haired knight hissing at my father, about to strike. Everything went black. I could hear the screams and feel the tearing of flesh in my hands.

I shook my head, clearing my vision and my senses. My breath came in great rasps and my heart pounded in my chest. Scared, I grabbed hold of the prayer beads around my wrist and moved them between my fingers, reciting the words Azra taught me. They were a focal point, something I could hold in my head instead of the images I was getting.

The hold on my control was tenuous and I shook with the effort to keep it in hand.

Disoriented, I slammed my back into the china hutch. The sound of shattering glass and porcelain filled the room. My hands flew to cover my head from the china and jewels falling to the concrete floor.

Leave it to my uncle to confuse fine china with jewelry boxes. A pair of emerald chopsticks and sapphire-encrusted sugar tongs toppled out of a Victorian bone china teapot and onto my head. Strings of precious gemstones spilled from one of the tureens and onto the ground around me. The noise was deafening against the silence of the building.

"Hey!" A voice shouted from the hallway outside of the storage shed.

Startled, I whipped my head up, bumping it on the ledge of the hutch. More pieces of china crashed down on top of me.

"Put your hands up!" The other voice sounded again, harshly.

When I was sure no more breakables were falling towards my head, I sat up. Through my blurry vision, I made out the fuzzy figure of a slightly rotund man in a uniform who held what looked like a stick in his right hand. I shook my head, trying to determine the extent of the damage the china hutch had done to me. Had I hit my head so hard that I was hallucinating?

"I said put your hands up!" The sharpness in the voice marked the person shouting at me as real; not a hallucination. I saw a uniform of a white shirt and black pants. The man yelling at me was a security guard, not a police officer. It took more than a moment to digest what was happening and more time after that to respond.

I guess I took too long to move because he stalked up to me and grabbed one of my hands. "You aren't supposed to be here. You're coming with me."

The second he touched me, I felt a spark inside ignite the anger I'd been bottling all day. After everything I found out about my mother—how my father and my uncle lied to me about it, as well as the memories from my own past flooding into me—this stupid human was the last straw. My fragile hold on my temper frayed and I reacted without thinking, kicking his legs out from under him. He released my hand, which caused his head to smack on the floor with a thud.

He rolled to his feet, wielding his club menacingly. He was a pudgy man; short with a balding head and squinty blue eyes. His pale skin was flushed from the exertion of being knocked around.

I flexed my fingers, balling them into a fist. A small part of my mind scolded me. Humans were too fragile for me to fight them like this. A tap from me could kill him. I wanted very badly to ignore the little voice. I was a lot more powerful than this pathetic being. It would be nothing to crush him and paint the walls with his blood.

That image disturbed me, almost as much as the realization that I really was ready to make it happen. It brought me to my senses.

"I forced myself to relax. My hands went up to show I wasn't going to hurt him. "Let me just—"

"Shut up!" The guard yelled, furious at being laid out. "You're under arrest for trespassing, breaking and entering, theft, and assault." He started forward to make a grab for me again.

I dodged him easily, placing a carousel horse between us. "You can't arrest me. You're just a rent-a-cop," I protested. The glare that the man gave me made me realize that had been the wrong thing to say. "I didn't take anything. This is my uncle's storage shed. He gave me the key earlier today."

The guard wasn't listening. He was too incensed at my previous comment. He lunged to the left. I went right.

"The cops are on their way now," he panted, still trying to snag a hold of me. "There's no use, kid. You're caught." He managed to snatch my shirt and, before I could get away, he had me by my wrists.

The sick urge to bash my head straight into his and see who would be left standing overtook me. Panic bloomed in my chest. I was losing it and fast. I had to do something to make him stop. I was desperate and so I did the first thing that popped into my head.

All angels have the power to influence humans. We can get into a human's mind and work them like a marionette. We can even make it seem as though it was the human's idea. This is how the war between Heaven and Hell was being played out on Earth. Angels from both sides were mentally controlling humans as their pawns in the fight. The circumstances varied, but there were really only two endings for the humans; their souls were either relegated to the Fallen Ones or ascended with the Heavenly Choirs. Neither option was better than the other since angels never cared much for humans while they were alive and I seriously doubted that they changed their opinions once they were dead.

That being said, I had never tried it before. I wasn't even sure if I could do it. But I had to do something because if this guard kept pushing, dental records wouldn't help to identify him.

I steadied my gaze at the guard and focused on his forehead, directly at his third eye chakra point. Chakra points were kind of like psychic pressure points. The one I was currently intent on would, if pushed right, allow me to get into the man's head to control his thoughts and his memory. I would be able to make him forget the entire situation. That was the theory anyway.

The angelic power I had within me flowed strongly and I had to fight to control the amount that poured into the man. I had to be precise with the force I put into controlling him. Humans were fragile; too much power and their heads would crack like an egg, too little and nothing would be accomplished.

Centering my attention to the guard, I said as confidently as I could, "Look at me."

I gave him a mental poke. It was like jimmying a

window open so that I was able to get inside of his mind with just a little effort. Breaking into his mind was like nothing I had ever experienced before. The sheer power I felt was intoxicating. I saw the strings that controlled this man, the delicately colored brainwaves and the electric impulses that made him function. It was exhilarating to know that, with just a thought, I could make him do whatever I wanted; I could manipulate those brainwaves, so easily. I could make him my slave.

A glassy expression came over the guard's features as I struggled to control myself. I wouldn't hurt him. I just needed to alter his memories. Exerting just a little more pressure, I pushed into his mind, searching for the right strings.

He fought against me. He pushed me to the side every time I advanced. In response, I poured more of my own energy into the fight. It wasn't long before the power streamed more quickly between us, faster than I could handle. My control was slipping. Suddenly, he broke free of my hold. I was violently shoved out of his head and slammed fully back into my own. As I stood there, disoriented and weak, the guard lunged over the carousel horse. In doing so, he ended up bringing it and him down on top of me.

The weight of both the horse and the fat guard both knocked the breath out of me and severed the mental connection between us. His hands grappled for my neck. Fighting off his hands, I couldn't stop my head from slamming into the concrete.

Reacting more on instinct than thought, I placed my hands under the carousel horse that pinned me and pushed. The guard and the wooden horse were propelled into the air. The guard slammed against the metal cabinets with a crash. The carousel horse narrowly missed him. Still, with the force that I had used, it wouldn't have surprised me if he had a few broken ribs and a decent amount of internal bruising.

That was why it was such a shock when he didn't stay

down for long. Within moments, he was back on his feet and charging at me. I was too disoriented from the attempt at mind control to stop him from tackling me to the ground. He drew back to pound on me. Everything was happening so quickly, but I gathered my strength to shove him off of me before he could land another punch.

"Freeze!" A powerful voice demanded. I heard the click of guns being armed and boots pounding over the concrete to where we were on the floor.

The guard threw his hands up in the air, a look of triumph on his face. "Hello, officers," he called out, sneering at me.

He moved to get off of me, but one of the officers barked at him, "Stay down. Put your hands above your head. Do not move."

"I'm the one who called you," he whined.

One of the officers took his arms and pulled the guard off me and out of the storage unit. I was hoisted to my feet. My head ached too much to care. Moments later, I was sitting on the pile of pirate paraphernalia, handcuffed and struggling to answer the questions that were put to me.

An officer stood over me and flipped open a spiral bound pad of paper. "What's your name?" He was a short, brown skinned man with balding black hair and a thick mustache. The name embroidered on his uniform said Pacheco.

That was an easy enough question. "Ryan Gregory," I answered, shifting uncomfortably on *The Goonies* merchandise. Everything was fuzzy and I struggled to focus. The after effects of attempted mind control sucked.

Another officer stood slightly to the left of Officer Pacheco, just in case I got out of hand. I couldn't see the name on his uniform and he didn't volunteer it. Another officer was gazing around at my uncle's things, clearly at a loss for words. I could sympathize.

"How old are you, Ryan?"

I debated on the answer to this and decided to go with the truth. "Five thousand six hundred forty seven," I said. That seemed about right.

"Don't be a smart ass," the officer next to Pacheco growled. "Answer the question truthfully."

Oh if he only knew. "I'm seventeen."

"Is this your storage unit?" Officer Pacheco had an easy going manner about him. He asked the questions directly, but also calmly and quietly.

"No, it's my uncle's."

"What's your uncle's name?"

Another easy question. "Azra."

"Azra. Does Azra have a last name?"

Oh yeah. "Gregory."

I watched him make some notes on his notepad. My head was beginning to throb. The energy loss was more intense than I thought it would be; I began to feel nauseated and disoriented.

Officer Pacheco asked, "Does your uncle know that you are here now?"

I shook my head and then regretted it when the thudding increased. "No," I said, closing my eyes against the pain in my head. Whether it was from bumping my head or the backlash of the mind control, I didn't know. It just hurt like hell.

"We're going to have to give him a call. Your parents too. What are their phone numbers?"

I sighed. "My parents are dead," I answered dully. "My uncle is my guardian."

Great. Uncle Azra would be here in no time and then I would have to explain all of this to him. The thought made me dread giving the officer his number. But I did it anyway, knowing that if I gave wrong information, it would be that much worse.

After noting the information, Officer Pacheco looked at me seriously. "Why are you here this late?"

This wasn't such an easy question. I glanced around at Azra's stuff, trying to come up with a reason. "I... I came up here to pick up something for a school project," I lied, returning my eyes to the officer. "Time sort of got away from me. I didn't realize the place had closed."

"Time got away from you, huh?" Officer Pacheco repeated skeptically.

In response, I jerked an elbow towards the mass of junk behind him. "Well, yeah. Look at all that. You try finding something specific in all of that."

Officer Pacheco raised an eyebrow. "Good point. So what happened then?"

I shrugged dramatically. "I don't know. I was just in here looking for the. . ." I wracked my brain for a suitable object. "My great-great grandfather's stereopticon—"

The officer held up his hand. "Wait. Your grandfather's what?"

"Stereopticon. It's like an old viewfinder. It was the precursor for the 3D movie. I needed it for my history class. I was looking for that and all of a sudden, that guard comes running in here, scaring me half to death and threatening to arrest me. He told me I was a thief and I was trespassing. I said I didn't think he could arrest me because he was just a security guard and that's when he attacked me."

"I see," Officer Pacheco made more notes. "Wait here. I'll be back for you in a little while." He turned to exit the crowded unit, presumably to compare notes with the officer that had questioned the security guard and to call my uncle.

I sagged against the ships helm, exhausted. The thought of Azra's reaction made me groan. He was going to freak out. Especially when he found out I attempted to influence a human. Not only attempted, but failed miserably at it. But then, why should I care if he was angry about it? I had more right to be angry with him than anything else.

At last, the exhaustion claimed my mind. I stopped thinking. I had only enough energy to sit quietly and watch as the police officers milled around looking at all of Azra's collection of junk.

It seemed like hours passed before Officer Pacheco

came back to check on me. "Alright, kid," he said in a serious tone. "We're going to have to take you down to the station. You were here after hours and trespassing is a crime, not to mention assault."

I protested, "He was the one who assaulted me!"

"It's his word against yours."

I wanted to argue, but he had me and I knew it. "Have you called my uncle yet?"

"Yes," Pacheco said, but he didn't elaborate any further. He helped me up and started leading me out of the storage unit and into the hallway. "You have the right to remain silent. Anything you say can be used against you in a court of law. . ."

I was so consumed with the dread of having my uncle come get me out of jail that I phased out the words. As we left the building, I looked up at the night sky filled with stars briefly before they put me into the back of a squad car. I wondered if Azra would ever let me see them again.

Chapter Eleven

They put me into a communal cell with the other people they had arrested that night. I spent the time in the corner waiting for Uncle Azra to burst through the door and make a scene.

But the scene never came.

My energy levels were at an all-time low. All I could do was lean against the wall and think about what happened. I didn't know trying to control and influence humans could take so much out of you. Or perhaps I was feeling this way because I hadn't done it right; it was hard to tell which. The hours dragged by and my dread of confronting my uncle grew steadily with them.

Police officers passed by the cell regularly, but none even glanced over. It was a curious way to keep guard. Hours later, a tired looking officer approached the cell and called in a bored tone. "Ryan Gregory."

I stood up as quickly as I could, jostling though the press of my sullen and angry cell mates. "I'm right here," I answered.

"Come with me," the officer said as he unlocked the cell door.

After I was out and the cell locked behind me, the officer led me through booking to the waiting area. Uncle Azra was there looking disheveled, as though he had been woken up abruptly and had rushed down to the station. Ironically enough, he was wearing more clothes than he usually did; his board shorts had been traded for khakis topped with a loud Hawaiian print shirt.

"Ryan!" He exclaimed in a falsely worried tone. He reached out dramatically and I had trouble hiding my embarrassment. Azra would make a wonderful B-list actor with his dramatics. "I've been so worried about you!" He took me in his arms for a firm embrace. "You and I have a lot to talk about, mister," he whispered into my ear. His clipped words were in Old Greek, the first language I had learned. That he chose to speak it made me realize just how angry he was. He tended to save the old languages for his more severe lectures. Pulling away, he declared loudly back in American English, "Don't you run off like that again. You gave Beth such a fright!"

"The goat was worried about me?"

"Don't call her that!" Azra ejected, scandalized. He turned to the officer who was smiling at us benignly, if not a little dazed. "Thank you so much for finding him for me. He hasn't been quite the same since his mother . . ." Azra trailed off, pausing in respect. "Well, we'd better get going. Thank you very much, officer."

My blood boiled at the mention of my mother and that this could in any way be her fault. Uncle Azra gripped my arm in one hand and hauled me out the door. On the way, he snatched the belongings the police had confiscated for evidence.

The goat was tied up to the bike rack outside. While I'd been rummaging through his stuff for evidence of my destiny, Azra had taken my advice and gotten her a collar and a leash. It was much to my chagrin that they were made of bright pink leather and that the collar had spikes protruding from it.

"You seriously got the goat a spiked collar?" I asked.

Azra spun around, eyes blazing, and hissed at me again in Old Greek, "You would do well to keep your mouth shut, Orion." He pulled a tan file folder from under his Hawaiian button down shirt and tossed it to me. "Put this in your backpack and destroy it as soon as we get you home."

There was no question about it—he was royally pissed off. "What is this?" I asked, doing my best to ignore his fury.

"That," Azra replied fighting to keep his voice level,

"is your police file. I'll not have everything ruined by a shitty mug shot and ridiculously biased witness statements." As he spoke, he untied Beth's leash with sharp, jerky motions like he was punctuating his speech with his elbows.

Azra untangled the goat and started forward, yanking Beth along with him. I followed in the wake of the clopping sounds her hooves made on the sidewalk. Trying to soften the stony silence radiating off him, I shuffled forward to walk next to Azra. Beth served as a safety buffer between us. "What did they say?"

"They asked if I had lost a sticky fingered nephew. A nephew who has a curious lack of respect for rules that were set in place for a reason. I told them no, that my perfect little angel for a nephew should be in his room. I told them my nephew couldn't possibly lie or steal."

I focused my gaze on the sidewalk in front of me, trying to control my own anger at the lies Azra had crammed down my throat all of those years. Ascher's version of my mother's death loomed largely in my mind. "Look, Uncle Az. I didn't. . ."

He stopped abruptly and turned to glare at me, his outrage lending his stare a certain amount of fire. "What part of 'you had best keep your mouth shut' didn't you understand, Orion? I'm not in the mood to listen to your excuses right now."

He wasn't in the mood to listen to me? He had the audacity to threaten me without even hearing my side of the story? My own leashed anger broke free. Without warning, I swung at Azra.

My fist was met with my uncle's palm as he easily deflected the hit. Not in the least deterred, I threw my weight towards him, trying to catch him off balance. He stood solid despite my attempted body slam and all I managed to do was fall hard on my stomach.

"Knock it off," he growled at me. "We will discuss this at home. You've caused enough public disturbances for one night." Yanking Beth's leash he headed in the direction of my apartment. I had no choice but to pick myself up and follow. I caught up, trailing just a few steps behind them, allowing the silence to overtake us.

Azra didn't so much as look at me the rest of the way to the apartment and that was just fine with me. Unspoken words dangled in the air between us. It wasn't until we were all inside (Beth as well, though I had cringed as her hooves pounded on each step) that Azra was ready to talk.

He sat me down on one side of the table while he took the other side. Beth wandered around, looking for something to eat. She settled on going through my garbage and consuming what was left of Uncle Azra's decorations for my failed date.

"Orion," Azra began, attempting to be considerably calmer than he had been on the walk home, "would you care to explain exactly what you were up to?"

I was still furious, but I took a breath and some time to think about how to best phrase things. "I get that you are angry, but—"

"No," Azra interrupted, holding up his finger. "No, I'm not angry that you betrayed my trust. I'm not angry about you going through all of my stuff and lying to me. I want to know about what happened with that guard. That's the part I need to understand, because I am *very* angry about that."

I bit my tongue to keep my reaction in check. "I didn't mean to. . ."

But Azra didn't let me finish. "You didn't mean to? Which part, Orion, didn't you mean to do? Break into a storage unit that you had no business in? Lying to me? Getting into a fight with a human when you know you're more powerful? Or how about almost erasing the entire memory of that guard's life? Really, Orion, I want to know what part you didn't mean to do!"

I clasped my hands tightly together on the table to keep from hitting him. In a slow and measured tone, I said, "I had to see if I could find it."

"Find what exactly?" Azra demanded, his voice elevated. He pounded his fist on the table in frustration. "What could possibly have been so important to put yourself in that situation? Do you have any idea what you did, or what could have happened?"

I couldn't hold it back any more. I snapped at him, "Do you know what you did? If it wasn't for you and my father, my mother would be alive right now! It's your fault she is dead!" I hadn't realized what I had said until the words left my lips.

Azra looked as though I had slapped him. He stared, slack-jawed, the redness of his fury draining out of his face. It was a full minute of us staring at each other; me in fully righteous anger and Azra in stunned silence before he asked, "Did Ascher tell you what happened?"

I didn't trust myself to speak, so I just nodded.

He swallowed. "Is that what all of this is about? You are mad at me for how your mother died, so you break into my storage unit and attack a security guard?" He didn't sound angry anymore as much as confused, but rage still flowed through me.

"No, that's not all. I need to make sure that the destiny you've been cramming down my throat for years is the one I'm meant to fulfill or if you are just delusional. I wanted more information on the prophecy. I don't want to sound like an idiot if Stella isn't involved in it." At some point during my emotional outburst, I'd gotten to my feet, knocking the chair down behind me. "And you know what? Yes, I am mad about my mother. If you and my father had stayed with her, if you hadn't pissed off some Archangel on one of your drunken revelries, she would still be alive. I would have had a mother."

My uncle rose to his feet slowly, not even looking me in the eye. His face was a neutral mask, scaring me more than I would like to admit. Still, I was angry enough to stand my ground.

He closed his blue eyes for just a moment and inhaled deeply. He was obviously doing his best to keep his slipping temper in check. After exhaling the same breath, he said, "Ascher never got the whole story. He was too angry at the time and he just assumed."

"So then what happened? I think I deserve to know."

Uncle Azra ran his hand through his hair. "Your father and I went out that night. Not to on a drunken revelry or whatever Ascher assumed we did, but to scout out the area. We heard about a collection of Fallen Ones that had banded together in the city. We never did find them. Instead, a couple of Choir Boys slumming down from Heaven decided to pick a fight with us. Rasheym killed one of them. The other ran back to Heaven, or so we thought. Really, what happened was that he hid and then followed us back to the villa where you and your parents lived.

"Your mother was furious at us being caught by Choir Boys. Really it was her way of showing how worried she was for us," he smiled at the memory. "It was kinda cute how much she fretted. Rasheym was convinced the other one would bring help down from Heaven. He wanted to go confront them, to finish the fight so to speak. Naturally, your mother was against the idea because she didn't want him to get himself killed for no reason. She didn't understand the pride we felt at the idea of besting a group of Choir Boys. Your parents fought and let me tell you, it was a big one. I'd never seen your mother so mad."

I frowned at Azra's tale, noting quietly the similarities and differences from Ascher's.

He kept his voice low and calm as he went on with his story. "Rasheym ended up storming out of the villa. As his best friend and partner, I couldn't let him go alone so I followed him. We stalked the streets, searching for the Heavenly Host that we were sure would come for us. But we never found them." Azra sank down into his chair, leaving me standing and unsure of my own rioting emotions.

"We got back to the villa in time to see an Archangel go inside. Rasheym didn't even hesitate. He ran after the

Archangel, screaming. I knew he would attack first thing and I was torn. Do I get Indra and you out first or do I help Rasheym? I teleported inside the villa with my weapon drawn and ready to fight. Indra and your father were both going against the Archangel. You were in your cradle, bawling your head off. I knew that the important thing was to make sure that you were safe. Rasheym and Indra could take care of themselves. They were a deadly pair when they joined forces and weren't fighting each other. Especially if they were defending you."

"So you grabbed me and got out of there," I said. "You didn't try to help them?"

He shrugged, "It was what they would have wanted. Just as you and I got out, something exploded and the entire villa went up in flames. We barely got away from the fire in time. A few minutes later, the Archangel emerged from the smoke and left. I didn't get a good look at his face, but I did see a lot of blood. Some of it was his and some of it wasn't.

"When Rasheym came out carrying Indra, it was almost surreal. I couldn't believe she was dead. Ascher had arrived moments before. When he saw your mother, he started shouting and threatening Rasheym. It was his way of dealing with it, I guess. Rasheym didn't even respond, it was like he didn't even see Ascher in front of him. I think he was in shock. He gave me one of his looks; the one that I knew lead to trouble, and not the good kind. He took off with Indra's body. I knew exactly where he was going and I wasn't sure if he would ever come back."

I shivered at the look in my uncle's eyes. The resentment was draining from me with every word of his tale. "Where did he go?"

"Both Heaven and Hell have entrances into this world. The ones that lead into Hell are called Hellmouths and the ones to Heaven are called Stairways. Your father went to one of the Stairways to confront the Heavenly Host. It was a suicide mission and I don't think he expected to survive. I know for sure that I didn't expect him to.

"Suddenly, I had to take care of you. Ascher was there too, but he was more concerned about going after Rasheym. It took some convincing, but I managed to get him to stay with me. I didn't have the first clue about taking care of a baby. Neither did he, but I guess he thought I would have just made a mess of it on my own because he stayed with us.

"Rasheym came back a week later. He was beaten black and blue and refused to talk about what happened. We left for what would eventually be called South America right after he came back. He couldn't handle staying anywhere near Rome after that."

"So that's what happened?" I asked, hollowly. The fire had gone out of my voice. While it hurt, I was glad to finally hear the story from Azra. His version had the ring of truth to it; more so than Ascher's cold retelling. "Thank you for finally telling me."

He shrugged and cleared his throat. "It was time. Now, you said you were looking for information. Why didn't you just ask me?" I detected a subtle hitch of emotion in his voice, a hoarseness that betrayed his forced serenity.

"Because you wouldn't tell me anything!" I retorted. Now that Azra wasn't as angry, I let some of my muted frustration out. "I've asked you and asked you, especially in the last few days since I met Stella! You give me the same answer: find the human. But you won't tell me how! You know so much more than you are telling me, I can feel it!"

"That's not true!" Azra shouted back, the tight leash he had on his anger had finally snapped. "I've told you everything I know. I'm not hiding anything from you."

"Then why don't I know some very basic things about the subject? Like how am I supposed to know when I find the human that is to help with the war? Why won't you believe that Stella might be the one? When will I have to be ready? What about the mirror?"

"I don't know!" Uncle Azra launched to his feet and stormed around the room out of aggravation. "It isn't as though you came with instructions. All I know is what your father told me long ago. I was able to do a little more research, but it was very difficult and by that time I had to take care of you. It's extremely hard to track down ancient rumors with a kid in tow, especially one that acts like a beacon for all of your enemies." He ran his fingers through his blonde hair, a gesture I had seen him make many times before when he was stressed out.

"Both my parents believed I was the one in the prophecy?" I asked.

He nodded quietly, his hand moving back and forth over his head.

"Ascher told me that my mother didn't care about any of that."

The sound of his old friend's name brought Azra's eyes to mine. A suspicious light flared in his gaze. "Instead of asking me about the prophecy, you ask *him*? He doesn't even believe it! For the love of everything sacred, why would you ask him about it?"

I decided that honesty was the best policy at this point because I was already in for it. There was no point in pulling punches to spare his feelings. "I was hoping he'd tell me what he knew about the prophecy and the Angelic War. What I got was how my mother died."

Uncle Azra's expression turned brittle. "So, based off of this one conversation you had with Ascher, you decided to go break into my storage unit and go through my stuff looking for. . . what? Some evidence of a prophecy you aren't even sure that you believe in anymore?"

"Not quite," I admitted. "I decided to break into the storage unit before I spoke with Ascher. I lifted your key on the beach yesterday morning." This information had Uncle Azra pacing once more.

"What then? You got there and you started rummaging through everything. Did the guard come up to stop you?"

I nodded. "He came in and scared me half to death. I tried to reason with him—"

"Was almost erasing his entire memory part of your reasoning?" Uncle Azra asked in a low voice. "Was tampering with his free will part of the negotiation?"

I said with more conviction than I felt, "I did what I had to do. I didn't have a choice."

"Didn't have a choice, huh?" Uncle Azra stalked over to the couch and grabbed my shirt again. "Let me make something clear to you!" He shouted as he pinned me up against the wall. "When it comes to screwing around with human minds, there's always a choice! You have no idea what could have happened."

I yanked his hands away, forcing him to let go of my shirt. "I do know what could have happened," I screamed back at him. "I know the risk I took. And you know what? It was worth it. That stupid guard had it coming!"

"You idiot," he seethed. "You sound like a Fallen One or a Choir Boy. You really don't understand what you could have done, do you?" He let go of my clothing and took hold of my ear instead. He used it to lead me to the bathroom. "Come on. You need to remember which side of this fight you are on."

"OW! Easy!" I maneuvered so the pain wasn't as intense. "Where are we going?"

"Ascher was right. You need this punishment for the stunt you pulled. Some lessons in morality are in order."

"You told Ascher?" I don't know why I felt so betrayed at the thought of them discussing me behind my back.

"I was with him when the cops called. I didn't agree with his suggestion at first, but after that smart-ass comment, that is what you are going to do."

"What?"

He shoved me into the small bathroom and shouted, "You are going to get showered and dressed. Then you are going to church. You will keep going to church until you understand that you do not mess with the free will of humans. Religion is how the whole Angelic War is being fought, so while you are there listening to whatever it is they do at Mass, think about how it can be twisted into fanaticism. Think of how many lives have been lost because of some angel prying into a human's mind to control them."

I knew better than to question the authority that came across in that one demand. He shoved me backwards into my small bathroom and slammed the door. "Hurry up!"

I stood there, absolutely livid. He was actually going to make me go. He was probably looking up churches in the phone book as I stood there. "Why church?"

"I don't hear that shower going!" Azra bellowed through the walls, ignoring my question. "Get going or so help me, you will go to Mass butt naked!"

I groaned in disgust. He would do it too. Resigned, I started up the water and looked at myself in the mirror. The places where the guard had hit me were angry looking. The bruises would fade soon enough. My eye, however, had a small cut from his knuckles. It wasn't deep or really even that big, but it was enough to be noticeable. No matter. It was one of the perks of being me; minor injuries healed rather quickly.

I showered and dressed as Uncle Azra had bid me to. He laid out a stiff grey suit and an audacious yellow tie that had ducks with small crosses printed on it. I glared at him as I tied it on.

"You will wear it and you will like it, young man," he warned. He was dressed in his usual swim trunks and flip flops.

"You aren't coming with me?" I asked.

"I'm not the one being punished. Besides, I don't do religion. I am, however, going to drop you off and pick you up. And Orion," he growled, "I will know if you skip out on this. So help me, you will be in even more trouble than you are now if you do."

I stared back at Azra defiantly and answered in a

short, clipped syllable. "Fine."

We left the apartment with Beth in tow. She was still gnawing on a large red paper heart from the garbage. To get down the stairs, Azra slung her over his shoulders and started down. I trailed behind, trying to avoid the goat's reproachful gaze and slowly moving jaw.

Chapter Twelve

The San Buenaventura mission was only a few blocks away from my apartment. It was painted creamy white and sporting a light brown roof with dark wooden beams as trim. There was a cross above the main entrance from Main Street, but the real attention-grabber was the stately bell tower next to the doorway. Beneath the cross, on the face of the building, was a circle of stained glass that was in the image of a book and a dove.

Cars pulled into the parking lot and families in their Sunday best made their way to the red doors. As they passed the threshold of the house of God, they were greeted by the smoky scent of Frankincense and Myrrh from previous services.

True to his word, Azra walked me all the way to the front step, earning us both strange looks from the other parishioners due to his lack of proper attire. Well, that and he had a goat on a spiked leather leash.

Azra grabbed my shoulder before I could go into the mission. Looking me directly in the eyes, he said, "You will go in there, sit quietly, and observe. Think about what you have done. If we were meant to control the humans, then they wouldn't have free will. Ascher said this was the best place for you to figure that out. You are not to leave until the services are over. Do not take communion, do not take confession. Don't take anything from anyone. It might be contaminated. I will pick you up here when it's over. And don't even think about sneaking out of this; Ascher has set up a specific ward that will notify us if you do leave. You won't get away with it." Uncle Azra turned, yanked on Beth's leash and left me standing in the doorway.

Heaving a sigh, I turned and went through the

wooden double doors just as the bell above called out to the faithful.

While the outside of the mission could be described as clean and simple, the inside housed all the trappings of a Roman Catholic Church. The vaulted ceilings showed decorative crossbeams and elaborate chandeliers hung down from silken ropes. The chandeliers themselves once held candlesticks but were now replaced with the more common electric lights. A large red carpet divided dark wooden pews in the large rectangular room and led to an elaborate altar.

I sat near the back, figuring it would be a quicker getaway than a pew closer to the front. I was pretty sure Azra was lying about the wards. I doubted Ascher had bothered at all and if that were the case, all I would have to do is make sure I was back before Mass ended. As soon as it started, I would sneak out.

I settled back to watch the faithful as they crossed themselves and went to find their own seats. Boredom and irritation crept over me. All at once, the anger and sheer injustice of my so-called punishment hit me. Why was I wasting my time here when I should be learning all I could about the prophecy? What I did couldn't have been that bad. Uncle Azra surely did it at some point too. The guard was fine; it wasn't as though I had killed him.

"Excuse me young man," a quavering voice spoke into my ear.

I nearly jumped out of my seat. When I turned, I came face to face with a frail looking old woman. Her long silver hair was tied back into a braided bun and was covered with a black lace shawl. Her dress was made out of a heavy satin-like material with long sleeves and a lace ruffle at the neck that was secured with a black and white cameo broach. She looked as though she belonged in the previous century. For a fleeting moment, I thought she was a ghost, but on closer inspection, she was as real and as tangible as the uncomfortable pew that I was sitting upon. I couldn't quite tell how, but she was strangely familiar.

"Would you be kind enough to help an old woman to her seat?" Her accent was foreign and thick, but I understood her perfectly. Italian, maybe?

"Yes, ma'am." I stood and held out my arm, still trying to place where I knew her from. Her touch was soft and light, as if what lay on my arm wasn't a hand, but a thin swath of silk.

I walked with her for a few feet before she yanked surprisingly hard on my arm. She tugged me down to my knees in the middle of the aisle as she sank into a half curtsey. She crossed herself, keeping her eyes serenely on the altar. In order to not appear out of place, I did the same, feeling vaguely like a traitor or at the very least a sinner. Wasn't it a sin to cross yourself in church if you weren't of that faith? Did that even apply to me?

We began walking again; she with her head held high while I took small, awkward steps so the woman wouldn't have to rush to keep up.

"Grandmother," I began in my most respectful whisper, "do you not have family to escort you?" The stares from the people in the pews made me uncomfortable. At least, I thought they were staring. I would if I saw a woman who looked as though she had come from a nineteenth century funeral.

"No," she shook her head. The lace covering must have been pinned very well because it stayed in place. "My family has other obligations today. It is the anniversary of my husband's death, so I come to remember him and to pray that La Bona Dia and her Son care for him still."

"I am sorry to hear that." The phrase La Bona Dia— the Good Goddess—caught my attention, making me realize that I had been right; she was Italian. Not only Italian, but of the rural folk traditions. They were the only ones who called mother Mary a goddess. It reminded me of what Ascher had told to me about the Creator and all of the religions being based off of the four Archetypes. Could this old woman know about all of that? I eyed her closely, wondering if she were somehow more than she appeared to be. The prophecy never mentioned how old the human had to be. I took another sly look at the woman. No, it couldn't be.

She smiled up at me. "You're a nice young man. I wasn't expecting you to be so polite. Sit with me." She gestured to the third row of pews to the left.

"Ah, no thank you. I am not staying," I said, trying to back away.

"I insist," the woman's grip on my arm tightened and she pulled me down to sit next to her. The thick skirts she wore rustled and billowed around her. She was stronger than she looked. "I have been waiting to meet you for some time. There is much for us to discuss about the future."

What was this lady talking about? She kept her hand firmly on my arm until I nodded my assent that I would stay. I placed myself next to the woman, allowing the black material of her dress plenty of room.

"Now, young man, what is your name?" she smiled up at me. When she did so, her wrinkles deepened and her grey eyes shone so much that they appeared to be silver. I thought I saw a spark of something in them, something powerful. It was gone in a flash and I wondered if I really saw anything at all.

"Ryan Gregory," I answered, trying to understand why I suddenly wanted to stay. The woman was lonely and wanted someone to talk to. I could afford to humor her. Uncle Azra was probably outside waiting in case I tried to leave anyway. Besides, there was something about the woman that nagged at me, something that I should have known immediately. It was frustrating to think I was missing it. I glanced up at the altar and suppressed a shudder. Being this close to the front of the church was unnerving.

The old woman's hand on my arm brought me back to the present. She spoke in a light manner, like she was happy for my company. "You may call me Sylvia. Thank you for humoring an old woman. I know Giovanni, may his soul rest in peace, he would be happy that you are here with me today."

I said, "It'd my pleasure, bella nona."

Her laughter was light and surprisingly rich. "Oh, I didn't realize you spoke Italiano. And such a flirt, too! Though, I suppose the two go hand in hand. My Giovanni was the same way, that dear man. My husband was a God-fearing man. He loved his religion with all of his heart, but it did nothing to save him." She said this in such a way that it was obvious she had made her peace with whatever had happened to her husband.

A bell chimed from the direction of the altar, calling the faithful to attention. Sylvia leaned closer to me and whispered, "Now, we had best pay attention. The priest is coming."

She struggled to stand up straight by resting her weight against the pew and lifting herself as best as she could with her arms. She refused my help when I offered it, clearly wanting to be independent. I could understand that. I strove for the same thing in my own life. Still, why did she want me to help her before then?

I looked at the altar to see two priests, one in a long white robe with a sort of thick embroidered tunic over it and one in a black cassock with a thin, white smock covering him from the waist up. They each knelt at the altar and bowed their heads. The congregation knelt on the little ankle-high benches. Sylvia, however, decided to sit on the pew at this part. I watched her with growing curiosity as she clasped her hands in front of her breast and bowed her head.

Latin words resonated through the acoustics of the mission. They echoed against the painted walls, falling on the ears of the faithful. I wondered if any of these people understood what was really being said.

I listened to the words, re-familiarizing myself with the lyrical cadence the sounds held. The priest saying the Mass had difficulty with Latin. Perhaps he was new and the mistakes I heard were the combination of mumbling and mistranslation. I had to fight to keep the laughter bursting from my lips when he misquoted the mass. Instead of calling Jesus the Lamb of God, he said he was the rabbit of glory. Sylvia glanced up at me questioningly.

"He doesn't know his Latin very well," I explained, my voice just barely a whisper.

An odd smile played about her lips. "Is that so?"

The priests performed a sort of shuffling of positions by moving the book from one side to the other. My mind rebelled against the senseless ceremony I was seeing. Humans actually believed this sort of thing got them closer to the Creator?

When I was younger, I had asked my father what the Creator was like. "You know," he told me with a faraway look, "I don't think the Creator is something that can be described."

"Please try," I had begged.

His dark eyes were full of sadness as he explained to me, "It was a long time ago, before the official outbreak of the Angelic War. I was with the Creator for only a short time, but I can say it was the most complete I ever felt. When I met your mother, it was an echo of what it was like in the presence of Divinity."

"So the Creator is love?" I asked. I knew my father loved my mother very much. He told me whenever I did something that reminded him of her.

"Yes," he confirmed. "In a matter of speaking, the Divine is love."

Looking back, that had to be the biggest load of crap he had ever given to me. If the Divine was love, then why had my parents been banished from Heaven, from their home, for simply being what the Creator made them? Why had the Divine allowed the Angelic War to be waged for so long? Even now, why was the Creator allowing all of the senseless violence that was running rampant around the world?

I kept my thoughts to myself and watched the people

around me as they prayed; some had rosary beads clutched in their clasped hands and some held only their bibles.

I broke out of my reverie when I saw a line of people heading up to the altar to receive communion. More senseless ritual. I looked over at my companion, who sat steadfastly in her seat and whispered to her, "Sylvia, would you like to go up there?"

"No," she made a slight shake of her head. "I'm in no state to receive the Holy Communion."

I frowned at that, but didn't argue. I supposed I wasn't fit either, so who was I to judge?

The rest of the Mass crawled by. It was hard to keep my mind on what was happening. Besides bemoaning silently about how much time this was wasting, I found myself considering my companion. Where did I know her from? The puzzle kept me in my seat more than anything else. She said that there was much to discuss about the future. Was it just a crazy woman's babbling or was it something more? Maybe whatever she had to talk to me about had to do with the Angelic War.

I groaned mentally. What was wrong with me? I was looking so hard for more information that I was starting to see it everywhere it wasn't. It made me think of how Azra described Ascher's quest for the mirror: seeing treasure everywhere, especially where it wasn't.

After the dismissal, people stood, filing down the aisle towards the door. I stood as well, feeling a sense of perverse accomplishment for sitting through an entire mass without any apparent negative side effects.

"Well, that was a nice service, don't you think?" Sylvia asked with a wink.

Being polite, I offered my hand to help her up. "It was interesting," I lied.

She accepted and allowed herself to be led to the main aisle.

Instead of heading for the exit, however, she pulled me towards a smaller altar with a large statue of the

Mother Mary. At the base of the statue were tiers of blue encased votive candles, some lit, and some not. Releasing her hold on my arm, she said, "Please, wait for me here. I must do one more thing and then we can talk." She eased herself onto her knees on the cushioned stool in front of the altar.

Not knowing what else to do, I moved to the side and watched her quietly. She went through the motions of crossing herself and lighting the candle, but something about the way that she did it was different than the others. There was something more mystical, more powerful about it. Her movements flowed as though they were conducting energy; her low murmuring voice could be weaving spells just as easily as offering prayers. I felt the power rise and fall with the old woman's breath.

I glanced around to see if anyone else had noticed. None of the other people even stopped to look. They were either on their way out or still sitting in their pews, whispering their prayers, and clutching their rosaries. My eyes strayed back to Sylvia. How was she doing it? I could swear that the air rippled with her intent.

My pocket vibrated and it took a moment to realize that it was my phone going off. I fished it out and flipped it open. Much to my elation, it was a text from Stella.

Hey. What are you doing?

She didn't hate me after all! I could have sung at the top of my lungs, right then and there.

Sitting in a church, I responded with a ridiculously huge grin on my face. It didn't matter what Sylvia was doing with the air now, or why she was familiar, and it certainly didn't matter that I was in a church for a stupid punishment. Stella was talking to me after that horrible, horrible date. Nothing else in the world could have made the world more right.

What? Why are you in a church?

My uncle wanted me to learn some morality. I laughed, picturing her confused face.

Ever-ready was her wit because she retorted before

I was able to return the phone to my pocket. *Is it working?*
I dunno. Is morality itchy?

Meanwhile, Sylvia had finished her devotions and was struggling to her feet. "Ryan, come here," she called. Reluctantly, I stuffed my phone back into my pocket and rose from my seat. Within a moment, I was there and able to steady her.

"Thank you dear," she patted my arm. "That's not as easy as it used to be. Now, I do need to discuss something very important with you, but I do not believe this is the right place for such a conversation."

We walked out of the church; I pretended to listen as I read Stella's quick response, which made me smile.

"Tell me," Sylvia said, eyeing my phone curiously, "do all young people have those contraptions?"

"Most," I replied. "I just got mine not too long ago."

She nodded. "I see. My granddaughter has one too. You would think it was attached to her hands. She never puts it down."

Taking her hint, I finished sending my response to Stella, closed the little black device, and stuffed it back into my pocket. When I looked up, I saw Uncle Azra in the crowd looking for me. The anger I had gone into the church with was still fresh and hot at the sight of him. I ignored his frantic gestures and turned to Sylvia, still with her hand on my arm.

"Sylvia, is someone coming to pick you up?" I asked, concerned. It didn't look as though the woman should be able to drive and I didn't want to just abandon her.

She smiled up at me. "My ride will be here shortly. But now that I have your attention, I was wondering if you would like to have supper with my family and I this evening? I'm making lasagna and, as I mentioned before, we have much to discuss about your future."

I blinked. "My future? What do you mean?"

Whatever she was going to say was drowned out by Uncle Azra screaming my name in a panic. "Orion!"

Sylvia saw him weaving through the crowd towards

us. "Who is that calling you?"

I didn't want to answer; I wanted to refuse any sort of connection with the mad angel running towards us. Turning to look, I was relieved to see that Beth was not with him. Distantly, I wondered where he had left her as I answered my new friend, "That would be my uncle."

Sylvia watched him come closer. "He certainly is in a hurry," she commented. "Supper is served promptly at six. Here." She slipped me a small folded piece of paper. "This is where I live." I wondered when she had had time to write down directions.

"Orion, I am glad I found you," Azra said loudly as he approached. "I thought you had left earlier than—" he stopped abruptly, realizing that I was arm in arm with an eighty year old woman who smiled at him knowingly. He recoiled physically at the sight. His back arched. He drew back one leg in the air and his shoulders hunched forward as his arms waved in the air. His hands turned to defensive claws pointing at Sylvia. The whole stance made me think of his Kung Fu movies or a cartoon character that had been scared out of its wits. "What in the name of all that is sacred are you doing with *that*?"

"What?" I was shocked. He very rarely reacted that much to anything, let alone an old human woman.

"Orion," Azra said in a voice that sounded as though he meant to soothe a feral animal, "drop the old lady's arm and come to me slowly. Don't make any sudden movements."

"Azra!" I admonished him. "Stop that!" My chastisement wasn't as effective as it could have been since Sylvia was chuckling next to me.

"It is quite alright," she assured me and patted my arm. "He doesn't know how else to react to me." I wondered at her cryptic answer as she slipped out of my grasp and smoothed her skirts imperially. "Be sure you are on time, Ryan." She delicately stepped towards the street. She had gone only a few feet when she turned back and called with much amusement in her voice, "It was nice to meet you as well, Azra."

As she turned away again, Azra glanced at me, half fearful, half angry, "How did it know my name?"

I rolled my eyes at him and started walking away from the mission. "You really are an idiot, aren't you? What is your problem? She was a nice lady."

"A nice lady?" He gasped after me. "You really don't know what that was, do you?" He shook his head. "You're lucky I found you when I did."

"I'm sure," I said acidly as I tugged on the tie at my throat. Brushing past him, I made my way to Main Street.

Uncle Azra rushed to catch up to me. His hand fell upon my shoulder and he said in his most serious voice, "Orion, that thing was hardly a nice lady. It was a witch. A Strega to be exact."

"Don't be ridiculous," I scoffed. "She's just a kooky old lady."

"No, she is a dangerous being and she has a lot of power. Couldn't you feel it around her? She was dripping with it. Witches have plagued humankind for generations. They're tricky, manipulative, and cannot be trusted. The Strega are the worst of them."

"Why are the Strega the worst?"

"Because they're Italian," Azra said vehemently.

I knew better than to question his logic, however flawed it was. "Sylvia was very kind to me. She invited me to dinner with her family tonight."

"It did what?" The alarm that colored his voice caused it to go up an octave.

"I'm having dinner with her and her family tonight," I repeated, opening the door to my apartment building. We ascended the steps with my uncle sputtering protests at me.

"I don't think so, young man. I'm not letting you anywhere near that den of vipers. Who knows what they are in league with. For all you know it could be a trap. Besides, you are still grounded from that stunt you pulled with that security guard."

"Uncle, please," I groaned as I opened my apartment door. "Sylvia isn't going to hurt me. Why on earth would she want to? We're just going to have dinner and talk. Plus, you already made me go to church for the security guard. My time has been served for that offense."

Azra slammed the door behind us and stamped his foot. "You are still grounded for the guard ordeal and especially since you won't listen to reason!"

I had removed my jacket and thrown it on the couch when he made his proclamation. I gazed at him as though I had never seen him before. "Excuse me?"

"You're grounded," he repeated folding his arms over his chest. He jutted his chin out in a decisively stubborn manner.

Full of outrage, I demanded, "Why, because I'm going to have dinner with a woman that you think is a witch?"

"I don't think she's a witch. I know for a fact she is. The energy coming off of her was astounding. It was more than a mere human could produce. Hell, it was more than a lot of other witches I've encountered. I can't believe you didn't pick up on it. Didn't you see the green in her aura?"

"You expect me to believe the little old woman I sat with, during Mass none the less, is really a dangerous . . . what's the word you used? Strega?"

Azra nodded.

"For Heaven's sake, the woman could barely walk on her own! There wasn't any abnormal energy coming off of her. She may be a little crazy, but she is harmless," I told him.

Something nagged at the back of my mind, though. There had been something odd going on when she was at the altar to Mary. The air felt different when she was praying to the Mother, not necessarily powerful, just . . . different.

"I know that look," Azra said walking towards me. "That look means that you aren't telling me something. Come on, out with it."

"It's nothing. Look," I said, "I'm going tonight and that

is it."

"No you are absolutely not! Don't you remember those horrible stories people told about witches? The Grimm brothers made a very lucrative business with those stories." He came forward and placed his arm on my shoulders to maneuver me so that I was sitting on the couch. "Don't you remember the witch hunts?"

I frowned, annoyed. "You told me the ones that died during that time were innocent people, that all of the stories and rumors were just that, stories."

"Well, yes and no," Uncle Azra hedged. "Some of the people killed in the hunts were actual witches. They had all of the powers they were accused of and more. Now, back to the matter at hand, you aren't going tonight."

I was about to protest when my thoughts were interrupted by another text message from Stella. *Want to see a movie tonight?*

Butterflies flapped in my stomach and all thoughts of the crazy old woman flew out of my mind. A movie, with Stella? I looked up at my uncle, his arms crossed over his chest in righteous indignation. "Fine," I agreed. "I won't go to Sylvia's."

Azra uncrossed his arms, confused. "Really? You believe me?"

"No, of course I don't believe you. I'm going to a movie with Stella instead."

"You can't go to a movie with Stella. You're still grounded," he informed me.

I narrowed my eyes at him. "What do you mean I'm still grounded? I told you. I'm not going to Sylvia's. I'm doing what you wanted."

He shook his head, obviously stuck in one of his parental kicks that he got into every so often. "I said you're grounded and you are. You can't just do things and expect not to have consequences. You can wait to see your supposed prophecy girl at school, because until I say you can leave this apartment, you stay put."

"That's so stupid! You sent me to church as

punishment for the guard and you grounded me only after you thought I was going to Sylvia's for dinner. Well, now I'm not, so I should be able to go out."

He didn't give me a chance to argue before he stormed out of the apartment, slamming the door behind him. The key entered the deadbolt and I watched the latch lock from the outside. I rolled my eyes. Did he really think that would keep me inside? I mean, come on.

I texted a response to Stella, *What movie?*

No one answered when I dialed the number below the address Sylvia had given me, so I left a message on the machine, explaining I wouldn't be there. After giving my apologies, I hung up and looked at Stella's response.

She suggested one of the new adventure films that recently came out and I quickly agreed. We were to meet at the theater at seven thirty.

According to my phone, I had a few hours to wait, but I was excited. More time with Stella after a completely bombed first date was definitely a good thing. I would have a second chance to determine if she was the one I was supposed to find. Admittedly, that wasn't the only reason I wanted to hang out with her, but I wasn't quite ready to face that yet.

I settled into the couch and flipped on the TV. After a while, I heard a loud pounding at the door. I peeked through the peephole and what I saw filled me with dismay. Uncle Azra was out there with planks of wood and a hammer.

"What are you doing?" I yelled. I know he heard me by the smile that crept onto his face. He acted as though he hadn't. I watched in alarm as he proceeded to nail the boards in place, making it impossible for me to leave.

He worked from the bottom up, coming finally to the part where the peephole was. He peered inside at me. When I tried to jerk the door open, it was stuck fast. He'd done something more than just nail boards over it. I should have been able to open the door to get at the boards if that had been all he had done.

My phone rang and I answered angrily. "Yes?"

"When I say you're grounded, I mean it."

I sputtered half-formed protests, but they were no use. He hung up and continued his work. Once he was done, he whistled as he left. I don't think I ever had a reason to hate my uncle before. Dislike, disagree with, certainly. But this, I decided, was definitely a good reason for the hate category.

It took fifteen minutes of flinging things against the door to calm down enough to think of an alternate plan of escape. There was a large pile of broken objects, most of them Azra's, in front of the boarded-up door. My uncle was long gone, which was a good thing. I had a feeling if I was confronted with him right then, only one of us would be left standing.

Still seething, but considerably calmer, I took stock of my options. I couldn't go out the door, so I looked to the small window and yanked back the curtains. Sunlight streamed through as confirmation that Uncle Azra hadn't thought that far. There was still some time before I had to meet Stella, but the oppressiveness of the small apartment coupled with the fact I was supposed to be trapped inside started to grate on me.

I couldn't wait anymore. I threw open the window and regarded the small opening. I would have to struggle to fit through, but it was possible. I tossed my skateboard and my backpack out before I hoisted myself onto the sill. It was a long way down. Taking in a deep breath I squirmed through the window, struggling only a little bit. When I was mostly through, I grabbed hold of the scaffolding and stood to get my feet under me. Four stories below, a cluster of oleander bushes sat. Hoping the bushes below would provide a soft enough landing, I jumped.

The foliage came up to meet me with scratches and the sound of snapping branches. On the last bounce, I rolled and hit the ground with a thud.

The bruises I would have promised to be colorful. I

brushed myself off with a wince or two and retrieved my bag and board. Casting a glance around to be sure my uncle wasn't lurking close by, I skated away from my would-be prison with a satisfied smile.

Chapter Thirteen

I spent the time before the movie tearing up downtown with my board. The constant motion and exertion of putting my body through the tricks helped me to relax. By the time I arrived at the theater, Azra's absurd parenting techniques were forgotten; or at least out of my immediate thoughts. As I approached the theater, I scanned the crowd of people for Stella. There was no sign of her yet.

Getting in line to purchase tickets for the adventure movie we agreed on, I kept a look out for her. She still hadn't shown up after I had bought the tickets, so I went to inspect the movie posters on the outside of the building.

I was pondering how incredibly genius it was to have horror flicks come out on Valentine's Day (sick but genius) when someone behind me said, "At least you didn't go for the cheesy romantic comedy. Stella isn't that kind of a girl."

I turned to see who was speaking to me, but there wasn't anyone in the area; just a couple of older women a few yards away discussing their last bridge game. Neither of them could have sounded like the Brooklyn man I heard. It was strikingly similar to the voice I thought I heard on the pier and out in the water when I was training.

"Who is there?" I asked, barely above a whisper. Even if I was being delusional, there wasn't any sense in advertising I was hearing voices. Maybe I really should ask Azra about this hearing stuff. I shook my head at the thought. All he did the last time I mentioned it was crack jokes about Stella. I could just imagine what he would do if I told him what the voice was actually saying.

Of course, no one answered. I looked at the area around me suspiciously. Out of the corner of my eye, I saw a figure stride purposefully towards me.

Stella called out surprised, "You're early."

I promptly forgot about the voice. I met her halfway, stopping about two feet away from her and resisted the urge to scoop her up in a hug. After the disaster of our last date, I didn't want to rush things.

"I got the tickets," I said, hiding my excitement behind a sedate smile as I handed one of them to her.

Stella put her hands on her hips and quirked her mouth to one side. She tsked at me. "You didn't have to get my ticket."

"Well, too bad. I got them, so there." I stuck my tongue out at her playfully. She laughed and my heart lifted at the sound.

"Fine. But I'll get the popcorn!" She rushed past me and into the theater before I knew what was happening. I ran to catch up to her, my skateboard dangling from my hands. She made it past the bored looking teenager tearing the tickets and was already in line by the time I got through the glass door.

"Third theater on your left," the ticket taker advised me as I sped towards the snack counter.

When I only had one person ahead of me in the snack line, Stella tugged at my sleeve. Two drinks and large popcorn were balanced precariously in her arms.

"Hey," she teased. "Would you help a girl out here?"

"You win," I conceded my defeat and grabbed the popcorn and a drink from her.

"Of course I do."

"You let her win," the voice from before chided. "Or are you really that slow?" It was right next to my ear and I nearly dropped the popcorn.

"You okay?" Stella asked, looking at me strangely.

Whipping my head around quickly and not seeing anyone, I straightened and cleared my throat. "Yeah, I'm fine. It's just I thought I saw a bee."

She looked doubtful, but didn't comment on my lie. Together we walked to our designated theater and then Stella led the way confidently to the middle of the seats. There was a couple snuggling in the top row and a few other people seated near the front. The giant screen flashed advertisements while the surround sound speakers belted out generic instrumental music.

We sat in the reclining red plush seats, arranged the popcorn between us and proceeded to wait for the feature film.

"What made you want to see a movie?" I asked, tossing a piece of popcorn into my mouth.

Stella shrugged. "I don't know. I thought it would be fun. Maybe give you a chance to redeem yourself for Friday night."

I groaned. "I'm sorry. That was a really bad night."

"Not all of it," she corrected me. "Skateboarding down the hill was a lot of fun."

"Good," I told her. I moved the popcorn away from the armrest between us and grabbed her hand boldly. "Thanks for getting me out of my apartment."

She squeezed my hand in response. "By the looks of the scratches on your arms, it seems you've been out and into some trouble."

"What?" I asked, looking down at my arms. A few scratches from my fall were ringed by already fading bruises. "Oh, those. Yeah. That was an accident."

Her eyebrow arched. "Really? Is it what were you sent to church for?"

I coughed. "Not quite."

"Going to church as a punishment is diabolical," Stella went on. She sounded torn between disgusted and impressed. "What did you do to be sent to Mass?"

I was very cognizant of her hand in mine. It was warm and soft. The soft prickling was still there, but it was suffused with warmth and belonging. It felt right. I tightened my grip and answered, "I got into a fight with someone. Uncle Az didn't approve and he pulled the parental shtick on me. He said I needed to learn that what I did wasn't very moral. The church, I guess, is a sort of parallel to the lesson he wanted me to learn. He wants me to be more aware of how influencing people isn't the best way to get my point across."

"Influencing people?" she questioned. Before I could explain, she said, impressed, "Wow. You must have really kicked the other guy's ass."

"I did land in jail for a bit." I tried not to brag.

Her eyes widened and her right eyebrow arched in surprise. "No wonder he thought you needed to learn morality."

I laughed. "You should know that I don't visit jail that often. This was my first time." I shrugged it off like it was no big deal.

"Well that's a relief. What was the fight about?"

I struggled with exactly how much to tell her. I decided it would probably be best to mostly stick to the truth. "It was all a big misunderstanding," I told her. "I was in my uncle's storage shed and a security guard thought I was a burglar. Things got out of hand and the cops were called."

Stella sighed. "And to think I just did some chores and wrote a couple of pages in my journal."

"Really?" I asked, intrigued. "What did you write about this time?"

"Nothing as exciting as your weekend," she shrugged, still holding onto me with her fingers. "Mostly about my impressions of Ventura so far."

"Anything about me?"

She laughed. "Maybe. Like I said, mostly it's what I think of this place."

I tried to be surreptitious about the intention of my next question. "And what exactly do you think of it, if you don't mind me asking."

Her grip tightened on my hand and she told me wily, "You'll have to read it to find out."

"Will I get to read it?"

The lights dimmed and the music was replaced by the booming dialogue of some trailer. A small secretive smile formed on her lips as she answered, "Maybe. Now, shhh. The movie is starting." We lapsed into a comfortable silence, our hands sweating from the heat of our bodies, but both of us refusing to let go.

I can honestly say I don't remember much about the movie. I spent most of the time wondering what the hell I was doing; sitting there and completely enraptured with this human without quite understanding why. Usually, humans were just something I had to deal with and, lately, they were mostly a borderline annoyance.

So why was I to the point of giddiness over holding Stella's hand?

I peeked over at her, the screen lighting her features. She was very attractive. I don't think anyone could dispute that, but what was different about her from the rest of the girls I'd been around? The attraction I felt had to be so much more than a reaction to the physical aspect of her. Sure, it was icing on the cake, but there was something else. It was a puzzle—a mystery, this fascination I had with her. I wanted nothing more to figure out why.

But did that fascination mean she was the one that was supposed to help me? Or was Uncle Azra right in thinking it was just a temporary infatuation? There had been a few humans before her that I thought had been the ones, but the difference here was that I hadn't been this drawn to any of them.

I looked at Stella closely, trying to understand the fascination I felt. It was foreign territory for me and, honestly, the part of me who held the stories of the Nephilim closely in mind was appalled. I knew what happened when a Grigori fell in love with a human, but the question that nagged at my mind was did that really apply to me? Like so many other little things that separated me from the other Grigori, this could easily be something that didn't affect me.

It made me doubt, and it made the possibility of something happening between Stella and me more realistic. I watched her more than the movie. She was completely outside of everything I knew.

As I tried to piece out the puzzle, something clicked inside my head. It didn't matter why I was attracted to Stella, it just mattered that I was. That should have been all I needed. I just didn't get this way over humans, so there had to be a reason for it. Things were going to turn out the way they should. I just had to have a little faith and follow my instincts and my instincts told me she was the one. All I had to do was figure out how to talk to her about it in order to become one hundred percent sure.

She leaned into me and whispered, "You aren't watching the movie."

I made an effort after that to pay attention, but I still snuck glances at her from the corner of my eyes. Every so often, I caught her looking back at me. We would both look away immediately, but her grip on my hand would squeeze mine for a moment in acknowledgement.

The movie ended all too soon. We stayed in our seats as the other people around us stretched and made for the exits.

Stella released her hand from mine. "Well? What did you think?"

I shrugged; too embarrassed to admit that I hadn't the faintest idea what we just saw. We watched the credits roll for a moment, taking in the music.

Suddenly, Stella burst out laughing. It wasn't just a polite chuckle or a quiet giggle. It was the kind of laugh that you did when something funny caught you by surprise. I looked at her questioningly. Her head was thrown back against the seat and her hands clasped over her stomach.

"What?" I asked, eager to be in on the joke.

"The best boy grip," she gasped wiping her eyes. "His name is Rocco Anderolle."

"Are you serious?" I snorted, looking back up at the screen for confirmation.

"You missed it," she said calming down a bit. "I never get over what some people name their children." I turned back to the screen speculatively, eyeing the names that went by.

"There's one," I cried out. "Harry Chin, the Electric Supervisor."

"What is your middle name?"

I blinked, not quite ready for the question. "I don't have one."

"What? How can you not have a middle name?"

I shrugged, not sure what to say. "Well, what's your middle name?"

She let out a derisive and un-ladylike snort. "I hate my middle name. It's antiquated and doesn't go with the rest of it."

"Come on. It can't be that bad," I reasoned.

"Oh, it is," she assured me.

"Yes it is. I don't know what her parents were thinking," the Brooklyn accented voice commented.

I was hearing things. I had to be. Doing my best to ignore my mounting insanity (because, honestly, what else could I do?), I told her, "Tell me what your middle name is." I glanced over at her to find that she was grimacing. She couldn't have heard the voice too, could she? I didn't want to ask. "Come on," I prodded. "It can't be any more ridiculous than my name."

"Ryan isn't embarrassing," she countered. "It's very common."

"You're right," I agreed. "That's why I go by it. But it's not my real name."

"What is your real name, then?"

I took in a breath. It seemed fair if I were going to pressure her for hers. "Orion."

"Orion?" she repeated. The sound of my name on her lips sent a chill through me. "Like the constellation?"

Making a face, I nodded. "Yeah. Ryan is easier. So

yours can't be that bad."

"I wouldn't count on that," she muttered.

"Tell me what your middle name is. I told you mine. Fair is fair."

The sigh she let out was heavy, but she told me, in a begrudging manner, "Seraphina."

The sound of the name of the highest Angelic Choir made me stop breathing for a moment. That couldn't be what she said. Choking, I asked, "I beg your pardon? It sounded like you said Seraphim . . .?"

The Seraphim were the choir of angels closest to the Divine. Their power outranked the Archangels hundredfold, except for the major seven. I had never encountered one since they mostly stayed in Heaven.

"Close," Stella said, causing my anxiousness to rise a notch. "It's the Latin version. Seraphina. It means the 'burning ones'. They're a type of angel." She made an exasperated face. "Nona wanted me to have a very celestial name."

"Stella Seraphina Evangeline," I said, rolling the syllables around my tongue. "It has a certain flow to it."

Finally, the credits ended and the music went dead. "What do you want to do now?" I asked.

"I'm not sure," Stella said. There was a muffled buzzing sound. Stella sighed and pulled out her cell phone. She pushed a few buttons, unlocking the keys and groaned. "Oh no. Nona called me four times. I better call her back."

We left the theater, squinting in the light of the lobby. Without pausing, Stella dialed a number on her phone and walked out of the theater. I trailed behind her with my skateboard in hand. Within moments, she was speaking rapidly in Italian.

"Now what, Romeo?" the Brooklyn voice asked me. "Gonna try to take her back to your apartment again?"

"Listen, whatever you are shut up and go away," I hissed. Stopping myself I shook my head. I couldn't believe I was talking to myself. Had I finally gone insane?

Uncle Az said that sometimes other Grigori do go insane. Was hearing voices the first step?

"Not a chance, mister. I've got my eye on you."

"Will you shut up?"

Stella gave me an odd look and I flushed in embarrassment. Great, she saw me talking to myself. At last she heaved a sigh and said in defeated sounding English, "Fine, Nona. I'm coming home then." She clicked off the phone without saying goodbye.

"Gotta go, huh?"

She looked as saddened as I felt. "I'm sorry Ryan. My cousins just came into town tonight and I'm supposed to be at dinner."

"Don't be sorry. I had a really fun time with you."

"I did too," she ran her fingers through her hair.

"Want me to walk you to your car?"

This time her smile was more heartfelt. "Do you really have to ask?" We walked down the way and towards the pier. "It's the only place I remembered where I could park," she explained when I looked at her in askance.

The moon was making its ascent against the quickly darkening backdrop of the night. "I wish we had time to walk on the beach. It's so relaxing at night."

"It is," I agreed. "But it's even better when the moon is full and you can see the reflection on the waves."

She brightened. "We will have to do that. The full is only ten days away. You up for it?" She peered at me curiously, expectation written all over her features.

"We could do that," I allowed.

Spike was parked in the same lot from Friday. It was only a few blocks away from the theater. The asphalt was coated in sand from the nearby beach and we could hear the roar of the water crashing against the shore. Stella approached her car with a slow gait, undoubtedly trying to put off the inevitable. We reached Spike and she unlocked the door, squeaking it open unhurriedly.

She brought her hands up with the shrug as if to say,

'that's it folks'. "See you in school tomorrow?"

"I'm counting on it," I told her sincerely.

She got into the driver's side and exclaimed, "Where are my manners? Ryan, did you want me to give you a ride home?"

I was touched by her thoughtfulness and was about to accept when I remembered I had to jump out a window to go out with her. "That's alright," I declined. "You have to get back to your house sooner than I do. I'll just see you tomorrow."

Her right eyebrow rose doubtfully. "Are you sure?"

"Yeah," I tried to sound sure. "I want to do some skating anyways." The excuse was lame even to me.

"Alright," she said. "I guess I'll see you tomorrow then." She closed Spike's door with a resonating slam.

"I'll be there," I promised softly as she pulled out of the parking space and drove off. I waved at her as she disappeared around a corner.

"I'm in the mood to skate?" I repeated loudly in disgust. "What kind of a chump am I?" Berating myself, I walked towards my apartment building holding the board from its trucks. I wasn't in any hurry in case my uncle was waiting for me and there was too much for me to think about. I trod through the streets, not really paying attention to what route I was taking. Before long, I found myself at a dead end of an alley. The windows of the adjacent buildings were dark and I stumbled on the abrupt incline.

"Great," I muttered, and turned back.

Out of nowhere, a peculiar shiver came over me and the hair on the back of my neck stood on end. Someone was watching me. I glanced up at the rooftops, expecting to see someone staring down at me. There was no one.

Warily, I heightened my senses, listening for even the slightest sounds. There were soft footsteps inching slowly and steadily towards me. Whoever was following me was coming up from behind. I swiveled around trying to catch a glimpse of it, but whatever it was kept just out of sight.

It only appeared out of the corner of my eyes.

I gripped my skate board with both hands, preparing myself to swing with all of my might. I just had to wait until they were a little bit closer.

"Ryan? Are you alright?"

I had to stop myself mid-swing before I hit Ascher. I was so surprised to see him that I ended up dropping my board. "What are you doing here?"

Ascher put his hands in his coat pocket. "Azra sent me to find you. He's not happy that you snuck out."

As I picked up my board, I made a face. "I'm not that thrilled at being boarded up in my apartment either."

"At any rate," Ascher said, stifling his laugh, "I'm here to collect you for another lesson. Don't worry; your uncle is sitting this one out. Are you ready?"

I shrugged, "Sure."

Together we walked out of the alleyway. "Where is your car?" he asked.

"What car? Azra won't let me near the things."

Ascher frowned. "You mean he won't let you drive? That's odd. He should have let you have a car decades ago, especially if you can't teleport places."

"I know! He's being too overprotective. I'm not a kid anymore. I can handle myself just fine."

"Yes, that was obvious with the little trick you pulled on the human security guard last night." His tone was sarcastic.

Instantly, my face flushed in embarrassment.

Ascher laughed. "It wasn't too bad for a first attempt. You need to practice a little more to get it down, but overall, not bad. As for your uncle, well, he treats you like a child because he still sees you as a child. It is hard for him to let go of the responsibility of raising you. For so long that has been his purpose. Now that you are grown, what else does he have?"

"It doesn't change the fact that I can take care of myself." Even that sounded petulant to my own ears. Ascher was right, but I hated to admit it. It felt better to hang onto the anger.

"No, you are right; it doesn't mean you can't take care of yourself," Ascher agreed. "Still, if you are trying to get into humans' heads, then I think I should teach you the proper way."

"Won't Azra get upset if you teach me how to do that?" I asked. "He wasn't too thrilled I had tried to do it in the first place."

Ascher gazed at me steadily. "Well, you are old enough. What do you think?"

I hesitated. "I don't know."

The older Grigori threw his arm around my shoulders. "It's time you started thinking for yourself, Ryan. You're old enough to have your own mind."

We had wandered into a parking lot. "You know, Ryan, I want to give you something," Ascher said.

"What? Why?"

"Call it a coming of age present, so to speak. You are old enough now to understand our role on this earth and to understand that there are certain benefits attached to that role." He released his grip on me and gestured to the cars that surrounded us. "Pick one."

"I'm sorry, what?"

"Pick one and it's yours."

I couldn't quite believe what I was hearing. "I don't understand. These cars belong to someone else."

Ascher scoffed, "Just a human. No one of consequence." He waited for me to react, to respond. I couldn't help but feel like I was being tested.

"I can't take someone's car," I said. "It's not right."

The disapproval on his face made me feel like I had failed. "Don't you understand we operate beyond human laws? We have to in order to survive."

The statement was contradictory to everything Uncle Azra had taught me. Sure, we did what we had to in order to stay under the radar, but we didn't blatantly throw the rules out of the window. "I don't understand," I answered, confused. "Stealing a car is wrong."

Ascher draped his arm around my shoulders again. "It's like this: we are Grigori, not humans, right?"

"Right." I focused on the ground as I listened to his explanation.

"Why would we, the higher species, stoop to follow rules that they put in place? It would be like wolves obeying the rules of a herd of deer."

"We don't eat humans," I pointed out. "We aren't in competition with them. We're here to blend in and keep the balance." The words came out and I thought I heard the echo of Uncle Azra in my head. It was the objective of the Grigori race, or so I had been taught.

"Balance," Ascher scoffed. "The Grigori are being hunted by both sides of the angelic factions. Do you think maintaining the balance is a top priority anymore? No. It's about survival by any means possible. If we are trying to survive, why would we allow ourselves to be constrained by the humans?"

I didn't have an easy answer to that. Ascher stepped away to peruse the vehicles. "Do you have a preference or are we just shooting in the dark?"

I watched the elder Grigori for a moment, trying to understand how he could hold such a view. As much as I hated to admit it, some of what he said made sense. Why should we follow the human rules to the letter to fit in? Not even mortals followed their own rules all the time.

But I wasn't a Grigori and I wasn't a human. I was something completely other.

"I'm not going to steal a car, Ascher." I stated firmly.

He gave a short, "Ha!" as he came back towards me. "You don't understand right now. But you will, in time. Come on then. It's time for your next lesson."

Chapter Fourteen

We arrived at an old abandoned shack set deep in dark hills. I wasn't even sure we were still in California. Trees were thick all around us, though I couldn't tell what kind. Snow blanketed everything around us, giving even the most ordinary rock a beautiful sheen that only ice could provide. Even with my body's ability to mute cold and heat, I could tell it was well below freezing. I began to shiver in my hoodie.

"What are we doing here?" I asked as I peered into the darkness. The nearest city was so far away that its lights couldn't even be seen on the horizon. The stars ruled the darkness. Nocturnal animals could be heard crunching in the snow not too far away. A screech of an owl pierced the night air as it claimed its prey.

"Orion, we need to know how you will fare if it comes down to fighting and defending yourself."

"What do you mean?" Something in the pit of my stomach squirmed.

"You're going to fight a Fallen One. On your own."

My eyes widened. "Excuse me?"

Ascher repeated calmly, "You will be fighting a Fallen One. The only way to test your abilities in combat is to put you in a combat situation."

"This fight is what my training is building up to, right? I mean, it's like a final? I've only had the one lesson so far. I don't think I am ready."

Ash indulged me with a slight upwards curving of his mouth. It couldn't be called a smile because it lacked any of the warmth that a smile gave. "No. You'll be facing the Fallen One tonight. I've already caught one for you."

"You've what?" I couldn't believe my ears. Ascher had

mind in the split second before he slammed into me; I dodged to the left. His body grazed mine as he sailed past. I crouched down to prevent from toppling over. The Fallen One landed in a heap but was back up in a matter of moments.

Quicker than thought, it struck out at me one, two, three, times. It was like its fists were attached to pistons aimed directly at my midsection, each with more force than the last. Its blows were like bricks, slowing me with pain. It kept punching until I moaned for mercy. Then it wrapped its hands around my neck and squeezed. The constriction was enough to make me panic and clutch uselessly at his arms.

I couldn't think. I just lashed out haphazardly and with every ounce of strength I had left. My struggling and kicking was enough to make him let me go and take a step back.

Launching myself at my enemy, I grabbed the collar of the red t-shirt while I brought my knee into his stomach. The Fallen One was too agile and he twisted out of my grip. I was pushed to the ground.

More punches landed on the back of my head adding to the already monstrous headache that was developing and the blurriness to the edges of my vision.

I was so tired. There was no sensation. Only pain. I couldn't do this on my own.

I squinted out to where Ascher stood watching. I saw the sick smile on his lips and the gleam of excitement in his eyes. He looked straight at the Fallen One who stopped pounding on me.

Ascher mouthed the words, "Finish him."

I braced myself for the final flurry of blows. Instead, the Fallen One grabbed a fist of my hair and forced my head up.

I remembered thinking about Azra. He had been wrong all along; I wasn't the one destined to end the Angelic War after all.

No. I couldn't let him down. I refused to die like this.

Fury rose within me, heating my blood and giving me new purpose. I took in a shaking breath. I would not be beaten. Everything was washed in red by the time I exhaled.

The Fallen one stepped in front of me, his hand still yanking my hair back. He looked into my eyes. What I saw gave me cause to smile viciously. Fear had found its way onto his face.

Then it all went black.

***

I awoke to a high-pitched whirring sound. It was so aggravating that I pulled a pillow over my face to muffle the sounds.

Wait. Pillow?

I opened my eyes to see the walls of Azra's bedroom. Daylight streamed through the sheer curtains of the windows.

What happened?

I was still in the clothes I'd worn to fight the Fallen One. They were smeared with dirt, leaves, and something that was an unsettlingly red . . . was that blood? I touched a rust colored spot hesitantly and found it to be dry and stiff. The mud had also dried and crumbled off of me at the slightest touch.

Climbing out of the bed, I wasn't surprised to find my muscles stiff and sore. I inched my way to the bathroom and flipped on the light. The person squinting back in the mirror looked as though he had been to hell and back. I was covered in mud and grass and what could only be described as dried gore. The sight was sickening. I turned on the shower and stripped off the grime encrusted clothes, shoved them into the garbage can next to the toilet. I didn't want to look at them, let alone try to wash them.

I stepped into the shower and let the hot water sluice over me. The heat did little to ease the tension of my muscles, but it was enough to get them moving more freely. As I rinsed, I probed my memories of the night before. Had it just been last night or had I been out for longer? Flashes of images teased and nauseated me at the same time.

Red dripped at the edges of my recollection. All of the flashes from the fight were drenched in the color; from the red of the Fallen One's hair to the red that had poured out of his corporeal body when I killed him. Wait. Had I killed him?

The images were shaky and inconsistent, like I was only seeing quick flashes of different movies that didn't quite go together. It all had to be part of a nightmare. None of the images made any sense and, apart from making my stomach turn, I couldn't get any sort of answers out of them.

I washed the dirt and the filth off of my body, using more soap than necessary. Afterwards I still felt disgusting, but at least looked halfway normal. Well, with the exception of a lot of fading bruises. There were a few scars that were growing faint. I wondered briefly what had caused those.

Once dressed, I took a chance and creaked open the bedroom door. The whirring sounds had stopped, but had been replaced by the sounds of Uncle Azra and Ascher arguing.

"If he doesn't wake up, it will be your head," Azra cursed. "I still can't believe that you set him up to fight a Fallen One on his own! And you didn't think that I would want to know first? I should have been there! Or at least I should have known about it!" Cabinets were slammed, punctuating his anger. "He could have been killed, Ash."

Ascher hissed. "But he wasn't killed. Not even close. What he did . . . Az, I've never seen anything like it. If you had been there, if you had known what was happening, then I don't think we would have gotten the results that we did. You would have held him back from his full potential yet again."

"His father asked me to take care of him. Me. I am responsible for the kid!"

"Then actually be responsible and let him figure out what he can do! He's got an unlimited potential! You can't coddle him for the rest of time. At some point he has to grow up."

"Grow up doesn't mean put him in life and death situations just for the hell of it, Ash!"

"Think, you idiot! His whole existence is a life and death situation. But because I put him to the test without interfering, we now know what he is capable of. We know he can do so much more than we imagined."

"Yes, now we know, but at what price?" Azra questioned. It sounded as though he didn't believe that I was going to wake up again.

I'd heard enough. I stepped out into the main room of the apartment to see Azra puttering around in the kitchen. With all of the curtains thrown open, the whole apartment was bright. I could see clear blue sky on the other side of the glass.

"Hey," I said and gave a little wave.

When he saw me, Azra dropped what he was doing and scooped me up into a giant bear hug. "You're alive!"

"Shhh," I told him, wincing at the echo my voice created. I pulled away from his hug and put my hand to my head. The pain was booming so much that everything was a little blurry. I shuffled over to sit on the couch. Ascher was in the recliner with a newspaper held in front of his face. As I flopped down on the soft suede cushions, the paper lowered and Ascher's dark eyes observed me.

"What?" I asked him roughly. I wasn't sure why, but the way he was staring at me irritated my already thin nerves. No. He wasn't just staring; he was evaluating me.

"Nothing," he replied nonchalantly and went back to his newspaper.

"Here." Uncle Azra came around the couch and pressed a drink into my hand. It was a thick sludge-like substance that was a revolting shade of greenish gray.

"Drink up, kid. You're gonna need your strength."

"What is this?" I asked.

"It's a protein shake. I picked it up at the health food store. It's supposed to replenish vitamins and nutrients."

I sniffed the concoction cautiously and wrinkled my nose in distaste. "It smells gross." I set the glass on the coffee table and shut my eyes. Would the room stop tilting already?

"Of course it smells gross—it's healthy. Drink it." My uncle sat on the couch next to me and I had no choice but to take a sip. It tasted as horrible as it smelled.

What do you remember from the other night?" Ascher's silky voice inquired above the rustle of papers.

I frowned. "The other night?"

"The night you fought the Fallen One," Ascher prompted.

"Wasn't that last night? How long have I been out?"

"Day and a half." The confirmation was given in unison by both Uncle Azra and Ascher. Their voices held a tenor that denoted both fear and amazement.

"Seriously?" I tried to move off the couch to get my phone. Stella must have texted me at some point. My body wasn't ready to move that quickly and I wound up back on the couch, suddenly nauseas and dizzy. Weakly, I asked, "Where is my phone? Did anyone call?"

"I have it over here," Azra called from the kitchen. "Stella called yesterday."

"What did you say?" I asked. I really felt sick, but now it was for a completely different reason. There was no telling what Azra had done.

He scoffed at my worried tone. "I just told her you were really sick and that you would call her when you were feeling better."

I couldn't quite believe that was all, but I let the matter drop right then. I'd have to call her and set things straight. Well, I would as soon as I could sit up without wanting to hurl.

"What do you remember?" Ascher repeated the

question. He was still as stone with a carefully blank mask covering his reactions. There no sign to give away the fact that he and Azra were fighting only moments before. My uncle tried to imitate Ascher but there was a slight crack in his rigid countenance, a small twitch in his eye. That, more than anything, told me their fight wasn't over by far.

I answered the question slowly, doing my best not to be sick at the images my mind provided. "Not a lot. I thought I was going to die."

The two Grigori exchanged a meaningful look. What it meant, I couldn't even begin to fathom. After a long, pregnant silence, Ascher spoke first. "Orion, you killed the Fallen One."

Whatever answer I thought was coming it certainly wasn't that. "I what?"

There was a glint of amusement in Ascher's eye. "You killed him. Ripped him to pieces with your bare hands. I've never seen anything so brutal before."

"Ash!" My uncle's eyes blazed in warning.

"He's got a right to know what he did," Ascher snapped back. I stared at Ascher, stunned. I couldn't tell if Uncle Az was going to punch him or not. The tension was radiating off of them.

"How dare you?" Uncle Azra began with his voice pitched low and menacing. "What the hell do you know about any of this?"

Ascher didn't flinch away from my uncle as he calmly replied, "Apparently, I know a lot more than you about what a growing angel needs. How many thousands of years has it been since he was born? You need to let him grow up a bit and make his own decisions in life."

"His own decisions?" My uncle repeated. His hands gestured wildly in the air, punctuating his points. "You think he's old enough to make his own decisions? Ash, he's just a kid!"

Ascher glanced at me pointedly. "He's not as much of a child as you think he is."

"Fine," Azra all but spat. "Walk in here, Ash, and tell

me everything I've done wrong in raising him. I doubt you could have done any better. I didn't ask for this, you know. It was all I could do to keep him safe."

Ascher nodded in agreement. "Now it's time for him to keep himself safe." He turned his gaze on me. "Now, tell me, what do you remember?"

"For the love of everything sacred, this is the first time he's killed a Fallen One! Would you just give the kid a chance to breathe!"

I've never seen Azra so angry at Ascher before. It only served to hit the enormity of the situation home.

Ascher fell silent and the image of him watching from beyond the ward that night flashed before my eyes. What exactly did I do to get out alive? Especially since Ascher had been counting on the opposite.

I killed a Fallen One? With my bare hands? It almost didn't seem real. It couldn't be right, could it? The haze of red images coupled with the phantom screams in my mind lent truth to what they said.

"I passed the test then?" I asked, still in shock.

Ascher snorted behind his paper and Uncle Azra give an appreciative, but hesitant chuckle. "Yes. You passed, kiddo," Uncle Azra confirmed.

I felt a mix of relief and apprehension. Relief because I was alive and apprehension because if that were true, then the orders Ascher had given the Fallen One was also true. He had orchestrated the entire thing in the hopes that I would end up dead. I didn't trust him anymore. I doubted I ever could again.

Ascher folded his paper and tossed it onto the coffee table. "Well, this has been fun. I have some business to attend to, so I will be back a little while later. Ryan, think you are up for another sparring match this afternoon?"

I hesitated. Luckily, Azra jumped in and answered for me, "He's still kinda out of it, Ash. Let's give him a day to rest, okay?"

Ascher shrugged as though it didn't matter. "Sure. I'll see you later."

My uncle nodded to Ascher as the Grigori walked out of the apartment. When he looked at me, the hard expression melted. "I'm so glad you are alright, kiddo."

"Me too. I didn't know Ascher hadn't told you about the fight. I just assumed that you weren't there because you were mad at me for sneaking out. I'm sorry."

He came to sit next to me on the couch. "Well, I was angry, but that wouldn't have stopped me from being there for you. If I had known he was going to train you like that, I'd have stopped it right then and there. I know we see Fallen Ones almost every day and it shouldn't be that big of a deal, but what if something happened to you? What if that sleazy Fallen One had managed to hurt you, or worse, kill you?"

I bowed my head. "I know, but it didn't. I survived."

A heavy sigh emitted from him. "You're right. You did survive." Abruptly, he stood, brushing away the emotions as best as he could. "Listen, I'm going to the store. You need anything while I'm out?"

"I'm alright," I said as I stretched out on the couch. "I'm still really sore, so I'm just going to stay here."

"Well, while you are doing that, you can read through all of this." Azra tossed something onto the coffee table. It was a file folder, papers spilled out of it and onto the floor around me. "It took me awhile to gather it all together. It's all the information I have on the prophecy."

My mouth hung open as I looked at the folder and spilled paper. "Seriously?"

"All of this is what you were looking for in the storage shed, right?"

Mutely I nodded.

"Well, there you go. Next time just ask and save us all a world of trouble." He took the leash that was hanging on the edge of a chair and said, "I'll be back." He left me with the mess of papers and locked the door behind him.

Stunned, I sat up and gathered the papers back into the file folder. Most of the information was scrawled haphazardly on heavily stained notebook paper. There didn't seem to be any sort of order to any of it. Still, the scraps of torn paper gave me hope. There had to be something in there that would help me figure out how to not only talk to Stella about all of this, but also how to fulfill it.

Chapter Fifteen

Azra and Beth returned to the apartment about an hour later. I was set up at the kitchen table, my legs propped up on one of the other chairs and the papers he had left spread around me. My hands covered my face. Behind my fingers, flashes of the night with the Fallen One danced in my head. I couldn't get the sheer mount of blood out of my vision. It was as though there was a red haze around me, coating everything I saw. I felt sick.

"Kiddo?" Uncle Azra asked as he placed a hesitant hand on my shoulder.

I groaned in response and dropped my hands to my side. Giving my head a little shake, I blinked away the memory. "Yeah, I'm fine. Just a little out of it right now."

"You've been pouring over all that stuff since I left, haven't you?" Azra asked.

"Yeah, but it isn't getting me any closer to the answers." I settled back into the chair and watched as he unloaded the groceries.

"Well, since you aren't getting anywhere with that, why don't we hit the beach and catch some waves?"

I gazed at the papers in front of me. "I don't know."

"Oh come on, kiddo. You can take a break for a couple hours. After everything that has happened in the last couple of days, I think we both need to relax and have some fun. Besides, Beth is making great progress. I want to show you how she can surf."

A wry smile graced my lips. "You really taught her how to surf?"

"If you don't believe me, then come and see for yourself!" He laughed and it reminded me of how much fun we used to have. I found that I missed those times.

"Alright then," I said and pushed the papers away. "Why not. Let's go surfing. I think the water is just what I need to make these aches go away."

Azra slapped the counter. "Fantastic! Go and get changed. I've got some boards at the beach ready and waiting for us to take them to the waves."

I did what he told me to do, but slower than usual because of how sore I was. Stretching the muscles did feel good though.

After a few moments, a knock sounded at the door. "Ready, kiddo?" Azra asked.

"Yeah." Despite the aches and pains, I was looking forward to this time. Maybe this afternoon of surfing would be exactly what I needed to keep the haunting images of the other night at bay.

Together, Azra and I teleported down to Leo Carrillo Beach.

As soon as we landed, I knew something was wrong. For starters, we weren't at the beach. Instead, we were in some sort of abandoned industrial complex. The slightest movement echoed against the rows of large metal storage containers all around us. No, not us; it was just me. Azra and Beth were nowhere in sight.

Something wasn't right with the air. It shimmered and was entirely too bright. A sick feeling roiled in my stomach. A lightheaded, dizzy sensation gripped me. Slowly, it dawned on me what was happening.

This was what happened when I was in the immediate presence of the Heavenly Host.

It had been centuries since I last experienced this sensation, but the feeling wasn't something you could easily forget.

"Well, well," a booming voice echoed behind me.

I whirled around to face where the voice resonated from. A blinding golden light, brighter than the sun flared. There, masked by the play of shadows and light, was the unmistakable stature of a Heavenly Host still in his astral body. Large white wings fanned out behind him. They were covered in what looked like feathers, but were actually more similar to scaled armor. The Heavenly Host sailed towards me and, as he came closer, he summoned his corporeal body. The magnificent wings faded away, his aura dimmed and his glide became the rhythmic tapping of feet encased in hard soled shoes hitting the pavement.

Adrenaline coursed through me. This shouldn't be happening. He shouldn't have been able to find me because of my disguise. I glanced at my wrist and panicked even more. My bracelet was gone! Where had I lost it? Frantically, I tried to figure out where it had gone. The last place I remembered seeing it was just before I fought the Fallen One. Damn it!

I was completely defenseless, but the angel didn't know that. Maybe if I put up a good front I would luck out. Bracing myself for an attack, I called out, "What do you want?" Much to my shame, my voice cracked on the last syllable.

Where the hell was Uncle Azra? Had he been hurt when we landed?

The angel wasn't intimidated in the least by my amateur stance. He halted a few feet away from me and said in a completely monotone voice, "I am Sariel. I am to exterminate any Grigori I find."

"By exterminate, you mean let go and never look for again, right?" I asked hopefully. It was difficult to keep my fear under control. Right then it was strong enough to make me tremble.

Sariel frowned even as he clarified, "Exterminate as in annihilate." He drew out a faintly glowing sickle-shaped blade.

The portion of my brain that wasn't gibbering with terror at the sight of the celestial blade thought, *great. I had to get one without a personality.* I fought the urge to run in panic. There was no way I'd be able to outrun him so I had to take care of this on my own. To do that, I needed to focus. With great effort, I cleared my mind and breathed in deeply while I edged backwards, out of the corridor of containers and into a sort of clearing with a couple of resting forklifts. I needed more open space.

With every step I took, the angel advanced two. As the distance closed between us, I tried to remember what Ascher had taught me. My mind had gone completely blank.

Without any other course of action, I succumbed to my panic-stricken urge to run. I intended to duck around Sariel to run to what I hoped was an exit. Instead Sariel caught my shirt and flung me backwards. Hitting the metal wall of a container, I fell in a heap onto the cold asphalt. The blow knocked the wind out of me. My back throbbed and all the aches I had before were amplified a hundred fold.

I attempted to stand, but Sariel grabbed me up by my shirt until I was suspended a good two feet off the ground. He brought the celestial blade up to my throat. I cringed at the electric power surging off of the weapon. At the same time, something rose within me. It felt similar to what happened the night I had fought the Fallen One.

The sensation was pure rage. The tension inside of me threatened to break free and unleash a maelstrom of power. It came faster today, more readily than before. Truth be told, it terrified me how quickly the power came this time.

He paused and I thought that he must have felt the building power. But the seconds he wasted served to bring enough confusion to save my life.

"You," the angel growled, bewilderment lacing his monotone words. "You are not one of the Grigori." His eyes widened as the realization what I was dawned on him. "You! You are supposed to be a myth!" The horror-filled accusation hung in the air between us.

I struggled to loosen his grip. Finally recalling Ascher's lessons, I forced myself to kick. My legs worked furiously, attempting to knee him somewhere that would hurt enough to let me go. But with the way he held me, it was nearly impossible to land a blow.

The surprise in his face had turned into indecision.

"I cannot destroy you. I will have to take you with me," Sariel stated. "Gabriel and Michael will know how to dispose of you."

True fright set in then, shoving my earlier panic into a corner. While this Sariel was unfamiliar, I had definitely heard of Michael and Gabriel. They were two of the main Archangels. Michael was feared in every choir and Gabriel was one of the main proponents of the Grigori extermination. The two of them alone were responsible for more Grigori deaths than all the others put together.

The angel held me tighter as a maniacal light shone in his pale eyes. "I did not know the time for you was almost at hand. Yes, you will come with me to see Gabriel and he will . . ."

"I don't think so, Featherhead."

Never in all of my life had I been so relieved to hear Uncle Azra's voice. Sariel removed the blade from my throat to confront the newcomer. I twisted as much as I could in the angel's strong grasp to see Uncle Azra standing next to a forklift. On her leash next to him, Beth pawed at the ground.

"Better put him down, Choir Boy, before someone gets hurt," Azra warned.

Beth bleated in agreement.

Sariel frowned at Uncle Azra's name calling. "Grigori," he stated, recognizing my uncle for what he was. Keeping his eyes on Azra, the angel released me. Again, I tumbled to the pavement below. This time I was ready and I landed on my feet. While Sariel's attention was elsewhere, I edged along the wall of the alley to get closer to my uncle.

"You know, this is stupid," Uncle Azra said conversationally as he moved to the left. This effectively turned Sariel's back to me. "All you Choir Boys don't seem to understand that we Grigori aren't the real enemy down here."

Sariel snarled at Uncle Azra's attempt at conversation, which surprised me. The Divine's servants weren't supposed to snarl . . . were they?

"You are filth, Grigori. Mucking about with the humans and fornicating with them. It's disgusting. You squander the gift that the Divine gave you."

A plan formulated in my head. Just keep him talking, Az, I thought. I needed him good and distracted.

As if hearing me, Azra tugged Beth's leash forward and into striking distance of the angel. It was a foolish move, but if there was one thing about my uncle it was that he's fearless when he fights.

"I'm going to let you in on a little secret," Azra told the angel. Whatever he was about to say was lost because his concentration was broken when he noticed the blade in the angel's hand. "Are you crazy, Choir Boy? You could gouge somebody's eye out. Put that thing away!" he admonished.

Defiantly, Sariel held the blade higher. Without a word of warning and faster than light, Azra flicked his hand. He hit the angel's wrist which sent the knife clattering to the ground a few feet away from me. *Perfect,* I thought. The dizziness took hold of me again. It caused the ground to tilt a bit, making me off-balance. I had to flatten myself against the wall for stability.

"There," Azra said calmly. "Now that you aren't waving that toad stabber around, we can talk like two civilized beings."

The angel stared at my uncle like he just grew a second head out of his elbow.

I seized the opportunity and dove for the knife. Even with landing wrong on my ankle, I managed to grasp the blade firmly by the handle.

The second my skin made contact it felt like I'd been hooked up to a generator. Electricity surged through my body from the celestial blade. I fought to maintain control as the overwhelming power threatened to overtake me completely. There was a scream of pure agony. It took my mind several moments to realize that I was the one screaming. I fell heavily to my knees under the weight of the energy. It was as though the blade had been soldered to my skin. My fingers refused to release the thing. There wasn't much else to do with it except to hold on and see it through. My body was about to blow apart any second due to the sheer amount of pressure.

Gritting my teeth, I held on and pushed past the pain. Soon, it lessened and an amazing elation overtook me; I was invincible, ready to take on anything. The overwhelming pressure was replaced with a sense of supremacy and unlimited power. The exhilaration was addicting. I yelled again but this time it was in triumph over the power flowing through me. I was in control and I was going to kick some Choir Boy ass.

I stood in a single, fluid motion. All of the aches and pains from my previous fight were gone. Hefting the blade high, I felt invincible.

The angel was busy fighting my uncle. He didn't see me aim for his head. I sprinted forward, a guttural scream coming from my throat. The angel dodged my attack. Azra had to jump out of the way of the blade.

"Watch it, kiddo!" he yelled.

I ignored him and continued my attack on Sariel. I swung the blade with more force and even more abandon. The knife nicked the angel in the arm. Luminescent light dripped form the wound—angel's blood, I supposed. The sight of it, blue and glowing, made me smile. The energy that suffused my actions pushed my attack onward.

Sariel growled as I advanced. He sidestepped and tripped me. I fell heavily to the ground. The blade was kicked out of my hand and all of the foreign energy abandoned me. All of the power drained as quickly as it had come. The loss of it left me weak and shattered. How could I have let go?

A fist caught me square in the jaw, pitching me backwards. Before I knew what was happening, the angel was on top of me, drawing his fist back to deliver another blow.

Despite how drained I was, my mind washed in red. I reacted. I heaved the angel backwards with more force than should have been possible. He toppled onto the ground, releasing me. As he struggled to regain his position, I tried to get to my feet. He reared up, the blade back in his hand. It plunged into my thigh, sending electric bolts of agony through my flesh. Sariel jerked the blade out for another try. Like hell I was going to let him stab me again. I punched him so hard that he sprawled on the ground and the blade skittered away.

The energy and the rage was completely gone— vaporized as soon as the red cleared from my sight. Confusion and exhaustion overtook me. I had trouble even standing. Despite my intentions of fighting more, I could only sink onto the concrete as I gasped for breath. Feebly, I clutched at the throbbing wound on my leg.

Casting a look around the clearing, I spotted Azra lying on the ground a dozen or so feet away, out cold. Blood dripped from a nasty looking cut on his head and on his shoulder. Beth knelt next to him bleating mournfully.

What had happened? Was Azra dead?

The sight of the faint glow of the celestial blade drew my attention. I had to get ahold of it. I had to protect myself. I moved for the knife. As I did so, the angel got to his feet and, with a shriek of outrage on his lips, came for me.

I wasn't quick enough to get out of the way. The angel picked me up by my shirt and pinned me against one of the metal containers. The ridge of it dug into my back painfully. There was a sickening pop and a sharp pain as my arm came out of its socket. My muscles, already sore, was positively screaming. He gripped the front of my shirt and his arm pinned my neck in place. I hung limply, too exhausted to do anything more than just watch, as he brought his closed fist towards my face.

Before his fist could connect, however, Sariel lurched

forward, hitting his head against the metal. My injured shoulder flared in another wave of pain. As he was straightening up, he lurched forward again. Thankfully, I was left uncrushed. This time I saw what was causing his forward momentum.

Beth, in all of her spiked collared glory, was tapping into her inner mountain ram and aiming to head-butt the angel right in the rear end.

Sariel realized what was happening at the same time I did. While keeping me immobilized against the wall, he grabbed the goat by the neck with his other hand and tossed her roughly to the side.

He refocused his attention on me. "Now. You and I are going to—" He cut off abruptly, making a wet, gasping sound instead of words. Immediately, his grip loosened and I fell unsteadily to my feet.

The angel stumbled backwards, his hand clutching at his chest. I saw the pale glow of the celestial blade shine at the point where his heart would have been. Sariel collapsed right where he stood. Uncle Azra panted heavily over the inert form.

A bright, golden light shone from the motionless shape of the angel's corporeal body. The light disintegrated into a million fragments no bigger than pinpricks which ascended into the sky, leaving behind only the knife.

"You alright, kid?" Azra asked, still laboring for breath. He shifted Sariel's blade into his injured arm and clasped his good hand over the still gushing shoulder wound.

I nodded. The throbbing pain in my leg was distant. What I felt was cold— a bitter, shocking cold that left me trembling. Azra offered me a hand up. I took it gratefully, gasping at the heavy pain from my wound. My uncle held me steady with his good arm.

Once I was on my feet, he helped me limp towards Beth. "C'mon," he said. His tone was distant and serious. "We have to get out of here. Who knows if more of the

Heavenly Host are on their way? We can't risk being caught by them."

Chapter Sixteen

Uncle Azra transported us in dizzying circles all over the globe, going as far south as Australia and as far north as Greenland, with easily three dozen places in between. I can't remember where we left Beth—Azra just said it would be safer than with us.

"It's to confuse our trail," he explained when we stopped somewhere in Moscow. "It'll buy us enough time to get out of dodge and blend back in with the humans."

I was in too much shock to listen. The world had a sort of surreal quality to it, like a waking dream. Had I really taken on a Choir Boy? And survived?

It was just before dawn when we arrived in France. I shook as we slipped furtively into one of Azra's many safe houses. The one in Paris was in the heart of Marais, one of the oldest neighborhoods in the city.

The house was dark, but clean, and the modern furniture was at odds with the old architecture. We stumbled through the dark and into the kitchen together. I sank into a high-backed chair, my knees trembling and the puncture wound in my thigh throbbing. We had taken care of our wounds at our first stop. While the cut continued to bleed, it was nowhere near as bad as it had been before we bandaged it. Still, I'd already lost a lot of blood, so weakness flooded through me. Azra was on his phone as he lurched to the cabinet and pulled out a shot glass and a hidden bottle of Heavenly Nectar.

"Ash, I need a favor. I need you to create a diversion for us. One of the Choir Boys almost got Orion. Yeah, we are alright. We are somewhere safe for now. No, I don't think we were followed, but I would rather be safe than sorry." There was a pause. "I don't care what you do; just aim it for the southern hemisphere. . . Alright, thanks buddy." He set the phone onto the counter with a clatter. Unstopping the Heavenly Nectar, he poured a liberal amount into the shot glass. He downed the golden liquid and slammed the glass onto the counter with a wince. He repeated the process once more and then poured one for me. "Drink up, kid. It will help calm your nerves." He sounded just as weary as I felt.

"Thanks," I said and threw back the liquid. It burned on the way down, causing me to choke and sputter. It tasted like a cross between motor oil, chicken livers, and mouthwash. "Ugh!" I wiped my mouth with my sleeve. "That's disgusting!"

"Good," Azra said with a certain triumphant note in his voice. "More for me then." He took the empty shot glass from my hand and returned it to the counter. He then grabbed the bottle of Nectar and plunked it onto the table between us and took a seat.

"What's Ascher going to do?" I asked.

"He's going to distract whatever Heavenly Host comes down to investigate that Choir Boy's death. He'll lay a false trail to give us time to settle somewhere. We won't stay here. I think we'll go up to Copenhagen. We haven't been there in a while."

"Copenhagen?" Alarm spread through me. We had to go back. Stella was still there. "I can't go to Copenhagen. I have to go back to California."

Azra shook his head as he prodded at the raw wound on his shoulder. "Not a chance. Our cover is blown. They know we were there and, more than likely, the Host is already crawling around the city waiting to see if we come back. It just isn't safe. And speaking of safe, where are your beads? You are supposed to wear them at all times!"

"They were lost during the fight with the Fallen One. Those beads are the last thing on my mind right now, Uncle Az. I have to go back to California. I can't leave Stella there alone!" I slammed my fist against the table out of sheer frustration.

The sound made Azra's head jerk up. His scowl was fierce and, if I had been younger and not so determined, that look alone would have made me waver. "You almost died back there! What in the world makes you think that I'll let you go back? We are going to Copenhagen, end of discussion," he growled.

"No, it is not the end of the discussion!" My uncle wasn't expecting me to fight back. He opened his mouth to put me in my place, but I went on with what I had to say. "You have pushed me for as long as I can remember to fulfill the prophecy and end the war. Now that I have found the human that can help me do it, you are refusing to help me. What gives?"

Azra's eyes blazed with barely contained anger. "You don't know for sure that she is the one, kiddo. You haven't even talked to her about it. Need I remind you that you were almost killed tonight? Why are you so sure this girl is worth getting annihilated for?"

I could barely keep my voice level. "Why won't you listen to me? Stella *is* the one!" Now that I had the wrath flowing in my veins, my trembling had ceased. Instead of the iciness, my limbs were enflamed with the heat of fury. I felt that power, that strength that had infused me before begin to creep back. "I just know Stella is the one, alright. She will help me stop the war. As for talking to her about it, that is the whole reason why I have to go back. I can't leave her."

Azra stared at me. The gash on his arm oozed past the makeshift wrappings and bruises formed under the layers of caked dirt and blood on his face. It would be awhile before he looked like he had before. While I hadn't had a chance to look in a mirror, I was sure I was in a similar state, if not worse. It would take some time for me to heal too. Celestial blades tended to leave more permanent damage if they didn't land a killing strike. I wasn't looking forward to the extended healing process.

Azra and I glared at each other for a solid minute. Neither of us were willing to budge until his tense posture relaxed and he took a healthy swig of the Heavenly Nectar.

"What do you want from me, kiddo?" Azra asked. "I can't take back what happened. I promised to keep you safe and I intend to keep that promise. I know we mainly run into Fallen Ones and they really aren't that big of a deal to handle, but the Heavenly Host are a completely different ballgame. We were lucky to get out of there with our heads still attached. If it wasn't for Beth throwing him off, I don't think we would be breathing right now." He took another long swig from the bottle, letting the statement sink in.

It was true that in our travels we encountered mostly Fallen Ones. I couldn't even remember the last time we had faced one of the Heavenly Host. The events of the last few hours were more than enough to prove that if we did go back and the Host were waiting for us, we might not make it out again.

Then Stella's eyes flashed in my mind, igniting my resolve. I remembered why I needed to stay and I held onto that reason with all my might. "I don't care. I have to go back. Stella shouldn't be left alone there—especially with the Host swarming the place. Who knows what could happen."

Azra argued. "She is a human who has no connection to the Host, Orion. They have no reason to go after her. That is, unless we go back and paint a target on her. Or did you not consider that as a consequence?"

Begrudgingly, I nodded, acknowledging his point. "Yes, but she is part of all this, so she is already involved. I know you don't believe it, but give me some time to prove to you she is the one. Please, just give me this chance to do what I am meant to do."

Uncle Azra remained silent as he thought over the options. After a while, he leaned forward to look me in the eyes as he said, "Orion, you've been acting really stupid lately. It seems like no matter what I do, you're thinking of twenty different ways to defy me. You've caused more trouble this last week than any other time of your life."

I refused to bow my head to the guilt he was throwing at me. I could concede I'd been a jerk, but that's not to say that Azra had been (forgive the pun) a perfect angel either.

He sighed. "If you say she is the one, then I need to believe you. I should trust you. You haven't been this persistent about anything for your whole life, so that has to say something. We will go back, but only for a limited time. You have two days. Count 'em, two days to get her to help you end the Angelic War. Once the forty-eight hours has passed, we are out of there. Do you understand?"

I shifted my gaze to meet his, not believing what he said. "Really?" Slowly the anger within receded, leaving me more tired than I was when we first arrived. He was going to give me a chance after all.

He gave a curt nod. "Yes, but there are rules. You're staying with me while we are there. We're going to stay in the condo in Camarillo. It's far enough away from where we were to be out of their immediate radar, but close enough so that you are still in the general area. Ascher's distraction, whatever it is, should be big enough to give us time to set that up."

"Fine," I conceded. "What else?"

"I go where you go. It isn't the smartest thing for you to be roaming around on your own."

I groaned. "You mean you are going to be with me everywhere?"

"Me or Ascher. If you don't like it, then we won't go back to California. Lastly, we have to do something about your lost beads. The last thing we need is for you to go all agro and summon the damn Choir Boys right to you."

I glanced down at my bare wrist. "How? You said you got those beads from some Shamaness years ago."

"Correction—your father picked it up from some Shamaness long time ago. I won't go near those creepy women. You know if they look into your eyes, they can get inside your brain and control you like you are their voodoo zombie. They are like witches, except witches are much, much worse."

There was no way to react to that statement other than to shake my head. For someone so worldly, Azra believed some ridiculously medieval superstitions. "Well, if we can't get another set of beads, what do we do?"

My uncle considered me for a long moment. "Maybe we don't need the beads. Maybe you can do it yourself."

"Come again?"

Azra stood and began shuffling around the room as he mused out loud. "The whole reason we got the beads in the first place is because we didn't know what Grigori traits you inherited; I mean angel genetics is an oxymoron. We didn't want to take a chance."

"So now you want to see if I have the ability to blend in with humans?"

"We don't really have a choice, now do we?" He glanced meaningfully at my wrist.

"Good point. So how do we test it out?"

Azra pursed his lips in thought. "Well, the disguise should kick in automatically—at least that is how it is for the Grigori."

"But if it doesn't just kick in, then we are going to be attacked as soon as we leave this house," I pointed out.

"Yeah," Azra said and lapsed into contemplative silence. "Our only other option is for me to put a ward on you. It's not going to last very long, but I think I can get you from one safe house to another. Ascher will have to redo it if you need to be protected for longer than that."

I frowned. "Why can't your ward last?"

My uncle actually blushed and bowed his head. "I'm not the best when it comes to that sort of stuff," he admitted. "My wards tend to fade really quickly."

I suppressed my immediate retort. If the topic hadn't been so serious, I would have laughed and teased him about it. Instead, I said, "You look like hell and you're bleeding through the bandages. Let's change your dressings."

Azra chuckled. "Have you looked in a mirror lately?

That gash on your leg looks like it hurts."

"You don't even know."

He glanced at his shoulder. "I wouldn't bet on that. I'll go get the kit. I think it's under the sink."

He went around to the kitchen cabinet to retrieve the small tackle box of emergency medical paraphernalia. He lugged it over to the table.

"Hey Kid," Az said as he rifled through the bandages for some antiseptic. "You did good out there. I mean, good for not knowing anything about self-defense. I'm proud of you."

"Thanks," I said, embarrassed. The adrenaline and fury were gone. The weakness made me shake as I tried to pour the antiseptic onto a cloth.

"Here," Azra took the rag and bottle from me and pushed me back into the chair. "Yours is worse." Diligently, Azra cleaned the rush stitch job on my thigh. It hurt, but not as bad as getting stabbed in the first place. I made a mental note to not let that happen again.

"Doesn't look that bad," he assured me. "Mostly it's the blood that made it seem worse than it was. You shouldn't even have any scars once it heals all the way." He finished wrapping the bandage and shifted to the table to see to his own wounds.

"Damn," I said with a smile. "I was hoping for a cool scar to show off to Stella."

Azra smiled, though tersely. His gash looked uglier than mine. Sewing together skin hadn't been high on my extracurricular activities, so my stitches were ragged and uneven. But they had gotten the job done. Azra inspected the stitches I had done earlier with a grim expression. He poured antiseptic onto the whole thing, letting out a loud hiss as it hit his skin. After slapping a thick gauze pad on it, he sat back and let me wrap it.

"Uncle Az? Can I ask you something?"

"Let me guess. You want to know why you reacted like you did to the celestial blade you touched, right?"

I nodded, thinking back to when I picked it up from

the ground. "It was like lightning. I couldn't control it. Why did it do that?"

"I wish I knew, kiddo. It's just one more mystery to the conundrum that is you." He patted me on the shoulder then grabbed for the bottle of Heavenly Nectar.

I snorted. "That helps. Really, it does."

Uncle Azra chuckled and went to sit back down. "I think it has to do with the fact that you are the only angel that's ever been born. Anything from Heaven is bound to affect you differently. Like Heavenly Nectar." He hoisted the bottle to his lips by way of salute.

"Or, it could just be that Heavenly Nectar is disgusting," I pointed out.

Uncle Azra shook his head. "It is not disgusting at all. Black licorice . . . now that's really disgusting."

I packed up the medical kit. "How long until Ascher gives the all-clear?"

Azra shrugged. "It will take as long as it takes. We aren't leaving here until he does, though." He got up and wandered into the living room. Turning on the TV, he stretched out on the couch and breathed deeply. I followed him and let myself be numbed by early-morning infomercials in French.

"Uncle Az," I asked after a while, "Are you sure Ascher will have to redo the ward to disguise me?"

He sighed. "Yeah. Believe me, I trust Ascher's wards over my own any day of the week."

The next question had trouble getting past my teeth. "Uncle Az? Do you trust Ascher?"

"What?" he glanced over at me incredulously. "Of course I do. Why would you even ask that?"

"Is it possible? I mean . . ." I hesitated, wondering how to think of how I could put this. "Maybe Ascher isn't the person we think he is."

Azra brushed off my concern airily. "It's not my fault if he is too rough on you in training."

"No, it's not the training. Well, it kind of is." I struggled to put my reservations into words. I had to make him understand. "Did you know that he believes that we are better than humans? The night I fought the Fallen One, he told me that Grigori were above the human's rules and laws. He says that is because we're the better species. Haven't you noticed how much he hates humans? He has nothing but contempt for them. He even tried to get me to steal a car with him."

"I don't believe that," Azra said as he took a sip of his Heavenly Nectar.

This wasn't going as well as I had hoped. Still, I pressed on, "Uncle Az, when I asked him about the prophecy he said my mission wasn't to save the world and get us back into Heaven. He told me that my sole purpose on this earth, in this life, was to bring the three realms crashing together to destroy everything."

He sighed. "Ryan, if he was one of the bad guys, don't you think he would have killed you by now? He's had so many opportunities over the years. Ascher wouldn't have done half of what he already has for you if there was even an ounce of truth to what you said."

I held my ground. "You still believe that after he set me up to be killed by a Fallen One? I saw him, Uncle Az. I told the thing to kill me."

"He said it was just a test; a training exercise. He wouldn't have allowed you to be killed."

"You weren't there! I'm telling you, he was hoping I wouldn't come out of that fight. I saw it in his eyes!"

"Yeah, well I know what I have seen," Azra shot back. "I know when your mother was killed, Ascher begged Rasheym not to go after the Archangel that did it. He pleaded for your father to let it go. He told Rasheym that you needed him. He pushed you into your father's arms and told him that you were all that was left of Indra now and he had better be there for you. Does that sound like a person that wants to destroy you? Or like someone who doesn't have your best interest at heart?"

The anger my uncle displayed crumbled with every word he spoke. His blue eyes teamed with the memories he was dredging up—the memories I had always been afraid to ask about. Azra continued talking with more emotion than I would have thought possible for him. "Did you know he was there when your father died? Do you remember?"

I did remember . . . sort of. My memory of my father's death had been rendered intentionally blurry. Even as I tried fight against it, he pulled it into the light. "Your father took you hunting. It was your first time tracking a Fallen One. He took you to England during the Wars of the Roses." Azra's eyes grew haunted and remorseful. "The Fallen One you had been tracking led you into the forest. Something happened. You lost control. It was the first time it happened and it turned you into a monster. Like someone hit the switch on you and we couldn't turn it off again."

Snatches of the memory broke free of their protective confinement. I saw the shadows of the trees racing passed me. Then the labored breathing of something large and angry following me. No. The panting was coming from me. I saw the Fallen One: a dark haired knight hissing at my father, about to strike. Everything went black. I heard the screams, felt the tearing of flesh in my hands. The smell of intense fear and blood filled the air.

"You've only done that three times in your life," my uncle told me quietly, breaking me out of the memory. "From what Ascher told me, the other night with the Fallen One was the third."

That explained the odd flashes of memory when I had woken up. I had literally torn the Fallen One apart, limb from limb. The red that had soaked the scene clips in my mind was the blood of the corporeal body I had shredded. Revulsion and horror filled me. How could I be such a monster? The abrupt understanding of exactly what I was capable of made me shake.

Azra kept telling the story, as lost in his words as I was in my memories. "Your father tried to contain you, but you had gone feral. The Fallen One escaped, but just barely. While Rasheym was trying to calm you down, one of the Choir Boys found you. Your temper tantrums always had one hell of a psychic range; yet another reason why you needed those beads. Anyway, Rasheym couldn't fight him off and keep you out of the way at the same time. He took quite a beating before Ascher showed up." He repeated the name with vehemence to press his point. "Ascher came and held you back so that your father could stand and fight."

I couldn't remember the Heavenly Host. In my mind, Ascher loomed in the forest, spitting out harsh words at my father, who was still holding me back.

"You deserve to die," Ascher screamed in my memory. Did I imagine the fury and the sick smile plastered on his face as he lunged to attack my father? The restraining arms released me and I was flung to the side to watch my father die. The hate inside of me grew stronger, more defined.

Azra swallowed hard, as though he were having trouble saying the next part. "I was too late to help. By the time I got there, Rasheym . . ."

"He was dead," I said for him. There was no emotion, just a quiet blankness. I was reciting words, keeping the torrent of feeling back.

Azra's eyes pleaded with me to understand, even as his voice was harsh, "I'm sorry I wasn't there to help your father. But you need to understand that Ascher was there. Ascher saved your life. Remember that the next time you want to go accusing him of trying to kill you."

I was quiet for a long moment, allowing my thoughts to settle and the hardness of my resolution to take hold. I asked in a quiet, but determined voice, "Do you want to know what I remember of that day, Uncle Az?" I looked him straight in the eyes. Their usual bright blue dotted with gold was filled with apprehension.

"I remember Ascher waiting in the woods, watching us. I told my father that I had seen him, but he didn't believe me. After the Fallen One had gotten away, Ascher came out of hiding and confronted my father and he killed him."

"No," Uncle Azra shook his head adamantly, the forcefulness of the denial bringing back his anger. "Ascher wouldn't have done that. How can you say these things, Orion?"

"I can say them because they are true. Why else would he not tell you that I would be fighting the Fallen One?" I stood, feeling lightheaded. The weight of the memories I had locked away so long ago was gone.

"I won't believe Ascher killed your father. I can't." Despite what he said, I could tell he was considering the possibility, double checking his own interactions with Ascher. He shook his head back and forth as if he were trying to prevent what I said from sticking.

We lapsed into silence, letting the noise from the TV fill the house as we waited to hear that it was safe to go back to California and to Stella.

Chapter Seventeen

We didn't talk much for the rest of the night. The all-clear came from Ascher a few hours after dawn. Before we left Paris, Uncle Az made me stand in the foyer of the house while he put on the disguise ward. His eyes were screwed tightly shut and he murmured under his breath. Sweat popped out onto his forehead out of sheer concentration. My skin felt dampened slightly, as if he was blowing bubbles at me. The whole experience was awkward for both of us. When he was finished, he stepped back and asked, "How do you feel?"

I hesitated before answering, "Damp."

He nodded briskly. "Fair enough. It should last until we get back to the Camarillo safe house. I already got the word out to Ash. He will meet us there."

I bit back the response I had to that. Instead, I asked, "I need to do one thing before we get to the house. I need to talk to Stella."

"I don't think that's such a good idea before we get you properly protected," Azra said.

"Look, I just want to make sure she is alright. Plus, I can ask her if she has plans this afternoon so we can get together and talk."

Uncle Az looked doubtful but he conceded with a nod. It was just at the end of first period when we arrived at Ventura High School. It took a bit of convincing before Uncle Az agreed to wait for me outside. I had to tell him that the front of the school was the best place to stand guard. Though I felt a bit of guilt for making my uncle stay outside, my mission to talk to Stella was going to be difficult enough without him shadowing my every move. In the end, he made me pinky promise to yell if there was any trouble.

I stood awkwardly in front of Mrs. Foster's classroom with a moderately sized bouquet of stargazer lilies in hand and feeling acutely idiotic. Nerves had my stomach tied in knots. This was a stupid idea. I should have just texted her instead of coming here. Or, at least, I shouldn't have brought her the flowers.

The bell rang. A swarm of teenagers came rushing through the breezeway, all trying to get to class. I leaned against the wall to stay out of the tide of bodies that flowed past. Several girls eyed the flowers enviously. They left muttering to each other and casting curious glances back at me.

This had been a really stupid idea.

"Hey." Someone tapped me on the shoulder. I turned and came face to face with Stella.

Today, a purple knit hat decorated with buttons covered the top of her head. She looked good in hats. But then, I couldn't imagine anything that she wouldn't look gorgeous in.

"Geeze Ryan! What happened to you?"

"What?" I asked. Then I realized she was probably reacting to my more than slightly beaten appearance. "It's nothing," I tried to say confidently. It fell short and I'm not sure I would have believed it myself.

"What happened?" She touched the side of my face in concern. "Did you get into another fight?"

Reflexively, I shied away from the touch and she dropped her hand as if stung. To her credit, she didn't push the issue.

"Who are those for?" she asked, pointing to the flowers in my hand. It was a good change of topic, but it wasn't quite quick enough to hide the hurt she felt when I winced.

I glanced down at the blossoms and then back to her. "They're for you." I offered them up and was rewarded with a big smile.

She closed her eyes, taking in a deep breath of the

perfumed blooms. The pleasure on her face made all of the awkwardness worth it. "Do you give all the new girls flowers?"

"Only the ones I like."

She looked at me with a brief unreadable expression. In an instant it was replaced with happiness. "That's so sweet. Thank you. How did you know that lilies are my favorite?"

"I didn't actually." It felt I could stand there with her for the rest of time. I wanted to forget about the prophecy, the Heavenly Host that were prowling around, and anything else that would have stopped this moment. But I couldn't forget about those things. Time had to move on and so did I. Uncle Azra was likely to storm in here like it was a rescue mission if I didn't get back to him soon. "I have to go. My uncle is waiting for me."

"What?" she asked, her brows furrowing together. "You aren't staying for class?"

"No, I have something important I have to handle. I just wanted to give these. Well, and there is something I really need to talk to you about."

"What is it?"

"I can't get into it right now, but it is very important. Is there any way you can ditch?"

She frowned, "What is so important?"

"I told you, I can't get into it right now. Can you ditch or not?"

She let out a frustrated sigh. "I can't until fourth period. Can whatever it is wait until then?"

I glanced around and saw several people staring at us. Damn it. "Yeah, it can wait that long."

Stella nodded thoughtfully and swiped a strand of hair back behind her ear. "Okay, well, I have an assignment for French class that I need to go to the Getty for. If I have to ditch, then we are making a trip down there. You can tell me whatever you want to tell me on the way."

"The Getty?"

"It's the art museum down in the valley."

My smile broadened. I couldn't have asked for a better place: public and open. "That would be perfect."

She bit her lip in an effort to keep the grin from her face. "Great. I'll pick you up at your apartment."

"Ah, actually, I'll be over at my uncle's place out in Camarillo. Can you pick me up there?"

"Text me the address and I will." She looked as though she wanted to ask what was going on again, but she held it back.

The second bell rang, alerting students that they had one minute to get to class before they landed in detention. "You better get going," I said to her. "I'll text you later."

She leaned up to give me a quick peck on the cheek that blossomed into a numb patch on my skin. Before I knew it, her lips were gone and so was the sweet sensation. She dashed into the classroom, either out of embarrassment or desire not to be late, I couldn't be sure which.

Backing away, I bumped into several people who were scrambling to class. I never took my eyes off of the door, hoping she would come back out. It was amazing the effect that girl had on me. She was the one. Now I just had to prove it.

True to his word, Uncle Azra had waited for me at the front of the school. "Are you done, Romeo?" he asked when I came closer. The earlier awkwardness between us had disappeared and we were again back to normal. Well, as normal as we ever were.

"Yeah. Thanks for the flowers. She loved them."

"Told you," he grinned smugly. "It never hurts to butter them up before you press them for information. Now, let's get you to the safe house before my ward completely disappears."

I was still thinking about Stella's lips on my cheek when Azra took my hand and we teleported out of the school parking lot and into the condo in Camarillo.

It was bright inside. A small square of pale tile at the

doorway was hedged in with brown carpeting that lead further into the place.

The entrance hall widened to a large living room. Immediately my eyes were drawn to the two large picture windows directly across from the front door on the west wall. Pale gauze curtains were draped over them and sunlight streamed through the sheer fabric. A mantled fireplace was angled at the point where the western and southern wall met making a sort of curved effect to the room. The walls themselves were pale beige with blue accents. A white sectional divided the room, distinguishing the kitchen from the living area. Blue throw pillows were tossed onto it. A round glass coffee table supported a small stainless steel abstract sculpture.

Across from the fireplace was the kitchen, neatly tiled with the island counters angled in such a way that they separated the kitchen from the living room. There was a lot of counter space both around the wall and on the island. To the right of the windows was a small wooden door paned in glass leading out to a balcony. In front of that was a tall, circular glass table encircled with four wooden bar stools.

My room was the doorway to the left of the kitchen and Azra's was to adjacent to the entryway. A large bed and an oversized dresser were crammed into the small space. I had my own bathroom and a walk-in closet, though, so it wasn't too bad.

"So what happens now? When are you going to talk to her?" Azra called from the kitchen.

Emerging from my new room, I rubbed my eyes and glanced at the clock on my phone. It was only nine thirty. "This afternoon."

Azra almost crowed in excitement. "What did she say? Did you tell her about the prophecy? Is she going to tell you how to stop the war?" Uncle Azra danced around me in his excitement. "How much does she know about us angels? The Grigori? Should I go get the maps? We need battle plans!"

I rolled my eyes. "We don't need battle plans. We are just going to an art museum and talk."

"Yes! That's perfect! A working date is just what you two need!"

"What kind of date? What are you babbling about?"

"Oh you know, it's like a working lunch, except there's more of a chance you can get to second base. Do you have an agenda? Does she know she has to come with ways to end the war? Should I make you two some snacks? Damn it, I forgot the Chex Mix! We can't save the world without Chex Mix."

"Will you stop?" I yelled. "I'm so nervous and this isn't helping. What am I going to do?"

"Orion," Azra shook his head in confusion, "you were so sure in Paris. What changed?"

"Nothing has changed. I'm just nervous."

Uncle Azra patted me on the back heartily. "Just ask her. I mean, we are risking our lives coming back like this and you haven't scared her away with your personality yet. This should be a piece of cake. Besides, when she laughs in your face, we can move on with plan Copenhagen. The sooner the better, too."

"Thanks for the confidence." I rolled my eyes.

"Hey, it's what I am here for. Alright, I've gotta go get Beth now that everything is quiet. I'm also gonna head to the store for some Chex Mix. You need anything?"

"Nah, I'm alright."

He strode towards the front door. "Remember, don't go anywhere until I get back. You are safe here, but the second you step out of this door, all that protection goes out the window."

"I know," I sighed.

"Ascher will be here soon and he can redo your ward. You should just rest a bit. I'll be back with some snacks in no time." He closed and locked the door to the condo behind him.

Left to my own devices, I decided to clean up a bit. My clothes were dirt smeared from my fight with the

Choir Boy and my bandages needed changing again. It was also a chance to reflect on everything that had happened in the last two days.

I had killed a Fallen One with my bare hands and I survived against one of the Heavenly Host. The truth of those words made me shake. It was the first time I had killed anyone. Not that Fallen Ones could be considered anyone. Could they?

For all of the brash talk from my uncle, the Fallen were still angels. They were still my family, weren't they? If so, then what did that make me? A killer? Some sort of psychopathic monster?

I wandered listlessly to the bathroom and turned on the shower. It took some time for me to take off the grimy and torn clothes because of my wounds. By the time I stepped into the hot water, my body was shaking from chills as well as grief.

I stood in the shower long enough for the scalding hot water to turn icy, as if it could wash away the overwhelming guilt I felt. But it must have worked somewhat because when I emerged and wrapped a thick towel around me, I felt slightly better. The guilt wouldn't just go away, though, and I expected to be feeling it for quite some time. But knowing that I had done what I had to do to survive made it bearable. I dried off and put on some new clothes with a fresh perspective.

By the time I emerged from my room Azra and Beth had returned.

"You smell a lot better," Azra told me, approvingly. He set the plastic grocery bags and one oversized canvas duffel down. He unhooked Beth from her leash. The goat wandered around the place, sniffing the furniture. I watched mutely as she took a surreptitious nibble of the couch. She stared back at me as if daring me to say something about it.

Just as I opened my mouth to let my uncle know what his pet was doing, Azra interjected, drawing my attention the large canvas bag he held. "Here. I have something for you. With everything going on lately and how much you are asking about your parents, I think it's high time that I give this to you."

"What is it?" I asked.

From the bags he withdrew a black leather scabbard and offered it to me.

I eyed the gift. The leather was tooled with a scripted rose and ivy design. The handle of the blade was slightly curved with the grip wrapped in a strip of black leather that made the ornate silver lions' head pommel stand out.

"Take it," he urged, offering it. "It was made specifically for you."

I put my hand on the hilt and felt the electric charge that signaled that it was a celestial blade. The difference from the previous one I held was significant. This time, I didn't feel like I was hooked up to a generator or that the power was going to completely overtake me. Instead, there was a steady hum of energy, a constant and subtle boost to my own power. The feel of it was vitalizing, not overwhelming; as if this blade was made to work in harmony with me.

Azra grinned as I pulled the blade out of its sheath. The faint glow of the curved short sword reflected off of the surface of the coffee table. "Nice, huh, kid?"

Mutely I nodded, too stunned to speak.

"This goes with it." He handed me a small rolled piece of parchment. Reluctantly I sheathed my new blade and set it down on the table as I accepted the rolled note. The parchment was sealed with red wax with an elaborate R imprinted on it.

Uncle Azra explained, "It's from your father. He meant to give it to you when you were old enough to start your training." He bowed his head sheepishly. "It's a little late, but that's my fault."

Speechless, I broke the seal and unrolled the note. Even though I was expecting it, I was still taken aback by the sight of my father's handwriting.

I hope this blade will help you in your destiny. Follow

your heart and you will not be led astray. I am proud of you and I love you, my son.

I looked at my uncle with tears watering my vision. "He made this for me?"

"Yeah," Az looked sheepish. "Well, he had it made for you. It took a lot of bribing and blackmailing of the last few contacts we had in Heaven. I should have given it to you sooner."

"Thank you, Uncle Az," I whispered, blinking away the tears that came.

Azra coughed and looked away. "It's nothing, really." I could see the pleased smile on his face that let me know that he was happy to give me my sword. "Listen, Ascher's been held up and he won't be able to get here to fix the ward. But, it's alright because I have the next best thing." Again, he reached into the canvas bag and pulled out a very old, weathered scroll. "I've got the instruction manual. I'll redo your ward and we can be sure it'll stick."

He waved the scroll around enthusiastically and a knot formed in the pit of my stomach. Azra couldn't even follow the instructions on a can of soup, let alone a complex disguise ward. Still, without Ascher, this was my only option.

"Well? What are you waiting for? Get naked, kiddo."

"Naked?" I swear, I didn't mean for my voice to squeak as much as it did.

"Yes, naked. This ward requires skin contact. I think that's part of why it didn't stick so long before." Azra went to the kitchen and started pulling out various things. "And, if I am reading this right, this will also make a killer risotto."

Chapter Eighteen

I stood in the middle of the living room, stripped down to my boxers, debating on just running back to the relative safety of my room. "I don't know about this, Uncle Az."

"Oh, come on," he admonished from his place in the kitchen. He had a pot of something boiling on the stove which he stirred constantly with an oversized wooden spoon. "There's no other alternative and I'm not letting you go anywhere without a ward, prophecy or no. You know that, don't you?"

I heaved a sigh and crossed my arms over my chest. "Yeah, alright. Can we get this over with already? Stella will be here shortly."

Azra shrugged as if to say 'whatever' and put a lid on the boiling pot. He grabbed the unfurled scroll and came into the living room. The parchment had browned considerably with age, but the inscriptions on it weren't faded at all. In fact, the ink was dark and glistened as though it were still wet.

"What are all of those symbols?" I asked as I peered at the foreign scribbles.

"That is the angelic language in its written form. It's beautiful, ain't it?"

I regarded the geometric shapes skeptically. "Can you read even it?"

"Of course I can read it!" Azra scoffed. "Well, I can kind of read it."

"Kind of?"

"Well, I mean, I remember some of it. You gotta understand, I haven't had to read this language for several millennia. Anyone would be rusty."

My doubts surged, but Azra was right; there was no other choice.

He went into the kitchen and spooned some of his concoction into a coffee mug. It steamed as he brought it over to where I was standing.

"What is that?" I asked.

"This is the pickled cherry lime risotto. According to the instructions, I've got to smear it over your skin." He must have seen my reticence because he told me smartly, "just shut up and stand still."

Without any other choice, I held my breath and tried not to grimace as he took the wooden spoon and dabbed hot, sticky globs onto my shoulders. The smell was pungent enough to make me gag.

When he was done applying the risotto, he set the cup aside and moved to stand in front of me. Without a word, he spit on his palms and rubbed his hands together. He hummed a few bars and peeked once more at the instructions. At last he closed his eyes and held his hands out in front, inches away from my chest.

Then he began to sing.

Nothing in the world could compare to Azra's singing. Even after being exiled for all this time, his voice conjured images of a Heaven and a Creator I've never known. While the words were alien to me, they were also hauntingly poignant. As the melody flowed around me, a center of warmth blossomed on my chest. It grew until it was about a hand span wide. The warmth intensified to the point that it felt like a sunburn. Then, the stinging tuned into burning. I smelled my hair and flesh singeing. The pain came secondary to the shock and realization that I was being branded.

As soon as that thought registered in my head, I gasped in pain and slapped his hands away. "What the hell are you doing?"

The singing stopped abruptly and I felt like the very air would shatter with the loss of the melody.

"Why did you do that?"

Glancing down at my chest, I saw an angry red impression of a ward—it was a large circle with several angelic symbols strewn throughout it. Luckily, I'd pushed Azra's hands away before it had gotten too deep.

Azra looked at the markings. "Oops. Sorry, kiddo. I don't think that was supposed to happen."

"You think?" Gingerly, I poked around the wound, trying not to get risotto in the burn.

"Well, at least we know this one won't fade away," he pointed out, helpfully.

I shot him a glare as I further inspected the burn. "But does it work?"

My uncle flushed with indignation as he ate some of the risotto. "Of course it will work," he said around a mouthful of the stuff. "I followed the instructions step by step. Consider the scar a bonus."

I thought it wise to keep my doubts to myself. "I've gotta go get cleaned up. I smell horrible and I don't want to risk bleeding on Stella when she gets here."

Uncle Azra rolled the parchment back up. "Oh that kind of wound won't bleed. The heat pretty much cauterized the blood vessels."

Turning towards the safety of my bedroom, I breathed out a loud, "Whatever." I grabbed my new sword on my way out of the kitchen.

As I closed the door behind me, I heard Uncle Azra giggling. I was going to have to do something to get him out of here within the hour. Who knows what sort of things he would say or do in front of Stella.

This time, my shower was short; just long enough to rinse off all of the foul smelling risotto. I took my time bandaging the ward on my chest. At least it didn't hurt anymore and hopefully it would actually keep me disguised when we went to the Getty.

I got dressed and was going to head out to the living room when I saw the sword Azra gave me laying on the bed where I had left it. I picked up the blade my father had made for me and tested it out with a few swipes. The balance was perfect and the energy of it enhanced my natural levels instead of overwhelming them like the other blades I'd handled.

Azra said that my father had this blade made especially for me, that he intended to train me before he died. Not for the first time, I daydreamed about what my life would have been like if he had lived. Would he be proud of me now? Would he like the person I've become?

I laid on the bed, my sword still in my hand. Resting felt so good to my aching muscles. Two fights in so many days had taken their toll physically. Even with my accelerated healing rate, mending was going to take some time.

I heard the front door open and close. Panicked that it was Stella, I leapt out of the bed, despite my protesting muscles, and darted out of the room.

The first thing I noticed was that Azra was nowhere in sight. What should have been relief coursing through me manifested into fear. As a general rule, I preferred knowing where my uncle was and what kind of trouble found him or what kind of trouble he was getting into as the case may be.

"Uncle Azra?" I called out. I was answered with silence. Even Beth was gone.

I realized that I had left my phone on the kitchen counter when I went to clean up earlier. "Shit," I cursed and dashed over to the counter. Just as I feared, it was missing. "Uncle Azra!" I yelled to the empty apartment.

The front door opened again and I swiveled around. Beth came in first with her leash trailing behind her. She was followed by Uncle Azra who was chatting happily on the phone.

"Uncle Azra!" I yelled again, this time with my target firmly in sight. The sound of his name screamed so forcefully caused him to jump. Warily and without taking his eyes off of me, he told the person on the line, "I'll have to call you back."

As he clicked off the phone, I snarled, "Give. Me. My.

Phone. Now."

His expression was that of pure innocence. "I don't have your phone." I eyed the one in his hand and he hastily brought it up for me to see. "This one is mine. Yours is on the coffee table."

I stomped closer to the couch so I could see over it. Sure enough, my phone was blinking on the coffee table, indicating waiting messages. It had been moved. I picked it up and flipped it open. I wouldn't put it past Uncle Azra to have sent something to Stella behind my back.

Quickly opening up the text messages, my apprehension mounted until I spotted one that made my heart leap: *I suppose we are dating . . . why?*

Before I could allow myself to get worked up, I read the following and final message: *On my way now. Are you ready?*

Frantically I thumbed through the outgoing texts. There were none. I rounded on Uncle Azra, "What did you say to her?" I was so furious I was shaking.

He was in the kitchen pouring the Chex Mix he had bought into two bowls. He didn't answer me right away as he leisurely set the smaller bowl on the ground next to the water dish for Beth. He then walked right past me, towards the living room. It was only after settling himself down on the couch with the other bowl in his lap that he addressed me in his best parental tone, "As your guardian, I like to know who you are hanging out with so I asked a few questions."

I clenched my fists, trying my best to restrain myself from choking the hell out of him. "What exactly did you say to her?"

"You'll see," he said with what I considered to be a wicked grin as he clicked on the TV. He munched on the Chex Mix as a show with a laugh track blared through the sound bar. He offered me some advice as he swallowed his first bite. "Just don't act surprised."

"What do you mean 'don't act surprised'? Az, I have to know because she thinks I'm the one who had the conversation! You didn't ask her if she was my girlfriend, did you?"

"Well, weren't you wondering the same thing? Chex Mix?" He offered me the bowl.

I knocked the container out of his hand sending the contents all over the living room.

"What the hell are you trying to do to me?" I shouted just as he exclaimed, "Hey! I just vacuumed!"

We glared at each other for a full minute and Beth started grazing on the spilled food. Our staring contest was broken by the sound of someone knocking loudly on the front door.

"Stella," I whispered. My expression of horror was mirrored by my uncle's gleeful smile.

"I'll get it!" He leapt off the couch and I was right behind him. I tackled him as he made it to the hall. Suddenly, we were on the ground with a loud thud. We scuffled, each trying to get at the door first.

My elbow connected with his jaw just as his knee jabbed me in the stomach. I'm not going to lie, it hurt, but I needed to get to Stella first. I scrambled past him, the echo of another knock urging me forward. My palm mashed his head down and I was finally able to get the leverage I needed to launch myself over him. He wrapped his arms around my wounded leg which made me scream out and smack against the floor. He took the advantage to scuttle around me. I copied his trick by nabbing one of his legs and brought him down again.

"Ryan?" I heard Stella's muffled voice call out.

I fought harder to get to the door. "Coming!" I replied just before Uncle Azra's fingers hooked themselves into my open mouth. I bit down on those fingers as hard as I could. A strangled yelp burst from my uncle's lips.

"Ryan, are you alright?" Stella called out.

Azra yanked his fingers away as soon as I opened my mouth to reply, I lifted my head to shout out the answer. My eyes were met with bright sunlight surrounding the shadowy figure of Stella. She held the door open and loomed over us. "I'm . . . fine," I said.

Both Azra and I froze in embarrassment. I looked up to see Stella's confused eyes stare back at me.

The only one of us who properly greeted Stella was the goat.

Beth wandered out of the front door, circling around our guest. Stella eyed the goat, surprise written all over her face.

"So. . ." Stella said, breaking the awkward silence of the moment. "Cute goat."

I dropped the arm that I had been twisting. Uncle Azra let go of my legs and hopped to his feet. I followed his example a little more slowly, my movements encumbered by the weight of mortification and my still healing wounds.

The smile on Uncle Azra's lips grew wider as he looked her over. I could tell he was reading her; digging around psychically to get more of a sense of her. By the way his eyes lit up I knew that he was about to say something that would humiliate me further. Instead of opening his mouth, however, his expression turned into one of fright and disbelief.

I didn't know what he saw that made him react that way, but it couldn't be good. The tension that sprang into the air around us was palpable.

Something wasn't right. Uncle Azra had opened his mouth, but then closed it again without so much as a squeak. Abruptly, he jerked me backwards into the apartment as he slammed the door in Stella's face.

"Hey! What is your problem?" I reached for the door again only to have my hand smacked.

"For the love of everything sacred, why didn't you tell me she was a witch?"

"She's not a witch! What is with you and thinking every human I meet in this place is a witch?" I yelled back. I didn't understand what he thought he would get from doing this.

"What is with you finding every witch in the city?"

Azra returned with just as much frustration.

"I don't know what you are talking about! Stella's not a witch and Sylvia isn't one either. You said you believed me! She is the human that will help end the war. Now let me go out there!" I moved for the door again only to have him wrench me back.

"It's too dangerous. I can't allow you to go with that thing out there. I don't know what sort of magic she's worked on you, but she can't be the one!"

I jerked my arm out of his grasp. "You said you believed me. You said you would give me two days to figure this out. Now my destiny is out there and I'm going whether you like it or not." I opened the door. Stella was still standing there, confusion written all over her face.

"Ready to go, Stella?"

"Of course," she answered. Azra gaped after us, speechless. She seemed more than willing to let the rudeness my uncle had shown her go. I was glad for that. Almost as if daring my uncle to stop her, Stella put her hand on my arm. The usual sensation was there, sparking my soul like an electric shock. Could she turn it on and off? I hadn't felt it earlier . . . or had I just been expecting it then?

"I parked Spike over here," she said, urging me to come with her. Azra didn't make a move, but I could see the fury in his eyes. His jaw clenched and his muscles strained uselessly. I thought that he was trying not to chase after me.

"Orion!" he shouted, "You need to be careful."

"Don't worry," Stella called out to Azra. "I promise to bring him back safe and sound."

My uncle and I glared at each other.

Stella and I climbed into trusty, rusty Spike, the tension from the awkward meeting of my uncle still hanging between us.

"Your uncle really is a piece of work. I thought you were exaggerating when you said he was crazy."

"I really wish I was," I said. As she started up the car,

the stereo came on full blast. "Is this Deftones?"

She nodded as she pulled out of the parking space. "Yeah."

"They are amazing live," I told her. "Have you ever had a chance to see them?"

Once we were out of the parking garage, carrying the conversation was easier. The tension had slipped away. The small talk flowed so smoothly that I took hold of her free hand and held it the entire trip, savoring the sensation where our skin touched.

Chapter Nineteen

Nestled at the edge of the Los Angeles basin resided the J. Paul Getty Museum. Due to Stella's expert maneuvering through the L.A. traffic, we arrived sooner than I thought we would. There was no time to even broach the subject of the prophecy or what I really was. What the small talk did do for us was to bury the awkwardness of Uncle Azra's introduction. In no time, we were back to flirting and joking around as though none if it had ever happened.

I paid for parking, which earned me a playful scowl and a threat of a souvenir. We got out of Spike and made our way out of the cavernous parking garage hand in hand and in relaxed silence. Holding her hand in mine reminded me of holding my new celestial blade; the energy wasn't overwhelming, but enhancing, almost energizing.

"What are you thinking about?" Stella asked, breaking me out of my thoughts. Her head tilted to the side and a curious expression graced her features.

A clean, white domed canopy shaded us from the sun. Uniformed employees monitored the flow of people coming through the elevator. We mingled among them, waiting for the tram that would take us to the museum.

I wasn't about to tell her how wonderful her hand felt, so I said, "This would be an awesome place to skate." I pointed to the gently sloping walkways and the yards and yards of metal railing.

"I suppose so," she agreed eyeing the features I pointed out. "But not for me and my long board. You and my cousins would get along well. They love to skate too."

"Yeah?" I asked, intrigued. "Are these the same

cousins that visited you?" The tram pulled up to the loading area on its electric track. Doors opened, letting people off.

As we meandered into the line that would allow us to board the tram, she said, "They're living with us now."

The doors on our side whooshed open and we were piled in with a group of other people who claimed seats where they could. Stella and I sat nearest the door with our backs to the opening.

"You don't seem too happy about that," I observed.

"It's not that I'm unhappy," she hedged. "They're just annoying."

"I'm sure it's not that bad," I consoled. Her eyebrow rose skeptically.

The tram lurched forward. Stella reached out and grabbed my arm to steady herself. I smiled at her and captured it underneath my own.

She blushed, but moved her hand so that we were palm to palm. "Well, the boys are my second cousins. They can be kinda fun when they aren't being stupid." She shook her head. "And Aurelia is nice enough. I think under different circumstances we could be friends. It's their mother, Donatella, who I have the problem with." She heaved a sigh and looked over her shoulder and out the window.

I followed her gaze and watched as the city of Los Angeles spread out before us. I was about to ask why she had such a problem with her cousin, but she spoke first, changing the subject.

"I miss the city," she told me. "Look, you can see the port from here." She extended her finger to point past the skyscrapers of downtown and the clustered mix of residential and industrial buildings at the distant hazy ocean. Her voice took on a wistful sound, "I love this view. Isn't it beautiful?"

"It is," I allowed. But instead of looking out at the scenery, I kept my gaze steadied on her. Her face turned to me and I locked eyes with her. "Do you know what's even more beautiful?"

Her answer was an almost imperceptible shake of her head.

I leaned in closer, so that we were cheek to cheek. The wisps of her hair tickled my skin and her breathing, rhythmically in and out, filled my ears. It was nothing short of hypnotic. Feeling like I was falling under some spell, I whispered in her ear, "You are the most beautiful creature I have ever seen."

A soft giggle and a squeeze of my hand was her response. "You're sweet. Cheesy, but sweet."

The tram slowed. I righted myself in my seat, still watching Stella's face. The quirk of a smile was back as she bit her lip and I could see the red flush on her skin. Then the tram rolled to a stop. The doors whooshed open once again and everyone headed out. Stella and I reluctantly stood, still clasping each other's hands.

There was a large open area with a gigantic metal sculpture made out of wires set before the tram docking station. I gazed up at it, squinting against the sunlight.

"Come on." Stella pulled me past the statue and towards the steps leading up to the museum entranceway. The travertine blocks that the place was made out of looked like a cross between white marble and a pale coral. There were fossilized leaves and shells in the surfaces of the floors and walls. Together, Stella and I went through the glass doorway.

As I looked around, impressed by the hanging art above us, Stella told me, "The paintings are up there." She pointed towards the upper level and headed confidently for a spiral staircase

"Why are we going to the paintings?" I asked, following her.

The stairs led us outside to an open-aired walkway overlooking the courtyard. People with cameras and maps milled below between strategically placed trees and benches.

"The assignment my French teacher gave us was to

research a piece of French art. It is a cultural background thing. The piece I want to do my report on is a painting. Plus, what a better excuse to come to the Getty with you than a school assignment."

"You didn't need an excuse to bring me here."

She laughed. "Sure, sure. Because most guys would want to be dragged to an art museum."

"Well, I'm here aren't I?"

"Yeah, only because you had something important to talk to me about. What is it, by the way?"

Well, I'm the son of two angels and I'm supposed to bring the end of the war between Heaven and Hell. Wanna help me with that? The words stuck in my throat with how ridiculous they sounded. I lost my courage. "Not yet. Let's see this painting first."

The art displayed in the North Pavilion was of a religious nature. There were medieval depictions of the saints, Jesus, Mary, even the Devil. Stella was quiet as we wandered through the rooms.

"What's wrong?" I teased gently as we stopped to contemplate a large rendition of the Crucifixion. "You don't like your men well-hung?" I bit my tongue as soon as the words left my mouth. Shit. Why had I said that? What was wrong with me?

She made a loud noise that was somewhere between choking and laughter that caused the docent assigned to the room to glare at us in warning. She looked at me with a sort of horrified yet amused expression. "That's awful," she rasped.

At least she hadn't just walked away from me in disgust. Eager to escape my ill-timed humor, I prodded her along and said, "Let's go."

We left the religious art section and passed through an enclosed breezeway. There was a small open terrace with a spectacular view of the city below and the surrounding hills. We pushed through another door and entered the East Pavilion where the paintings were of the neoclassical genre.

"What piece are you doing for your report?" I asked, peering at the displays. We passed by them quickly. She obviously knew exactly where she was going. I wondered how often she came here.

"It's a piece by Jacques Louis David. I fell in love with it a couple of years ago."

"Oh? Why is that?"

"You have to see it to understand." Stella slowed our pace to a crawl until we eventually stopped. She rummaged through her bag as she made her way to a painting set in an ostentatious gilt frame. From the depths of her purse, she pulled out a sleek silver camera. Aiming it at the canvas in front of her, she took several pictures in rapid succession. I took the time to reflect on the painting while Stella was gathering her information.

The composition was beautiful. The scene depicted a girl clinging to a boy with her head on his shoulder. Her hands were clasped around his neck in a sad embrace. The boy gazed at his audience with a resolute expression. His hand rested on the girl's knee and his other hand held a spear. A hunting dog stared at the boy with impatience.

Only half of the girl's face was visible against the youth's shoulder. From her closed eyes and the slight frown upon her lips, her stance was sorrowful and of one who knows the embrace would be the last one. Resignation and sadness emanated from her.

Stella came to stand at my side and turned her attention to the canvas as well. "It's called 'The Farewell of Telemachus and Eucharis'. Have you heard the story?"

It sounded familiar, but I wasn't sure if I remembered what happened correctly. "Telemachus was Odysseus' son in the Odyssey. He went searching for his father. But I'm not familiar with Eucharis. I don't think she's in Greek mythology."

"No, she isn't," Stella agreed. We sat on the cushioned bench in front of the painting, allowing the other guests roam past us with their slow gait. She put the camera back into her bag as she spoke. "You see, the story that this painting is based off of is actually a French novel called *Les Adventures de Telemaque.* In it, Telemachus is shipwrecked on Calypso's island. Eucharis is one of her attendants and he falls deeply in love with her. The problem is that Telemachus is duty-bound to find his father, so he has to leave her."

I looked at the painting again, this time seeing the scene completely. "She knows he isn't coming back, doesn't she?"

Stella nodded. "He has to fulfill his destiny. There's a fine balance between love and duty. It's a line not easily walked. Sometimes you have to realize that just because you feel for someone it doesn't mean they're who you are meant to be with." The sadness in her voice made my heart ache. All I wanted was to make her smile again.

I urged her up off the bench. "Come on. Wanna go play in the kids' area? There should be one around here, right?" I put on my goofiest Azra-esque smile.

It had the desired effect; she laughed, her embarrassment melting away as I tugged her out of the East Pavilion and down a flight of steps and into the central courtyard. To the left was a fountain with large marble boulders sticking out of the water like miniature mountains. Around the fountain were shallow pools with travertine stepping stones down the center.

In the spirit of wanting to hear her laugh again, I decided to do something stupid. I walked over to the pool and hopped onto the ledge surrounding the water. I practiced my balance on the very edge of the concrete as I heard Stella draw in a sharp breath, "What are you doing up there?"

"Balancing," I replied. Then, to impress her, I leaped to one of the boulders in the center of the fountain. Water bubbled at me from one of the jets nestled beside the rock. The sound of the water slapping against the stone was loud enough to muffle Stella's gasp. I grinned and kicked my legs up so I was supported on the slippery surface only by my hands.

"You're crazy," she called.

Other people started to gather around and watch my balancing act. Stella covered her mouth and glanced around. I could tell she was starting to get embarrassed, so I bent my elbows and pushed off, landing precariously on the ledge I had started on, wobbling a bit. I regained my stability after a moment and then hopped onto solid ground. There was sporadic applause for my trick as people started moving on.

Her laughter made me grin. The sound of it was like music and I longed to hear more of the melody.

"You're insane," she repeated, but she linked her arm in mine and I knew I was forgiven for the embarrassment. "Come on, the kids' area is over here. That's where you wanted to go, right?"

"Right," I affirmed.

It was a small maze of a room designed to let imaginations take over as they learned about the art that could be found in the museum. Exploring the kids' section was fun. There were magnets you could arrange on a giant picture of the city, a giant lighted white board that was overlaid with illuminated script with spaces you could write your own messages.

There was even a replica of a bed that was located down in the decorative arts exhibit. It was done in powder blues and its head and footboard supported a towering canopy that was accented with white ostrich feathers. The replica in the kids section was shortened to fit in between a couple of walls and did not have the canopy. What it did have, however was a mess of children's books.

Giggling, Stella climbed in and I followed, getting as close to her as I could. I was too tall for it, so I had to bend my knees up to sit sideways against the roll of pillows. She picked up a book and started leafing through the pages. I snatched the book away from her and held it up high.

"Hey!" she protested. "Give that back!" She reached for it, but I angled it away from her. Soon, she was using my shoulder as leverage to try to get the book from my hands. The closeness to her was electrifying and the prickly sensation was a consistent low humming in the background of my thoughts. Playfully, I shifted my shoulder out from underneath her hand. That caused her to lose her balance and to tumble down on me in a heap. We were both laughing.

Her face was inches away from mine as we quieted. Tension filled the air, urging me to do something reckless and yet instinctual. I swept a strand of her hair away from her face and hooked it behind her ear. Ever so slowly, I edged forward, giving her plenty of time and opportunity to turn away if she wanted to. She stayed where she was. When we were less than an inch apart, she came forward and our lips met.

The kiss was long and lingering. The tip of her tongue found mine and they danced as the electrifying sensation intensified. My hands, as though they had a mind of their own, roamed over the skin on her arms. The heat between us was incredible. It was as though we had caught fire.

Unbelievably, we separated. Her eyes locked onto mine and I saw the same electrified feeling reflected in her that was inside of me. Her heartbeat pounded in her chest as she lay against me. As I pulled her close to kiss her again, the sound of giggling made our heads turn.

At the edge of the bed were a group of girls, about eight or nine years old, smiling widely at us and whispering to each other behind their hands.

Stella blushed scarlet and immediately backed away from me and climbed out of the display. I followed her, sticking my tongue out at the girls. This caused them to burst into a fresh fit of giggles

"I'm sorry," Stella said when I caught up with her outside. "That was. . ."

My lips interrupted the apology on her lips and my arms drew her closer. My fingers trailed down her spine until I gripped her waist pulling her against me. She kissed me back, her fingers reaching up and threading themselves through my hair. The soft pressure of her fingernails grazing my scalp sent shivers through me. No kiss in the world would ever stand up to it again, as long as I lived.

Reluctantly, we separated, gazing into each other's eyes and pressing our bodies close. As much as I didn't want the moment to end, I had made her a promise and now I had enough courage to follow through with it.

"Let's go to the garden," I suggested, letting her go. "It's time to tell you about me."

Brushing her hair behind her ear, she walked quietly by my side as we circled around the courtyard to the sloping lawns. We chose a spot that overlooked the waterfall into the garden maze that was planted in the center of a large circular pool. Above us, a terrace full of people enjoyed dinner in the café.

We settled onto a comfortable patch of grass, each of us facing the other with a shyness that was almost painful.

Stella began. "What did you want to tell me?"

I squeezed her hand, summoning all of my courage. "I've been looking for a very long time for someone who could help me. See, I'm supposed to save the world and I think you are the person who is going to help me do it."

The confusion in her face made me waiver. Was I doing the right thing? Well, it was too late to stop now. "I—I'm something that shouldn't even exist."

The lines in her brow deepened.

I searched for a different way to explain. "Remember what you said about angels the other night? You know, the real ones, without the halos?"

She remained quiet, but some of the confusion left her face.

"Well, I am one. Or rather, my parents were. It's hard to explain. I'm the only angel in existence who has been born."

Stella shifted her eyes to the ground. I wasn't sure if that was a good thing or a bad thing, so I blundered onwards. "The war between Heaven and Hell you described is real. I'm supposed to be the one who will stop the war. The prophecy states that I need to find a human to help me and I think that it's you." I held my breath, waiting for her reaction.

The confused look was completely gone. It had been replaced with a carefully neutral mask. I couldn't tell what she was thinking and I feared the worst. Her silence scared me more than a fight with both a Fallen One and one of the Heavenly Host combined. Everything was riding on her reaction to this confession.

Silently, she extracted her hand from mine and my heart began to sink. This was a mistake.

I watched mutely as she reached into her purse and pulled out a small silken drawstring bag. She wasn't running, she wasn't screaming that I was insane. That was a good thing, right? While her lack of a reaction encouraged me, it terrified me at the same time. Her face was drawn tight with concentration. "I know what you are. I've known for some time now."

"What?" I couldn't believe what I was hearing. "What do you mean you knew?"

"I've been looking for you too. It has to do with this," she said as she pulled open the dark blue cords.

I focused on the bag in her hand. There was a subtle glow about it. Something unworldly. It was the same sort of glow that the celestial blades had, except slightly different; I couldn't take my eyes away from it.

"This has been passed down through my family for generations. It isn't just a mirror," she explained, keeping her eyes cast downward.

I didn't know what to think. She had the mirror. The same mirror Ascher was looking for. I don't know how I knew, but I did, without a doubt. The power that emanated from it was astounding. It practically screamed "danger" now that I was paying attention.

"I know what it is," I croaked. Out of the corner of my eye I noticed a man break away from the café crowd. I didn't pay that much attention to him at the time; I was too engrossed in what Stella was about to say next.

That turned out to be a mistake.

When he haltingly shuffled close enough to us, his movements became more purposeful. Suddenly, he knocked me to the side and snatched at the hood of Stella's sweatshirt. He yanked her to her feet, grasping for the mirror. "Give it to me now!" he demanded.

Stella had the presence of mind to stuff the mirror into her pocket as she screamed. Once the mirror was out of sight and secure in her pocket, she started kicking and hitting as hard as she could.

I leapt to my feet and charged the man, intent on getting Stella away from him. The aches and pains in my body were now nonexistent. Adrenaline and that strange fury swirled inside of me, giving me the energy I needed to fight. I seized his arms and pried his fingers off of her. I was so enraged that the loud snap of his arms dislocating barely registered in my mind.

Even with dislocated limbs, the man was undeterred. It was as though he hadn't felt a thing as he continued to struggle. He pitched himself forward, knocking me off balance. Staying on his feet with his useless arms hanging at his sides, he stomped after Stella who backed out of the way the moment she had been released. The way he moved, the ignoring of the pain, the dull look in his eyes. It was just how Ascher described an influenced human. But who was controlling him and why would someone do that?

I chased after the human, tackling him to the ground just inches from Stella's feet. I didn't hesitate even for a second before I started whaling on him, my fury completely unchecked. Red washed my vision. All I felt was wrath and the need to protect Stella so intensely that nothing else mattered. This was what I was meant to do: protect her to the point of death. His or my own. It didn't matter which so long as she was safe.

"Please, stop," the man moaned. His pleading was wasted on me. He was being controlled. His begging could have been a trick.

A hand on my shoulder made me swing around, growling at whoever dared to touch me.

Stella's terrified eyes brought me back to myself. The red faded from my vision at the sight of her. "Orion," she said my name, my real name. The fear in her voice brought me up short. She shouldn't fear me. She shouldn't ever fear anything. "Orion, stop this now."

Through the bestial creature I had become, I listened to her, this beautiful human girl who held my heart. I couldn't imagine disobeying her. She was the only one on Earth who could bring me out of my fury. Slowly, I became more cognizant of myself, controlling it again. I let go of the man who attacked her. He rolled over to his side and curled into a whimpering ball. Blood flowed from the cuts I had inflicted. His arms were twisted in the wrong directions. Bruises began to flower on his skin

I stood stupidly to the side and watched Stella take in the damage I had done. Needing something to calm me down, I reached for my bracelet only to remember that I no longer had it. The crowd I hadn't noticed before came into focus. A face in the back of the throng of people made my heart thump hard against my ribs. It was Ascher and he looked absolutely livid.

For one moment, our eyes locked and I saw the full measure of the Grigori. He was every bit as evil as I suspected and he was furious. I didn't have time to wonder what he was doing there or what his game really was because the museum security officers in blue blazers rushed to the scene. I left the man on the ground and ran away.

Stella ran away from the crowd as well. I followed her, narrowly dodging the security officers in the confusion. My injured leg made me slower than I normally was. Stella made it to the tram just as the doors closed. I was far enough behind that I didn't have a chance of catching her.

"Stella!" I yelled. She stared at me through the window, her eyes big and terrified. She was visibly shaking and tears stained her cheeks.

The tram rolled out of sight, taking not only my only hope at fulfilling the prophecy, but my heart with it.

Chapter Twenty

I didn't have time to stand there and stare after Stella. Security guards burst through the main doors of the museum and were heading straight for me. I did the only thing I could think of: I ran.

Even with my bum leg I had a decent enough head start and was able to easily keep ahead of them. Shouts followed me into the steep downhill brush that surrounded the tram route.

There wasn't much time until the real cops would show up. The human I attacked was hurt pretty badly. An ambulance was probably on the way as well. The man had been controlled by Ascher, I was sure of it. All of the signs indicated that's what happened. There wasn't much else I could have done. At least that is what I tried to convince myself.

The sound of the guards traipsing through the brush grew louder. They were close.

The decision that I made then was probably one of the more stupid things in my life, but my choices were limited. Settling into a particularly thick patch of foliage and hoping no one could see me, I prepared for something I hadn't done by myself in centuries. I was going to teleport out of there.

As I said before, teleporting isn't the best of ideas for me. The process magnified my psychic presence exponentially. Even if I still had my protective bracelet, any angelic being within two hundred miles would be able to find me in a matter of seconds. That was why I only transported with Azra and even then it only happened in emergencies.

The crunch of shoes over the rough gravel told me if

I was going through with this crazy idea, then I'd better hurry. I closed my eyes and focused on Stella, tuning everything else out as best as I could. My heart raced.

A fluttering sensation began in my stomach and moved throughout my limbs as it intensified. I didn't dare open my eyes for fear of breaking my concentration. Suddenly, I was floating. The advancing security guards were no longer a concern; nothing concerned me. I marveled at the sheer freedom not only of my mind, but also of my body. This was so much different than travelling with Azra. For a terrifying moment, I felt myself start to disperse in a million different directions. Feeling only a muted tremor of panic, I drew myself together again, picturing where I wanted to end up. It took a tremendous amount of effort to keep my mind trained on Stella. After what seemed like an eternity, the fluttering feeling in my stomach solidified, creating a center point for the rest of me to rally around.

The first physical sense to return as I coalesced at my destination was my hearing. Even before I could see where I was, a shrill shriek assaulted my ears. My body, still fuzzy with the apparition, slammed against something hard. The squeal of tires and blaring horns made it obvious that I was in a car.

"What the hell? Ryan? What are you doing? Where the hell did you come from?" Stella's voice screamed. I blinked her into focus. She was stunning in her rage. The scowl she wore would have withered a lesser person. The car swerved, narrowly missing a minivan in the next lane. Without thinking, I grabbed for the wheel, aiming the car back into safety. Furious, Stella smacked my hands away from the wheel. She returned her attention to the road and straightened the car's trajectory.

"How the hell did you get here?" She repeated once the car was back under control. The tone of her voice made me wince.

"I'm sorry about what happened back there," I said, doing my best to stop the nauseated feeling that washed over me. "I lost control and I shouldn't have let it happen. I should have been able to keep calm."

"You almost killed that man!" Stella exclaimed.

Shame colored my face. "I'm sorry. Look, if it helps, that man was being controlled by another angel. I had to do something protect you."

As if punctuating my point, a loud THUMP sounded above us. Rust particles rained down from Spike's roof. Stella let out curses at the top of her lungs and fought to control the vehicle.

Glass shattered and arms reached through the hole in the window next to me, grasping blindly. At the sight of those limbs reaching for me, panic bloomed in my chest. The aura I saw around those arms was the metallic sheen of a Heavenly Host. They had found me after my little teleportation stunt, even with the ward burned into my skin. My uncle wasn't kidding when he said he was terrible at casting wards.

I shouted wordlessly, doing my best to fend off the attacker. The arms that found their way through the broken windows managed to grab hold of my shirt. I was lifted out of my seat.

Abruptly, the car jerked from side to side. Tires squealed even louder and more horns sounded. Stella was trying to shake them off the car. I fought against the iron grip that held me. The angel adjusted to get his hands around my throat. My vision blurred and breath became shortened and strained.

Beyond the pain, I heard Stella begin chanting in a strong, confident tone. I couldn't make out the words— they flowed together almost lyrically, making them difficult to distinguish.

I had to do something, anything. Without really thinking it through, I focused what energy I could into my hands. I was still exhausted from the teleportation, but the thought of what the Host would do to me if I just gave up drove me to push past my limits.

My hands became warm as more and more energy

was forced into the digits. Uttering a strangled, guttural cry, I placed my hands on the arm that held me. The energy sizzled as I let it loose. There was a shout from the roof and the hand released me, disappearing through the car window once again.

"Are you alright?" I wheezed at Stella.

A sheen of sweat had developed on her forehead. Her mouth never stopped moving with her low chant rolling off her lips in a steady stream of syllables.

"Stella?" I reached over to make sure she wasn't hurt, but she waved me off.

A few more thuds on the roof made rust fall like snow onto us. Stella jerked the wheel to the right, abruptly taking the nearest exit. The angel on the roof must have lost his balance or something. There was a startled cry and the sound of wings unfurling.

Stella's chanting increased in volume and intensity. I didn't know what she was doing or why. At last, she pronounced the last word and settled into an angry silence. As we exited the freeway, I turned to watch out the back window to see how far away the angel was. There was nothing.

"Where did he go?"

Stella didn't answer me. Instead, she pulled into a half empty parking lot and turned off the engine.

The alarm at standing still when I should be running for my life crept into my voice. "What are you doing? We have to keep moving."

"They won't be able to find us." I was about to argue, but Stella held up her hand, effectively silencing me. She looked angry, but there was something else to it, a sort of distraction in her eyes. When she spoke, it was low and serious. "I'm giving you one chance. Explain yourself. What happened back there? How the hell did you end up in my car, and what just attacked us?"

I blew out a breath I didn't know I had been holding in. "I know this is hard to believe. The man that attacked you, he was being controlled by another angel. If the angel is who I think it is, then he was after your mirror. At least that's the only thing that makes sense right now. I had to do all of that to save you."

The severe frown she wore softened at the edges. "What just attacked us, Ryan?"

I met her gaze as steadily as I could, even as I turned the explanation over in my mouth. The words even tasted crazy. Still, it had to be said. "Remember when I told you my parents were both angels? Well, that's a big deal in the angelic community. In their opinion, I shouldn't exist. What just attacked us was an angel, one of the Heavenly Host in fact. They don't like me any more than the Fallen Ones."

"So in order to protect me, you decided to appear out of thin air, scare the living shit out of me, and lead a homicidal angel straight for my car?" Her volume rose with each syllable and a red flush colored her cheeks.

I winced. "I'm sorry. I didn't mean to. It's just . . . now that I've found you I don't want to lose you."

This seemed to bring her up short because I heard an intake of breath as though she were about to start yelling again. Not that I didn't deserve it. Hindsight, they say, is twenty-twenty. Right about then, it hit me how much danger I had put her in.

Something still wasn't right, though. The Heavenly Host didn't just give up. We should have been swarmed by now. Not that I wanted to be fighting for my life, but it was certainly strange that I wasn't right then.

Stella's voice broke through my concern. "It seems I also owe you an explanation."

"What?"

Worry creased her brows as she stared at the dashboard, deep in thought. My question hung in the air, unanswered. Finally, she blinked and the creases were gone. It was as though she made up her mind about something. Starting the car and revving the engine to life, we pulled out of the parking lot and made our way back to the freeway.

As we merged into traffic, I began asking questions. "What do you know about the prophecy? Where did you get the mirror? How did you know that I am an angel?"

She cast me an annoyed look. "I told you I owed you an explanation, not that I wanted to play twenty questions. I'm trying to concentrate. If this shield drops then that angel will be able to find us again."

"What are you talking about? What shield?"

"It's what I tried to tell you before. I can't explain right now. I just need you to trust me for a bit, okay? Once we get there, I'll explain everything."

"Where are we going?" I asked. I wasn't at all sure what was happening. My heart thudded in my chest and my eyes kept sneaking glances out of the windows. "I have to know, Stella. Are you really the one that will help me end the Angelic War? I don't want to get you involved if you aren't."

I was serious when I said it, but her reaction was a loud burst of laughter with a smidgeon hysteria.

Deftly maneuvering the rusting vehicle through the traffic, Stella said, "Ryan, It's a little late if you don't want me involved."

The red flush of chagrin colored my face. She was right. "You still didn't answer my questions," I pointed out in an attempt to change the subject.

The return of the stern, almost angry set of her mouth and the certain slant to her eyes made me drop the subject. My own anger took hold in response. It took all I had to keep my mouth shut; Stella's rigid posture made it clear she wouldn't answer anything until she was ready, regardless of how angry I got.

Settling into my seat, I stared out of the window. Now our lives weren't in danger, the adrenaline left and the exhaustion caught up with me. We had travelled only a few miles in awkward silence before the abrupt jangling of my phone ringing made me jump. I fished it out of my pocket. It was Uncle Azra. He had probably sensed my sudden transport.

I didn't really want to answer, but because of the tension in the car and Stella's lack of conversation, I chose to pick up the phone.

In usual Azra fashion, he started screaming before I could even say hello.

"Are you alright? What's going on? I FELT you transport! Are you safe? Where are you?"

His yelling grated on my nerves and I had to hold the phone away from my ear. "I'm fine, I promise. I'm—"

"What the hell were you thinking? You aren't supposed to be doing stuff like that! Haven't I told you how dangerous that is?"

Stella raised her eyebrows at the sound of Azra's voice, but her gaze never wavered from the road ahead. It made me realize that I would prefer silence. This wasn't a conversation I wanted to have with her listening in. "I'll call you later, Uncle Az." I hung up as he drew in a loud breath. The silence reigned again.

"So that sudden appearance you did, I gather you aren't supposed to do that either?" Stella ventured. Her tone conveyed curiosity and something else that I couldn't quite define.

It seemed unfair that she could ask questions, but refuse to answer mine. My response to her was more clipped than it should have been. "Yes."

"Why is that?"

"I told you. When I do, the other angels—both the Heavenly Host and the Fallen Ones—can find me. I've kinda got a price on my head."

Stella frowned. "Because you shouldn't exist?"

"Something like that."

My phone sounded again and I turned it off. I didn't have the time or the patience for Uncle Azra right then.

Stella bit her lip and didn't ask any more questions. After fifteen minutes of scanning the skies through the window, it was confirmed that we had lost whatever Heavenly Host I had attracted with my unauthorized apparition.

As I settled back into the seat, I tried to quiet the clamoring of my thoughts.

"I can't believe you are bringing him home. Your grandmother is not going to be happy about this." It was the Brooklyn accented voice. I whipped my head around, expecting to see someone in the back seat. There was nothing. But what was strange was that, for once, the voice wasn't talking to me. Which meant that it couldn't be in my head.

"Did you hear that?" I asked Stella.

The frown she wore deepened and when she spoke, it wasn't at me. "Max, tell her I am almost home. We need to talk to her."

The voice didn't respond, and all I could assume was that it went to do as Stella said. With nothing but silence reigning between us, I demanded answers again. "Who are you talking to? Who is Max? What in the hell is going on here?"

Like with all of my previous questions, she didn't bother to reply and I was left to make my own connections. If the voice was, in fact, associated to Stella, did it mean that whatever it was had been spying on me? Was that how Stella knew that I was an angel? Whenever the voice had been around, I hadn't sensed anything out of the ordinary. If it was some sort of spirit, I should have felt something. So what was it?

We took the next exit off of the freeway and cruised into a well lived-in suburb. A few turns later, Spike was parked along the curb of a ranch style house. The driveway was large enough to fit a pop-up camper, an old suburban and a truck plastered in several skate company stickers.

A garage poked sideways out into the front yard, making the patchy grass mound seem small in comparison to the neighbors' yard. The front door was almost hidden within a small covered porch.

Stella got out of the car and I followed her, squinting at the neighborhood. Nothing stood out as an immediate danger, but something prickled at my skin nonetheless. It was an odd sensation, whatever it was; not necessarily wrong, but not quite right either.

"Wait here," Stella said. I stopped at the edge of the sparse lawn as she advanced to the front door. Different lamps and candle holders hung from the peeling eaves of the aged roof around the porch, flickering in anticipation of the coming night. A little flower bed bloomed next to the concrete steps giving bright splashes of red and purple against the darkness of the soil and the pale gray of the concrete. Along the wall that hid the porch and most of the outer walls, were thick vines of ivy. There must have been another type of plant intermingled with the ivy, because yellow buds were interspersed throughout the green. Even in the dead of winter, the blossoms and leaves flourished.

The odd sensation intensified causing an almost surreal perception of my surroundings.

Stella was gone only a few moments, but I was already itching to leave. This place, whatever it was, made me uncomfortable. I didn't like the feeling of whatever altered state this was.

The screen door jangled open just as I made the decision to go. Stella held the mesh and wire open for a slow moving, stooped figure. She beckoned to me and, even though I was ready to run in the opposite direction, my feet propelled me forward. I reached the mailbox at the edge of the porch and halted, not wanting to go any further towards the house.

I could hear male voices laughing and slinging good natured insults at each other coming from inside the house. I raised my eyes first to Stella, then the figure in the doorway.

"Hello, Ryan." In the shadows, I could barely make out a benign smile on a withered face.

My mouth hung open in complete surprise as I blinked in confusion. What was she doing here? My lips formed the name in a whisper. "Sylvia?"

The elderly woman brought her bony finger to my chest and poked me with more strength than she appeared to possess. "You never came to supper the other night."

"You two know each other?" Stella sounded as surprised as I felt.

The old woman answered, "Yes. This is the young man I met at church last Sunday."

Instantly, I felt like an idiot. How had I not realized that Sylvia was Stella's grandmother? The similarities between them were striking now that I saw them standing side by side.

Sylvia shuffled around, intending to return to the dark depths of the house and she called out, "Come in, come in. Supper is almost ready. Better late than never, I suppose."

"No. I need answers now, before I go another step." I crossed my arms over my chest, determined to get the answers I sought.

Sylvia and her granddaughter stared at me, the elder one with an amused expression and the younger with anger.

The old woman spoke first. "I understand there are many things you want to know, Ryan. But these answers will be revealed in their own time. Now is the time for supper. You shall know all there is to know afterwards."

I stayed where I was, unmoved by her promise. "There's no time for that, Sylvia. There are others after me that could find me at any moment."

My argument meant nothing to the woman. "You are protected here. Now, stop being so stubborn and come eat." With that said, Sylvia turned back to the entrance of the house.

Stella dutifully held the door open for her grandmother once again, but all the while she glared at me, as though re-evaluating what she saw. When I didn't move, she hissed, "Come on, Ryan." She gestured for me to hurry up.

As soon as I crossed the threshold, the pricking sense of danger evaporated, but the aggravation remained. I paused in the dark, still not sure if I wanted to go on. The door shut with a harsh clang and Stella gave me a nudge forward.

"We aren't going to bite." She slid past me in the narrow hall that led to a bright room. I followed, feeling awkward and more than a little perturbed. When I reached the living room, Stella gestured to the blanket covered couch that was already occupied by two boys playing video games. They looked to be a few years older than she was.

"Hey guys, we have a guest. This is Ryan. Ryan, this is Nathan and Justin," Stella said. It didn't make any difference to them; they kept on playing without so much as blinking at me. She shrugged and left me standing off to the side of the TV. I wasn't sure if I should sit, so I remained on my feet and observed Nathan and Justin— Stella's skater cousins, no doubt. They were identical twins. Each had a dusky glow to their skin that only came from being out in the California sun every day. Thick strips of multicolored hair went down the center of their heads. The sides were shaved close enough to see their scalps, but not bare enough to miss that their original hair color was a shade or two lighter than their brown eyes.

It took me a few minutes, but soon I was able to discern the difference in them. The one with the Rancid shirt had more rounded cheeks while his brother had wider set eyes. It also helped that their Mohawks were dyed different colors. Rancid had red and blue stripes while Authority Zero had electric green with black roots and tips. The only problem was that I wasn't sure which one was Nathan and which one was Justin. I doubted they would tell me even if I did ask.

They paid me no attention whatsoever. As unobtrusively as I could, I chanced a look around the room. The couch where the twins sat was directly across from the large entertainment center. Just left of that was a decent sized brick fireplace.

A colorful woven rug rested on top of tan-colored carpet. When I looked to the right I was confronted with small piano complete with music on its stand and a plain looking bench underneath it. Like most of the surfaces in the room, the piano held picture frames and a variety of small knick-knacks.

I took in all of these details to distract me from the questions I couldn't ask yet. The whole charade of dinner felt ridiculous to me. I would have rather spent the time finding out what Stella's involvement with the prophecy really was. I worried that at any moment, a whole gaggle of Heavenly Host would pound through that door. I really had been stupid to teleport like I had, even with the supposed protection of Uncle Azra's ward.

"Boys, where is Aurelia? Supper is ready," a woman interjected as she came out of the kitchen. Sylvia was with her, but Stella wasn't. As they stood side by side, I could compare the angle of the chin, the highness of the forehead, the prominent nose. The younger woman had the same dusky coloring with the exception of the deep red hair that cascaded over her shoulders. I wondered if she knew about what was going on as well since both Stella and Sylvia seemed to know more than I did.

The twin with the Authority Zero shirt didn't take his eyes off the game as he mumbled, "She's probably in her room."

"I'm right here," a girl said from behind me. I twisted to find a thin girl with blonde hair woven into two braids that ended just at her shoulders. She had piercing blue-gray eyes that locked onto me in a serious stare.

Someone grabbed my hand, pulling me forward. I whipped my head around to see who it was. Stella had hold of me. "I'll—"

Whatever she was about to say was cut off by a deafening popping noise and a bright flare of light in the center of the living room. The twins cried out, but I couldn't be sure if it was because of the sudden intrusion or the interruption of their game. Instantly, Stella's hand released mine and I stood alone, blinded and terrified. This was it; the Heavenly Host had found me. My first instinct was to run. Then it was to fight, but I had no weapon. I cursed myself for leaving my sword on my bed at the apartment.

Suddenly, the sound of chanting rose around me, creating a buzz that was almost palpable in the air. The hair rose on the back of my neck and the odd prickling sensation flooded back into me full force.

The brightness receded and the living room came back into focus. In the center of the room, surrounded by Stella and her family, was a force field that shimmered blue, green and yellow. Inside that force field was none other than my dear Uncle Azra.

Chapter Twenty-one

"Where is Orion, you sleazy sorceress? What have you done with him? If anything happened to him, you will be more than sorry!" Azra railed within the bubble of energy that contained him. Every time he hit the barrier, sparks flew around the contact point which made him jump away with a loud curse. The more he shouted and flailed about, it was obvious he couldn't see beyond the bubble.

"Let him out," I demanded. "It's my uncle."

"He attacked us. Why should we let him go?" The unnamed woman shot back. As the words left her lips, the blue in the force field waned. When she returned her complete attention back to the matter at hand, the blue surged back into the energy barrier. That's when I realized the women of the family controlled the trap.

Uncle Azra pulled out his celestial blade. He slashed it through the air and started threatening the room in general in a long-dead language. When the celestial blade hit the bubble, there was a tearing sound and small gaps appeared in the energy.

Sylvia's voice rang out, loud and clear. I could see her distorted figure through the bubble barrier that contained my uncle. "Stella, Aurelia, Donatella, don't break. Keep focused."

Stella was positioned with her hands lifted towards the force field in front of her. Beads of sweat made her skin glisten in the soft light of the energy. Her brows furrowed and she bit her lip in concentration.

The girl with the pigtails, was in a similar stance on the other side of the bubble. The older woman, Donatella apparently, grunted and put forth more energy than before. For a second, the blue energy threatened to overtake the green and yellow swirls, but at the last moment it faded back, muted. By the translucency of her colored energy, Donatella was tiring fast. It marked her as a weak link; easily taken out first.

My fists were balled at my sides as I considered how to get my uncle out of there.

"Nathan, make sure Ryan doesn't do anything foolish, now," Sylvia said, reading my thoughts.

Immediately and without question, the twin with the green mohawk moved closer, presumably for my own safety. He didn't try to grab hold of me yet.

"Stella, please. Just let him go. He isn't going to hurt anyone. The only reason he came here was because he thinks I'm in trouble."

The girl shifted her eyes to me for a split second. She was considering what I said.

Something passed between us—a sort of understanding. I needed her help with the prophecy and she needed mine. This standoff was a waste of time and it wasn't going to help either of us.

"Trust me," I pleaded.

She gave a barely perceptible nod of her head before her hands dropped to her sides. Suddenly, the green energy that formed the crux of the cage disappeared.

At once the whole structure wavered, blinking in and out of existence. With startled cries, Donatella and Aurelia dropped their hands too. It seemed that even working together, they weren't powerful enough to keep the barrier up without Stella.

Interesting.

Once the bubble of energy was gone, Azra acted immediately. He sprang towards me with a shout worthy of a fierce warrior on the battlefield. In the blink of an eye, he sent Nathan sprawling onto the floor and deflected the twin who rushed to help his brother. Uncle Azra crouched in front of me, ready to take down anyone else who dared come too close.

Donatella took an angry step forward only to be halted by Sylvia's abrupt order. The woman with the red hair looked as though she were ready to kill.

I had to hand it to Sylvia; she maintained her composure. Her face remained neutral if not inquisitive when she asked her granddaughter, "Stella, why have you put us at such risk?"

Azra stood up a bit straighter, though still at the ready. He grabbed hold of my wrist. "On my signal, we bail out of here, okay?" he murmured.

"No way," I whispered back. "I'm here for a reason. They can help me with the prophecy."

My uncle made a face, but he didn't contradict me. I knew that once we were out of here, though, there would be a fight between us for sure. He didn't want to expose any sort of division between us in front of an enemy.

Stella, meanwhile, had edged as close to me as she dared, separating herself from her family. "We aren't going to get anywhere acting like this. We need his help. Keeping his uncle trapped isn't the way we should go about it."

"His uncle invaded our home. He is armed and, from the looks of him, deranged and dangerous. We have every right to protect ourselves from outside threats," Donatella said. Even though Sylvia had commanded her not to, she was still ready to fight.

"Let's be clear, witch. I came only for him. If you hadn't coerced him here for your own nefarious reasons, I wouldn't be anywhere near your viper's den." Azra spat the words out contemptuously, but I knew him well enough to detect the timbre of fear in his voice.

"There is a simple answer to this," Sylvia interjected before anyone else could speak. "Ryan is here because we, I mean to say, Stella, can help him. As I understand, it is Ryan's choice whether or not to accept Stella's help. Do you agree that this is the situation, Mister Azra?"

My uncle scowled at the logic presented to him. To drive the point home, I muttered in ancient Greek,

"Remember how you said you were going to start trusting me?"

He responded in a whisper, "Yes, but I didn't think it would mean allowing you to put yourself in this sort of situation. Don't you know what these people are? They are witches. Powerful and dangerous witches."

"Does it really matter what they are if they have information on ending the war? Uncle Az, I can't keep running at the first sign of trouble. I'll never fulfill my destiny if you don't let me take some risks. Plus, they won't tell me anything with you waving your celestial blade around like a madman."

He glanced around the room, his lips puckered in thought. When he heaved a loud sigh, I knew I had convinced him. "Fine," he exhaled in English. "I'll trust you this time. But if you are not at the meeting spot in one hour, I am coming back here to get you and I will bring more than just my sword. Got it?"

I nodded, not wanting to press my luck. Uncle Azra gave a final, warning glare to the other occupants of the room. "If you so much as hurt his feelings, you will have to deal with me, got it?"

"I assure you, he will be perfectly safe. You have my word," Sylvia inclined her head to Azra.

He accepted the gesture with a nod of his own. "One hour," he reminded me before disappearing into thin air.

My eyes met Stella's as Donatella and Aurelia dashed over to inspect the twins for injury. Neither of the guys had more than a couple of bruises from how they landed. Once she was sure her boys were alright, Donatella rounded on Stella. "How dare you bring him here? How could you put us in that much danger without even a warning? What on earth were you thinking?"

Stella didn't flinch from her cousin's wrath, nor did she dignify it with a response. "Nona, are you ready? We are kind of on a time limit now."

Sylvia watched her granddaughter holding my hand with an unreadable expression. The old woman sighed. "I suppose supper will have to wait then, won't it? Donatella, you and the children go ahead and eat. Stella and I have some business to attend to with our guest."

The majestic bearing Sylvia had when facing my uncle melted away, leaving in its wake a tired, withered old woman. She shuffled her way to the narrow, dark hallway that led deeper into the house. Stella followed her grandmother, motioning for me to come along.

There was no telling what I was walking into, but I was duty-bound to follow the two women. There was a closed door at the end of the hall, but to the left of that were two additional doors that were open. I didn't have time to even peek into the open rooms before they steered me into the one room that had been closed off.

Heavy bookcases lined one of the walls. The shelves held a myriad of trinkets, books, candles, vials and crystals. There didn't appear to be any rhyme or reason to the order of it. Four straight-backed chairs with thick cushions were clustered around a lace-covered table. A heavy candlestick made out of wrought iron rested in the center of the round space. Plush carpeting softened my footfalls as I was ushered to a seat next to the lace-curtained window.

Peeking out through the glass, I could see a magnificent garden. Trees and vines managed to hide the distinctly suburban concrete wall that separated their backyard from their neighbors.

Amazed, I returned my attention to the room. Oil paintings lined the bare walls.

As we settled into our respective chairs— Stella beside me and her grandmother in front of me— Sylvia began to speak. "Ryan, do you understand what we are?"

"Witches." I answered, confirming my thoughts and Uncle Azra's analysis.

Stella peeked at me, her face pinched with apprehension. Did she think I would run screaming? I bit back a laugh. After everything had divulged to her and everything I had put her through this afternoon, she was worried I would run away because she was a witch?

"Yes," Sylvia answered. She kept her face neutrally curious, but I could tell that she was watching me carefully. "Does that frighten you?"

"Not at all," I answered truthfully. "What I want to know is who or what Max is and why he has been following me for the last few days."

Stella let out a sigh. I wasn't sure if it was from relief or resignation.

The old woman chuckled. "I am glad you do not share your uncle's superstitions. And you are very observant." She lifted her chin ever so slightly to address the room at large. "Max, would you please come out?"

Silence overtook the room. Then, ever so slightly, I felt the air shift, as though it were being stirred. In the corner across from the door, a shimmery figure appeared. He was short; the long, brown trench coat he wore almost touched the ground. His long, dark hair slicked back into a tail at the nape of his neck and was covered by a dark brown fedora with a tan band above the brim. He had the face of someone who could easily disappear in a crowd; nondescript features that more or less guaranteed anonymity.

"Max," Sylvia greeted him with a smile. "I believe you know Ryan?" She gestured towards me imperially. "Ryan, please meet Max."

The specter nodded briskly at me. "Hello. I suppose it is time we met officially."

I was dumbfounded. He looked like a ghost, but not one I that had ever experienced before. Usually I could feel their presence and they were rarely, if ever, this solid. The ghosts that I encountered were more ideas than actual substance. Max was nothing like any of that. There was absolutely no evidence that he existed, no trace of his energy patterns. Nothing. Everything: ghosts, humans, animals, plants, they have an energy signature, something that announces that they are here, that they exist. Max, for some reason, didn't. Trying to get a sense of him was like looking into a void.

"What the hell are you?" I blurted out. "Why have you been following me?"

Max blinked at me then rolled his eyes at Sylvia. "He's not the brightest halo in the bunch, is he?"

"Max," Sylvia chided with a slight chuckle. She addressed me in my indignation and explained, "Max is a ghost. He has been with our family for quite some time."

I wasn't sure if I bought that explanation. "Why can't I sense him? I can usually tell when there's a ghost skulking around."

"He has been part of our family for several years now. As part of our family, he enjoys all of the protection I and my coven can provide. As to why he was following you, I have to admit that was my fault. I was curious as to whom Stella was spending her time with. Then I discovered what you were. I don't think you realize how important you are to everything we have been working for. Naturally, I wanted to keep an eye on you. Max was kind enough to assist me with this."

"You know what I am? Stella, you've known all along?" I glanced back and forth between the two women, incredulously.

Stella laughed. "It's kind of obvious, Ryan."

I wasn't sure how to feel about that. How had they seen through my disguise? Well, when I still had my beads, that is. Was it because they were witches? What else did they know? I shifted uncomfortably in my seat, making the chair squeak.

Sylvia pressed on. "Now then. Are you ready to know your destiny?"

I gave a curt nod, casting a wary glance at the specter in the corner. He gave me a laconic smile and tilted his hat lower over his brow. His form shimmered and faded until he was no longer there. Well, he didn't appear to be, at least. I knew all too well that he could still be lurking around, listening to everything that transpired.

Stella remained beside me, quiet, yet alert. I had the

sudden urge to take her hand, but felt odd for wanting to. With all of these revelations about her and her family, there was too much I wasn't comfortable with.

Sylvia told me, "It is good that you are willing to face your fate so confidently. Not many do, especially with a fate as important as yours."

"You said you knew about the prophecy," I said, wishing she would get to the point.

Sylvia bowed her head. "Yes, I know it. 'An angel twice born within the realm of man. A Father's creation stands guard over the Divine hand. A human blessed with the Mother's gift. The catalyst of the healing of the rift. Together will bring forth the next stage. Summoning the start of the new Age. Return what was lost when the stars were formed. The family united that once was torn. Sacrifices made cannot be undone. End the war and three realms come one'."

I found myself moving my lips to the familiar words. Their meanings were still shrouded in mystery.

"Let me tell you a story," the woman began.

"I didn't come here for stories, Sylvia. I need you to tell me what you know about us angels, the war, and how to end it." My agitation earned me a stern look from Stella.

Sylvia laughed. "My dear, this story has everything to do with your prophecy and so much more. A long time ago, before my grandmother's grandmother's time, there lived a woman named Aradia. She was a very powerful Strega who taught the Old Ways in the height of the Church's influence. She was despised among the clergy, but very loved among her followers. There are many stories I could tell you about Aradia, but the most important thing you should know about is her vision.

"She told her followers about a child that would come after years and years of persecution that would bring an end to the Age of the Son."

My head tilted in question. "Age of the Son?" The phrase tickled my memory. Where had I heard that expression before?

Stella answered for her grandmother, "The Son is the son of God that is worshipped in this world. The Christians are a prime example of Son worship, though they certainly aren't the only ones. The Son has many different faces, like most deities. The Age of the Son is what we are in now, though His influence is waning."

I nodded, finally remembering Ascher's explanation of the ages. At least he hadn't lied about everything.

"The Son's diminishing influence on this world is a sure sign that His reign is coming to an end," Sylvia interjected. "The child Aradia spoke of will be the catalyst for the Age of the Daughter. She will bring about great changes in the world. The Daughter will create a new society that is truly equal among all men. She will end all wars with the rebirth of the old ways. The Daughter is the Witches' Messiah."

I shifted in my chair, making the old wood creak beneath me. "The Witches' Messiah." The idea was difficult to swallow for me. Even with my angelic background, my stance on religion had been more of a spectator. Even Uncle Azra didn't encourage religious participation, except for his recent attempt at punishment. "What does any of this have to do with my prophecy?"

"It's not just your prophecy," Stella said as reached into her pocket and drew out the blue drawstring bag with the mirror. My muscles tensed at the sight of it.

She placed it on the table in front of me as Sylvia asked, "Do you know what this is?"

I nodded, still thinking about everything that Ascher had told me. "That's the mirror that was stolen from Heaven. According to some, it's what caused the Fall. How did you get it?"

Sylvia removed the mirror from the bag. She turned it in her wrinkled hands, almost lovingly. The silver shone in the dim light. "It has been passed down in our family for countless generations. The legend is that the Goddess appeared to some of her worshippers. She spoke of a war

Kira Shay

that was brewing in Heaven and how it would be played out on Earth. She gave the object to my ancestors for safe keeping; a gift, if you will. She said that one day, the object would be needed to stop the war. One day, someone would come for the object who would be completely unique. He would be of this world, but also of Heaven. The Goddess charged my family with the protection of the object. They were to keep it safe throughout the generations until it was needed.

"She left only after giving my many times great grandmother, already a powerful enchantress, the knowledge and the power required to use and to protect the object. The enchantress was to be the guardian and would pass the object to her daughter or granddaughter who would give it to her own daughter and so on." Sylvia gave a partial smile to Stella as she set the mirror back on the table. Raising her eyes to meet mine, she said, "The power has been passed down from generation to generation just as the mirror has. It appears as though you have come for the mirror at last."

I sat quietly for a moment, allowing the information to sink in. "Okay, I get that the mirror needs to be returned to Heaven. I suppose I am the one who is supposed to do that. I understand that will probably stop the war. What I don't get is what the Age of the Daughter has to do with me."

The two Strega exchanged a meaningful glance. Stella spoke first, heading off whatever her grandmother was about to say. "You are looking for a human, right? A specific person that has been 'blessed with the Mother's gift' to help fulfill the prophecy? Well, that would be me."

I hadn't been expecting the confirmation to come so easily. I paused for a couple of heart beats, trying to figure out how to proceed. "Okay. So how are you going to help me? What is the next step?"

She glanced at her grandmother who nodded. "Go on. Tell him."

Stella took in a deep breath. "Nona believes that I am

destined to be the leader of the Age of the Daughter. She—
we— believe that if we can get the mirror returned to
Heaven where it belongs, then it will be revealed to me
what actions I need to do in order to become the Goddess
made flesh. That will end the war and the Age of the Son."

There was something she wasn't telling me, some
reservation she was holding back. If I hadn't been reeling
from all of the information that was just laid at my feet, I
would have pressed for more of an explanation. "Alright,"
I said, still sorting through everything they had laid at my
feet.

Stella let out a sigh of relief. "Then you'll help?"

"Of course. This is my destiny. We have to figure out
how to get this thing back to Heaven."

"There is just one more thing we need to check. We
want to be sure," Sylvia interjected.

"Oh, Nona, do we really have to do this? He's already
agreed to work with me."

Stella's grandmother frowned at her. "This is an
important decision. You must never assume your will is
the will of fate."

She reached over to one of the shelves behind her
and grabbed hold of a small purple bundle of velvet and
unwrapped the material in slow deliberate movements.
Once all of the fabric was out of the way, she set what
appeared to be a deck of cards on the lace table covering.

Murmuring, Sylvia placed her bony hands over the
deck. Energy swirled around us, breaking into the muted
atmosphere like colored dye injected into water. Tendrils
of power wrapped around the three of us. She plunked the
deck of what I now knew to be Tarot cards in front of me.

Sylvia watched me with a glimmer in her eye. "Cut
the deck, if you are brave enough to find out what is in
store for you."

Chapter Twenty-two

I shifted my gaze down to the cards in front of me. The energy coming off them was thick and bright. Holding my breath, I placed my fingers on the sides of the deck and lifted, taking roughly half of the cards with me. The power surrounding them encircled my hand, sparking against my own aura. Exhaling, I set the cards I had selected to the right and sat back, waiting.

Sylvia gathered the stacks to form a single deck again. She placed three cards face down on the table. After giving me a significant look, she flipped them over, one by one.

The pictures on the cards were old and appeared to be hand-painted. The edges of the cards were well worn. It showed how often they had been used. The images on the cards meant nothing to me. Stella, though, paid rapt attention to them, drinking in whatever details that were presented by them.

"You see? You are destined to do this. You are destined to end the war. But you cannot do that without Stella's help, just as she cannot fulfill her destiny without yours. Everything is closer. The choices have to be made. You must act soon or we will lose everything."

How she got that out of pictures of a wheel, a naked woman with stars above her and a depiction of a knight riding a pale horse I will never know. I couldn't care less about the cards. What convinced me was the gut feeling I got. This *felt* right. This was where I was supposed to be. Stella was the one I was supposed to meet and together, we would do what had to be done.

"I believe you," I said. "We will do what we can to figure this out."

The lights in the room flickered and Sylvia closed her eyes. She said in a loud, clear voice, "It's settled. The path has been chosen. The time is coming closer. I have seen it in my cards. You two don't have much time. May the Lord and Lady watch over you as you both claim your destinies."

As if that parting phrase were a dismissal, Stella rose from her seat and headed to the door. "Come on," she said and beckoned me into the hall. "The hour is almost up. Your uncle is waiting for you. I'll go with so we can explain what's going on."

As we emerged from the hallway and headed for the front door, the sounds of zombies biting the dust and the animated shouts of the twins became louder. The abrupt shift back into everyday life was disorienting. With all of these new revelations and with everything that was about to happen, how could they just sit there and play video games?

The sharp jangle of the bells and the slamming of the door punctuated our exit. Stella continued walking down the driveway and stopped just short of where Spike was parked.

I followed, unsure what to say or what to do.

When I reached her, she said, "Look, Ryan. I'm sorry about tonight. I really wasn't expecting things to happen like this."

"It's okay." I laughed as a sudden thought flashed through my mind. "I've been making a fool out of myself trying to impress you while I tried to figure out how to tell you about me. Stella, you're the first human I've wanted to talk to about what I am. I was terrified about how you would react. And you knew all along."

She laughed along with me as she shook her head. "You must think I'm such a dork. First my Nona at church, then my cousins..."

"Have you forgotten about my uncle?" My question made her sputter and laugh even harder, which is what I was going for. "Your family has nothing on mine."

"I guess that's true," she giggled. She looked up at the darkening sky and at the half full moon rising higher and higher. She asked, suddenly pensive. "So where does that leave us? Are we friends? Co-workers of sorts?"

"Of course we are still friends," I confirmed and before I could stop it, the next thought came sliding past my lips. "Actually, I was hoping we could be more than just friends."

Stella squeezed my hand in hers. Leaning into me, she whispered impishly, "That depends."

Bending down, my lips brushed hers in a hesitant kiss. She returned it with more passion than I expected and it took me aback. I covered my surprise by holding onto her and focusing on the sensation of her lips.

"I hope you two aren't going to do that often," the Brooklyn-accented voice interjected, sounding very annoyed. Max materialized next to Stella's car, looking fairly disgusted.

Startled, she broke away from the embrace; I coughed nervously and looked at the ground, uncomfortable at being caught by a ghost. His silent and sudden appearances were going to get very annoying very quickly.

"We better go find Azra," I said, feeling like a complete tool. "He's probably getting ready to send out a search party for me."

"Yes," Stella agreed. Did I detect embarrassment in her voice, or was it something else? She got into the car and I followed her lead. Max appeared in the back seat. I supposed Sylvia had sent him along to keep an eye on us.

Once we were out on the main streets of the city, she asked me, "Where am I going, Ryan?"

"The condo in Camarillo where you picked me up. There's something I want to get before we meet up with my uncle."

The ride to Camarillo was quiet. There was much I wanted to say, but knowing Max was in the background made it hard. "So the mirror . . ." I started. "I know the one who is after it."

The streetlights passed over us as we sped down the freeway. The headlights from the other side of the divide highlighted the worry on her face. "His name is Ascher. He was my uncle's friend. He's was the one at the Getty today. That's who possessed the human who came after us."

"How is that even possible?" Max piped up from the back seat. "I thought only spirits and ghosts could possess a human."

Max was invisible again, but his voice sounded just behind me. I kept my eyes on the road and the cars we passed. "Angels can do it too. There's this mental trick, a mind control sort of thing where they gain control of the body and use it like a puppet."

"That's sick," Stella whispered. "Who the hell would do something like that?"

It was with shame that I pursed my lips together. I didn't want to mention that I had tried it because I was fairly sure that sort of information would have gotten me kicked out of the car right then and there.

"I don't know how many others are looking for the mirror," I changed the subject. Why hadn't I gotten more information out of Ascher when I had the chance?

Stella asked slowly, "If this guy is your uncle's friend, then what's to stop your uncle from trying to take the mirror from us when we talk to him?"

"She brings up a good point," Max piped up. "How do we know we can trust your crazy uncle? He did attack us back there."

My teeth clenched. "I told you. He only did that because he thought I was in trouble. Ordinarily he wouldn't go anywhere near a witch, let alone a coven of them. He won't take the mirror because Uncle Az doesn't believe in it. He thinks it's just an old legend. Besides, I know why Ascher wants it so badly."

"Why is that?" Stella wanted to know. Her hands gripped the steering wheel.

"Redemption. He believes that if he finds the mirror,

and deliver the humans who stole it to the Heavenly Host, that he will get back into Heaven."

"My family didn't steal it! The Goddess gave it to us for safekeeping." Stella protested sharply.

"That's not how the story goes according to the angels," I pointed out.

Silence filled the car as we travelled through the night. We arrived at the condo after what felt like both an eternity and only a matter of seconds. Stella parked the car and I opened the door to get out.

Stella grabbed my arm. "Be careful."

I nodded. "I will. Wait here." I got out and closed the door securely behind me.

The condo was dark and quiet. No one was there waiting for me, which was a relief. This wasn't the spot Azra was referring to, but I had a feeling I would need something that I had left behind earlier. Without turning on any lights, I went into the room and withdrew the celestial blade hidden between my mattress and box spring. The hum of the weapon was almost audible in the quietness of the apartment.

I strode back to the car, gripping the blade firmly in my hands.

Stella had left the car running and the rumble of Spike echoed through the parking garage like a warning growl of an angry wolf.

"Did you get what you came for?" Stella asked as I climbed into the passenger seat. The closing of the door sent a rain of rust on top of me.

"Yes," I replied, brushing the specks of rust from my clothes. "Let's go find Uncle Azra."

"Where is he?" She put the car into reverse and expertly maneuvered the beast towards the exit. I gripped the scabbard of my blade, hoping that I wouldn't need it later on.

"Leo Carrillo Beach in Malibu," I answered. "He'll be there teaching Beth how to surf."

"Beth?"

"He means the goat," Max piped up from the back seat of the car.

Her eyes widened and I thought I saw the crack of a smile appear on her lips. "Are you serious?" she asked, fighting the laughter that threatened to come out.

"Deadly," I replied letting my own grin through.

She couldn't keep it in any longer. She burst into a fit of giggles. "Poor Beth. She must be so frightened out there in the water."

I smirked. "Maybe, maybe not. It seems as though she's pretty tolerant."

We could joke and laugh, but the weight of what we were going to do was still there, looming in the distance. Equally heavy was the fact that we had no idea how to go about it. Stella grabbed my hand in hers as we sped through the night. The feel of her skin against mine and the gentle squeeze she gave me let me know everything would be fine.

Chapter Twenty-three

We approached Uncle Azra's favorite stretch of beach on foot, having parked Spike off the side of the highway. The climb down the shrub-filled sand and rock was difficult in the dark. Max glided over the terrain easily and unconcerned.

I helped Stella over the trickier parts of the narrow path and soon we stood on the soft sand near the water. The waves sent the sounds of their lulling rhythm into the night. The lapping of water onto the shore was peaceful and serene.

As we walked, I scouted the shoreline looking for the telltale signs of Uncle Azra's usual set up of a beach chair, an extra surfboard or two, and a cooler. Suddenly, a prickling sensation crawled up my neck. We were being watched.

Just as I was about to tell her so, Stella reached over and put her hand on my shoulder. "Um, Ryan?"

I turned. From under the same bridge we had just crossed through, a large group of Fallen Ones stalked towards us. They were dressed similarly in dark cargo pants, boots and black tank tops. On the whole they looked like a group of soldiers going into a combat mission. I didn't see weapons on them, but I was sure they were somewhere. Each of them had violent, flashing eyes and permanent grimaces contorting their mouths. I had never seen so many Fallen Ones together before; usually, they were solitary creatures. Seeing them banded together like this meant something nefarious was at hand.

I maneuvered in front of Stella, keeping my eyes trained on the advancing group. My right hand palmed the hilt of my blade. I wasn't willing to pull it out quite yet, but

I wanted to be ready for the instant I needed to. Max vanished quicker than thought and I fought down my irritation. Of course the ghost would disappear at the first sign of a fight. It was all up to me. I struggled to remember the few short hours of training Ascher had given me. Would it be enough to keep these thugs away from Stella?

"Ryan?" Her voice rose in panic. "What do we do?"

Before I could answer, the horde let out a chilling battle cry and raced directly at us. Instinctually, I grabbed Stella's hand and dragged her over to the mound of rock jutting out in a cliff from the ocean. We circled around it, our feet splashing in the waves as we came to an alcove of rocks. It was solid; something we could put our backs against to force the enemy though the bottle-neck opening. Smooth pebbles, wet from the ocean, rested beneath our feet.

I searched for something—anything—I could give Stella to use as a weapon. I didn't want her to be defenseless in case they got past me. There, a few paces away was a hefty-looking piece of driftwood. I splashed over to pick it up. I swung it a few times, getting the feel of it in my hands. Perfect.

Max's voice was scathing at my left. "A piece of driftwood, seriously? What damage can you possibly do with that?"

I growled. "It's for Stella and it's the best I can do for the moment. I thought you ran away."

"Ryan!" Stella shrieked.

The Fallen Ones were funneling through the opening and pinning us against the rock face sooner than I thought they would. I scrambled back to Stella with my makeshift weapon.

"Here," I shoved the driftwood at her. It fumbled in her shaking fingers before she gripped it firmly. She held it up over her shoulder like a baseball bat.

I drew my celestial blade and tossed the scabbard to the side. I readied my stance as the Fallen Ones came at us. "Max, keep her safe. Do whatever you have to, but don't let them touch her."

There was no time to wait for his acknowledgement. I charged forward with my blade held high, ready to slice anyone who got in my way. There wasn't room to think. All I knew was that I had to direct the fight out and away from Stella as best as I could and as quickly as I could.

The first Fallen One I met received a vicious slash to the head. Well, that was the plan anyway. In actuality, the blade grazed the Fallen One's cheek. The slice had barely scraped away some skin but it wasn't deep enough to draw blood. The sting certainly got his attention though, because he lunged straight at me. I managed to jump out of the way.

As he fell, I kicked him in the stomach. He flipped onto his back in the sand. I lifted my blade high over my head, intending to bring it down squarely in the middle of his neck.

I hadn't paid enough attention to who was around me because as I started swinging, something hit my hand, causing the blade to fall out of my grasp. It clattered against the pebbles as someone's foot connected with my side. It sent me sprawling onto the ground.

The impact jarred me, but the real pain came with the boots that kicked into my gut savagely. My blade was just out of arms reach behind me so I twisted around the kicks to get a better angle on it. Someone stomped on my outstretched arm, sending a sharp shooting pain up through my body.

Gritting my teeth so I didn't make a sound, I latched onto the boot. I punched the kneecap that was attached to the foot. Bone shattered beneath my knuckles. The Fallen One toppled on top of me.

The Fallen Ones kept attacking, not seeming to care about the well-being of their comrades. Nevertheless, when I took that first Fallen One down, I could finally reach my blade. I gripped the hilt tightly and just started swinging. A few of them were caught off guard and tumbled down, but others simply backed out of my range.

I jumped up, careful to kick the ones on the ground away from me. They rolled to their feet as though my blows were nothing more than a stiff wind. I was surrounded.

At least they are away from Stella, I thought. *She'd have a chance to run.*

A loud thunk sounded and one of the Fallen Ones that encircled me crumpled, hissing in pain. Something flew past me at record speed; the raw energy coming off of it almost seared me as it went by. Two more Fallen Ones fell. I looked in the direction where the projectiles came from. There was Stella, her lips moving silently in time with the hand movements she needed to complete the charge of the rocks in her left hand. The energy she summoned was pooled at her feet and flowing up through her with every gesture. The renewed hope at the sight of her fighting back made me smile.

Something blurred the air around her. Any of the Fallen Ones who got too close were swiftly rebuffed out of the way. It was a tight radius, but it worked to keep her safe. Silently I thanked Max for listening to me.

"Stella!" I called for her attention I shoved a Fallen One into her trajectory. One of her charged rocks hit him in the chest. He reacted as though he had been shot. He grappled at the hole in his chest. I continued the fight, not stopping to watch what happened to him. I punched and clawed my way towards Stella. More charged rocks flew past me, eliciting startled pain-filled cries.

At last I was with her again against the cliff side. "Take out as many as you can. I'll help Max keep them off of you." An imperceptible nod of her head and she began firing the charged and blessed rocks at the Fallen Ones.

It held them back for a while, but they were persistent. For each Fallen One that Stella, Max, and I were able to take out, another appeared. Where were they coming from?

"We have to do something," I told her. "This isn't working."

Stella looked back at me, her eyes expressing only

exhaustion. Her hands trembled and she sagged against the rock face. The green energy coating her ammunition was faded and pale. Just looking at her, I could tell she was almost at the end of her rope.

"What would you suggest?"

Her fatigue hit me like a slap in the face. She was draining herself by slinging pebbles. Why was that little effort draining her so badly?

"Her power is running out," Max said, seeming to read my thoughts. Another Fallen One went flying and the Brooklyn voice grunted with the effort.

"I thought she was blessed with the power from some goddess."

"Technically, she won't be until Sylvia passes on. That is when the mantle of power is transferred to her. Until that happens, she is stuck with a limited power source," Max explained. Somehow the ghost was out of breath.

"Stella, we have to get you out of here," I told her. "We can't keep this up much longer. Max, if I create a cover, can you help her get out of here?"

"No," she said fiercely. Her eyes blazed. "I'm not going to leave you."

Part of me was relieved to hear her say that, but another part cursed her stubbornness. The Fallen Ones were getting closer and more insistent. "You don't have a choice," I replied.

"Like hell I don't! Give me your hand!" She dropped the pebbles and reached for me.

"What? Why?"

"Just shut up and do it!"

I shifted my sword to clasp her outstretched hand in mine. I cast a worried look towards the advancing horde of Fallen Ones.

"I'll cover you," Max assured me. "Just do what she says!"

Stella looked scared, but her grip on my hand was tight. "Focus. Envision a ray of energy coming out of our hands, like a fire hose. I'll do the steering. You just keep focusing your energy. Okay?"

"Are you sure this will work?"

The look on her face said she wasn't at all sure. Instead of answering me she said, "On the count of three! One! Two! Three!"

I flung everything I had in me outwards. The crackle of power nearly knocked me off of my feet. Our energies merged and instead of forming the beam Stella intended, a giant purplish-green bubble wrapped itself around us. It looked like the bubble trap that Azra had been caught in, except this time I was on the inside. Confusion threatened to break my concentration. What happened?

The attackers surged forward all at once, thinking we were vulnerable. I was shocked when they hit the barrier they shrieked in agony and reeled back, wounded. Whatever body part had come in contact with our bubble simply disintegrated. It wasn't just their corporeal body either. As they tried to reform the illusion of the lost limbs, it became apparent that their astral bodies had been maimed as well. Those who collided fully died, their bodies turning to the sticky tar-like substance and pooling onto the sand. Our shield was acting like a celestial blade.

"We did it," Stella breathed. Beads of sweat rolled down her face.

"Yes, you certainly did," an achingly familiar voice called out from beyond the enraged troop of Fallen Ones. The sound of clapping accompanied the pronouncement of, "Wonderful job, Orion. I didn't know you had it in you."

The Fallen Ones halted their attack and fell silent at the voice. The horde parted, bowing slightly in deference and making way for what was apparently their leader.

Ascher strode through the crowd, trailed by even more warriors. This group weren't just comprised of Fallen Ones either. A diverse representation of all of the angelic races, all sides of the war stood before us. From Fallen Ones with their dark, murky auras to actual Choir Boys with their metallic ones, I could even spot a couple of Grigori in the mix, their vibrant bluish auras standing out against the others few and far between.

"What are you doing? How did you find us?" I yelled at Ascher. Seeing him at the head of such a formidable army like this compounded the betrayal somehow. It confirmed the hazy memories of my father's death and the attempts on my life in a way that nothing else could have.

A smile stretched across his drawn, sallow features. "You aren't that difficult to track. Especially without these." He spun my protection bracelet around his finger with nonchalance. "I see you've met my associates. I'm sorry you had to be introduced under these circumstances." He stepped over the wounded Fallen Ones as he advanced on our defensive barrier. "It seems the three of you have something I want." He didn't come close enough to touch the shield, but his eyes reflected a certain amazement. "This really is excellent craftsmanship. It's a very powerful ward. I didn't know you had it in you."

Hate made my tone quiet and menacing. "What do you want?"

He tsked at me, as though he were disappointed. "Now, Orion, you were taught more respect than that." He paced in front of us, still too far away for me to try to strike out at him. He pivoted on his right foot and took three paces back to me, closer than he had dared come before, but still just out of reach. "You know why I am here. I want the mirror, Orion. Give it to me."

"No," Stella wheezed, her head shaking. "Ryan, don't tell him."

"You aren't getting it Ascher," I replied, squeezing Stella's hand reassuringly.

He looked genuinely disappointed. "You realize you're going against your destiny by denying me the mirror, don't you?"

My mouth settled into a grim line.

"You exist to find the mirror and return us to Heaven.

You don't have to be afraid of what you are anymore. You were born to do this. Join us. Fulfill your potential."

"You're a liar," I told him.

He laughed. "Am I? The prophecy states 'Return what was lost when the stars were formed.' This is our chance to go back home, to start new again. We will finally be able to leave this damned place to the humans. Home is calling. Your mother would be so disappointed to see you fighting so hard to keep things the way they are. She would have expected you to do your duty."

"Shut up!" I shook with rage. "You're talking about the entire annihilation of all life. My mother wouldn't have wanted that."

The smile on his face became cruel and embittered. "It's too bad you never had the chance to know her, Orion. She would have taught you your proper place in this world instead of allowing you to mix with inappropriate company." He sniffed at Stella as though she were a bug deserving nothing more than his disgust. "Honestly, the creatures you choose to associate with. A witch and a ghost? It has to be Azra's influence at work here. He never could discern from the trash. Your mother, on the other hand, believed angels were the superior race and the war over these insignificant creatures was a waste. She knew getting the mirror was the only way to get us back into Grace."

I shut my eyes in a vain attempt to block out his words. It couldn't be true what he was saying. She wouldn't have believed that . . . could she?

The image of my father as he was murdered flashed before my eyes. "Is that why you killed my father?" I shouted. "Because he didn't agree with your insane notion that we would be welcomed back into Heaven if we found a mirror?"

Ascher drew in a deep breath. "Rasheym was an unfortunate accident. Your mother fell in love with him, even after I warned her against it. She said she would win him over to our way of thinking. Indra could be very persuasive when she needed to be." He sighed. "Sadly, she didn't succeed. After he let her die, there was no one to convince him of our plans." He stopped moving and looked me straight in the eye, all traces of amusement gone. "What is done is done. The present, Orion, and the very near future, is what concerns me now. My employer is very interested in the whereabouts of the mirror. I cannot disappoint him in this, so I am going to ask you nicely. Where is it?"

"I don't know," I lied. There was a waiver of doubt in my voice. He must have heard it because he smiled again.

"You know, Orion. I think you're lying to me. Look at your companion, the Strega girl."

Almost unwillingly I did as he said. She shook from head to toe with exertion to keep the barrier up. Sweat dripped off her and it was a struggle for her to keep standing.

"Do you see what I see?" Ascher's voice made my teeth clench. "Your little witch is tiring. What do you think will happen when she finally passes out from using too much energy?"

The sight of Stella straining so much wrenched my heart. I faced Ascher again.

"I'll tell you what will happen. Your barrier will come crashing down. Then I will take both of you. I'll make you watch as I torture her, as I drive her mad by using her own thoughts against her. That is, unless you give me the mirror."

What he promised terrified me. There was no doubt in my mind that he would do it. And he was right; it was only a matter of time before Stella was too exhausted to carry on. I cast a saddened look at her, hoping that she would understand.

She saw what was in my mind and screamed, "No! Don't you dare! You stupid—"

"It's not here," I told Ascher, cutting off her protests. "We don't have it. After the incident in the museum she sent it to a friend in Italy."

"What are you doing?" Stella's defeated wail was convincing. I was relieved that she picked up on my lie so quickly.

"Good, Orion. Perhaps we can do business after all." Ascher's approval was accompanied by a snarled order to one of the angels to his left as he turned his back to us, "When the shields break, kill the Strega."

"What?" I roared. "You promised you would leave her alone!"

Ascher cocked his head to the side. "Is that what you heard? No, no, no. I told you if you gave me the mirror, I wouldn't torture her in front of you. You really should listen more to what people are saying." He gave a nasty smirk and turned to walk away.

"Stop right there, Ascher!" someone cried out from above us. I squinted at the rock face.

Uncle Az leapt down from his perch, landing just in front of where Stella and I stood. He was still dripping from his swim, dressed in a pair of white board shorts with the Superman logo printed on the back. He held his celestial blade relaxed in his hand.

"Well," Ascher sneered, "if it isn't my good old buddy, Azra. Catch any bitchin' waves tonight?"

Azra stood resolute and tall, impervious to Ascher's sarcastic insults. "You know it won't work, right? That plan you have about 'making a level playing field' crap? It's a stupid theory. Frankly, I'm surprised you got so many idiots to buy into it." He cast an imperious look over the gathered assortment of angelic beings.

The said crowd of idiots burst into angry muttering and snarls. Ascher held up his hand and they lapsed into silence again. "Is there a point to your rabble rousing?"

Azra pointed his blade directly at Ascher's face. "You killed Rasheym. You lied to me about it for all these years. You made me think that you were my friend and you tried to kill the one hope we have left in this world." The list of wrongs was delivered in a deadly calm voice. I had never seen Azra this focused before, never this determined to fight. He usually went about things so haphazardly that I wondered if it was just luck that was saving his skin. But now, seeing his poise, his control at not leaping immediately at his target, I began to think otherwise.

Ascher laughed. "I did all of that and more. You couldn't possibly fathom the reasons behind it all."

"Then you and I have something to settle." Azra's stance didn't falter.

Ascher chuckled. "Do you not see the army I have behind me? You can't possibly take all of us on at once."

Uncle Azra tilted his head, as though considering what Ascher said. "Maybe not, but I am not challenging them. I am challenging you.

"And if I refuse?"

"Believe me, Ash, there's no way you're getting away from this fight."

Stella's shaking worsened as the connection between us started to crumble. I missed Ascher's reply, because she fell to her knees. She heaved for breath and her eyes were shut tight in concentration.

"Hold on," I whispered to her. "Just a little while longer, please, Stella."

When I looked back, Ascher had drawn his own blade, the same self-satisfied smirk upon his face. Though they didn't say anything, both materialized their wings at the same time. In a single, fluid motion they took off, launching themselves into the air.

"Ryan?" Stella's voice came out a hoarse whisper, "I can't hold it any longer."

"Try," I pleaded, but I knew it was useless. She'd been entirely drained. Her shaking turned into a violent spasm and she gasped in ragged breaths. The last sparks of her power sputtered through our clasped hands. The shield flickered like a light, turning more purple than green, and then vanished entirely. Seconds later, she collapsed at my feet.

I gathered her in my arms and held her close, shifting my gaze to the crowd of warriors. Most of them had their attention locked on the aerial battle happening between Ascher and Uncle Azra. A couple, however, were eyeing us in wicked anticipation.

"Stella," I whispered, hoping the cries and the clashes of the battle happening above us would cover my voice. "You have to get up. Come back."

"She can't. She is completely out," Max told me. The ghost flickered into sight, a testament to how panicked he was. His hat was askew and his long coat was torn and frayed. The evidence of his fight was shocking.

The few Fallen Ones who had been waiting for their chance started inching forward. Their movement caught the attention of a few more.

I risked a quick look up at the sky. Uncle Azra and Ascher were fiercely clashing their swords against the other, swirling in an intricate pattern. There was no way for me to tell who was winning. I couldn't expect Uncle Azra to save us this time. The crash of the waves onto the shore reminded me of a ticking clock counting down for the attack waiting to happen.

With great care I laid Stella onto the sand. "Max, how are you at possession?"

"No dice. It's not in my bag of tricks. What about you? Can't you mind-meld them or something?"

It was a good question, but it was one that I didn't have an answer for. I almost lost control the last time I had tried taking over a human. What would happen if I lost control when trying to take over an angel? There was a good chance that I would end up dead and Stella would be left defenseless. I cursed the fact that I hadn't had more time to train.

"No," I finally answered the ghost. "It's too risky. We have to keep her safe. Are you up for this?"

"I have to be," came the resigned answer. "Sylvia would not be happy if something happened to her granddaughter."

"Fair enough." Facing Ascher's army of angels, I summoned all of my courage. I would protect her until my last breath. I just prayed it would be enough.

Chapter Twenty-four

As Ascher's soldiers advanced, my mind raced with possible strategies for any advantage I could get. There wasn't much in my corner. The one thing I did have was my rage. If I could tap into that and control it enough to direct it towards the advancing soldiers, then I might stand a chance.

The first wave of the enemy came and I had no more time to think. Reaching deep down inside, I wrapped the fury around me like a blanket. The only reservation I had was that I might hurt Stella.

"Keep her safe. Even from me," I told Max. I didn't give him time to question me before I launched myself into the advancing army.

It was a whirlwind of activity. Somehow, I did more damage with my small blade than ever before. The rage made my attacks vicious and deadly. I danced through them like a shadow, assaulting them from every direction. It seemed that the fury more than made up for my inexperience in the battlefield.

At one point, I picked up another celestial blade from the bloodied sand. The agony of holding it was crippling, but I let it fuel my rage. Skewering it through the nearest Fallen One, I released the handle. Immediately the pain receded. If I kept my contact with the stolen blades short, then I could take the enemy out in half the time.

I don't know how many of them I killed. All I can recall is the wash of their blood spilling onto the beach. I was in a daze. The one consistent thought that kept me from losing the last shred of control I had left was Stella. I had to protect Stella. More soldiers came forward, replacing the ones I had killed. The focus I started with began to slip. It only took one mistake and I was off balance. One rogue Grigori took the opportunity to cut my arm with his blade. The pain was enough to make me scream furiously into the night air.

As I fell to my knees, a mass of angels surrounded me. Each of them aimed their blades at me, ready to kill. The rage diminished and was instead replaced with fear. This wasn't supposed to happen. I wasn't supposed to die without fulfilling the prophecy.

That's when I heard it; the distant bleating of a goat coming from the right. I looked through the forest of bodies towards the water. What I saw made my jaw drop. Beth rode a small wave through the rocks and to the shore on her yellow surf board. As soon as the board touched the sand, she lowered her head and charged straight for me. She pushed through the attackers taking them by surprise.

Never in my life would I have thought a goat could go Rambo, but that is exactly what Beth did. She head butted, kicked, and bit her way around me creating a barrier of goat fury. The angels surrounding me broke apart as she advanced on them. No doubt they were in as much shock as I was. She didn't stop though; Beth knocked the enemy down like bowling pins.

With the threat of being killed momentarily paused, I took a quick look at the cut on my arm. Blood ran freely and the bone was visible at the bottom of the gash. Instinctively, I clamped my hand on the wound. There was no time to attend to it now. But with Beth giving me a minute to breathe, I risked a glance upwards to check on the battle above.

The clanging of steel and the shouts of anger and pain punctuated the night sky. Uncle Azra attacked, his sword swinging down above Ascher's head. He brought up his own blade in time to block the blow and lock swords. With faces inches from each other, their wings pumped furiously to keep them steady in midair. The crossed blades wavered back and forth from the pressure on either side. They stayed still with the struggle for a minute before they sprang apart. The dance between them continued, circle, attack, block, attack, dodge, circle.

A loud yell brought my attention back down to earth. As entrancing as the fight between Uncle Azra and Ascher was, I had my own battle to deal with.

An angel ran at us, his blade held high. Automatically I brought my celestial blade up from the ground. In a single fluid motion, I lopped off his hand at the wrist. As he screamed and clutched at the bloody stump, I jumped to my feet. Without any hesitation, I slashed his throat.

My pain fed my anger, forcing me to move. Stella was still inert against the cliff face. I had to get to her to make sure she was protected. The blur of Max moving around her slowed; he was tiring. I couldn't risk him allowing one of the enemy slip past him and get to her.

Time slowed as I shoved and slashed through Ascher's army. I used the bodies of the dying soldiers I'd killed to block the attacks of their comrades. I ripped off limbs and tossed them into the crowd. Beside me, Beth fought so viciously that I wondered how it was possible she was just a goat. The bloodshed didn't phase her in the least.

The carnage I left in my wake was massive. It took the bodies of the Fallen Ones I killed more than a few moments to absorb back into the earth and even longer for the angels to ascend into the sky. The other Grigori, the few that Ascher had managed to convince of his plan remained where they lay since they belonged to neither Heaven nor Hell. Eventually they would crumble to dust or the ocean would carry them out.

At last, Beth and I reached the rocks. I could see the rise and fall of Stella's chest. She was still alive and I intended to keep her that way.

I didn't know how long Beth, Max and I held our position protecting Stella. Wave after wave of angels attacked. Somehow, miraculously, none of them managed to get past us. With their numbers dwindling and without any more reinforcements, the remaining soldiers slowed their assault to a standstill. Their glares were calculating.

Max and I exchanged a wary glance. Both of us were still poised for another attack. It never came. Instead, they silently turned their backs on us and calmly walked away. They trudged off of the beach and made their way to the highway. Some teleported away instead. The sudden and calm retreat made me nervous. What were they up to?

A rushing sound of feathers and the thump of feet on rocks made my head jerk up. Azra had landed above us. He watched what was left of the army disappear with a stern frown. Blood dripped from his wounds onto the stone. In the moonlight, the bruises he had sustained darkened his skin like oddly placed shadows.

"The bastard got away," he said, his eyes narrowed at the retreating army. "He's going to withdraw while he can. This little fray cost him too much. He hadn't been expecting you to fight back so well." My uncle spat.

"Orion." The sound of Stella's strong and confident voice calling my name took me by surprise. I turned towards the cliff to find her standing tall. Her dark eyes glittered in the moonlight. She walked to the water, stopping at the cliff that jutted out of the ocean.

"You should have given him the mirror."

She shouldn't have been able to move like that, having been out cold only seconds before. Fear paralyzed me as I began to suspect what happened. Denial made it that much harder to find the telling signs of a human being controlled. When she was close enough, she placed her hands upon my shoulders. Leaning in close, she whispered in a seductive yet menacing tone, "It would have been so much easier if you just gave me the mirror."

I yanked myself backwards. Instead of her warm brown eyes, I found myself staring into back discs. A sneer marred the beauty of her face as she backed away. Stella, or rather, Ascher, continued heading to the tall pile of rocks.

My strength faltered as the reality of the situation hit

me. "No," I shouted. "Ascher, you can't do this. Get out of her right now!"

Stella's head twisted back to look over her shoulder at me. She had reached the base of the mountain of rocks and was about to climb. "Don't presume to make demands, Orion. You are hardly in control. If you don't do what I ask, then your girlfriend will suffer, I promise you that."

I stumbled forward, my body refusing to move quickly enough. I knew I wouldn't be able to get to her in time. That fact was almost too much to bear.

"Kid?" Uncle Azra called down from his perch. When I didn't immediately answer, he hopped down to stand next to me.

Stella ascended to the top of the rocks and teetered at the edge. "You know what I want," Ascher shouted over the noise of the water. "Don't make your girlfriend suffer, Orion. You don't want her to end up like your mother and father."

The words coming out of her mouth were excruciating. There was nothing I could do. If I gave him the mirror, he would kill her anyway and then he would have the most powerful weapon in Heaven, Hell and Earth. I remained silent and I felt as though I were drowning in my helplessness.

"Fine. Have it your way."

Stella-Ascher stretched her arm towards me, almost longingly. I couldn't help it, I darted forward. Stella-Ascher took the impossible step that led to the jagged rocks and pounding waves. The girl I loved pitched herself head first towards the shallow, swirling water below. Her head smashed against the rocks that jutted out of the thundering waves. It was surreal how slowly time moved as I stood there, helpless as her body was swallowed up by the water.

"NO!" I roared. Time sped up and I couldn't move fast enough. Azra was behind me, questions on his lips that I didn't have time to answer. I made it to the water just as the wave receded and dragged her limp body out to sea.

"STELLA!" I splashed into the icy waves, rushing to her before the current could sweep her out of sight. Distantly, I heard Uncle Azra come after me. It didn't matter; my sole focus was getting to her.

When I reached her, she was bobbing face down in the surf. There was blood in the water around her. When I flipped her into my arms, I saw the large gash on her head. Panic set in as I thrashed to get her back to the shore. Her limp form was difficult to hang onto in the tossing current.

Then, Uncle Azra was there with Beth's board. Together, we lifted her onto it and guided her back to safety. I couldn't look away from the blood congealing on her face. Her arm was twisted at an unnatural angle, most likely broken.

"I don't think she's dead. Not yet. We have to get her to the hospital," Uncle Azra informed me after checking her pulse and her breathing.

I wanted so badly to believe Stella wasn't dead, but I couldn't take Azra's say so. I had to be completely sure. When the surf board was close enough to the beach, I pulled her out of the water to check for myself. I would make Ascher pay for every scratch, every bruise that he dared inflict on her.

"Orion!" Uncle Azra shouted, trying to get me to listen. "You can't help her."

I hadn't realized I was crying until I felt the tears fall down my cheeks. I clutched Stella's prone form to my chest. For the first time in my life, I prayed. *Please*, I thought as I buried my face in her wet hair. *Let her be alright. Please!*

I don't remember how we got to the hospital. At one point Azra tried to take her from me, but I refused to let her go. It took all of the doctors and the nurses to pry her out of my arms. I felt so broken and useless as they wheeled her away.

Uncle Azra clamped a hand on my shoulder. "It will

be alright, Orion," he assured me. "They know what they're doing."

I could only stare after her. The big blue doors at the end of the hall opened and the hospital staff walked her through. Icy numbness overtook my limbs. I whispered under my breath, more a promise to myself than a prayer, "If she dies, I will make him suffer beyond all measure."

Chapter Twenty-five

The sterilized hospital room they kept her in was a sharp contrast to the tumultuous emotions raging inside of me. The thoughts that darted through my mind were not clean, organized, nor hypoallergenic. My knee jangled up and down with the force of trying to contain them. I had to remind myself that the emergency staff had done everything they possibly could to help her. The doctors knew what they were doing. If they said all we could do was wait, then I would just have to wait.

At first they hadn't wanted to tell me anything; I wasn't really her family, after all. But since I was stubborn and I refused to leave her alone, the nurses took pity on me and let me stay.

When they tried to treat my wounds—the vicious cut on my shoulder and the other lesser cuts and bruises I had obtained—I wouldn't to let them touch me. My hand remained wrapped around hers as they interrogated me on what had happened. I spun some lie. They must have believed it because no more questions were asked.

The nurses explained that she was in a coma from her head injury. She had some internal bleeding as well. I was told several times how lucky we were that she hadn't died. Each time they said that, I wanted to disagree. Stella wasn't lucky at all. The day we met should have rightfully been the worst day of her life.

I breathed in time with the soft beeps and harsh rhythm of the machines monitoring her. Stella's eyes were closed, but who knew if she could still sense me. They had given her morphine for any pain she might have been in. The white bandages wrapped around her looked stiff and brought out the color of the bruises developing on her skin.

I wanted to shout, to yell, to rage, but I held it back. Causing a scene wouldn't be the best idea. I couldn't risk not being there when she woke up. Or even if she didn't wake up at all.

I gave the hospital staff Sylvia's name. They called her and said she was on her way. Max had probably already filled her in on what had happened; at least that's what I assumed. I hadn't seen or heard anything from the mouthy specter since the fight.

I dreaded the moment Sylvia walked through the door and she saw firsthand what I had done to her granddaughter. What would I say to her? How could I possibly explain?

Azra had gone to patrol around the hospital hours ago. He said it was in the off chance that Ascher had tracked us here. I think it was because he didn't like being in a hospital room with a witch. He was probably also visiting Beth who he had left tethered in the field next to the hospital. I barely acknowledged it when he left me alone with Stella and my oppressive guilt. His promise to check in on me fell on unresponsive ears.

"Why didn't you protect her? How in the hell could you let this happen?" I demanded of myself. Only the beep and whir of the machines answered me. The words echoing in the room stung, but they didn't hurt any more than they had in my head. I rose to my feet, too upset to remain seated.

As I paced, the door to the room opened and Sylvia, Donatella, and Aurelia appeared.

Immediately, I stopped moving and watched. I waited like a deer in headlights to see how her family would react.

At first they didn't see me. The sight of Stella lying still as death on the bed held their complete attention. It elicited a sharp breath from Donatella and a murmured prayer from Sylvia. In seconds, the three women surrounded the bed, bypassing me completely. There was a frenzied conversation in Italian that I didn't have the energy to follow. Seeing Sylvia at her granddaughter's hospital bed was heartbreaking.

Only one thought echoed in the wake of my crushing remorse: this was all my fault. I put her in that situation. I made her vulnerable to Ascher. I was responsible for her being in a coma.

The shame of it was too much to stand.

Even though I didn't want to let Stella out of my sight, I quietly left the room. It was best to let her family be with her now.

Unwilling to go farther than the nurse's station, I hovered just outside the room. I couldn't leave; not yet. I had to make sure Ascher wouldn't come back to finish the job. I had to know that Stella would live.

Aurelia, Stella's soft spoken cousin, was the first to emerge from the hospital room. She approached me with her head bent towards the ground. I knew she was around Stella's age, but right then she looked a lot younger. When she stood next to me, she asked, "Are you alright?"

I blinked. That was the last question I expected anyone in Stella's family to ask me. "I'll be okay."

She accepted my curtailed answer with a nod. She leaned against the wall beside me. There was a long, pregnant silence before she asked her next question. "Would you tell me what happened?"

The worry in her voice was genuine, but there was something else in the question. It sounded like a sort of grim satisfaction to her tone. Almost as if she was glad Stella had been hurt.

That tenor in her voice didn't make any sense to me. I chalked it up to my own exhaustion and shame.

"Well . . ." The word hung in the air as I searched for how to tell her what she needed to hear. Donatella burst into the hallway, lips pressed tightly together and her eyes blazing.

"What happened?" she demanded as she placed herself in front of me. It was as if she dared me to run for it. "How could you let her get hurt like this?"

"Donatella!" Sylvia's voice was sharp and reproving. The elderly woman inched out of the doorway. "Stop making a scene. It wasn't his fault."

Donatella whirled on her grandmother, her anger only barely muted. "How can you possibly know that? You saw her lying in there. She's hooked up to machines and barely breathing. Who knows if she'll ever wake up? Meanwhile, here he is, with barely a scratch on him."

The glare Sylvia gave her granddaughter was withering. "Stop blaming Ryan for what happened. He didn't cause this tragedy."

While Sylvia's rebuke silenced Donatella, I disagreed with the statement. Donatella shot me dirty looks, but I didn't bother returning them.

Her glares were the least I deserved. I wasn't sure if Sylvia really knew what happened, but her confidence was misplaced. I was solely responsible for Stella's condition.

As if the old woman heard my thoughts, she spoke with a heavy resignation, "We're all very tired and none of us are thinking straight. It's been a very eventful night. Donatella, Aurelia, come with me to find a doctor. I want to hear what they have to say about Stella's condition first hand."

Donatella bit her lip, visibly forcing herself to keep back her protest. Aurelia's gaze remained trained on the linoleum under her feet and didn't say anything.

"What happens if she wakes up and we're not here?" Donatella argued, finally unable to stay quiet any longer. I was amazed Sylvia remained so calm at the woman's aggressive persistence given the situation at hand.

"She won't be alone. Ryan will be here with her, won't you dear?"

I nodded at Sylvia's encouraging and hopeful smile. She knew I wouldn't leave Stella— not when Ascher was still out there and could come back at any moment.

"Him?" Donatella's tone was incredulous. "You're

going to trust HIM? Nona, the last time you trusted this boy with your granddaughter, she wound up in a coma."

Sylvia's kindly features turned hard and imperial. "You would question me, granddaughter?" Donatella's head bowed at the sound of power. The elderly woman, still harsh with her rebuke, addressed the girl standing next to me in a cold voice. "Aurelia, go get a few strands of your cousin's hair. We will do the spell tonight."

The quiet girl next to me bobbed her head and disappeared into the room.

Donatella, with her lips pursed so tightly they turned white, silently stalked in the opposite direction, presumably to hunt down the doctor on shift. I was left with the elder Strega, too guilt-ridden to even offer up an apology. "Sylvia, I—"

She shushed me. "Don't. I know you would never intentionally hurt Stella. I don't believe that what happened out there was your fault." Her voice became sad. "You have to do what you have to do. I won't stop you if you feel in your heart that it is the right thing to do. All I ask is that you think long and hard before you make your choice."

Her warning made me pause. What was she talking about?

Aurelia returned to the hallway with her fist closed tight. Sylvia took hold of her great-granddaughter's arm and they walked away together. I was left to puzzle over what Sylvia's words meant.

Chapter Twenty-six

After Sylvia and the cousins left, I returned to Stella's room. She was no different than before. I paced around the small room in an attempt to tame the nagging guilt. The sight of her still and lifeless on the hospital bed made me sick. But I still couldn't look away. If I hadn't insisted on talking with her today, if I hadn't been interested in her from the get go, if I hadn't told her about the prophecy, what would she be doing right now?

I had been such a fool to wear my emotions on my sleeve. I may as well have handed her over to Ascher on a silver plate. He knew that I loved her and he knew that I would do anything to keep her safe. That meant he would be searching for her. If I stayed, she would always be in danger because Ascher would never give up the hunt for the mirror.

If I wasn't with her, how could I ensure that Ascher would leave her alone? There wasn't any guaranty that he wouldn't try to attack her in the future, unless . . .

Unless he thought Stella was dead.

The glimmering of an idea stirred in my head.

I slowed my pace as my mind raced with possibilities. There was no way Ascher stayed inside of her when she hit the rocks. He wouldn't have exposed himself to that sort of pain. If he stuck around to watch from a hiding spot nearby, then he would have only seen her still body. Ascher was arrogant enough to assume he had killed her without bothering to check. Even if he hadn't expected to kill her, I could still draw him away from her and make sure she'd stay safe.

There had to be absolutely no doubt that Stella Evangeline had died in order for this scheme to work.

What would make him believe the lie completely? I glanced around the room, waiting for inspiration. My eyes fell upon Stella's ripped and damp clothes and the idea struck me like lightning.

The mirror! Ascher just wanted the mirror. So that's what I would use to keep him away from her.

A fleeting worry about what I was risking with this idea crossed my mind. I was putting the world at risk in the hopes of saving Stella. Honestly, it was what I should've done in the first place.

In two strides I had her clothes in my hand and was rummaging around in her pockets, searching for the little blue drawstring bag. Relief filled me when my fingers brushed against the wet material. Soon, I had it clenched in my fist. The shock of the energy emanating from it almost made me drop the cool metal. It was powerful alright— a million times more so than a celestial blade. Gingerly, trying not to touch it more than I had to, I picked it up with the sleeve of my hoodie and stuffed the mirror into my pocket. My plan formed with every movement I made.

I would hide the mirror somewhere safe. It would be far away from Stella and somewhere Ascher would never dream to look for it. This object was too dangerous to be in Ascher's hands and, even though Stella was its keeper, it was far too dangerous for her now as well. I was stealing the mirror in order to save her life.

I would go with Ascher, just like he wanted me to on the beach. I would make him believe I was on his side, just to make sure he didn't have a reason to return and find her alive.

Stella was the most important thing in my life, even more important than the prophecy. If she was lost to this world, then I couldn't have anything more to do with it.

I looked back at the bed, embedding the sight of her into my memory. Every smile, every glance and every kiss we shared shone like a million suns in my mind. The realization that those memories would be all I could have of her was bitter and painful. I couldn't tell her about my plan. The more she knew the more danger she'd be in. As much as it hurt, it would be better for her to think I stole the mirror and ran off than for her to know the truth when she woke up.

But I couldn't leave her without saying something. I couldn't walk away without a word. She meant too much and I owed her some sort of explanation.

I returned to the chair next to Stella's hospital bed to ponder what message that would be. Uncle Azra returned moments later. He didn't say much. After all, what could he say? He sat down in the chair across from me, pulled out a bag of Chex Mix and started munching on his snack loudly.

"Chex Mix?" he offered me the bag.

I shook my head declining it as a sudden comprehension gripped me. In order to truly deceive Ascher, it wasn't just Stella I had to leave; I would have to leave Uncle Azra behind as well. If I abandoned everything, it would convince Ascher that I bought into his beliefs, that I was willing to take that dark winding path with him.

The concept of leaving town without Azra was strange. He was the one person I could count on to be there for me. He was the only family I had left.

There was a long stretch of silence between us as these thoughts percolated in my brain. Feeling regret for what I was about to do to him, I said, "You did good training Beth. I never thought she'd do it."

He looked over at me quizzically. "Do what?"

"Save us. She surfed into the fight and took on Ascher's entire force. It was a pretty damn impressive stunt for a goat."

"She surfed? And I missed it?" Uncle Azra threw the bag of Chex Mix and cursed. "That's just not fair!"

I allowed myself a crack of a smile, but I couldn't bring myself to laugh. This was it. It was time to put my plan into action. I had to get him out of there before he changed my mind. "Uncle Az? Can I have a few moments alone with Stella? Sylvia is going to be back any minute now and there's something I need to say to her."

Compassion softened his features and sorrow gave his blue eyes more depth. He got up and patted my shoulder consolingly. "Of course. I'll be outside." I studied Stella's face as my uncle got up, crumpling the Chex Mix bag. A lump formed in my throat as he walked out the door.

Stella and I were left alone.

It was now or never.

I got paper and pencil from the stand next to the bed and started sketching, mindful of each line. I used the time to think, to refine my plan.

In order to make Ascher believe I was sincere, I'd have to do things I was against. Stella's life and my own would depend on my ability to forget I ever had morals. I was about to embark into madness.

I paused to inspect my handiwork. What had come out was a rendition of Stella's favorite painting. The one she showed me at the Getty only a few hours ago— *The Farewell of Telemachus and Eucharis*. It was a hastily-drawn copy, done in sloppy sketch marks and shadows. The important difference was Stella's face reflected in what should have been Eucharis and my own in Telemachus.

I looked up from the paper to Stella's bandaged and bruised face. Remorse and determination flooded me. I had to do this. There was no other way. Once I stopped Ascher, once I was positive he would never be able to hurt her again, only then could I come back and beg forgiveness. If I failed . . . well, then forgiveness wouldn't be needed.

It still felt like I was about to abandon her, not protect her.

Shoving the thought away, I decided what message to leave. Madness was where I was going, so I made the first reference that came to mind. I penciled at the bottom of my sketch: "Doubt thou the stars are fire, doubt that the sun doth move, doubt truth to be a liar, but never doubt I love."

In Shakespeare's play, Hamlet gave that message to Ophelia so she would have faith in him while he pursued his quest for revenge. It was a message for her to not believe the madness and to remember that no matter what he did, no matter how it seemed, he did love her and he always would.

It was the only way I could get her to understand without putting her in danger of knowing too much. I signed my name at the bottom, folded it carefully and buried it deep in one of the pockets inside of her bag.

Originally, I wanted to wait and make sure she was going to come out of the coma. But the more my plan came together, the more it became obvious I couldn't be there when she woke up. If she saw me, I wasn't sure I could gather enough determination to leave her afterwards.

My resolve was set. There was just one more thing I had to do. I went to Stella's side to gaze on her for a last time. My fingers brushed strands of her hair out of her face. Dark shadows under her eyes made her skin seem paper thin. But despite all of the bandages, and the cuts and the bruises, she was still the most beautiful creature in the world. Overcome with a strange mix of remorse and determination, I leaned down and brushed my lips against hers in a chaste, sorrowful kiss.

As I straightened, a soft groan came from her inert form on the bed.

I froze, my heart rejoicing and breaking in the same instant. Like Sleeping Beauty in the fairy tale, she emerged from her death-like slumber. Wasn't I just a sorry excuse of a Prince Charming?

Another noise and a fluttering of her eyelids provoked me into action. I couldn't let her see me. Taking a deep breath and casting a final, longing look back, I walked out the door and hoped I was making the right choice to protect her.

It was cold outside; the chill in the air penetrated my skin much more than it should have. The sun hadn't yet made its appearance. I circled around the entrance of the hospital, being sure to keep an eye out for my uncle. He would stop me if he even suspected what I was about to do.

As soon as I reached the parking lot, I pulled out my phone. With it came the small drawstring bag and the mirror. After dialing the number, I fingered the blue fabric, slowly untying the knots in the cords.

"Hello, Orion." Ascher's voice sounded smug.

I didn't return the greeting. "I've made my decision. Meet me at the Serra Cross in an hour." I didn't wait for his reply before I clicked the phone off. I flung it as hard as I could into a nearby dumpster. I couldn't be connected to anyone in my former life and I couldn't be tempted to contact them. It was just too dangerous.

Clutching the mirror in my hand, I left the hospital and everything I had ever known behind.

***

Once again I watched dawn brighten the sky as I leaned against the old Serra Cross. Below me, the downtown area awoke to the rhythm of the waves against the shore. It was a déjà vu moment. The only difference was this time I knew what was coming.

I didn't have to wait long. Ascher descended the steps of the empty parking lot slowly. His echoing footsteps let me know he was there. I turned to face him.

"Orion." He inclined his head.

"Ascher." I replied in kind.

"Do you have the mirror?" He stepped closer, but not close enough to be within striking distance. He was playing it safe.

"No, but I'm willing to help you find it."

He tilted his head, intrigued. "Really? Why the sudden change of heart?"

I shrugged. "Your theory makes the most sense. I should be doing something, not paddling around the ocean and watching Kung Fu movies. My destiny is more than that. I understand now what my mother wanted from me."

"And the Strega?" He took another step closer. Ascher was still wary, but he was listening.

Again I shrugged like it didn't really matter. I forced my tone to be neutral and uncaring. "Dead."

"Your uncle?"

I looked Ascher in the eyes, willing myself to be convincing. "It's time I made my own choices. He was holding me back from my true purpose."

This statement, this declaration of intention, seemed to satisfy him because a smile stretched across his thin lips. He crossed the distance and stared into my eyes. I prayed he wouldn't be able to see my deception.

After a moment, he put his hand on my shoulder. "You made the right choice, Orion." Taking me by surprise, he forced me onto my knees and grasped my wrists tightly behind my back. From the edge of the hill, two of his henchmen came with ropes. They took hold of me as Ascher let go.

Stepping in front of me, he straightened his jacket and said coldly, "You will forgive my doubt. It will take quite some time before you give me reason to trust you."

Through the pain of being bound, I growled, but nodded. I hadn't really expected open arms. He jerked his head at his lackeys and they hoisted me to my feet, aiming me towards the waiting car.

"There is a lot you and I need to discuss," Ascher promised. A bag was put over my head before I was shoved into the back of the car. For a second I wondered if I was doing the right thing.

As the car began to move, I banished all of my doubts. It was far too late to turn back now.

Kira has been telling stories for as long as she could talk and writing them down as soon as she could hold a crayon. While her chosen writing implement has matured, she still enjoys weaving stories that both entertain and make people think. She is one of the founders of FSF Publications. Kira currently lives in Arizona with her husband, Will.

CPSIA information can be obtained
at www.ICGtesting.com
Printed in the USA
FFOW01n1855260417
34990FF